**Praise for Malorie B**

***Noughts & Cross***

'A book which will linger in the mind long after it has been read'
*Observer*

***Knife Edge***

'A powerful story of race and prejudice' *Sunday Times*

***Checkmate***

'Another emotional hard-hitter . . .
bluntly told and ingeniously constructed' *Sunday Times*

***Double Cross***

'Blackman "gets" people . . . she "gets" humanity as a whole, too.
Most of all, she writes a stonking good story' *Guardian*

***Boys Don't Cry***

'Shows her writing at its best, creating characters and a story which,
once read, will not easily go away' *Independent*

***Pig-Heart Boy***

'A powerful story about friendship, loyalty and family' *Guardian*

***Hacker***

'Refreshingly new . . . Malorie Blackman writes
with such winsome vitality' *Telegraph*

***A.N.T.I.D.O.T.E.***

'Strong characterisation and pacy dialogue make this a real winner'
*Independent*

***Thief!***

'. . . impossible to put down' *Sunday Telegraph*

***Dangerous Reality***

'A whodunnit, a cyber-thriller and a family drama: readers of nine or
over won't be able to resist the suspense' *Sunday Times*

**By Malorie Blackman and published by Doubleday/Corgi Books:**

**The Noughts & Crosses sequence**

*Noughts & Crosses*
*Knife Edge*
*Checkmate*
*Double Cross*

*Boys Don't Cry*
*The Stuff of Nightmares*

*A.N.T.I.D.O.T.E.*
*Dangerous Reality*
*Dead Gorgeous*
*Hacker*
*Pig-Heart Boy*
*The Deadly Dare Mysteries*
*Thief!*

*Unheard Voices*
(An anthology of short stories and poems, collected by Malorie Blackman)

**For junior readers, published by Corgi Yearling Books:**

*Cloud Busting*
*Operation Gadgetman!*
*Whizziwig and Whizziwig Returns*

**For beginner readers, published by Corgi Pups/ Young Corgi Books:**

*Jack Sweettooth*
*Snow Dog*
*Space Race*
*The Monster Crisp-Guzzler*

**Audio editions available on CDs:**

*Noughts & Crosses*
*Knife Edge*
*Checkmate*
*Double Cross*

# THE DEADLY DARE MYSTERIES

malorie blackman

CORGI BOOKS

THE DEADLY DARE MYSTERIES
A CORGI BOOK 978 0 552 55353 7

This collection first published in Great Britain by Corgi Books,
an imprint of Random House Children's Books
A Random House Group Company

First Corgi edition published 2005
This edition published 2012

DEADLY DARE
First published in Great Britain by Scholastic Ltd, 1995


COMPUTER GHOST
First published in Great Britain by Scholastic Ltd, 1997


LIE DETECTIVES
First published in Great Britain by Scholastic Ltd, 1998


1 3 5 7 9 10 8 6 4 2



The Random House Group Limited supports the Forest Stewardship Council (FSC®), the leading international forest certification organization. Our books carrying the FSC label are printed on FSC®-certified paper. FSC is the only forest certification scheme endorsed by the leading environmental organizations, including Greenpeace. Our paper procurement policy can be found at www.randomhouse.co.uk/environment.

Set in Bembo

Corgi Books are published by Random House Children's Books,
61–63 Uxbridge Road, London W5 5SA

www.**randomhouse**.co.uk
www.**kidsatrandomhouse**.co.uk
www.**totallyrandombooks**.co.uk

Addresses for companies within The Random House Group Limited can be found at:
www.randomhouse.co.uk/offices.htm

THE RANDOM HOUSE GROUP Limited Reg. No. 954009

A CIP catalogue record for this book is available from the British Library.

Printed in the UK by CPI Group (UK) Ltd, Croydon, CR0 4YY

*For Neil and Lizzy,*
*with love*

# CONTENTS

# DEADLY DARE

## Chapter One

# Dear Diary

### 23:35 hrs Wednesday, 14th May

I don't know what to do. Tom just won't listen to me. He says we need the money and this is the only way to get it. I told him I didn't like his friends – especially that Robbie. He's the kind who'd cosh you over the head for a packet of crisps. In fact, he'd cosh you over the head for free, just 'cos he'd have fun doing it. But Tom just laughs at me when I say that.

What am I going to do?

It's past midnight and all I want to do is go home. Tom's still down there with them – his so-called friends. He looks up every ten minutes or so and smiles at me. He doesn't notice that I don't smile back.

I wish I could get through to him. I wish I could keep him away from them.

*What am I going to do?*

I've got to do *something*. If I don't, Tom will end up in trouble – in prison, or worse. I've got to look out for my brother. He may be a lot older than me but he sure isn't smarter. Anyone with half an eye could see that he and the rest of that lot are up to something. Knowing Scott, Robbie's brother, it's something illegal. Scott doesn't say much but you can see his mind never stops working.

I don't like him either. He gives me the creeps.

He's always smiling, smiling, smiling. I don't trust people who smile all the time when there's nothing to smile about. In a strange way, I think he's worse than Robbie. I know

Tom and the rest are up to something bad, something dangerous. Someone's going to get hurt. Knowing Robbie, it wouldn't surprise me if someone ended up dead. I just don't want it to be Tom – or me.

## Chapter Two

# The Game Begins

This was it! Today was the day! Theo was about to make some *serious* money. His brown-black eyes gleamed at the thought. Today was definitely *his* day! And if his head would just stop pounding and his body would stop aching, then there'd be no doubt about it at all!

'Ai . . . ai . . . aischoo!' Theo's sneeze rang out through the classroom. Followed by another, then another.

Mrs Daltry glared at him. 'How much longer d'you intend to inflict your cold germs on us, Theo?' she snapped.

'Sorry, Mrs Daltry.' Theo took an already soggy tissue out of his trouser pocket and wiped his nose.

'Sorry isn't good enough. You should've stayed at home.'

Ricky, Theo's best friend, kicked him under the table.

'Ow!' Theo yelled.

'What's the matter now?' frowned the teacher.

'Er . . . I got a sudden pain in my . . . er . . . leg,' Theo mumbled.

He glared at Ricky, who was bent over his workbook, writing furiously.

'Theo, if your flu isn't any better tomorrow, stay at home! And if I catch your germs, I won't be best pleased,' said Mrs Daltry.

Moany old trout! Theo scowled at her as she turned away. But what did he expect? Sympathy?

'Bless you!' Ricky whispered. It was better late than never!

Theo nodded and sniffed heavily. There was no doubt about it. His rotten cold was getting worse. But there was no way he was going to let a cold stand between him and how much? Over fifty pounds? Maybe even sixty? And what an easy way to get it! All he had to do was perform a couple of dares and the money was his. It was already as good as in his pocket. What would he do with the money? Theo closed his eyes and smiled as he considered all the possibilities. He could put it towards the cost of a games console, or start saving up for a new bike, or maybe he could buy that cool jacket he'd seen down the precinct.

Theo glanced over at the clock on the wall. Mrs Daltry's maths lesson was dragging on even more than usual today – something Theo wouldn't have thought was possible.

'Angela, that's the third time you've yawned in five minutes,' Mrs Daltry frowned.

'Sorry, Mrs Daltry,' Angela said quickly.

'Keeping you awake, am I?' the teacher asked with sarcasm.

Barely! Theo answered Mrs Daltry's question in his head. He could well understand why Angela was yawning!

'What each of you learns here in this classroom will serve you for the rest of your lives. You children need to realize that life is not a bowl of cherries.'

A few indistinct murmurs floated in the air. Mrs Daltry had inflicted her favourite saying on the class yet again. Not a day passed without her commenting on life and bowls of cherries at least three times!

'Come on. Come on,' Theo muttered, his eyes returning to the clock. Why didn't the buzzer hurry up and sound?

'Theo, did you say something?' Mrs Daltry enquired.

'No, Mrs Daltry,' Theo replied quickly.

Today was not the day to wind up the teacher. Already, Theo could feel the others in the class glaring at him. He quickly looked down at his workbook, his face burning. He hated being looked at.

'Hhmm!' Mrs Daltry pursed her lips. Just as she opened her mouth to add more to her suspicious 'Hhmm!', the lunch-time buzzer sounded.

'Exercise 24 is homework. I want it in first thing on

Monday morning from *everyone* and no excuses. And for those of you who haven't already done so, don't forget to bring in your consent forms signed by a parent or guardian for next Friday's trip to the Irving Museum to see the Astral Collection. That's the Greek and Roman jewellery exhibition that's on there at the moment. It's very interesting. Some of the pieces are priceless.'

The muttering that filled the classroom showed that not many people agreed with the teacher's assessment of the jewellery exhibition. Words like 'dull', 'tedious' and 'yawn' floated down to the front of the class.

'There's also a computer exhibition, hands-on experiments and a space technology exhibition,' Mrs Daltry added drily.

The class gave a collective sigh of relief.

'That's more like it,' Ricky whispered to Theo.

Theo nodded, watching with everyone else as Mrs Daltry rushed out of the classroom, her packet of liquorice allsorts already out of her jacket pocket.

Cathy ran to the door and popped her head out, looking up and down the corridor.

'All clear,' she said at last, giving the rest of the class the thumbs-up. She closed the door and leaned against it.

Ricky whipped his black baseball cap with 'CHILL!' written on it out of his bag and put it on. Mrs Daltry didn't let him wear it in class – at least, not when she was teaching.

'OK everyone. It's time to play Cash or Dare! Anyone who's not playing has to leave the class now.' Angela Tukesbury made her way to the front of the class.

'Can't we stay and watch?' asked Carl.

'No way. It's against the rules,' Angela replied firmly.

Reluctantly, four or five others in the class got to their feet and moved to the door. Ishmar, the last of the non-players, left the classroom, slamming the door petulantly behind him. Cathy leaned against the door again.

'No one's allowed to ask for help from anyone who's just left,' ordered Angela.

As Theo watched the new girl he couldn't help frowning. She'd only arrived at the beginning of the week and already it was as if she'd been there for years. There was something about her that Theo wasn't quite sure about. Something about her that he didn't quite like. She had dark brown, almost black, hair and the palest blue eyes Theo had ever seen. Eyes that always seemed to be silently watching you – watching and waiting.

'Theo, are you staying?' Colin asked, surprised.

Theo frowned. He looked at Colin, then around the room. Colin wasn't the only one who was surprised to see him still there.

'Yes, he is staying. What's it to you?' Ricky answered before Theo had the chance.

Theo sighed. Ricky was a great friend but he did sometimes wish that Ricky didn't insist on fighting all of his battles for him. Theo looked at Ricky, who was still glaring at Colin. Theo and Ricky looked so different. Theo wore round glasses which made him look like a wise owl and was small for his age. He was also too quiet – according to Ricky, Mrs Daltry *and* his parents! No one could say the same thing about Ricky. Ricky was massive, solidly built and almost as tall as Mrs Daltry. He had a loud voice and a louder laugh and no one messed with Ricky. Theo really envied that about him. Nothing and no one scared Ricky. Theo still hadn't given up hoping that maybe just a little of it would rub off on him.

Theo could feel another sneezing fit coming on. He dug into his pocket for his tissue again. It fell apart, damp and clammy around his fingers.

'Ricky, have you got a tissue?' Theo asked, sniffing heavily.

'I've only got the one we used for Legs' hammock this morning,' Ricky answered.

Theo wrinkled up his nose. He didn't fancy using the tissue that Ricky's pet tarantula had been swinging in, but beggars couldn't be choosers.

'OK. That'll do,' Theo said.

Ricky handed it over.

All at once, a funny-peculiar feeling tickled the back of Theo's neck. He frowned. He knew at once what it was. He was being watched! Theo's head shot up. He was right. Angela was looking straight at him. He knew it! He just knew it! His frown deepened. Angela's eyes burned into his before she looked away, waiting to get everyone's attention. Theo shook his head slowly. There was definitely something about Angela Tukesbury . . . Still, Cash or Dare was her idea – and Theo had to admit, it was a good one.

'There's twenty-five of us,' Ricky said, excitedly. 'At two pounds each, that's fifty pounds.'

'And all that money is going into *my* pocket,' said Theo, wiping his nose.

'Dream on!' Ricky scoffed.

'This is a great game. We used to play it in my old school,' said Angela. 'Let's get the money bit over first.'

Each member of the class queued up to drop their pound coins into Angela's plastic cup. Theo and Ricky deliberately stood at the back of the queue. When it was Theo's turn, he peered into the cup before dropping in his money from a greater height than necessary. It made a satisfying *plink* as it hit the other coins. Slowly, he filed back to his desk. Angela smiled and put the cup down beside her.

'The winner of the game will get all this money,' she said.

Theo stared at the money cup. Pound coins danced before his eyes. Gold-coloured coins, heavy and glistening.

'The first rule of this game is no one is allowed to let anyone outside of this classroom know what we're doing. Do that and you'll be disqualified immediately.' Angela's voice was cool, almost cold.

'These are the other rules of the game,' she continued. 'We each write down a dare on a piece of paper, fold it twice then drop it in this bag.' She held up a carrier bag. 'You mustn't sign your name to it – it's got to be anonymous. Then I'll shake the bag and we each pick out a dare. If you won't or don't do exactly what's written on the paper, then you're out of the game and you lose your money. No excuses, no reasons, no explanations. If you tell anyone, anyone at all, what your dare is, you're automatically out of the game. Those left after the first round then write out new dares and we go through the whole thing again until only one person is left. And that person gets all this money.'

'That's going to be me!' Ricky muttered.

'Hang on a minute. If we're not allowed to tell anyone what our dare is, how is anyone to know whether or not we've done it?' Sarah asked from behind Theo.

'Yeah . . .'

'That's right . . .'

All eyes turned towards Angela expectantly.

'If the dare involves someone else, then that person will be a witness. If it's a dare you have to do by yourself, you have to be able to prove that you've done it. Otherwise I'll act as a witness,' Angela explained.

'Why you?' Darren asked.

''Cos this was my idea and it's my game,' Angela replied. 'And one more thing – two kinds of dares aren't allowed,' she continued. 'Spiteful ones and dangerous ones . . .'

'What d'you mean by spiteful?'

'And what d'you mean by dangerous?'

Theo was wondering that himself.

'Spiteful is like daring someone to thump someone else. And dangerous is something stupid like daring someone to run out in front of a car or a train. No dorky dares like that are allowed. They've got to have a little imagination behind them. If anyone writes down a dorky dare, the person who picks out that dare doesn't have to do it and automatically goes through to the next round,' Angela explained.

'Who's to say whether a dare is dorky or not?' Theo asked.

'I am,' Angela replied instantly.

Angela and Theo looked at each other. Theo wanted to ask who'd died and put her in charge, but he didn't. If someone else had said it first, then he would've backed them up. Only no one else spoke up either. It looked like everyone was waiting for someone else to do it.

'Remember – no one's allowed to tell anyone outside this class what we're doing. It's our secret,' said Angela.

Sarah leaned forward over her desk and tapped Theo on his back.

'Bossy, isn't she?' Sarah whispered.

'That's one word for her,' Theo agreed sourly.

'If it was me, I'd let you decide with me whether a dare is dorky or not,' Sarah added.

Theo and Ricky exchanged a look. Theo grimaced, kicking Ricky under the table as Ricky put two fingers in his mouth and mimed being violently sick. Theo wondered why Sarah always had to show him up like that? He'd known her since infant school and she was constantly drooling over him. It was *so* embarrassing.

'OK, everyone.' Angela smiled silkily. 'Write down your dares.'

Just at that moment, with that secret, silky smile, Angela reminded Theo of Legs, Ricky's tarantula spider, just before it pounced on some unsuspecting insect and gobbled it up.

'What're you going to put?' Ricky asked.

Theo shrugged. 'I don't know yet.'

'Mine's going to be really *bad*,' Ricky gloated. 'No one's getting all that money thanks to me!'

'You'd better be careful. You might get your own dare!' Theo pointed out.

Ricky's face fell. 'I hadn't thought of that,' he said.

'Yeah, well,' Theo replied. 'You can think of it now!'

Ricky's face dropped even further. Theo chewed his pencil whilst he thought. He hadn't thought of much else since Angela had told everyone about Cash or Dare two days ago. He needed something really good. Something that wasn't dangerous but something that was really difficult. Then it hit him.

'Got one!' Theo announced.

'So have I. A good one,' Ricky replied.

Ricky and Theo smirked wickedly at each other. They each bent low over their sheets of paper, their hands cupped secretively around what they were writing. The scratching noises of many pens and pencils moving rapidly across paper filled the room. Cathy, still guarding the door, leaned against it to write down her dare. Theo got a tickle in his throat and coughed impatiently, then coughed again to get rid of it. He'd be glad when his rotten cold went off to torment someone else!

One girl in the class looked around slowly. Everyone was too busy writing to notice her. She slipped an already folded piece of paper out of her skirt pocket. Frowning deeply, she looked down at it. Indecision clouded her face.

Come on. Don't chicken out now, she thought sternly.

That was why she'd written down her dare in advance. She knew that if she had to write it down in the class, she'd never go through with it. Her dare was dangerous. Very dangerous. Someone could end up getting hurt, but what other choice did she have?

Do it. Just do it, she told herself.

Her face cleared. Her indecision passed. Lips pursed with stubborn resolve, she held her pre-prepared dare in her hand, ready to drop it into the carrier bag.

You don't have any choice. She kept repeating that thought in her head, over and over. *You don't have any choice.*

But the frown never left her face.

## Chapter Three

# Theo in Trouble

'I feel sorry for the person who gets my dare,' Ricky announced to no one in particular.

All the dares had been dropped in the carrier bag. Everyone was jostling for position – no one wanted to be the first or the last to pick one out.

'Right then. I'll give them out now,' Angela declared.

'Can't we pick them ourselves?' Sarah protested from beside Theo.

'No, or we'll be here all day,' Angela replied. 'But first . . .'

Angela picked up the cup filled with pound coins and tipped all the money into a small brown envelope before sealing it. She put the envelope in the money belt around her waist. Then she walked about, fishing into the carrier bag and passing out the pieces of paper to the crowd around her. When she gave Theo his dare, she looked at him without smiling, without blinking. Theo frowned. He wished he knew what her problem was. Angela moved on, without saying a word.

Theo stepped back from the crowd and surreptitiously began to unfold his dare. He coughed wearily, wishing his head would stop pounding – just for five seconds.

'Remember, you're not allowed to tell *anyone* what your dare is or you're immediately disqualified,' Angela reminded everyone. She took the last dare out of the carrier bag for herself.

No sound could be heard except that of pieces of paper being rustled as they were unfolded. Moments later the protests erupted virtually simultaneously. Theo's mouth fell open. He gasped. Groans and cries like 'What ratbag wrote down this one?!' filled the room. Theo looked at Ricky. Ricky's face was all scrunched up as if he was chewing a lemon, peel and all.

'Your dare can't be any worse than mine,' Theo informed him.

'Wanna bet?' Ricky scowled.

No, Theo didn't want to bet. It would be too easy to win. He grimaced as he looked down at his dare again.

*At exactly ten minutes to six tonight, you must enter the deserted warehouse at 117 Buzan Road, behind the shopping precinct. You must enter the ventilation shaft at the right side of the building and crawl inside QUIETLY. Crawl to the end of the tunnel – no turning off into the tunnels which branch to the right or left. Keep straight. Once you've reached the end of the tunnel, you must wait for an hour until 7 p.m. then leave QUIETLY. If you don't stay for the full hour, you lose. I'll be watching . . .*

*Who'll be watching*? Frowning, Theo looked around the room. Who could've written this one? Theo caught Sarah's eye and she smiled at him. Theo quickly looked away. Was it her? But hang on, how could Sarah know that he would get her dare? So that couldn't be right.

Somehow he had to get past his mum and dad and get out of the house to be at – where was it again? – 117 Buzan Road just before six. It might've seemed like more of an adventure and less like mission impossible if his head and nose hadn't felt like they were stuffed full of cotton wool. The aches in his arms and legs were spreading to his fingers and toes. Everything was hurting! Even his fingernails.

'What's going on in here?'

Theo was so caught up in his dare that he hadn't even heard the classroom door open. Cathy had abandoned her post the moment Angela had handed her a dare and here was the result. Mrs Daltry stood in the doorway, her eyes narrow slits of suspicion.

No one spoke.

'Angela, tell me what's going on in here,' Mrs Daltry commanded.

'Nothing, Mrs Daltry. I was just telling everyone about my old school,' Angela replied.

She looked so convincingly innocent that she almost had Theo believing she was telling the truth, and he knew better!

'It must have been riveting for everyone to give up their lunch to hear it,' Mrs Daltry said.

'I was just telling everyone about a boy in my old class who insisted he'd been kidnapped by aliens. He said he'd been away for over a year but that the aliens went back in time to return him to his bed only an hour after they'd taken him. But the funny thing was . . .'

'That's quite enough of that nonsense, Angela,' Mrs Daltry frowned. 'Everyone – out! All of you! I shouldn't have to tell you to go to lunch.'

The teacher waited by the door as everyone trooped past her. Ricky and Theo were practically the last to leave. Mrs Daltry snatched Ricky's cap off his head.

'Don't wear this in the classroom, Ricky. I've told you that before,' she snapped, waving the cap above Ricky's head.

'Sorry, Mrs Daltry,' Ricky muttered. 'Can I have it back?'

'No. I'll return it at the end of the day,' Mrs Daltry said tartly. She shoved Ricky's cap into her jacket pocket.

Angela leaned against the wall in the corridor, watching. She waited until Mrs Daltry strode by them, chewing on yet another liquorice allsort, before speaking.

'Theo, you're not allowed to tell anyone your dare,' Angela said urgently. 'That goes for you too, Ricky.'

'You didn't have to wait behind to tell us that. We know the rules,' Ricky frowned.

'Yeah, you've told us often enough.' Theo sniffed resentfully.

Who did Angela think she was – staying behind to show

them up like that? Did she think they were going to cheat the moment her back was turned?

'Just saying,' Angela replied. And with that, off she marched.

Theo took a look at Ricky. Ricky looked how Theo felt – annoyed!

'Never mind her. She's just a weevil head and three-quarters,' Ricky said.

'A weevil head and seven-eighths.'

'A weevil head and fifteen-sixteenths.'

Ricky and Theo made their way to the lunch hall. By that time Angela was a weevil head and two hundred and fifty-five, two hundred and fifty-sixths!

Theo felt horrible. More horrible than he'd ever felt in his life before. Dad placed a hand on Theo's forehead, tutting over and over as he did so.

'You are burning up,' said Dad.

'Bu' I feezin',' Theo protested.

'What was that?' Dad took the thermometer out of Theo's mouth.

'But I'm freezing,' Theo repeated. 'And everything aches. And my headache's getting worse. And I feel like this tissue here.' Theo held up a tissue which he'd only used twice and already it was on its last legs – soggy and falling apart!

'A few days in bed and you'll be back to your normal gungy, grungy self,' said Dad.

'But I can't stay in bed . . .'

'Theo, it's not a cold – you've got the flu and moaning about it won't change that,' Dad interrupted, popping the thermometer back into Theo's mouth.

Theo groaned. What about his dare? What about his fifty pounds? It wasn't fair. It was all Mrs Daltry's fault. She was the one who'd sent for Dad after the afternoon break. Theo was sure he could've made it to the end of the day but his teacher disagreed.

'You look terrible, you sound worse and I'm not going

to let you pass your germs on to everyone else in the class,' Mrs Daltry had told him testily. 'You're going home.'

Ordinarily, Theo would've been glad to go home. But not today of all days. Now Mum and Dad would be watching him like a hawk. How would he ever get out of the house to get to 117 Buzan Road? Theo took the thermometer out of his mouth.

'Dad . . . I don't suppose you and Mum will let me go out this evening – just for an hour?' Theo asked.

Dad stared at Theo. 'You must be crazy out of your head! You're not going anywhere tonight.'

Theo sighed. He had his answer. The doorbell rang.

'And keep that thermometer in your mouth,' Dad ordered. 'I'll be right back.'

Dad left the room, still muttering incredulously at Theo's request. Theo twisted and turned in his bed, trying to get comfortable. He pulled his duvet up past his neck. He was freezing, and yet perspiration was dripping off him like rain-water. He'd never felt so lousy. It was as if every drop of blood in his body was hurting. And he was going to lose the dare contest. That was what hurt the most.

A minute later, Theo's bedroom door opened. The peak of a baseball cap appeared first, followed by Ricky's head.

'Can I come in?' he asked softly.

Theo took the thermometer out of his mouth. 'If you don't mind catching my germs,' he sniffed, reaching for yet another tissue from his bedside table.

Ricky walked into the room, carefully closing the door behind him.

'Your dad said I can't stay long,' Ricky whispered.

Theo frowned and struggled to sit up.

'Ricky, why're you whispering?'

'Am I?' Ricky's voice was even quieter than before.

Theo raised his eyebrows. Ricky laughed.

'Sorry,' Ricky said ruefully, his voice back to normal. 'How're you feeling?'

'Like a plate of week-old spaghetti,' Theo replied. 'Ricky, I'm in trouble. What am I going to do about my dare? I was meant to do it this evening.'

'Can't you put it off until tomorrow or some time later this week?'

'No. It's got to be tonight or never. I'm meant to go somewhere later and I feel terrible. Besides, there's no way Mum and Dad will let me get past the front door. If it wasn't for this rotten cold, I'd have won the fifty pounds for sure,' Theo said glumly.

'You reckon? You're sicker than I thought!' Ricky replied. 'It's affecting your brain!'

'I'm too ill to argue with you.' Theo reached out for another tissue. He had another coughing fit, followed by one sneeze after another and another. After that, Theo collapsed back against his pillows.

'You sound like a frog on a bad day and look like year-old spaghetti, not week-old spaghetti,' Ricky said, with his version of sympathy.

Theo nodded. 'I know.' He wiped his nose. 'So what was your dare like? Have you done it yet?'

Ricky shook his head. 'Just thinking about it makes me want to chuck!'

'Is it really that sick-making?' Theo asked.

Ricky nodded, his face long. Theo and Ricky watched each other. Theo was dying to know what Ricky's dare was. And from the look on Ricky's face, he was thinking the same thing. Suddenly Ricky stared at Theo, his eyes huge and bright. A slow smile crept over his face.

'I've got it!' He waved his hands in the air.

'Got what?'

'The perfect solution.' Ricky grinned. 'Your dare has to be done tonight and mine doesn't. So why don't we swap dares?'

'Swap? But Angela said—'

'If you don't tell her, I won't,' Ricky interrupted. 'Come on. If we keep it to ourselves, who's to know?'

'Isn't it cheating?'

'No. All we're doing is swapping. I won't help you with yours and you won't help me with mine,' Ricky replied. He had it all figured out.

'What's your dare?' Theo asked suspiciously.

'Oh, no, you don't,' Ricky said. 'If you agree then we swap dares and we don't swap back.'

'Can't I see it first? It might be worse than the one I've already got,' Theo argued.

'You can't leave your house to do the one you've got, so what difference does it make?' Ricky pointed out.

Theo thought for a moment. 'And it's strictly between us two?'

'Yep!'

'Promise?'

'Promise.'

'Oh, all right then. Hand your dare over.'

Ricky fished into his jacket pocket and took out a now crumpled piece of paper.

'Where's your one?' he asked.

Theo lifted up his pillow and took out his dare. Ricky walked over to Theo. He tentatively held out his piece of paper. Theo did the same. Their hands were about twenty centimetres apart but neither of them moved closer.

'After three?' Ricky suggested.

Theo nodded.

'One . . .'

'Two . . .'

'*Three!*'

They each grabbed for the piece of paper in the other's hand. His heart hammering, Theo smoothed out Ricky's crumpled piece of paper.

*You will ask Sarah McWilliam out for a date. You must take her for a meal or to the pictures before the end of next week – your treat!*

Theo stared in total horror. Sarah! The worst girl in the class! The worst girl in the whole school! It was bad enough that she sat behind him and was constantly tap-tapping on his shoulder, but now he had to take her out as well? Not a chance! Not in this lifetime!

'I want my old dare back,' Theo said immediately.

'No way!' Ricky laughed. 'We made a deal.'

'I'm not taking Sarah out anywhere. I'd rather eat one of Mum's fish pies. I'd rather mow the lawn for the next ten years. I'd rather have the flu for the next one hundred years!' Theo shook his head so hard, his neck started hurting.

'Tough!' Ricky grinned. He looked down at the dare in his hand. 'This is easy compared to taking Sarah out! I'll have to sneak out of our flat but that's no problem. I'll wear my action man kit – trainers, black jeans, black jacket, black baseball cap . . . It'll be fun!'

'Stuff fun! Give me my old dare back,' Theo demanded.

'Not a chance.'

*'Please!'*

Ricky shook his head, not even trying to hide the victorious smirk on his face.

'But Sarah probably wrote this herself!' Theo tossed the dare aside as if the paper were suddenly burning his fingers.

'Tough and two-thirds!' Ricky replied.

Dad came into the room with a glass of orange juice.

'I think that's enough for this evening, Ricky. Theo needs his rest,' said Dad.

'OK, Mr Mosley,' Ricky said. 'I was just going anyway.'

Ricky practically sprinted to the bedroom door. 'See you tomorrow, Theo,' he smiled.

'Ricky . . .'

Theo attempted to get out of bed. Too late! Ricky was gone. Moments later, Theo heard the front door slam shut.

'Where d'you think you're going?' Dad asked. 'Back in bed.'

Reluctantly, Theo swung his legs back between the sheets.

'Mum'll be home soon.' Dad smiled as he tucked Theo in, before sitting down at the edge of the bed. Then he spotted the thermometer on the duvet.

'Oh, yeah! I forgot about that,' Dad said, popping it back in Theo's mouth. His smile turned into a sudden grimace and he groaned. 'I've just had a horrible thought. As you're ill, Mum'll probably insist on doing one of her fish pies for dinner. Why does she always wait until one of us is sick before inflicting it on us?'

'Some form of torture so we'll hurry up and get well?' Theo suggested grimly, before putting the thermometer back into his mouth.

'Or maybe she reckons that's the only time we'll eat it, when we're too weak to argue,' said Dad.

Dad and Theo sighed at each other in total sympathy.

Theo sagged back against his pillows. What had he done to deserve Sarah *and* Mum's fish pie, all in the one day? Being sick was the pits!

## Chapter Four

# I Did It . . .

### 17:00 hrs Thursday, 15th May

Well, I did it. Theo will be at the warehouse at six tonight and I'll be watching. He'll be all right – I hope. Please God, let him be all right. Please don't let anything go wrong. Don't let him get caught . . .

Chapter Five

# Ricky Disappears

Theo took a deep breath, held it and pressed the button to take one more step. He died instantly! A huge snake's head appeared on the screen and grinned maliciously at him. Theo hated the way the snakes always grinned at you when you stepped on them. But at least he didn't have to listen to the snake sniggering at him because the telly volume was turned right down.

'Stupid game anyway,' he muttered to himself.

Theo went over to the games console and took out 'Combat Rattlesnake', which at that moment was one of his least favourite games! Then he went through all his other games disks. What should he play next? It would've been great if Ricky was there to play the games with him. Playing by yourself got a bit tedious after a while. Never mind, Ricky was bound to come and see him after school.

'Theo, I hope you're resting in there.'

'Yes, Mum,' Theo called back.

He'd had a real battle persuading Mum to allow him downstairs. He'd been in bed all morning and most of the afternoon but Mum seemed to think he should stay put, remain still and not even blink unless it was absolutely vital. Theo'd grumbled on and on for so long that Mum finally let him come downstairs just to shut him up. But she insisted that he kept a blanket wrapped around him and stayed put on the sofa.

'No telly. No CDs. Read a book or sleep,' Mum ordered.

That was why the volume on the telly was turned right down. Mum'd taken the day off to stay with him, but she was still working from her PC in the front room. Theo didn't want to disturb her – that way she wouldn't find out he was playing games!

Theo had decided that he'd play 'Timeslip' next, when the doorbell rang. He glanced at the LED display on the DVD. Who on earth could be calling at half past three in the afternoon? He went out into the hall as Mum opened the door.

It was the police – a tall, black man and a woman with brown hair, both in uniform. And Mrs Burridge, Ricky's mum.

Theo stared. The police . . . They hadn't yet said a word and already his heart was beginning to thump in an odd, hiccupy way. And Ricky's mum – she looked terrible. There were dark rings around her glistening eyes, her lips were a thin, pinched line and her hands circled each other constantly. Her eyes darted back and forth, taking in every part of the hall as if searching for something.

'Mrs Mosley?' the policeman enquired.

'Ricky? RICKY?' Ricky's mum called out at the top of her voice.

Theo's mum switched her puzzled gaze from the police to Ricky's mum. 'Etta, Ricky's not here. What's wrong? What's the matter?'

Ricky's mum's eyes filled with tears which spilled over onto her cheeks.

'Ricky . . .' she began hoarsely. 'Ricky's disappeared. He's gone missing.'

Theo gasped, winded as if he'd been kicked in the stomach.

'What d'you mean – he's gone missing?' Theo's mum asked, shocked. 'Look, come in. Come in all of you.'

Mum led the way to the living room. Theo stepped out of the way but the grown-ups were all too preoccupied to take any notice of him.

'We understand that Ricky arrived home safely after visiting Theo yesterday afternoon but . . .' The policeman didn't get any further.

'We both had an early dinner, then watched telly. He went up to his room after that, but this morning I found that his bed hadn't been slept in. I . . . I don't know what to do. I've tried his mobile but it just goes straight through to his voicemail.' Ricky's mum kept clenching and unclenching her hands – over and over. As if suddenly aware of what her hands were doing, she hugged her arms tightly about herself before speaking again. 'Are you certain Ricky isn't here? I was hoping . . .'

'Oh, Etta, I'm so sorry. We haven't seen him since he left yesterday afternoon,' Theo's mum said. 'I wish we had.'

'Oh. I see. Are . . . are you sure?'

Theo's mum nodded unhappily. 'I'm sure there's a perfectly reasonable explanation for all this. Ricky will turn up soon, I'm sure he will.'

'Yes, of course he will,' Ricky's mum agreed, her voice barely audible.

Theo's mum put her arm around Ricky's mum's shoulders. Neither of them spoke. A tangible fear descended on the room. Theo swallowed hard, then swallowed again. Fear clogged his throat. Ricky . . . The policeman and woman exchanged a look, their faces sombre.

'Theo, we understand that you and Ricky are very good friends. Did he say anything to you about going somewhere last night or this morning?' asked the policeman.

Theo was burning up – from the top of his head to the tips of his toenails. And he couldn't breathe. No matter how hard he tried, he just couldn't catch his breath.

'It's all right, Theo. Don't be afraid,' said the policeman. 'I'm sure we'll find Ricky safe and sound.'

Theo gasped audibly. He still couldn't get his breath. It was as if he was underwater, fighting to find a way up and out, fighting not to drown. Ricky was missing.

*Ricky was missing . . .*

Was it the dare? It couldn't be the dare. It'd been so simple. A matter of spending an hour crouched in the ventilator shaft of a warehouse behind the precinct. Nothing spiteful. Nothing dangerous . . . But maybe the ventilator shaft had collapsed. Maybe the whole building had collapsed. What if Ricky was trapped, or hurt, or worse . . .

'Theo?'

Theo turned his stricken gaze to his mum.

'Theo, d'you know where Ricky is?' Mum asked slowly.

Theo's tongue was frozen to the roof of his mouth and it refused to budge.

'Theo?' his mum prompted softly.

The dare contest. They weren't meant to tell anyone about it. But Ricky . . . Where was Ricky? Theo swallowed hard.

'117 Buzan Road. The warehouse.' Theo's breath came out in a desperate rush.

None of the grown-ups spoke.

'It was a dare.' Theo fought to keep his voice steady. 'Ricky had to spend an hour at 117 Buzan Road from six yesterday evening.'

'A dare?' Ricky's mum asked, sharply. 'You dared him?'

'NO! No. It's a game and practically everyone in our class is playing. He didn't get my dare.' Theo shook his head. He couldn't get his head clear. His words were coming out in a horribly confused jumble, but in spite of that, the grown-ups seemed to understand him.

'And Ricky was dared to go to 117 Buzan Road?' The policewoman frowned.

Theo nodded, his left hand cupped inside his right to hide the fact that he was crossing his fingers. He was seconds away from being sick – actually being sick on the living-room carpet. If Ricky was hurt or trapped then it'd be all his fault.

*Because the dare had originally been his . . .*

'I'll radio in this new information,' said the policeman.

He took out his radio and walked into the hall.

'Mrs Burridge, I don't suppose we can persuade you to go home and wait for us to call you?' the policewoman asked.

'No. I'm coming with you,' Ricky's mum argued. 'If you don't take me, I'll run all the way there if I have to.'

'Calm down, Mrs Burridge. We'll take you,' the policewoman soothed.

The policeman came back into the room. 'Well, there's been nothing untoward reported from Buzan Road in the last twenty-four hours, but we'll check it out anyway.'

'Etta, let me know . . . what happens . . .' Theo's mum struggled to find the right words.

Ricky's mum nodded.

'We may need to come back to get more information from Theo,' the policeman warned.

'I understand,' said Theo's mum.

She escorted them to the front door and let them out. Theo watched, afraid to blink or move in case he missed something. He felt so strange. So peculiar. So *calm*. But it wasn't real. It was as if there was a storm raging all around him and slowly but surely closing in on him.

The moment the front door was shut, Theo's mum turned to face him, her eyes filled with worry and concern and the anger that sprang from both.

'Right, young man. I want to know all about this dare business and exactly what you've been up to,' she demanded.

And the storm descended.

## Chapter Six

# An Omission and a Find

On Monday morning, the weather was horrible. The weatherman on the radio had called it a 'marvellous Mediterranean scorcher'. As far as Theo was concerned it was hot and sticky and it wasn't even eight-thirty yet. It would make what he had to do that much more difficult.

'Theo, are you sure you're able to go to school?' Mum asked.

'That's the umpteenth and a half time you've asked me that,' Theo said. 'I'm fine.'

'You sure you're over the flu?' Dad frowned.

'Course! I'm super fit,' Theo smiled. 'I've only got a little bit of a sniffle left.'

'Hhmm!' Mum wasn't convinced.

'Hhmm!' Neither was Dad!

'I wouldn't be going to school if I didn't feel OK,' Theo pointed out.

'Hhhmmm! I guess not. You know you can stay home for another day if you want to.' Theo's mum still wasn't completely satisfied.

Theo forced his smile to widen. 'No, thanks.'

'Are you sure?'

'Mum, Dad – chill!' Theo said, exasperated. 'What's this meant to be? Nagging in stereo?'

'We're only asking . . .'

'I want to know why you're in such a rush to get to school.' Dad raised an eyebrow.

'Because I'm fine,' Theo said firmly.

He'd never had to act so hard in his life. His head was

pounding and his body still ached, and as for 'a little bit of a sniffle' – it was more like the river Thames running through his nose! But he knew there was no way Mum and Dad would let him out of the house unless he convinced them that he'd got over his flu.

And he had to get out of the house.

Because Ricky was still missing.

Ricky's mum had phoned late on Friday night to tell them that Ricky hadn't been found and that the police had found 117 Buzan Road empty and deserted. She hadn't phoned back since to say otherwise. On Sunday evening, Dad phoned the police who told him that they were stepping up the search for Ricky. Dad asked again about the warehouse on Buzan Road. As far as the police were concerned there was no sign that Ricky had ever been near the place.

But Theo felt there had to be more to it than that – the sick, anxious feeling in the pit of his stomach told him so. Ricky's disappearance had something to do with the dare – Theo was sure of it. Now it was up to him to find Ricky and prove it. He'd already lost the weekend because Mum and Dad wouldn't let him out of the house. There was no way he was going to lose yet another day. He'd lost too much time already. He had to find Ricky – he just had to.

'See you later, Mum. 'Bye, Dad.' Theo fled out of the house before his parents could say another word.

He glanced down at his watch. He'd have to hurry if he was going to make it to Buzan Road before school started.

117 Buzan Road was a huge, two-storey warehouse with dirty-grey, barred windows and a heavily padlocked front entrance. The roof was flat and the whole building looked what it was, derelict and neglected. Theo stood outside the front doors. He wiped the perspiration from his forehead, wondering vaguely if it was the weather or the tail end of the flu or what he might find that was causing him to sweat so much. Theo looked around. How could he get past the

front gates for a closer look? Had the police got into the warehouse? They must've done. They'd probably contacted the warehouse owner, got the keys and walked in. Theo would have to find another way.

'Come on, Theo – think!' he told himself sternly.

How would Ricky have got in?

'Of course!' Theo mentally kicked himself.

*The ventilator shaft!*

Theo turned and walked to his right, scrutinizing the building for the ventilator shaft mentioned in the dare. Nothing. Surreptitiously, Theo looked around again. He wanted to make sure he wasn't being watched. No, he was safe. Everyone was in a hurry, their eyes on the road straight ahead as they rushed to work or school. Theo ducked around the side of the building. Was the ventilator shaft here? He carried on walking and searching. Still nothing. And he couldn't get round the back because a big double gate blocked his way.

The entrance to the shaft had to be round the other side of the building. Blowing his nose, Theo strolled out onto the main road, fervently hoping that he didn't look suspicious. The last thing he wanted was to attract attention. He walked past the front entrance, still searching for the elusive ventilator shaft. He turned round the corner and searched along the other side of the building. Eureka! There it was! A half-metre high mesh grille in front of the ventilator shaft.

Theo took a quick look around again. It was all clear. He crouched down.

'Ricky?' Theo whispered through the grille. Silence. 'Ricky?' He tried again, louder this time.

Theo ran his fingers along the top of the grille, then down the sides, looking for a gap into which he could work his fingers to pull the whole grille off. Nothing doing. The grille was tight against the wall. Theo sat back on his heels and frowned. Something wasn't right . . . Something was *missing*. Then Theo realized what it was. Dust! There was no dust on his fingers. There was no dust on the grille. That proved that Ricky had found a way to move the grille and the dust had fallen off it. Or maybe the dust had fallen off when the police moved it – if they had . . .

Theo's eyes widened with shock as he realized something else. He *hadn't* told the police about the ventilator shaft. Theo frowned deeply as he tried to remember just what he *had* said. He'd told them about the dares and the address of the warehouse but not about the ventilator shaft – he was sure of it.

'RICKY?' Theo called urgently through the mesh.

Even if the police had searched the warehouse, they might still have missed Ricky if he was injured in this shaft somewhere. Theo swallowed hard, the sick feeling in the pit of his stomach intensifying. Lacing his fingers into the holes in the mesh, Theo pulled as hard as he could. He winced as the wire mesh cut deeply into his fingers, but he didn't stop. One corner of the grille shifted. Theo pulled harder. Suddenly, unexpectedly, the grille came right away from the wall. Theo fell over backwards, hitting the ground with a hard THUMP! Quickly he looked around. It was all right, he was still alone.

Theo sat upright and peered into the shaft. After about a metre, it melted into darkness. Theo knelt closer.

'Ricky . . .' His voice was a whisper again.

A bird rose from his stomach to flutter in his throat – at least that's what it felt like. He didn't fancy going into the shaft at all, but if Ricky had gone in there then he had to too. He had to find out what'd happened to his friend. Theo glanced down at his watch. He'd have to hurry, or he'd be late for school.

Taking a deep breath, Theo crawled into the shaft. It was filthy-dirty and full of dust which made him sneeze – and the stink! It was like diesel fumes and cigarette smoke and rabbit, mouse and elephant droppings all mixed up into a noxious cocktail. The smell whistled up his nose like a sharp wind, in spite of his cold.

The floor was littered with bits of dirt and debris, some too small to see in the half light of the tunnel but not too small to dig into his palms and knees and shins as he moved forwards. But that wasn't the thing that slowed him down. No, what made him hesitate was the darkness sweeping over him like a slow tide, in spite of the bright sunlight outside. The light in the shaft was a darkening grey with swirls of dust like a mist dancing all around him. Theo crawled on, waving his hand before him every so often in a vain attempt to keep the dust out of his eyes and nose. And the tunnel grew narrower as he crawled on, until he had to tuck his head and elbows in to make sure he didn't hit the top or the sides of the tunnel.

After crawling what felt like half the length of a football pitch, the shaft split into three, with tunnels to the left and right as well as straight ahead. Theo looked down each tunnel in turn. Each one looked like the others. Theo dug out a tissue and wiped his nose as he considered. Straight ahead. He'd try the tunnel straight ahead first. He carried on crawling.

Minutes passed. Theo's back was beginning to ache from being hunched up for so long. He longed to stand up straight and stretch out but it wasn't possible, not in that narrow shaft. Theo was beginning to think about maybe turning back when he saw a strange light ahead. He moved faster, his eyes still on the light. His right hand landed on something soft – like material. Instantly, Theo drew his hand away in case it was something yucky! It was a black baseball cap. Theo snatched it up and turned it over. 'CHILL!' was written across the front. Ricky's cap . . . There was no doubt about it. Shock, like a flash of summer lightning, shot through Theo's body.

Ricky *was* here. In this shaft.

'RICKY!' Theo hollered at the top of his voice. 'ARE YOU IN HERE?'

Silence. Dust swirled madly around him, but nothing else

stirred. Theo took up Ricky's cap and stuffed it into his trouser pocket. He moved towards the light in front of him. At last he could see where it was coming from – grimy windows up and down the opposite wall, flooding the deserted warehouse floor with an eerie blue-yellow light. And from Theo's position he could see that the warehouse was deserted.

Theo sighed with disappointment. He sat for a few moments, frustration washing over him. But what did he expect? The police had already been here and they hadn't found Ricky.

But they hadn't known about the ventilator shaft. So Ricky could still be in one of the tunnels somewhere. Theo tried to turn around to go back the way he came. He couldn't. The tunnel was too narrow. Panic, like a sneeze, began to tickle at him.

'Don't you dare,' Theo muttered sternly. 'Don't you dare lose your head and panic and flip and lose your cool and be a doof and . . . and let Ricky down.'

The last one seemed to do the trick! Then all at once, Theo realized what he had to do. He started crawling backwards. Each second seemed to last for ever as Theo made his slow, careful way backwards through the tunnel. It took twice as long as before. The dust was worse, swirling and spinning up into his mouth and nose and eyes. And it was getting unbearably hot. His chest was tight and his head was beginning to hurt, but Theo couldn't give up. Not now. Not yet. Ricky might need him.

At last Theo reached the place where the shaft branched off in three directions. Here at last he could turn around. Now it wasn't so bad. But even so, Theo wanted to leave, to get out into the open and breathe air that wasn't full of dust and dirt. He looked ahead longingly, then turned and crawled along the tunnel now on his left. This tunnel also ended with a grille looking out over a warehouse floor, but to Theo's surprise, it looked out over the darkened basement level rather than the ground floor. The ceiling was a metre above him, whilst the floor was three metres below. Theo backed up and tried the only tunnel he hadn't yet explored. This one just led to another part of the ground floor. There was no further sign of Ricky. Theo didn't know whether to be sad or grateful. But not finding Ricky unconscious in the shaft meant that Ricky was all right. Ricky was safe . . . *wasn't he*?

Theo couldn't leave the ventilator shaft fast enough. He emerged from it, coughing and spluttering, his mouth full of goodness only knew what. After the shaft, the sunlight was warm and welcome.

'I'm not going in there again,' Theo muttered.

And he certainly wasn't. Not if he could possibly help it. He glanced down at his watch, then stared.

*Nine-thirty!*

How did it get so late already? Theo took off up the street, oblivious to the startled looks being directed at him. Mrs Daltry was going to bite off his head and play football with it!

Chapter Seven

# Someone's Lying

Theo took a deep breath, then another. Might as well get it over with, he thought.

He opened his classroom door, his eyes on the ground. He didn't want to watch Mrs Daltry winding up for attack. He'd seen it plenty of times before.

But the attack never came. The room was totally silent. Theo looked up and immediately his breath caught in his throat.

Two policemen stood in the room, at the front of the class. One of the policemen was stocky, the other was beansprout thin.

'You've found Ricky?' Theo asked eagerly.

'No, they haven't. And where on earth have you been? You're covered in dust. No, never mind. Just hurry up and sit down,' Mrs Daltry said in a rush.

'You're Theo Mosley, is that right?' asked the stocky policeman.

Theo nodded. He looked around. All eyes were on him.

'Theo?' Mrs Daltry prompted impatiently.

Theo stumbled to his desk and plonked himself down. The chair next to him seemed ominously empty. Ricky's chair . . . Theo tore his eyes away from it. Why were the police here? Why weren't they out looking for Ricky?

'Now we know from Theo that some of you were playing a dare game. How many of you were playing?' the stocky policeman asked, his tone light and friendly.

Theo's face started to burn. What would everyone else think about him telling the police about the dare game?

Theo straightened up in his chair, his lips set. It didn't matter what everyone else thought. Ricky was more important than some stupid game. It was just tough and three-quarters if the others didn't like it.

'It's all right, I promise. We just want to know how many of you were involved in this game?' The stocky policeman smiled. He was the only one of the two policemen doing any talking.

Reluctantly, hands started going up into the air.

Both policemen looked around the room slowly. The policeman who seemed to be in charge turned his attention to Theo. 'Theo, what was Ricky's dare? Try to remember.'

Theo swallowed hard. 'It said something like – "Around six o'clock, enter the deserted warehouse at 117 Buzan Road, behind the shopping precinct. Go into the ventilation shaft, wait for an hour, then leave. If you don't stay for the full hour, you lose." Something like that.'

'Oh, so the dares were written down?' the policeman said, surprised.

Theo nodded. 'We all had to write down anonymous dares and put them in a carrier bag. Then we each got a dare which we had to do.'

'So who wrote Ricky's dare?' asked the policeman.

All the hands came down. Theo looked around. He'd been wondering that himself. The hands stayed down. Then Theo remembered something else. He put his hand up.

'Yes, Theo?' Mrs Daltry prompted.

'I've just remembered what Ricky's dare had written at the end of it,' said Theo. 'It said, "I'll be watching."'

Silence. The classroom was as still as a cemetery at night for a few moments. It was as if everyone in the room was holding their breath.

'Let me say again that we're not interested in blaming anyone or getting anyone into trouble,' said the stocky policeman. 'At this stage we just want to find Ricky. So please, who wrote that dare?'

Theo looked around again. No one moved.

The policeman in charge walked over to Mrs Daltry and they muttered together for a few moments. Theo strained closer to hear what they were saying, as did everyone else, but the words were indistinct.

Mrs Daltry shook her head, then pointed to the white-boards at the front and side of the classroom. The policeman reluctantly nodded before turning around.

'We'd like each of you in turn to write out the dares you made up last week,' the policeman explained. 'And please put your name next to your dare once you've written it down.'

Theo risked a curious glance at the skinny policeman. He still hadn't said a word and it didn't look like he was going to either. Was he just there to watch – to see if anyone gave themselves away?

'Claire and Robert, you can start,' Mrs Daltry said, handing out blue pens to the two pupils closest to her.

Robert and Claire rose unwillingly to their feet. They walked over to the whiteboards, their arms lying like wet socks at their sides.

'Well?' Mrs Daltry prompted.

Hesitantly, they both started to write.

'If you're a boy, I dare you to wear a frilly dress and walk around the block in it. You must be seen by at least one other person in the class or it doesn't count. If you're a girl, I dare you to get one of the boys in the class to wear a frilly dress and walk around the block without telling him why,' Claire wrote.

'So that was *you* was it, you bat-breathed dweeb? I got that one!' Tony said with disgust.

Everyone creased up laughing. Theo read Claire's dare enviously. He wished he'd thought of that one!

'That's enough,' Mrs Daltry said sternly. 'All of you just remember Ricky and why we're doing this.'

The laughter died away instantly.

'Write a letter asking Mrs McMurtry if she's bald under her wig and sign it.' Robert's writing got smaller and smaller towards the end of the sentence, but not small enough! It could still be read, even from the back of the class.

Everyone reckoned the headmistress, Mrs McMurtry, was as bald as an egg because of the funny-peculiar way her hair sat on her head. No one would deliberately style their hair like that, so it had to be a wig – at least, that was the consensus. Mrs Daltry tutted heavily but didn't comment on either of the dares.

'OK, leave the pens up there and sit down,' she ordered. 'Chris, Danny, you're next.'

One by one, everyone had to go up to the front of the class and write down their dares. Theo'd been right about the dare Ricky had swapped with him. Sarah *had* written it herself!

She must've reckoned that even if a girl got her dare, she'd still get to eat and see a film for free, Theo thought with disgust.

Many minutes passed before the last dare was written down. Both whiteboards were covered from top to bottom with scribbled dares. And not one of them mentioned Buzan Road or being there at midnight. Angry, Theo looked around the room again. Someone was lying.

'Theo, you're sure about what was written on Ricky's dare?' asked the stocky policeman doubtfully.

'Positive,' Theo replied. 'That's what it said, I promise.'

The grown-ups turned around to read the dares again.

'Someone didn't write down their real dare.' Theo voiced his thoughts.

'Right then. I'd like each of you to come up here in turn and write your name next to the dare you *received*. Not the one you wrote, the one you got,' said the policeman.

Theo understood at once. The person who'd lied and written down a brand new dare would be found out when no one claimed their dare. Clever! He looked quickly around the class. No one looked particularly anxious or upset – at least, not as far as he could see.

'The dare I got isn't on the board,' Janice complained.

'Then we'll assume your dare was written by Ricky,' the policeman smiled.

Five minutes later, every dare had the writer's initials and the receiver's name next to it. Theo sat back, puzzled. He couldn't understand it – unless there were *two* people lying? But that couldn't be right. No, Ricky's dare had been written by someone working alone – Theo was sure of it. But then, how come each dare had a name written next to it? There weren't any left over. Unless . . .

'Could those people who received the dares they wrote themselves please put their hands up,' said the policeman lightly.

That was just what Theo was thinking. If he'd written out a new dare to cover his tracks, he'd have no choice now but to claim it as the one he'd also picked out. And he was sure that was just what the person who was lying had done.

As Theo looked around, three people put their hands up. Colin, Angela and Emily . . .

'Hhmm! I see.'

The two policemen turned their backs on the class and whispered together.

When the policeman in charge turned back to the class, he said, 'You can put your hands down now.'

Angela's arm was already at her side. Colin and Emily put their hands down.

'I think all I'd say at this juncture is if any of you see or hear from Ricky or remember anything, anything at all that could help us, please phone the police or get your parents to phone us,' said the policeman.

'Is that it? Is that all you're going to do? Someone's *lying* . . .' Theo protested.

'Theo, that's enough,' Mrs Daltry admonished.

The policeman opened his mouth to speak, then closed it, looking thoughtful.

'I'd also like to say this.' He waved his hand in the direction of the two whiteboards. 'Playing so-called games for money can be very dangerous. I see that none of these dares is out-and-out dangerous but a lot of them are . . . dubious, to say the least. And apart from anything else, you might start out as friends playing these kinds of games for money, but that's not how you'd end up – I guarantee it. It's not worth it. So my advice is – don't do it. And consider the consequences. Ricky Burridge is *missing* . . .'

'Thank you, Sergeant Ridley. I'm sure we've all heard and understood every word you've said.' Mrs Daltry looked around the room slowly, her blazing eyes sending laser bolts into anyone brave enough to return her gaze. Looking at her, Theo was sure that none of them had heard the last of this dare business.

'We have to go now. We have other classrooms to visit,' said the stocky policeman. 'But if anyone remembers anything that might help find Ricky, get in touch with us. It's very important that you do.'

As Mrs Daltry saw the two policemen to the door, Theo took out Ricky's crumpled-up cap from his trouser pocket and laid it on his lap beneath his table. He looked down at it.

'Ricky, where *are* you?' he mouthed to the cap.

A strange tingling appeared at the back of his neck. Theo rubbed his nape impatiently. Then he realized what it meant. His head whipped around. Angela was watching him. The moment he caught her gaze, she looked away. Theo glared at her. She probably hated him for spoiling her dare game. Tough and fifteen-sixteenths! What did she want him to do? Say nothing to the police?

The moment the door closed behind the policemen, Mrs Daltry turned to the class.

'We all have some very serious talking to do,' said Mrs Daltry. 'Or rather I have some talking to do, you lot will listen . . .'

The mid-morning buzzer sounded. The whole class gave a collective sigh of relief.

'This isn't over yet. I want to see each and every one of you back here as soon as the break is over,' said Mrs Daltry.

And she left the classroom. Theo could tell she was more than upset because she didn't pop a liquorice allsort into her mouth. Everyone else trooped out of the classroom after her, very subdued. Everyone except Theo.

He walked over to the whiteboards and examined every dare in turn. The dare he was after might not be on the board but what about the handwriting? Theo studied each written dare twice, then three and four times. It was no use. There were at least ten very likely samples of handwriting and at least another five possibles. Huffing with frustration, Theo dug his hands in his pockets. What should he do now?

Of course writing on a board was different from writing on a piece of paper. Except how would he get to see samples of everyone's handwriting as written on paper? And what about Ricky's cap? Should Theo hand it over to the police or not?

Soon, Theo decided. Very soon – but not now.

Theo still needed the cap. It was his only way of keeping close to Ricky.

## Chapter Eight

# Wrong

### 11:05 hrs Monday, 19th May

I'm sitting in the loos writing this. The smudges on the paper are from where I've been crying. I cry all the time now. The least little thing sets me off. I feel all alone and so frightened. It all went wrong. As wrong as can be. Tom guessed that it was all my fault. He told me not to tell the others – under any circumstances. I must never tell anyone. That's what he says.

Robbie is madder than a kicked dog about it and is ranting non-stop. Scott says nothing. Somehow that's worse. I've caught him giving me strange looks, but he hasn't said a word – at least, not directly to me.

Does he suspect me? From the way he keeps looking at me, he must do. But Ricky can't have told them yet that he and I go to the same school – otherwise Scott and Robbie would've said or done something by now. Ricky doesn't . . . shouldn't know I'm involved in this. He doesn't know about Tom being my brother, so maybe I'll get away with it. Maybe. If, as Tom says, I keep my mouth shut. Tom says if anything happens, he can handle the others. But he's just fooling himself. He wouldn't stand a chance against Robbie, and Scott's the sort to stab him in the back – literally. Dylan's a complete waste of space, so he wouldn't help. Dylan couldn't help himself out of the shallow end of a swimming pool.

I can't stop thinking about Ricky. I wish I could, but I can't. It's not my fault Ricky got caught up in the middle of all this. It's not my fault Ricky got caught at all. Who told him to come prying and poking around and sticking his nose in where it wasn't wanted? That's not my fault. It has nothing to do with me.

They're going to do the job the day after tomorrow. Robbie keeps going on about how nothing and no one is going to stop them now. Not the police, not the army and certainly not some little snot-nosed kid – as he calls Ricky.

Tom says they didn't mean to hurt Ricky but they didn't have any choice. Just thinking about it make me feel sick. There's a solid lump of something hard and heavy sitting in my chest. It's there all the time now.

I think it's fear.

It's not fair. Ricky getting caught was his own stupid fault. I can't do anything to help him – I wish I could, but I can't. I . . . I . . .

I've got to sign off. I can't stop crying. I wish I could just freeze the world and everything in it – just until I'd had a chance to sit down and think. I'm so frightened.

When will I stop feeling so frightened all the time?

## Chapter Nine

# Don't Tell

'Theo, sit down!' Mrs Daltry was close to going nuclear! Theo was driving her nuts!

Theo walked the long way round the class to get to his desk. He stopped abruptly at Emily's table and snatched up her workbook. Flicking disdainfully through the pages, Theo then held the book by its spine and turned it upside down.

'Mrs Daltry, Theo's grabbed my book. Tell him!' Emily complained.

'Theo, I'm not going to warn you again. I don't know what's got into you this afternoon but I'm not going to stand for any more,' Mrs Daltry thundered.

Theo dropped Emily's workbook back down onto the desk from a great height and swaggered back to his seat. On the way he caught sight of Angela, yawning again. Before her mouth was closed, he grabbed her workbook and started looking through it. Angela sprang to her feet and tried to seize it back.

'Give me back my book, you toad!' Angela demanded.

'Make me,' Theo scoffed.

'Theo, that does it. You can sit outside in the corridor for the rest of the lesson,' Mrs Daltry ordered.

Slowly, Theo handed Angela her book back, his eyes never leaving her face.

'Serve you right!' Angela hissed.

Theo didn't reply. He walked around the back of the class, now taking the long way round to get to the door. He passed Colin's table and looked over his shoulder to see what Colin was writing in his workbook. Colin turned his head and scowled at Theo.

'Yes?' he asked curtly.

'Nothing.' Theo shrugged.

And he walked out of the classroom, feeling Mrs Daltry's furious eyes boring into his back. He was careful to close the door quietly behind him, not wanting to bring down any more of Mrs Daltry's wrath around his ears.

Relieved, Theo sagged against the wall. He'd done it! One way or another he'd seen the normal handwriting of everyone in the class. He'd managed to take a look at most people's workbooks during the lunch break when the classroom was deserted. But some people had put their workbooks in their shoulder bags and taken their bags to lunch with them. For those people, Theo'd had no choice but to devise a way of seeing their books before the day was out, without arousing anyone's suspicions as to what he was really doing.

So here he was, in trouble with Mrs Daltry, but at least now he knew who'd written his original dare. Theo shook his head as if to clear the doubts that were beginning to creep into his head. If he was right about who'd written the dare, then it didn't make any sense. He still couldn't figure out *why* they'd written it. So the only thing to do now was confront them and demand to know what had happened to Ricky.

Should I go to the police . . . ? Theo wondered.

No. Not until he had some concrete proof. The police would never believe him otherwise. So first Theo had to find out what was going on. He'd get proof – and then he'd talk to the police. That made more sense.

The minutes dragged by until the buzzer sounded for the start of the afternoon break. Theo turned to face the door. He breathed deeply, trying to smooth out the knots in his stomach. He'd have to follow the person he suspected out of the school building and wait for a suitable moment before confronting them. It wouldn't be easy, but the more Theo thought about it, the more convinced he became that he was on the right track.

Mrs Daltry was the sixth or seventh out of the classroom. Theo peered past her, wondering where the person he was waiting for had got to.

'Theo, follow me,' Mrs Daltry commanded.

'Pardon?'

'You'll be sitting outside the staffroom this breaktime,' said Mrs Daltry.

'Oh, but . . . but I've got things to do,' Theo protested.

'Too bad. You waste my time, I waste yours – that's the way it works,' said Mrs Daltry.

'But . . .'

'Keep arguing and you'll be outside the staffroom during all the breaks for the rest of the week,' Mrs Daltry warned.

Theo's mouth snapped shut.

'That's better,' said Mrs Daltry. 'Now follow me.'

And Theo had no choice but to trail along beside his teacher as she strode down the corridor, surreptitiously popping a liquorice allsort into her mouth as she did so.

So much for his wonderful plan! It'd just have to wait until after school. He sighed impatiently, then again with total frustration. But there was nothing he could do except wait.

When they both reached the staffroom, Mrs Daltry turned to Theo.

'I realize you're worried about Ricky, but that's no excuse for your behaviour today. You're usually so quiet and now I've seen the alternative, I want the old Theo back. Do I make myself clear?' asked the teacher.

Theo nodded.

'We're all worried about Ricky.' Mrs Daltry rested a hand on Theo's shoulder. 'You're Ricky's closest friend and I know how you must be feeling – that's why I'm not sending you to the headmistress.' Mrs Daltry's arm dropped to her side. 'But no more unruly behaviour – OK?'

'OK,' Theo agreed. He didn't need to play about any more – he had what he wanted. 'Can I go for my break now?'

'No. Cause and effect, Theo. Cause and effect.'

Theo sighed. Cause and effect! Mrs Daltry's second favourite saying!

'You misbehaved, Theo and the effect is?' the teacher prompted.

'No breaktime,' said Theo glumly.

Mrs Daltry shrugged. 'You have to learn that life is not a bowl of cherries.'

And there it was again – Mrs Daltry's favourite saying! Theo watched his teacher enter the staffroom, popping yet another liquorice allsort into her mouth.

Theo sat miserably watching as the others in his class made their way past him on their way out into the sunshine. Colin frowned at him. Emily glowered. Some others grinned. And then Angela came out of the classroom, her head bent as she tried to fasten her bag. She stumbled along the corridor, still fiddling with her bag. Her head snapped up as she suddenly became aware that she was being watched. Theo took a quick glance around, then leaped to his feet. Angela walked towards Theo, her head held high as she went to swan past him.

'I want to talk to you,' Theo said.

'What makes you think it's mutual?' Angela sniffed.

She marched past Theo as if a particularly obnoxious smell had just developed under her nose.

Furious, Theo called after her, 'Where's Ricky?'

Angela froze. Neither of them spoke. Theo didn't dare blink in case he missed something vital. Every word, every gesture, every move Angela made from now on would be important. Theo's heart thump-thumped slowly in his chest. This was it. What if he was wrong . . . ?

Angela turned slowly. 'What d'you mean?' she frowned. 'How should I know where Ricky is?'

'Because you're the one who made up his dare in the first place,' Theo replied softly. 'I saw the dare and I saw your handwriting in your workbook. They were both exactly the same.'

'I haven't a clue what you're talking about.'

'You were watching that night. Just like you said you would in the dare. You know what happened to Ricky,' Theo insisted.

'You're off your head . . .'

'Where is he?'

'I don't know.'

'I don't believe you.'

'That's your lookout.'

They both spoke faster and faster, rushing out their accusations and denials. Everyone else in the school had ceased to exist as Angela and Theo verbally battled with each other.

'I said, where's Ricky?' Theo demanded.

'And I said I don't know. I don't know anything about it,' Angela replied harshly.

'Oh, no? You wrote Ricky's dare, I know you did.'

'No, I didn't.'

'You're a liar. We both know you're lying. Ricky's dare . . .'

'Shut up! Shut up about that stupid dare,' Angela interrupted, her hands over her ears. 'And it wasn't even Ricky's dare. It was yours and you . . .' Angela's mouth snapped shut.

Silence.

Theo stared at her. 'So it *was* you,' he breathed. 'And you wanted *me* to disappear instead of Ricky.'

'It wasn't like that.'

'Why don't you tell Mrs Daltry and the police what it was like, then?' Theo replied furiously. 'And if you don't, I will.'

'No one will believe you.' Desperation crept into Angela's voice.

'Yes, they will. I can prove you know where Ricky is.'

'You're lying.'

'You wanna bet?'

'I'll deny it.'

'You can't. I . . . I . . .' Then Theo had a brainwave. 'I've still got the original dare. The police can compare the handwriting. They'll know I'm telling the truth.'

Angela stared at him, horror-stricken.

'Where's Ricky?' Theo's low voice rumbled like thunder.

'I don't know.'

'WHERE'S RICKY?'

*'I don't know.'*

'I've had enough of this. If you won't tell me, you can tell the police.' Theo marched over to the staffroom door.

'Don't tell on me. You . . . you can't tell on me . . .' Angela whispered.

'Watch me.' Theo raised his arm to knock on the door.

Angela moved like lightning to stop Theo's arm in mid flight.

'Don't,' she pleaded. 'If you tell Mrs Daltry or the police, they'll kill Ricky. They promised they would.'

## Chapter Ten

# The Next Step

Stunned, Theo stared at Angela. Her eyes shimmered with unshed tears, her mouth quivered, she had trouble catching her breath. In that moment, Theo knew that she was telling the truth. She'd lied about other things – so many other things and he didn't understand everything that was going on, but in this, she was telling the truth.

'Who's going to kill Ricky?' Theo whispered.

'I . . . I can't tell you.'

'It's me or the police,' Theo warned.

'Ricky heard and saw some things that he shouldn't have,' Angela said miserably.

'Like what?'

'I can't say . . .' Angela began. 'I really can't,' she added desperately as Theo's hand once again reached out towards the staffroom.

'D'you know where Ricky is?' Theo asked coldly.

Angela shook her head, brushing the back of one hand across her eyes.

'D'you at least know if he's all right?'

'Yes he is, I promise,' Angela said eagerly.

'So what's going on?'

'I . . .'

Theo shook his head quickly. 'And don't bother telling me that you can't tell me!'

Angela sighed but didn't speak.

'All right, then, answer this. Is Ricky being held against his will?' asked Theo.

Angela didn't reply.

'He must be – or he'd go home.' Theo answered his own question. 'We'd all have seen him by now.'

Still Angela said nothing.

'Look, I'm sorry but I don't have any choice in this.' Theo shook his head. 'Ricky's being held somewhere against his will. I have to tell the police. If something bad were to happen to him, I'd never forgive myself.'

'Nothing else will happen to Ricky, I promise. He'll be released soon, I'm sure of it.'

'How can you be sure? You don't even know where he is,' Theo said, exasperated. 'I'm sorry, but I'm telling someone.'

'*Please*. You don't understand. Ricky's safe for now.' Angela looked down at the floor, unable to meet Theo's gaze. 'Tom's looking out for him.'

'Who's Tom?'

'My brother,' Angela admitted. 'That's why you can't tell the police. Tom will get into trouble if you do.'

Theo and Angela watched each other silently. A few others in the corridor passed by, directing curious looks at them but neither Theo nor Angela saw them.

'What did I ever do to you?' Theo asked bitterly.

'I don't understand,' Angela frowned.

'You gave your dare to me – deliberately passed it to me,' Theo said with ice-cold fury. '*I* should be where Ricky is now. *I* should be the one being held against my will.'

'I gave my dare to you because I thought you could help me. I th-thought you could tell me what Tom and the others are up to. It wasn't to set you up, I swear it wasn't. Why would I do that?' Angela asked, aghast.

'What made you think I could help you?'

'Because . . .' A slow blush crept up Angela's neck and across her cheeks. 'Because you . . . you're quiet and quite small and I didn't think you'd get caught if you sneaked into the ventilator shaft at the warehouse. And . . . and I thought I could persuade you not to tell anyone but me what you found out.'

'Oh, I see . . .' And Theo did see. He was the classroom mouse – scared of his own shadow. That was what everyone thought. Angela had only just joined the class and already she thought so too.

'You looked the most likely to help me. That was all there was to it,' Angela said.

'Yeah, sure,' Theo said resentfully.

'It's the truth.'

Theo didn't reply. He turned his thoughts back to Ricky and this girl before him. He still wasn't sure of Angela and he certainly didn't trust her, but at that moment she was his only lead to his best friend. Theo leaned against the wall, still watching Angela. After a brief moment, she walked over to him and leaned against the wall beside him.

'Can you help me get to Ricky?' Theo asked softly. 'I must see him. I want to make sure he's OK.'

'I can try. I'll have to ask my brother where he is.'

'Will he tell you?'

'I don't know,' Angela said miserably. 'I don't know anything any more. I don't know who to talk to or trust.'

'You can talk to me. You can trust me,' Theo said.

Angela regarded him, then turned away.

Tell me what's going on. *Tell me.* Theo willed Angela to talk to him. He didn't want to push her. He sensed that she would clam up altogether if he did that.

'M-My brother Tom and three of his friends are going to do a job on Wednesday.' Angela's voice was so low Theo had to strain to hear it.

'A job?'

'They're up to something . . . dodgy. I don't know what. They were still planning it last week. Tom doesn't like to leave me alone when he's not at home unless he doesn't have any choice so he . . . he took me to his last meeting . . .'

'Meeting?' Theo prompted.

'The meeting where Tom, Scott, Robbie and Dylan made all their plans. I had to stay in the office up on the first floor. It's glass fronted so they could see me from the ground floor but with the door shut I couldn't hear what they were saying. That's why I wanted you to go into the ventilator shaft and listen to them for me. I thought you could be my ears.'

'And Ricky went instead of me . . .'

'And got caught,' Angela said. 'He's exactly the last person I would've asked to do something like this. He's not exactly quiet, is he? They probably heard him making a noise within the first five seconds that he arrived.'

'Don't you dare make it sound like it's Ricky's fault,' Theo exploded. 'If anything happens to him, I'll never forgive myself – or *you*.'

'I didn't want him to get caught. I didn't want anyone to get into trouble. I just needed to know what was going on, what Tom was getting himself into,' Angela insisted.

Theo bit back the harsh words ready to explode from his mouth. He counted to ten quickly, then added another fifteen for good measure.

'So how much do you know about what your brother and his friends are up to?' he asked at last.

'Not much. I know that whatever it is, it's going to happen on Wednesday. Wednesday night,' Angela said. 'Tom said that Ricky would be released on Thursday morning if everything went according to plan.'

'Thursday? What about Ricky's mum? She's going through hell and you're going to make her wait until Thursday before letting her know that Ricky's all right?' Theo couldn't believe it.

'I've got no choice. Robbie and Scott already think I'm involved. Theo, you don't know them. If the police or anyone else for that matter tries to move in on them, Ricky will get hurt – or worse.'

'Your brother's got some really charming friends!' Theo wasn't impressed.

'Don't you judge him.' Angela rounded on Theo like a

rabid dog. 'Tom's had to look after me all by himself since I was seven. He even stood up to our social workers when they wanted to put me in a foster home. So don't you say a thing against him.'

'I'm not going to argue with you,' Theo replied frostily. 'All I want to do is rescue Ricky.'

'Rescue? I thought you just wanted to make sure he was safe . . .'

'I want to get him away from your brother and his friends.'

Silence.

'Are you going to help me do that or not?' Theo urged.

'I'll . . . I'll try.'

'Not good enough,' said Theo immediately. 'Either you're with me on this or you're not. And if you're not, I'll go to the police.'

'That's blackmail,' Angela protested.

'Angela, wake up! Your brother and his friends aren't up to something dodgy or cagey or shady or any other stupid word like that. They've kidnapped Ricky. And God knows what they're going to do on Wednesday night. But whatever it is, it's obviously illegal. Not dodgy, cagey or shady. *Illegal!* When are you going to open your eyes and see that?'

'I'm not listening.' Angela put her hands over her ears.

Theo tried to pull Angela's arms down by her sides. She battled to keep her hands where they were.

'All right! All right! We'll play it your way. There's nothing *illegal* going on at all! Your brother and his friends are angels!' Theo said with biting sarcasm. 'So what's the next step?'

Slowly, Angela's arms dropped back down to her sides.

'I'll talk to Tom when I get home, then I'll meet you afterwards and tell you what I know,' she sniffed.

'When?'

'Six thirty?'

'Fine. Where?'

'The park. The swings in the playground.'

'I'll be there,' Theo said.

Angela walked away down the corridor. Theo watched her go for a few moments before calling out to her.

'Angela?'

Angela turned her head.

'If you don't turn up . . .' Theo left the rest unsaid.

Angela's eyes blazed at him with a hatred that would have knocked Theo backwards if he hadn't already been up against the wall. Without a word she turned her head and carried on walking. Theo's frown deepened as he watched her turn the corner. He didn't like blackmailing her, it left a nasty taste in his mouth and a horrible churning feeling in his stomach, but what else could he do? There was no way Angela was going to help him unless he cajoled and bullied and coaxed her every step of the way.

So what would she do? Suppose she didn't turn up? Theo sighed. In a way that would make things a lot easier. Theo could then just go to the police and let them find Ricky. If Angela *did* turn up, then Theo would be letting himself in for goodness only knew what.

But, hang on – suppose Angela didn't turn up but sent someone else instead? What if she told her brother or his friends what Theo was trying to do? They'd be waiting for him in the park and then he might end up in exactly the same place and predicament as Ricky. A fat lot of good he'd be to his friend then. Theo didn't trust Angela, not one bit. She could easily tell her brother about him and then what?

'So what're you going to do?' Theo asked himself.

But he already knew the answer. He was going to take a chance and turn up at the park at six thirty. And he was going to be very, *very* careful.

Chapter Eleven

# Theo Knows

## 17:30 hrs Monday, 19th May

Theo knows . . .

I have no choice now. I've got to tell Tom about Theo. I have to. Tom's my brother and I can't let Theo spoil things for us. Since I wrote in here this morning, things have got worse, not better. When is it all going to end? *Where* is it going to end? I have to stop writing now.

I'm smudging the ink across the paper again.

## Chapter Twelve

# Betrayed

Theo crouched down before taking a look around. The warning bells in his head wouldn't stop clanging.

*Go to the police . . . Go to the police . . .*

On and on they rang. Theo shook his head. Try as he might, he couldn't get over the feeling that he was being really, *really* stupid. Here he was in the park at five minutes to seven – and all alone . . . How much longer should he wait? It looked like Angela wasn't coming. Maybe she never had any intention of turning up. Maybe she'd just send her brother and his friends . . . And what if Tom and the others *did* turn up? Theo wouldn't know any of them from Adam. He could easily end up in the same predicament as Ricky before he had time to blink.

Theo checked his position again. He should be safe where he was. He was crouched down behind an oak tree on a slope leading down to the fenced-off stream. At the first sign of anything suspicious he'd leg it down the slope, hop over the fence and he'd race down the shallow stream towards the woods. He'd move so fast, Tom and his friends wouldn't see him for the water spray!

Theo frowned down at his watch. He'd give her until a quarter past seven. After that . . . Hang on! That man over there . . . Could he be Angela's brother? They looked quite similar. Theo crouched even lower. Had she betrayed him?

'Come on, Angela,' he muttered.

*Where was she?*

As if the thought summoned the person, Angela turned into the park and started walking down the path towards the children's playground. Theo froze. He didn't dare risk showing himself. Not until he knew she had come alone. He looked around again to see if anyone was watching her or acting suspiciously. There were plenty of people in the park, children and adults. It was hard to tell who was with whom.

Angela was getting closer . . . In a couple of minutes she would draw level with his hidden position behind the tree. Theo stood up slowly, careful to still keep himself hidden. A tall, slim man with dark hair and wearing a T-shirt and faded jeans turned into the park and immediately raced towards Angela. The man called out to her and she spun around. The moment she saw him, they launched into a fierce argument. Theo was too far away to hear all they were saying but they were obviously both very angry. Theo moved further into the shadow of the tree.

'Gotcha!' A vice-like hand descended on Theo's shoulder, the fingers digging into his flesh like talons.

Theo jumped out of his skin. He turned and the world was filled with the bearded face of a stranger. A stranger whose eyes burned into Theo with angry satisfaction. Theo's whole body felt like it was being held together with paperclips. Only the stranger's hand on his shoulder kept him upright and on his feet. He'd been set up. Angela *had* betrayed him . . .

'What d'you think you're doing – skulking about, hiding behind trees? I've been watching you. I want to know what you're up to.'

Theo hardly heard a word. The only sound in the world was that of his heart racing at light speed. The only sight was the stranger's angry glare. Theo felt the stranger's moist breath whisper over his face. It smelled of fresh coffee and stale cigarettes. Theo opened and closed his mouth like a fish out of water. The stranger drew back slightly and frowned.

'Are you all right?' he asked.

Slowly the world stopped crazily rocking. Theo blinked, then blinked again.

The stranger's words replayed in his mind. Theo took in more of the stranger's appearance now. He was the park-keeper! It wasn't just his uniform that gave it away – the badge on his lapel which said PARKKEEPER was another big clue!

'What's the matter? Are you ill?' asked the parkkeeper.

Theo nodded. It wasn't a lie. The churning in his stomach was only just beginning to slow down.

'What're you doing?' asked the parkkeeper.

'Waiting for someone,' breathed Theo. He shrugged out of the parkkeeper's grasp.

'What were you going to do? Leap out at them?'

Theo didn't answer. The parkkeeper took a step back.

'Look, are you OK? I didn't mean to scare you. I thought you were one of those yobbo boys who's been jumping out at people from behind trees – upsetting people, scaring them half to death,' the parkkeeper sniffed indignantly.

'Well, I wasn't doing that,' said Theo. 'You're the one who frightened *me*.'

'Hhmm! Well, I'll let you off – this once,' said the parkkeeper.

'You can't let me off if I wasn't doing anything in the first place,' Theo pointed out.

The parkkeeper was in the wrong but he couldn't bring himself to apologize to a kid. He was a typical grown-up, Theo fumed.

'Just watch yourself,' said the parkkeeper.

And off he marched. Theo glared after him. Then he remembered. Angela! Theo turned around. Angela and the man she'd been arguing with had gone . . .

## Chapter Thirteen

# The No-show

Theo pushed against the front door. It closed with a click that had him holding his breath. It was almost eight. He was meant to be home by seven at the very latest. So much for all his plans. So much for finding out where Ricky was being held and devising a plan to rescue him. Theo's head was spinning. He just wanted to lie down for a while, clear his head and think about what he should do next. Anxiously, he looked towards the living room. Nothing. Theo tiptoed to the stairs, then stopped. What should he do now? Tiptoe or charge? The stairs creaked horribly. If he tiptoed he was bound to get caught. But he'd get caught for sure if he charged. Theo sighed. He was going to get caught, no matter how he went up the stairs, so he might as well get it over with. Theo started walking upstairs normally. Charging required too much energy and tiptoeing required too much effort. He'd barely got his foot on the third stair when his mum and dad flew out of the living room.

'Where on earth have you been?' Dad raged.

'I went to the park,' Theo said.

'Until nearly nine o'clock? We were worried sick.'

Theo glanced down at his watch. It was five to eight not 'nearly nine', but Theo prudently decided not to argue.

'Sorry . . .' he began.

'Sorry! Sorry! Is that all you have to say?' Mum asked.

'I didn't realize it was so late.' Theo tried to explain.

He got no further. A policeman with wispy brown hair and a short, neat beard came out of the living room. Theo stared. What had happened? Why was the policeman here?

'As I was saying, Mr and Mrs Mosley, when children disappear, nine times out of ten there's a perfectly reasonable, logical explanation!' said the policeman.

'I'm sorry. We seem to have wasted your time,' Dad said grittily.

'No trouble. I'm just glad Theo turned up safe and sound,' said the policeman.

Theo's breath caught in his throat. The policeman was there because of *him*.

Dad escorted the policeman to the front door.

'I'll radio it in that your son has been found,' the policeman said.

'Yes. Thank you,' said Dad. 'I'm sorry you were called out unnecessarily.'

'That's OK. Good night.' The policeman opened the door and cast Theo a sympathetic glance before shutting the door behind him. Theo looked at his mum and dad. They glared back at him. It was like standing at the edge of an erupting volcano. Theo's whole body was burning up.

'Where's your watch?' Dad asked, his dark eyes glinting like chips of granite.

Reluctantly, Theo held out his left wrist.

'You had your watch on and you didn't know what time it was?' said Dad.

'I . . . I didn't look at it,' Theo replied.

'Theo, how could you be so thoughtless?' Mum asked. 'Ricky's disappeared and you've seen what his mum is going through. How could you put us through the same thing?'

Mum's voice was quiet and sad. Somehow that was worse than her yelling at him.

'What were you doing in the park?' Dad asked.

'I . . . I was just thinking. I was trying to help Ricky.' And that was the truth, even if it wasn't the *whole* truth.

'Trying to help Ricky – how?' said Dad.

Theo struggled to find the right words. What was he supposed to say? I went to meet a girl in my class called

Angela, because her brother is holding Ricky against his will, only she disappeared before I had the chance to speak to her. Maybe that's exactly what he *should* say. Get it all out into the open. He had to think of Ricky.

Just as Theo opened his mouth, the phone rang. Still frowning at Theo, Dad walked across the hall to answer it.

'Hello?'

Dad's frown deepened as he listened. Theo took a step down the stairs. Was it something about Ricky?

'I'm afraid he's busy at the moment . . . It is rather late to be phoning my son . . .' Dad said tersely.

Theo stepped forward again. He instinctively knew who was at the other end of the phone.

'It's someone called Angela. This is the third time she's called in five minutes. She says it's important,' Dad said.

Theo stepped forward, reaching out for the receiver.

'We want to see you when you've finished,' Dad said, before handing it over.

Theo waited until his mum and dad went back into the living room before lifting the receiver to his ear.

'What happened?' Theo hissed.

'I tried to sneak out but Tom came after me.' Angela's voice was so low that Theo had to strain to hear it. 'He insisted on taking me home.'

Theo checked. His mum and dad weren't listening. Even so, he turned his back to the living room and lowered his voice.

'What about Ricky? D'you know where he is?'

There was a noticeable pause before Angela answered.

'No. I don't know where he is now, but I do know where he'll be tomorrow night. With your help, we can get him away from Robbie and no one will get hurt.'

Theo took a quick glance around to make sure that he was still alone.

'Why should I believe you? Why don't I just tell Mum and Dad what I already know about you and your brother and Robbie and all the others?'

'Because you don't have any proof,' Angela replied immediately. 'Because it'd be my word against yours. And the moment another grown-up gets involved, you'd never see Ricky alive again – Robbie will make sure of that. Is that what you want?'

Theo clenched his free hand, totally frustrated that he could do nothing else.

'A-Are you still there?' The quiver in Angela's voice revealed that she wasn't quite as in control as Theo had first thought.

'Yes, I'm still here,' Theo replied. 'So where will Ricky be tomorrow night?'

'I'll tell you when I see you,' Angela said at last. 'I'll meet you outside the park at the main entrance.'

Theo understood at once. What he didn't know, he couldn't tell anyone else.

'But you'll really help me get Ricky away from your brother's friends?' Theo asked.

'I said so, didn't I?' Angela snapped.

'Then I'll see you at school tomorrow morning,' said Theo.

'After school,' Angela contradicted.

'What d'you mean . . . ? Hello?'

The continuous purr of the telephone line was the only answer. Angela had hung up on him.

'Theo?'

Theo spun around at the sound of his mum's voice. Had she heard . . . ? No, her expression was still the same as before the phone call. He followed her into the living room.

'I'm sorry I was late home, Mum and Dad,' Theo said quickly. 'I didn't mean to worry you.'

'Well, you did,' said Dad, still not placated.

'I know. I won't do it again,' Theo said. 'I promise.'

'Hhmm! I want you home straight after school every night this week. Is that clear?' said Mum.

But Theo was meant to meet Angela after school the next day . . .

'Theo, answer your mother,' Dad ordered.

'It's clear,' Theo mumbled, his fingers discreetly crossed at his sides.

'D'you want something to eat?' Mum asked reluctantly. She was still angry with him but she was always, always worried that he hadn't eaten enough – no matter what time of the day or night!

Theo shook his head.

'. . . the hunt for Richard Burridge. This report from Julia Bartless.'

Instantly all eyes turned towards the TV screen. The image switched from the newscaster to a black woman reporter. Theo's mouth dropped open. He pointed at the block of flats behind the reporter.

'That's . . .'

'I'm standing outside the flats where Ricky Burridge lives with his mother,' the reporter began. 'Ricky, aged twelve, disappeared three days ago.'

Ricky's photograph filled the screen.

'Police are very concerned about Ricky and are mounting a house-to-house investigation in the area, but they admit that hope and time are running out,' the reporter concluded.

The newsreader in the news studio appeared again on the left-hand side of the TV screen with the reporter on the right. The newsreader asked the reporter, 'Have you had a chance to speak to Ricky's mother yet?'

Julia Bartless shook her head. 'Mrs Burridge was too upset to speak to us and is currently being comforted by relatives.'

'Do the police have any clues at all?' asked the newscaster.

'Not as yet, but as one policewoman told me, they're going to intensify their search until Ricky is found.'

Theo's stomach churned. His blood roared throughout his body. It was horrible – worse than horrible. Ricky's mum had to be going through hell. Theo remembered what she'd looked like on Friday morning and now more days had gone past. Theo's mum came over to him and put an arm around his shoulders.

'Your dad and I can't watch you every single second of the day so we just have to trust you to be careful and sensible,' she said.

Theo nodded, searching desperately for something to say.

'Ricky will turn up all right, I know he will,' he said at last.

Mum smiled faintly.

'Let's hope so, Theo,' Dad sighed. 'Let's hope so.'

And in that moment, Theo's mind was made up. He *was* going to meet Angela after school tomorrow and deal with the consequences afterwards.

But later, as Theo cleaned his teeth, he couldn't get a phrase out of his head. It kept repeating like a song he couldn't get out of his mind.

*Fools rush in . . .*

## Chapter Fourteen

# The Escape

### 22:55 hrs Monday, 19th May

I hate him. HATE, HATE, HATE him! When I got home from school today, they were all in our house. I'd barely got my key out of the front door when Robbie said he was going to lock me in my room. And Tom let him. Tom looked down at the ground, at the walls, at his shoes – anywhere but at me. Scott and Dylan didn't say a word either. No one stuck up for me. There was no one on my side. Tom asked Robbie if locking me in my room was 'really necessary'.

Really necessary! I think it's just as well I didn't tell Tom about Theo and what happened at school today. He'd have run straight to Robbie. It's as if he's afraid to think for himself unless Robbie tells him when and how.

I told Robbie I was meant to be meeting someone in the park. D'you know what he said?

'Tough! You'll stay in and do as you're told.'

And then he had the extra nerve to tell me that I couldn't go to school tomorrow.

'We've got something lined up for tomorrow evening and we can't risk anything or anyone lousing it up for us,' he told me.

'How does my going to school louse things up for you?' I asked.

'You're not going to school tomorrow and that's final,' Robbie replied.

And all the time, Tom said nothing. I was so furious I

threw a tantrum on the bed and beat up my pillow. How could Tom let Robbie do that to me? How *could* he?

I racked my brains all evening to think of some way of getting out of my room without any of them downstairs finding out. I finally had to sneak out of my bedroom window, across the flat roof and down the drainpipe. I was positive that at any moment, I'd feel Robbie's fingers digging into my arms.

I HATE HIM!

I scraped practically all the skin off my knees and there's hardly any left on the palms of my hands either. But I got out. Only, Tom caught up with me in the park before I'd a chance to talk to Theo. Tom was furious. And he said that Scott and especially Robbie were spitting nails! I just hope Theo didn't see us. Theo doesn't trust me as it is. Goodness only knows what he would've thought if he saw Tom with me. I had to beg Tom to at least let me phone my friend to let him know why I didn't show up. I refused to budge until he agreed.

When we got home, you should've heard Robbie's language. I'm surprised the air around his head didn't turn bright blue. Tom hustled me straight to my bedroom, even though Robbie wanted to question me. For once Tom stood up for me. That happens so rarely – no wonder I'm writing it in my diary.

Tom sneaked me the telephone directory and let me use his mobile phone. I got through half the Mosleys in the book before I reached Theo's house. I think I got to him just in time. I hope I managed to convince him not to do anything stupid.

When the other sharks had left, Tom tried to tell me not to worry. I asked him what was going on.

'Nothing that concerns you. But after tomorrow we'll be on easy street. We'll have money enough to last us the rest of our lives. I'll be able to look after you properly, without social workers sticking their noses into our business every five seconds.'

My heart sank at that.

'Tom, I don't know what you're up to, but whatever it is that Robbie wants you to do, don't do it. You're going to get into trouble. I can feel it.'

'Don't talk wet,' Tom laughed.

'What about Ricky?' I asked. I could feel the tears pricking at my eyes then.

'I don't want to talk about . . . about the boy,' Tom said icily. 'After tomorrow he'll be fine.'

'But how d'you know that? How d'you know . . . ?'

'I don't want to hear it,' Tom interrupted.

He had that funny, glassy look in his eyes and I knew he'd stopped listening to me. He always does that when someone says something that he doesn't want to hear. So I just gave up after that. There's no point in talking to Tom when he switches off. He tried to change the subject and make me laugh the way he always does when I'm feeling sad but I didn't laugh and I didn't say a word. He soon took the hint. I'm still mad at him. He's like a sheep when it comes to Robbie. It's like his brain just melts away every time Robbie gets within a kilometre of him.

But I'm not going to let Robbie have things all his own way. This business with Ricky has gone far enough.

## Chapter Fifteen

# Watching the Warehouse

Theo looked up and down the street.

*Where was she?*

Right! That's it, Theo thought angrily. He'd had more than enough of all this messing about. He was going straight round the nearest . . .

'Theo? Theo!'

Theo turned his head. Angela came running down the street at full pelt towards him. He took a quick look around. No grown-ups were lurking – at least none that he could see. It looked like Angela was alone.

'I wasn't sure if you'd turn up,' Theo admitted once Angela caught up to him.

'To be honest, I wasn't sure either,' Angela confessed.

They both looked at each other and tentatively smiled. Then Theo remembered Ricky and his smile faded to nothing.

'We'll have to be very careful,' Angela said. 'Robbie's brought the job forward to tonight.'

'Tonight! How d'you know?'

'Tom's had me packing our suitcases all day. We're supposed to be going on holiday first thing tomorrow morning.'

'On holiday? Where?'

'Tom didn't tell me. He said it was a surprise,' Angela replied grimly.

'And what *is* this job they're doing tonight?'

'I don't know.'

'But we can rescue Ricky – right?'

Angela nodded, crossing her fingers behind her back where Theo couldn't see.

'Then let's get going,' said Theo.

Angela turned around and started walking back the way she'd just come.

'Where're we going?' Theo asked, falling into step next to her.

Angela looked at Theo steadily. 'To the warehouse on Buzan Road.'

'But . . . but the police have already searched that place,' Theo frowned.

'Which is why they've moved back there. The police have searched it once so they won't search it again. Scott reckoned it'd be safe for tonight.'

'How d'you know all this?' Theo asked suspiciously.

'I heard some of what they were saying in the kitchen when I climbed out of my bedroom window last night,' Angela explained. And that wasn't all she'd heard. Most of Scott's conversation had been about Ricky – and it was terrifying . . .

'You climbed out of your window? Why did you do that?'

'It was the only way I could meet you in the park. Robbie locked me in my bedroom,' Angela explained.

Theo gasped and stared at Angela. 'Robbie sounds like a real prince and two-thirds.'

'He's that all right,' Angela said bitterly.

'What happened when you got back home? Are you OK?' Theo asked, concerned.

Angela shrugged. 'Yeah, I'll survive. Thanks for asking.'

Theo's face began to burn. His face set hard and he glared at Angela.

'I was only being nosy, that's all. It doesn't mean we're engaged or anything.'

'I never said it did.' Angela's smile broadened.

Other thoughts bubbling up in Theo's mind refused to stay buried.

'Now d'you see why I want to get Ricky away from Robbie and the others? What makes you think that Robbie's going to keep his word and release Ricky?' The words erupted from Theo like a volcanic explosion.

'Tom wouldn't let anyone hurt Ricky . . .' Angela began.

'Tom couldn't stop Robbie from locking you in your room. What makes you think he could stand up to Robbie and Scott and the other one?' Theo said. 'What makes you think he'd even want to?'

'Shut up! SHUT UP!' Angela screamed at him.

They glared at each other like two enemies having a show-down in one of the old Western films. Theo carried on walking first. Angela fell into step with him. They walked in silence to the end of the road.

'Wait a sec,' said Theo. Then he took out his mobile phone and pressed the button to switch it on. He groaned.

'My battery's dead. Can I borrow your phone?'

Angela shook her head. 'I don't have one.'

'How come?'

''Cos I don't,' Angela snapped.

It took another five minutes before Theo and Angela found a phone box. Stepping into the kiosk, Theo picked up the receiver and began to dial, pressing more and more firmly on each numbered key.

'Who're you phoning?' Angela asked warily.

'My mum and dad. Neither of them will be home from work yet – at least I hope not.'

'I don't understand.'

'I'm going . . . Hang on!' Theo listened intently to what was going on at the other end of the phone. 'Hi Mum, Dad. A girl in my class, Angela Tukesbury, asked me to help her with her homework. I'm going round to her house now. I hope that's all right.'

Angela realized what was going on. Theo was talking into an answering machine.

'It shouldn't take too long. Angela said I could have dinner at her house and then her mum or dad will give me a lift home,' Theo continued at a rush. 'See you soon. 'Bye.'

Theo put the phone down quickly as if he was afraid that the receiver itself might start arguing with him.

'You shouldn't have said that about my mum and dad,' said Angela.

'Why not?'

'I live with my brother, Tom. There isn't anyone else. I told you that before.'

'What happened to your parents?' Theo asked curiously.

'Mum took off when I was five and Dad died a couple of years later.'

'How old was your brother then?' said Theo.

'Old enough to take care of me,' Angela rounded on him.

'OK! OK! Don't bite my head off. I only asked,' Theo said quickly.

'Sorry,' Angela mumbled. 'But ever since Dad died that's all I've heard. Tom's not old enough, Tom's not responsible enough. Everyone's so desperate to get me into a children's home.'

'Tom's not going to do you much good if he and his friends are caught on this job they're doing and sent to prison,' Theo pointed out.

'It won't come to that. And don't be such a smart alec doof ball,' Angela fumed.

Theo opened his mouth to argue, only to snap it shut without saying a word. The last thing he wanted was to antagonize Angela, and besides, it *had* been the sort of thing a doof would say!

Theo and Angela lapsed into silence until they reached Buzan Road. Each step that took them closer to the warehouse had Theo's heart pounding just that bit harder. About ten metres away from the warehouse, Angela's hand on Theo's arm stopped him in his tracks. They both stood in silence.

'What happens now?' Theo asked, still looking at the warehouse.

'We have to get into the ventilation shaft and wait. When they leave tonight to do their job, that's when we rescue Ricky.'

'They're all inside the warehouse now – right? Tom, Robbie, Scott and . . . ?'

'Dylan.'

'And Ricky?'

'And Ricky.'

'And whatever it is they're up to, it's definitely going to happen tonight?' Theo asked.

Angela nodded. 'That's why Tom left me at home instead of taking me with him as usual. He said he wanted me to get a good night's sleep for once – as if I'd believe that! He's dragged me to the warehouse with him almost every night for the last two weeks whilst they've been planning whatever it is they're up to.'

'Why didn't he just leave you at home?'

'Tom worries about me,' Angela shrugged. 'The house might catch fire, it might get hit by lightning, crushed by an alien ship landing on it – anything.'

Theo raised his eyebrows.

'That's how Tom thinks,' Angela smiled ruefully. 'He reckoned I was safer with him. Except for tonight when they're going to do whatever it is they've been planning for so long. I haven't got to sleep before three in the morning in over a fortnight.'

'So that's why you're always yawning in class,' Theo realized.

'No, I'm not,' Angela frowned.

'Yes, you are.'

'I don't yawn in class,' Angela said belligerently.

'If you say so.' Theo shrugged as he regarded her.

What was it with Angela anyway? If there was anything she didn't like or didn't agree with, she'd say it didn't happen, or deny it or just blank it out. Like drawing the curtains on reality and saying that the world beyond her window didn't exist.

'What're you looking at?' Angela scowled.

Theo shook his head.

They both turned to look back at the warehouse, each of them burning with a different kind of anger inside. Apart from the occasional car the area around the warehouse was practically deserted.

'How d'you know they're not going to take Ricky with them tonight?' asked Theo.

'I heard Tom trying to persuade the rest to leave Ricky behind. He said Ricky would only be in the way.'

'Did he succeed?'

'I hope so. We'll soon find out,' Angela replied. 'Scott . . . Scott mentioned something about taking Ricky with them to use as a hostage in case anything went wrong.'

Theo stared at her. Fear like a giant wave crashed over him, leaving him breathless.

'But maybe Tom managed to change his mind,' Angela continued desperately.

Silence. Theo took a deep breath.

'Come on. Let's get Ricky out of there,' Theo said at last.

Cautiously, they both approached the warehouse. Theo looked up and down the street. No one *seemed* to be watching them.

'Are you sure they haven't posted a lookout?' Theo whispered.

Angela looked up and down the street as well. 'I don't see anyone.'

They peered down the side alleyway where the ventilator shaft was situated. Two cars were there now which hadn't been there before. One was a metallic grey hatchback. The other was dark blue, but Theo couldn't see what make of car it was. After a brief look at each other, Angela and Theo tiptoed down the alley.

'Oh, no! Look!' Theo pointed when they were a couple of metres away from the grille.

Angela saw at once what the problem was. The metallic

grey car was parked too close to the grille. It would be a real battle to try and get the grille off, let alone squeeze into the tiny space left between the car and the ventilator shaft.

'What do we do now?' Angela whispered.

Theo's eyes narrowed with determination. 'We don't give up. Not now we're so close.'

Reluctantly, Angela nodded.

'Come on, Angela.' Theo beckoned, moving forward.

They both eased their way between the car and the wall. Leaning back against the car's front wheel arch, Theo interlaced his fingers into the grille. He could get his fingers into the mesh all right, but he was so close to it, he couldn't get enough force behind his attempts to pull.

'Help then!' Theo urged.

Angela tried, but it was no use. The grille didn't budge.

'We're going to have to think of something else,' Angela sighed.

On the main road, someone coughed, then sneezed violently.

'Why don't you get something for that?' a man's voice asked irritably. 'You've been coughing all over us for the last two days.'

Angela's eyes widened with horror.

'Move! Quick!' she hissed.

'What's the ma . . . ?'

'MOVE!' she ordered urgently, pushing Theo away from her.

Theo fell onto his hands and crawled away as fast as he could.

'What's going . . . ?'

'Quick! Please . . .' Angela implored.

Theo ducked behind the grey car, immediately followed by Angela. They both squatted down as low as possible between the two cars, just as footsteps turned into the alleyway.

'I don't like it, Dylan. What's Robbie up to in there?' A man's voice accompanied the sets of footsteps that turned into the alleyway.

'I don't know and I ain't gonna ask,' came the reply.

'Who . . . ?' Theo began.

Angela shook her head quickly, her finger over her lips. She turned and pointed to the second car behind them. Theo nodded. He peeped his head out from his side of the car. It seemed all clear. The two men must be walking on the other side of the alleyway. He could see the swinging arm and shoulder of one of the men and the side of his face but that was it. To be honest, Theo didn't want to see any more than that. He beckoned with his head and started crawling alongside the second car. The men were still talking and getting closer and closer. Theo was so busy concentrating on the men behind him that he didn't see the sharp piece of rubble beneath him – but his knee felt it. He only just managed to bite his lip in time to stop himself from crying out. Theo raised his knee slightly, brushing the debris off his jeans. He wasn't surprised when his hand came away smeared with red. His knee was bleeding. Grimacing at the pain, Theo carried on moving until he reached the back of the second car with Angela only moments behind him. They both sat back against the car, making themselves as low as possible.

'What's Robbie going to do with the boy?' the first man asked.

'Dunno,' Dylan replied, brusquely.

'I hope he's not stupid enough to bring him along,' said the first man.

'Look at it from Robbie's point of view. That boy knows all our plans, everything we're up to – and he's seen our faces . . .' Dylan's words trailed away into silence.

'But he can't hurt us after tonight. Besides, who'd take the word of a boy over four grown-ups?' the first voice argued.

'I don't like it any better than you,' said Dylan. And from the sound of his voice, he really didn't. 'But are you going to argue with Robbie? 'Cause I sure as hell ain't.' Then the same man had a coughing fit.

Theo didn't realize he was holding his breath until his

chest started to hurt. And still he didn't dare to breathe. The pain in his knee was sharp and intense, his lungs were aching fit to burst and he didn't dare twitch an eyelid.

'Let it go,' Dylan continued. 'Unless you've got a death wish.'

'But that boy . . .'

'That boy is none of our concern. And we'd better not still be here when Robbie comes out or we'll be in trouble ourselves,' Dylan interrupted.

Theo heard a clunk, then the sound of car doors opening.

'I still don't like it – not one little . . .' The rest of what the first man was saying was cut off by the car door slamming. Moments later the engine started. Only then did Theo release his breath in an audible hiss, dragging air into his tortured lungs with the next gasp.

'We've got to move – fast,' Theo whispered as he turned to Angela.

Angela stared straight ahead, tears overflowing from her eyes and running down her cheeks to drip onto her lap.

'Angela . . . ?'

'That was Dylan who got into the car,' Angela whispered. 'Dylan and my brother, Tom . . .'

## Chapter Sixteen

# Gotcha!

'Angela? Angela, listen to me,' Theo pleaded. 'Your brother's all right. He's safe, but you heard what they said. Ricky isn't. D'you hear me?'

'Tom said he wasn't really involved, he said he was just helping with the planning . . . but he's up to his neck in all this,' Angela sobbed.

'Your brother's not up to his neck. He passed that when they kidnapped Ricky. He's in way, *way* over his head,' Theo argued. 'Angela, you've got to help me. We don't have much time.'

'He lied to me. Tom lied to me . . .'

Theo squatted down in front of Angela, took her by the arms and shook her.

'Angela, help me – *please*.'

Angela looked straight through him.

'Right then. I'll do it myself. You sit there!' Theo said, angrily.

He leaped up and ran over to the grille. The grey car had gone so now he could use all his strength to pull it off – and he needed to get the grille off in a hurry. From what Dylan and Tom had said, Robbie would be out next and he was the very last person Theo wanted to meet. He *had* to get to Ricky. Theo interlaced his fingers in the grille and pulled as hard as he could. Nothing happened. He tugged harder, leaning back so that his whole weight could be used to pull the grille off. The metal bit into his fingers even worse than before but Theo couldn't give up. Not now. Angela laced her fingers into the grille and pulled alongside Theo. Theo looked at her, then got back to the task in hand.

'Really pull – after three,' Theo panted. 'One . . .'

'Two . . .'

'Three!'

There came a faint grating sound and then the grille flew off its mounting. Angela and Theo ended up sprawled on the ground, still clutching the grille.

'Let's get going,' Theo said, disentangling himself.

He took a deep breath, then another, before crawling into the shaft. He wasn't looking forward to being in that musty, dusty, cramped space again, but now not just minutes but seconds counted.

'Theo, help!'

Theo turned his head to see Angela struggling with the grille. Making himself as small as possible, Theo turned around. He and Angela struggled to pull the grille back on. Theo's fingers were already red raw from pulling at the grille but he couldn't risk Robbie or anyone else coming out of the warehouse and noticing something was wrong. With one last effort, he and Angela heaved the grille back in place.

'Will it stay put?' Angela asked, doubtfully.

'Let's hope so,' Theo said. 'Come on.'

They crawled together side by side until the tunnel became too narrow, then Theo led the way. The dust danced around them, the light grew dimmer and the smell was even worse than before – something Theo wouldn't have thought possible. When he reached the section of the tunnel which branched off to the right and left as well as straight ahead, he stopped.

'We need to get to the basement,' Angela whispered from behind him.

Theo looked up and down the tunnels, his eyes narrowed with concentration.

'This way,' he said at last, turning to his right.

'How d'you know that?' Angela asked, surprised.

'I've been in here before,' Theo replied.

'You have?'

'Yeah, on Monday morning.'

'So that's why you were late,' Angela breathed. 'I wondered.'

'Shush!' Theo whispered nervously.

The end of the tunnel was in sight. Cautiously, they moved towards it. Once there, Theo looked through the mesh down towards the basement. Three or four low-wattage light bulbs provided the only light. Though it was bright outside, Theo's eyes took a few moments to adjust to the gloom in the basement.

A white man with light brown hair tied back in a pony-tail stood below, his back towards the ventilator shaft. A smallish table, a large mattress and a couple of rickety, wooden chairs were the only bits of furniture that Theo could see – furniture that hadn't been there before. He turned his head this way and that, searching for Ricky.

'What's going on? Budge over,' Angela whispered.

'Shush!' Theo urged.

There was barely room for him, let alone enough for Angela to see what was going on as well.

'Budge up,' Angela insisted.

Angela pushed Theo's legs out of her way. Theo had to lie on his side to allow Angela to crawl forward. They both watched through the mesh as the man with the pony-tail packed a dark holdall with assorted items off the table. He picked up something and Theo caught a quick glimpse of it before the man put it in his jacket pocket. A gun . . .

'There's two men down there . . .' Theo whispered.

'That's Robbie.' Angela nodded towards the man with the pony-tail. 'And that's Scott, Robbie's brother.' She pointed to the other man. Scott's hair only just covered his head, it was so short. He was tall and broad and wore army combat clothes and what looked like Doc Martens. Theo didn't like the look of him at all. He was definitely *not* the sort of guy you wanted to meet on a dark night – nor even in broad daylight come to that. Neither of them were. Robbie picked up the holdall.

'All set?' Scott asked his brother.

Robbie nodded, then said something about 'the boy' which Theo didn't catch. Theo inched closer.

'What about Dylan and Tom?' Scott asked.

'What about them?' Robbie replied.

The two brothers regarded each other, before they both burst out laughing. Theo's blood ran ice-cold in his veins at the sound. He glanced at Angela. The grim look on her face reflected what Theo was thinking. Robbie and Scott were up to something . . . evil. Something that even Dylan and Tom didn't know about.

'Take care of business, Scott. And don't be late to the Irving. I need you. I'll take care of the boy.' And with that, Robbie headed for the exit at the far end of the basement. Theo and Angela watched him leave before either of them spoke.

'What did Robbie mean by that – "I'll take care of the boy"?' Theo asked.

Angela didn't answer.

'I don't see Ricky,' said Theo.

'He should be here.' Angela looked around. 'Maybe they've got him tied up on the ground floor somewhere. I'll go and take a look.'

'No, don't. We should stick together . . .' But Theo was wasting his breath. Already Angela was wriggling backwards.

'Angela!' Theo called after her.

It was no use. Theo shook his head. Angela was going to get them into real trouble at this rate. With a start, Theo realized what he'd just done.

He'd called after Angela *out loud* . . .

Theo ducked his head immediately. Had Scott heard him? Theo's stomach churned. He could taste fear, bitter as bile, in his mouth. Don't start panicking, he told himself sternly. Scott probably hadn't heard a thing. Theo raised his head slowly and looked down through the dust-covered mesh.

'I see you . . .' Scott said softly.

Scott stood directly underneath the grille, staring straight up at him. Theo's breath caught in his throat. His blood froze. In that instant, his whole body went numb.

Slowly, Scott raised his hand and pointed at Theo. 'Stay there!' he ordered.

Theo didn't wait to hear anything else. Panic-stricken, he pushed himself backwards. Stay? Yeah, likely! He had to get out of there – *fast*. In the shaft, he was a sitting duck. Ahead, Theo heard footsteps hurrying, then the sound of something being dragged across the concrete floor.

He's after me, Theo thought desperately.

Digging his elbows and knees into the floor, Theo used them to propel himself backwards. Ignoring the pain that the hard flooring and the bits of debris and rubble caused him as they bit into his skin, Theo could think of nothing else but getting out of there. How he wished he could turn around. Scott wouldn't be able to see him for the dust – literally! – if he could just turn around.

'Where d'you think you're going?' Scott's face appeared at the shaft.

He's standing on the table, Theo realized. Within moments, Scott wrenched off the grille and threw it behind him. It crashed to the floor, the sound echoing throughout the warehouse and straight through Theo's head. Now there was nothing between him and Scott.

'Gotcha!' Scott lunged at Theo, just missing him.

With a gasp of pure fear, Theo scurried back faster, using every part of his body, wriggling like a snake.

Scott placed both hands in the shaft and heaved himself upwards, trying to get after Theo. Only he cracked his head on the top of the shaft and sank out of sight, swearing fluently.

'I hope you've split your head wide open!' Theo called after him, still scurrying backwards.

Ahead, he heard the sound of running footsteps, but strangely enough they were running away from him rather than towards him. Puzzled, Theo slowed down, then stopped. Where was Scott going? Why wasn't he coming after him?

Theo got up on all fours, wondering why he hadn't done it sooner. It would've been so much easier to move. He leaned forward and listened very carefully. Silence. What was Scott up to? The silence stretched on for ever.

Then Theo realized. Scott was going to come up behind him. That was the only explanation. He hurled himself forward, not stopping until he got to the grille opening. The basement seemed all clear, but maybe it was a trick. And where was Angela? Theo could only hope that she was safe and hiding somewhere where Scott wouldn't find her.

'*Do* something . . .' Theo muttered to himself.

But what? Scott might be hiding somewhere behind one of the pillars in the basement, just waiting for him. But on the other hand, maybe Scott had left the basement and was entering the shaft from another entrance, trying to cut him off. Theo looked around again. How could he get down without breaking his neck? A fat lot of use he'd be to Ricky then. The table was underneath the shaft but it looked a long way down. A very long way down.

Theo swallowed hard. Jump . . . That was easier said than done, but he couldn't hang about in the shaft all day, especially with Scott after him. Theo curled himself up into a ball, manoeuvring so that his feet were under him. He leaned back, kicking his legs out before him so that they dangled out of the shaft. Then he sat up, his legs dangling out over the wall, but now came the hard part. Theo took a deep breath and held it. He swivelled the top part of his body and kicked off with his legs, letting his feet slap into the wall to absorb the impact before the rest of his body. He now dangled down from the tunnel, facing the wall with only his fingertips holding him up – and his arms were already aching.

Theo pushed off with his hands. Barely a second passed before he made contact with the table. He bent his knees the way he'd been taught in PE but a shock like lightning zapped up his right leg. Theo grimaced and slid down off the table. The moment his right foot touched the floor, pain like nothing he had ever felt before flamed through his leg. He dropped to the floor, clutching his foot. Beads of perspiration dampened his forehead and trickled down his back. The basement started to swim around him. The light rocked back and forth, growing more and more dim.

'Don't pass out. Don't you dare pass out,' Theo muttered, fighting down the waves of nausea that threatened to overwhelm him.

He had to get up. He had to *move* before Scott caught him. Most people already thought he was pretty feeble. Was he going to prove them right or wrong now? Theo struggled to his feet. He touched his right foot down onto the ground. Sharp, intense pain speared through his leg again. His mouth filled with cool saliva, which he swallowed convulsively. He had to get out of there. Gritting his teeth, Theo hopped towards the exit doors at the far side of the basement. With a little luck, Scott would be busy searching for him in the tun—

The exit doors burst open. Scott stood stock still, filling the doorway. He took a step forwards. Theo took a step backwards, never taking his eyes off the man before him. Scott took another step forwards. Theo took another step back. It was like some strange dance between the two of them. Then Scott broke into a run. Theo turned, stumbling, before he picked himself up and pelted towards the shaft. The pain in his ankle was distant, low down on the list of his current priorities. His heart hammered and his blood roared in his ears. But where was he running to? There was nowhere to go. The entrance of the shaft was far too high to get to, even if he managed to jump up onto the table. He'd just have to . . . But Theo got no further.

In the next moment, he found himself swept off his feet. He lashed out, flailing with his feet, his elbows, hitting backwards with his head. Scott groaned and swore viciously, but his arms were like a vice around Theo's chest.

'Let me go! LET ME GO!' Theo shouted, struggling harder.

Scott held him up higher, his arms wrapped around Theo's chest in a bear hug. Theo's feet were a good thirty centimetres off the ground. In amongst all the panic and fear, Theo felt the pain of his ribs being squeezed tight. He had to *do* something – before Scott broke all his ribs, before he passed out. Theo stretched his legs out in front of him, until they were almost at right angles with the rest of his body. Then he bent his head and bit as hard as he could into Scott's arm, kicking back with his legs at the same time. As Theo's heels made hard contact with Scott's shins, Theo ignored the pain dancing in his ankle and kicked back again, biting down harder into Scott's forearm.

'Oww!' Scott hollered, dropping Theo to the floor.

Theo sprang up immediately, ready to leg it, when he heard a clunk and a crash, followed by the sound of wood splintering. He turned and leaped to one side – just in time. Scott hit the floor like a felled tree. And there behind him stood Angela, still holding what was left of the wooden chair she'd applied to Scott's back and head. Her face was paper white as she stared down at Scott.

'Is . . . is he dead?' Angela whispered.

Theo squatted down and cautiously felt Scott's wrist. 'I can feel his pulse beat – and he's still breathing,' he replied at last.

Angela breathed a huge sigh of relief. Only then did she realize that she was still holding what was left of the chair. She dropped it as if it was suddenly burning her hands.

'We'd better tie him up before he wakes up,' Theo decided.

'Do we have to?' Angela backed away.

'I think so. It'd be safer. You look through the holdall, I'll keep an eye on him,' Theo said. 'Oh, and Angela?'

'Yeah?'

'Thanks!'

'You'd do the same for me,' Angela shrugged. And she and Theo smiled at each other.

Minutes later, Scott's feet were bound and his hands were securely tied behind his back using some stout rope from his own holdall. And in all that time he hadn't moved a muscle.

'Will he be all right, d'you think?' Angela asked.

'Yeah, of course. Anyway, who cares?!' Theo dismissed. He had a lot more on his mind than some criminal scuzbucket who'd tried to separate his head from his body. 'Did you find Ricky? Is he somewhere else in this building?'

Angela shook her head. 'I didn't get the chance to search properly. I was having a hunt around when I heard you shout something about hoping someone had split their head. I reckoned I should duck down and keep out of sight after that.'

'OK then. Let's search this place from top to bottom,' Theo suggested. He took another look at Scott. 'We should gag him first.'

Theo took out the hankie that Mum had insisted he carry with him until he was totally over his cold and twirled it around until it was a thick cord of none-too-clean material. Squatting down, he pulled it between Scott's teeth and tied it in a double knot at the back of his head.

'And stay there!' he ordered the still unconscious body.

He and Angela set off towards the exit, but Theo had barely taken a step when his ankle made its presence felt. He winced, immediately raising his right foot off the floor.

'What's the matter?' asked Angela.

'I did something to my ankle when I jumped down from the ventilator shaft,' Theo explained.

'Is it broken?'

'I don't know. I don't think so,' Theo said doubtfully. When Scott had chased him, he'd still managed to use it so it couldn't be broken. Mind you, his adrenalin level must've been off the scale so maybe he just couldn't feel it then.

'Wait here. I'll go and have a look,' said Angela.

'But . . .'

'You can't do much with a bad foot. Besides, you'd only slow me down,' Angela pointed out.

She didn't even wait for Theo to reply, before running off.

Theo watched her go, his lips a hard line across his face. Angela had no right to treat him like a spare tyre, like he was totally useless. Why did people always do that? It was as if everyone in the universe only remembered his name when they wanted something from him. Otherwise he didn't exist. He was always one of the last to get picked when sides were being chosen for football. When he put his hand up in class to answer a question, he practically had to jump up and down on his desk before Mrs Daltry even knew he was there. The only sure way he could get her attention was to have a cold and sneeze all over her. Everyone ignored him – except Ricky. Ricky didn't think he was a waste of space . . .

Theo waited and waited, gently twisting his foot first one way, then the other. It wasn't too bad now.

Time passed. Where was she? Theo didn't hear a sound from anywhere in the warehouse.

'You idiot!' he suddenly hissed to himself.

Angela was probably out of the warehouse and well on her way to warning her brother by this time.

But she couldn't. She *wouldn't*. She knocked Scott out, Theo reminded himself.

So what? All Angela cared about was her brother. And she certainly wasn't going to let Theo mess things up for Tom and herself.

'Angela?' Theo hobbled forward. 'ANGELA?'

No reply. She was obviously long gone. But what had Theo expected?

'Moron!' Theo berated himself through gritted teeth.

Now what? Angela had gone. And where was Ricky? He'd failed again . . .

Chapter Seventeen

# The Irving Museum

Behind him, Scott groaned. Theo turned. Scott was still lying on his stomach, his hands behind his back. He raised his head and shook it, as if to clear it. Theo instinctively backed away, ignoring the sudden sharp pain in his ankle. Scott turned his head, his eyes chips of ice when he saw Theo.

'Llmm . . . m . . . ou . . . plem . . .' What he lacked in coherence, Scott made up for in volume.

Theo increased the distance between the two of them. Scott tried to crawl like a caterpillar towards Theo, but gave up after moving only a few centimetres. Even though Theo couldn't make out what he was saying, there was no mistaking the blazing fury in his eyes or the tension which kept his whole body rigid.

'Llmm . . . m . . . ou . . . ymm . . . toa . . .'

'The same to you, mate!' Theo replied.

He turned and hobbled to the door. Surprisingly, with each step, the pain was growing slightly easier. He opened the door and hopped out into the small hall. There were toilets on the left and a staircase leading up to the ground floor on the right.

'ANGELA . . . ?' Theo tried again.

'What's the matter?' Angela called from the top of the stairs. 'Ricky's not here. Robbie must have taken Ricky with him when we were still in the ventilator shaft.'

'So what do we do now?' Theo asked.

'No police. Not yet,' Angela said quickly. 'I don't want my brother to get into trouble.'

'Isn't it a bit late for that?' Theo asked.

Angela shook her head. 'Not necessarily. Once Tom sees that Robbie decided to use Ricky as a hostage after all, he might see sense.'

'I'm fed up waiting for your brother to grow a brain,' said Theo with contempt. 'This job – whatever it is – is going to happen at the local museum so I think we . . .'

'Museum?' Angela interrupted.

'Before Robbie left the warehouse he told Scott not to be late to the Irving. The only Irving around here is the Irving Museum,' Theo explained.

'Of course!' Angela breathed. 'That explains those drawings I saw.'

'What drawings?'

'I'll explain when we get there. Theo, we can do this. We don't need anyone else. We can get Ricky and Tom out of there.' An uncomfortable pause followed as Theo considered his next move. 'Theo, are you coming with me?'

'What d'you think?' Theo replied, his voice hard. But uncertainty gnawed at him like a hungry dog with a bone.

Angela nodded, relieved. Theo wriggled his ankle again. It didn't feel too bad now. He could only hope that it would last out until Ricky was safe. Theo glanced at Angela. If it came down to a choice between saving her brother or saving Ricky, which one would she choose? Theo slowly shook his head. No contest . . .

'Let's go. We don't have much time,' Angela said.

'Lead the way,' Theo replied. 'I'm right behind you.'

Where you can't stab me in the back! Theo kept that bit to himself.

As they walked up the stairs, Theo wondered out loud, 'I wonder what they intend to do at the museum?'

He turned to Angela. The light of realization was on her face too.

'The Greek and Roman jewellery collection . . . Of course.'

There was meant to be a school trip to the Irving Museum

on Friday but if Robbie and his friends got their way, there would be nothing left to see!

'I don't understand. That collection must be guarded night and day. How do they hope to get away with it?' Theo asked.

'They've got someone on the inside working for them,' Angela admitted.

'Who?'

'The security guard. My brother Tom is a security guard there . . .'

Theo stared in amazement. Talk about setting a wolf to watch the sheep!

He shook his head. 'I don't like this – not one little bit. This is getting more and more dangerous, Angela. We should phone the police.'

'When we've got Ricky and my brother out of there. We can't call them until then,' Angela insisted.

'We should phone them now. We might not get another chance,' Theo replied.

'What d'you mean?'

'Robbie had a gun – I saw it. For all we know, your brother and that other guy Dylan could have guns as well. Someone could end up hurt – or killed.'

'Tom won't let that happen,' Angela said firmly.

There it was again – that total faith in her brother. She just couldn't bear to hear anything said against Tom. It was as if Theo's words entered her ears but couldn't get to her brain. Theo gritted his teeth with frustration. It was decision time.

'Sorry, Angela, but I think it's best to call the police. Tom and the others are all in the one place now. The police can handle it from here.'

'You can't do that . . .'

'I've got no choice.' Theo turned to walk away.

'If you go to the police, I'll phone my brother on his mobile and warn him that the police are coming,' Angela called after him. 'Tom, Ricky and the others will be long gone by the time the police get there.'

Stunned, Theo turned back to Angela. 'You'd do that?' he whispered.

'If you don't leave me any choice – yes,' Angela said through thinned lips.

'Well, now we both know where we stand, don't we?' Theo said quietly.

'Yes, we do.'

Silence.

'All right, we'll play it your way. But I'm warning you, Angela. I'll go to the museum with you but that's it. If anything goes wrong, if we don't get Ricky out, I'm going to call the police and nothing you can say will stop me,' Theo said.

Angela frowned at him.

'I mean it,' Theo said, his voice quiet.

'OK. OK.' Angela nodded reluctantly. 'What about Scott?'

'What about him?' Theo dismissed. 'As soon as we get Ricky, we'll phone the police and tell them where to find him.'

They left the warehouse by the front gate and set off.

'How do we get into the museum?' Theo asked.

His ankle was making him limp slightly but the pain was bearable.

'The same way Tom and the others will – using the delivery entrance.'

At Theo's thoughtful look Angela added reluctantly, 'I heard Scott talking about it when I climbed down from my bedroom.'

'I see,' said Theo. 'And how're you going to get your brother out of there without alerting the others?'

'You leave that to me,' Angela replied.

'OK then. Tell me how we get Ricky out of there when we know that at least Robbie has a gun?' said Theo.

Angela frowned. 'That's a bit more tricky. But we'll think of something!'

'I'm glad you think so,' sniffed Theo.

Fifteen minutes later they both stood before the Irving Museum. The evening was still light and bright with hardly a cloud in the sky. Theo looked around. Unlike around the warehouse there were quite a few people milling about. He turned back to the museum. The Irving was the biggest museum in the town. Mrs Daltry always saw to it that her class visited the museum at least once a year. Theo didn't think it was too bad. There were always plenty of experiments that you could do for yourself – always plenty of buttons to press, and levers to pull and plenty of gadgets to put together. And the exhibition of Greek and Roman jewellery was one of the biggest exhibitions the Irving had ever staged. What had Mrs Daltry called the collection? Priceless?

How did Robbie and the rest plan to rob the museum? Theo would've thought there'd be more than just one security guard looking after all that priceless ancient jewellery. He'd leave it to the police to figure out how Robbie and the others planned to do it. Right now, all he was concerned about was Ricky.

Angela glanced at her watch. 'It's past seven. The museum has been shut for over an hour.'

'D'you think they're in there?'

'They must be. They're probably wondering what happened to Scott,' Angela replied.

Theo looked up at the imposing building with its high colonnades and its huge double-doored entrance. It would've been so wonderful to have X-ray vision. Theo didn't really fancy blundering into the museum and getting caught before he'd even taken two steps. What were Robbie and Dylan and Tom doing at that precise moment?

'This way,' Angela said, whispering even though they were several metres away from the museum.

Without a word, Theo followed her. Angela veered off to the right and turned the corner to walk down the side of the building.

'D'you know where you're going?' Theo asked.

Angela looked back at him and sheepishly shook her head. 'Not exactly.'

'That's what I thought!' said Theo, ruefully.

'The delivery entrance must be around here somewhere,' Angela mused.

They walked all the way around the building, which occupied the entire block. There were plenty of doors around the block which looked likely but there was only one problem – they were all locked.

'You're sure . . .'

'Yes,' Angela snapped before Theo could get any further. 'Listen, I know you don't trust me and I suppose in your shoes I wouldn't trust me either! But I told you the truth. Tom was going to enter the museum as normal and then open the delivery door for them. That's all I know.'

'Why can't the others go through the same entrance as Tom?' asked Theo.

'Because all the ways into the museum – except the delivery entrance – have close-circuit TV cameras monitoring them. Everyone who enters or leaves the building is taped,' Angela explained.

'So where is this delivery entrance?'

Angela looked up and down the main street, perplexed. 'Wait a minute . . . Across the street . . . I remember now. I overheard Dylan say something about a long corridor in the basement leading to the ground floor. He was complaining that he only had thirty seconds to run one hundred metres, deactivate some special alarm and knock out the close-circuit monitors before all the bells went off. Tom couldn't do that bit for some reason. It needs an electronics expert.'

'One hundred metres? But that's well into the next block on every side,' Theo pointed out.

'The delivery door must be in one of the other blocks then,' said Angela.

'We'll be here all night,' Theo complained. 'And suppose we still can't find the entrance?'

'I'm all ears if you've got any better suggestions,' Angela frowned.

'All right. Let's try that block first,' said Theo, pointing to the next block across the street on the right.

Theo and Angela crossed over the road and started looking.

'I would've thought the delivery entrance would be quite big,' Theo thought out loud.

'Maybe. But don't forget the front doors are huge as well.'

'Even so.'

They examined every door they passed, particularly those that weren't attached to shops. Turning first one corner, then another, then the last one in the block, it looked like they were going to be unsuccessful until Theo spotted a huge set of doors with no number on them and no shops on either side.

'Angela, look,' Theo pointed.

They both ran up to the doors and studied them. The doors were high and made of wood painted black, with a huge door knob on each. There was no bell or knocker on or beside them. Nothing which indicated how you got someone on the inside to open them.

'What d'you think?' Theo asked.

Angela shrugged. 'Could be . . .'

They looked at each other.

'Go on then,' urged Angela.

'Last chance to call the police?' Theo tried.

'No,' Angela replied vehemently.

Slowly, Theo stretched out his hand towards the doors. That hot, queasy, uneasy feeling in the pit of his stomach was back.

'Oh, let me,' Angela said impatiently.

She pushed at one of the double doors as hard as she could, then the other. Nothing happened. Angela tried harder, groaning at the effort. Still nothing.

'It's no good.' She straightened up, panting. 'The doors won't budge. We'll have to think of something else.'

Theo frowned stubbornly. He wasn't going to turn back now. No way. He looked up and down the huge double doors, then at the door knobs. Stretching out his hand, he grasped one door knob and pulled it towards him. The door opened easily and silently. Theo turned to look at Angela, his eyebrows raised.

'OK! OK! Don't rub it in!' said Angela.

Theo looked past the doors. The darkness inside spilled out onto the pavement. He took a tentative step forward. There was a lift and some stairs but that was it. No corridors, no rooms, nothing else.

'This must be it,' Theo said doubtfully.

He stepped inside. It was immediately cooler and quieter. In the space of a couple of steps, the traffic noises outside all but disappeared, even though the door was still partially opened.

'Well? Aren't you coming?' Theo asked Angela.

With extreme reluctance, Angela followed Theo inside. As the door swung shut, Theo said quickly, 'Don't let it slam.'

Angela caught the door just in time. A centimetre at a time, she let it close with a faint click. Theo and Angela walked over to the lift. Angela reached out to press the button when Theo caught her hand.

'No,' he said, shaking his head. 'I think we should take the stairs. Someone might hear the lift moving. We don't want anyone to know we're here.'

As there was a staircase leading down to basement level and no other staircase leading up beyond the ground floor, Theo and Angela walked down the steps side by side. The stairs were grouped in sets of ten before they levelled off and started down again.

'I can't hear anything,' Angela whispered.

'Neither can I.'

After Theo and Angela had walked down for at least a

minute, the stairs finally stopped. They were in some kind of storage area. Mummy cases, display cases, odd bits of PCs, a cross section of a small plane leaning against a high wall, a strange looking engine, a two-metre-high model of an eye – as Theo looked around he felt like Ali Baba in a cave of bizarre treasures. Assorted items were scattered here, there and everywhere but with a definite gap leading through them, forming a corridor.

'At least we know we're in the right place,' Theo whispered. 'This is a lot more interesting than the museum itself.'

'Come on,' Angela beckoned. 'The museum must be that way.'

Weaving their way through the strange items, Theo and Angela made their way along the corridor. Theo looked around this way and that, keeping his eyes and ears as wide open as possible. He wanted to find Ricky, not any of the others. Angela's brother Tom was robbing the museum along with the rest of his gang and as far as Theo was concerned, that made him just as dangerous.

'We must be underneath the street,' said Angela, looking up.

Theo looked up and listened. He couldn't hear a thing, even though there had to be traffic roaring over them. They carried on walking to the far end of the corridor. There was another lift and another set of stairs. The echo of a distant, rhythmic knocking filled the air. Theo put his fingers over his lips and pointed to the stairs. Angela nodded. They both crept up the concrete stairs on tiptoe, their steps slowing the further up the staircase they got. The knocking grew louder and louder.

Theo was scared. He admitted it to himself and felt strangely better for it. He was close to Ricky – he could feel it, and he was scared.

At the top of the staircase, there was another lift entrance and a set of double doors. They tiptoed over to the doors. Theo listened hard, then pushed one open very, very slowly. He peeked out, then carefully let it shut again.

'We're on the ground floor of the museum,' he whispered. 'Where's the Astral Collection being held? Which floor?'

'No idea. Ask me another,' Angela whispered back.

'Not including Scott back at the warehouse, there's two of them, plus your brother, plus Ricky – so we'll have to be very careful and fifteen-sixteenths,' Theo said. 'There might be other guards in the museum working with them for all we know.'

'I don't think so.'

'Well, we can't take any chances.'

'Should we split up?' Angela asked.

Theo looked at her. 'I don't think so. I think it'd be safer if we stuck together.'

Angela regarded him steadily. 'You don't trust me at all, do you? What d'you think I'm going to do? Run off and warn them.'

'I never said that.'

'But that's what you meant . . .'

'Can we discuss this once we've got Ricky out of here?' Theo asked, exasperated.

'Ricky and my brother,' Angela reminded him.

'Hhmm!' was all Theo said.

He listened at the door again, then pushed it open a fraction to peep outside again. Nodding to Angela, he crept out as if he was walking through a graveyard at night. Angela quickly followed him. They ducked down behind the nearest display case and listened. Theo tried to focus in on the knocking sound which echoed almost eerily all around them. It was definitely coming from somewhere on the ground floor but the museum was filled with ante-rooms and alcoves leading off the main hall which could disguise where the noise was really coming from.

'Think!' Theo muttered sternly.

He'd been to the museum before on many occasions – so think! The Astral Collection . . . Where would they put a big, important display like that? Of course! The Irving Room.

Where else? Whenever the museum put on an important exhibition like – what had it been last year? – The Chinese Terracotta Army – then they always put it in the Irving Room towards the back of the museum.

'This way,' Theo whispered.

'Where're we going?' asked Angela, anxiously.

'The Irving Room.'

Theo didn't give Angela a chance to ask any more. He didn't want to stop or slow down for too long. That gave him too much opportunity to ask himself just what on earth he thought he was doing! Theo made his way towards the back of the museum. Behind him, Angela made scuffling noises as she followed him. Theo turned his head to glare at her.

'Sorry!' Angela mouthed.

They carried on moving, scurrying from display case to display case until, from round the side of a case, Theo could see the entrance of the Irving Room only a couple of metres away. And that's not all he could see.

Ricky was there. He was sitting down outside the entrance to the Irving Room. He was tied up like a supermarket chicken, with his hands tied behind his back, his feet bound and a big piece of sticky plaster covering his mouth. But it was definitely Ricky.

Excited, Theo opened his mouth to call out to him, only remembering where he was when he heard the loud knocking sound again. Then Theo really saw Ricky, really took in his appearance for the first time.

Ricky looked terrible.

There were streaks running down his face from his eyes which were red and sore. Ricky had been crying – a lot. His eyes were cast down and he looked so miserable and lonely and frightened that Theo felt anger rising up in him – and it was far stronger than the fear he felt.

Cautiously, he raised his head above the display case and looked around. The main display hall where he and Angela were hiding seemed to be all clear but there was some definite activity in the Irving Room. Theo ducked back down behind the display case.

'Wait here.' Without giving Angela time to argue, Theo crept out from behind the display case and raced for the wall adjacent to the Irving Room where there was no cover. If one of the thieves came out now, he'd be caught for sure. Squatting down, Theo took another look around. He had to find some way of untying Ricky and getting him out of the museum without the others seeing. The problem was, Theo was on one side of the entrance to the Irving Room and Ricky was on the other.

'Psssst! Psssst!' Theo couldn't risk saying it any louder in case he was overheard. 'Pssssst!'

Ricky looked up. His eyes widened with shock and surprise.

'Umm . . . The . . . Ge . . .' Ricky struggled to sit up, nodding in the direction of the Irving Room.

Frantically, Theo shook his head, putting his finger over his lips.

'The . . . ru . . .' Ricky struggled harder against the ropes that bound his hands and feet.

'I thought you tied that boy up and gagged him?' said an angry voice.

'I did,' another man protested.

'Go and see what's the matter with him,' the first voice ordered from inside the Irving Room.

Footsteps sounded on the wooden floor, getting closer and closer. Theo looked desperately at the nearest display case. There was no way he could run back to it without being seen. The footsteps were almost out of the room. Theo crouched down lower against the wall, knowing with absolute certainty that he was going to be caught . . .

## Chapter Eighteen

# Choices

'Dylan, it's me.' Angela stood up and ran over to the entrance of the Irving Room.

She stood between Theo and the entrance, just as a man whom Theo couldn't see came out into the main hall. Theo made himself as small as possible, crouching down against the wall. If he could've merged with it, he would have. He didn't dare blink, he didn't dare breathe. His heart was pounding so loudly, surely it could be heard throughout the entire museum?

'Angela! What the hell are you doing here?' Dylan exclaimed. 'Tom, it's your sister.'

Theo stared at Dylan's shoes, visible just past Angela's legs. He couldn't bring himself to look up. If he didn't look in Dylan's direction, maybe Dylan wouldn't look in his. Angela put one hand behind her and waved at Theo to stay back. Another set of footsteps sounded on the floor. An arm emerged and pulled Angela into the Irving Room. Theo crept forward slowly, still holding his breath.

'Angela, what're you doing here? And this had better be good.' The low, deep voice held quiet menace.

'Robbie, I . . . I wanted to make sure that Tom was all right . . .' Angela's voice trailed off into a miserable silence.

'Angela, you shouldn't have come here. I'm fine.'

Theo peeped around the corner. Tom was looking worriedly from Robbie to Angela and back again.

'Tom's right. You shouldn't have come here,' said Robbie. There was more in his voice than just agreement with Tom. Nervously, Tom moved to stand nearer to his sister. Angela was the only one directly facing the entrance. The others were too busy glaring at her. Theo caught Angela's eye. They both knew she was in deep trouble. Angela looked up at her brother, so as not to give Theo away. Theo had to act NOW. Summoning up all the courage he possessed, Theo raced across the entrance, keeping low and on tiptoe. He flung himself against the wall as soon as he was clear of the entrance and waited.

'Robbie, listen. It's not a problem,' Tom said earnestly. 'I'll take care of her. I'll make sure she stays out of our way.'

'Angela, how did you know where we were?' Robbie asked. There was no mistaking the menace in his voice.

'I listened when you were all in our kitchen,' Angela admitted. 'That's how I knew how to get in.'

Theo stepped behind Ricky and bent down to try and untie his hands and feet.

'Shush . . .' Theo whispered softly in his friend's ear.

'And where's Scott? He should've been here by now,' said Robbie.

'How s-should I know where he is?' Angela tried and failed to keep her voice steady.

'What's going on, Angela?' Robbie's voice was even softer than before.

Theo's fingers had all turned into thumbs and the knots felt like they'd been superglued in place. At last they began to give. Moments later, Ricky's hands were free. Ricky pulled the tape off his face, suppressing a wince of pain as he did so. Then he quickly untied his feet.

'There's nothing going on,' Angela replied. 'I told you, I just wanted to be with Tom. I've got to look out for him. You lot sure won't.'

Theo pointed towards the nearest display case in the main hall and the ante-room behind it. Ricky nodded, understanding. Ricky got to his feet and they both dashed for the display case. Theo turned back to see what was going on in the Irving Room.

'I'm tired of falling over kids every time I turn around,' Robbie said.

'Calm down, Robbie,' Dylan soothed. 'That boy was just an accident. And Angela is Tom's sister. We can trust her. She wouldn't betray us.'

'You reckon?' Robbie chided. 'If I was drowning in a bathtub, I wouldn't trust that girl to pull the plug out.'

'You got that right!' Angela replied, frost in her voice.

'Angela! You're not helping,' Tom pleaded.

Theo indicated the next case down and he and Ricky made a dash for it. Theo wanted to put as much distance as possible between them and Robbie but really they needed to be on the other side of the main hall where the exit to the basement was. The problem was how to get there. Robbie and Dylan were now standing side on to the Irving Room entrance. If Theo and Ricky risked darting across the hall, they'd be spotted for sure. And besides, Theo didn't want to leave Angela behind with that lot. If she hadn't come out into the open like that, he'd have been caught for sure. He had to admit, Angela was brave if nothing else.

'What's going on? What's Angela doing here?' Ricky whispered. 'How come she knows all of them?'

'Tom, the one with the dark brown hair, is her brother,' Theo explained.

'Her *brother*?' Ricky said, aghast.

'Yeah. Shush! I'll explain later.'

Theo looked around. He had to get himself, Ricky and Angela out of there in a hurry. But how?

*How?*

'Ricky where's your phone?'

'They took it off me,' said Ricky.

So much for that idea then. Theo racked his brains. A diversion. He needed a diversion.

'Ricky, listen,' Theo whispered quickly. 'See the door behind that display case?' he pointed across the hall.

'Yeah?'

'There's a staircase and a lift beyond that door which lead down to a basement corridor. You've got to get to the other end of that corridor and up the stairs on the other side. That'll take you out into the street on the opposite side of the museum. Then leg it to the nearest phone box and phone for the police.'

'What about you?'

'Don't worry about me. I'm going to run interference for you.'

'Huh?'

'I'm going to create a diversion. Wait until the coast is clear, then make a run for it,' Theo said.

'But Theo, Robbie's got a gun. You can't outrun a bullet,' Ricky exclaimed.

'D'you know if any of the others have guns?'

'No, they don't. Just Robbie.'

'OK then,' Theo said grimly. 'I'm still gonna go for it.'

'But Theo . . .'

'Ricky, we've got no choice,' Theo countered.

'Angela, if you've done anything, *anything* to mess up my plans . . .' Robbie took a step closer to Angela, who immediately backed away from him.

'Watch out, Angela,' Dylan said quickly.

'Don't touch those cases. I haven't deactivated the alarms on them yet.'

Angela turned to look at the Astral Collection, sparkling in the five display cases behind her. She took a step towards them. Robbie leaped forward and grabbed her by the arm.

'Oh, no, you don't,' he hissed.

'Ow! You're hurting me,' Angela protested, trying to prise his fingers off her upper arm.

'Robbie, let her go.' Tom tried to pull Robbie away from his sister. Robbie turned and, without letting go of Angela, he pushed Tom away from him.

'It's now or never,' Theo whispered to Ricky. 'Duck down and keep out of sight until you can make a break for it.'

'OK,' Ricky replied doubtfully. 'And Theo?'
'Yes?'
'Am I glad to see you!'
It took a moment for what Ricky had said to sink in.
'What're friends for?' Theo smiled ruefully.
Without further delay, Theo made his way on all fours down the hall, using the display cases as cover. At the end of the hall, he raced up the stairs to the first floor, keeping close to the wall. On the landing he picked up a blue and white pottery vase off a plinth and ran along to stand just above the Irving Room. Theo held out the vase over the banister, striving to keep his arms out – at least for the moment.
'Oi! I know you're there and I'm going to call the police,' Theo shouted out.
'What the hell . . . ?'
Theo heard footsteps charging out of the Irving Room. The moment he saw a head below him, he released the vase. He didn't miss, either! Dylan was just looking up when the vase cracked him on the top of his head. He crumpled up like wet newspaper and was out like a light. On impact, the vase shattered into a thousand pieces which rained down around him.
'I hope that vase wasn't expensive,' Theo murmured.
Tom emerged from the Irving Room, followed by Robbie who was still holding a struggling Angela in his vice-like grip. Frantically, Theo hunted around for something else to drop, but it was too late. Tom and Robbie had seen him. They both jumped forward, already out of the range of anything else Theo might drop.
'Go and get him,' Robbie ordered Tom.
Theo stared down in frustrated panic. This wouldn't work if Robbie didn't come after him as well. Robbie looked up at Theo. His green, cat-like eyes narrowed. Already Tom was running down the main hall on his way to the stairs.
'Angela – RUN!' Theo shouted.

Angela didn't need to be told twice. She gave Robbie a kick in the shins that Theo felt from up on the first floor. Robbie yelped and released her immediately, clutching his leg. Angela took off like a bolt from a crossbow towards the door where she and Theo had come in.

Time to follow her example, Theo decided. Tom was on the stairs and gaining fast. Theo ran along the upstairs landing, darting into a large room off the walkway. This room was full of pictures and models of dinosaurs. Various display cases were filled with dinosaur paraphernalia. This had always been one of Theo's favourite rooms but now was not the time to relax and enjoy it!

'Angela, take one more step and I'll shoot. Your choice.' Robbie's voice froze Theo in his tracks.

Robbie was going to shoot Angela. He was actually going to shoot her . . .

'Robbie, no,' Tom called out from the first-floor landing. At the sound of Tom's retreating footsteps, Theo ran out of the dinosaur room, edging along the landing until he could see down into the main hall. Robbie was holding a gun and pointing it straight at Angela who stared at him, horror-stricken.

'Robbie, no! Don't!' Tom charged down the stairs and ran towards Robbie, stopping only when Robbie turned to point the gun at him.

Theo ran silently along the landing and down the stairs, careful to keep to the wall and out of sight.

'Robbie, calm down,' Tom soothed. 'It's only my sister.'

'She kicked me,' Robbie hissed.

'You probably frightened her.' Tom shrugged with careful nonchalance. 'You know she's got a bit of a temper. But she can be trusted. She'd never do anything to hurt me, to hurt us.'

'No? Then why am I up to my armpits in kids? Where did that boy Ricky come from?' Robbie nodded in the direction of the Irving Room. 'And where . . . did . . . ?' Robbie's voice trailed off as he realized Ricky was no longer by the entrance. Eyes blazing with rage, he turned back to Angela who recoiled from his look as if it was a physical slap. There came a loud click as Robbie drew back the hammer on his old-fashioned revolver.

'Where is he, Angela?' he asked.

'I don't know. I swear I don't. I didn't let him go . . .'

Robbie took a step towards her. Tom ran to stand between his sister and Robbie.

'Robbie, listen to me. We can still do this. We can still take the jewels and blow.' Tom spoke rapidly. 'Ricky and my sister aren't the important ones now. The Astral Collection is. And it's *ours*. Robbie, listen!'

'Get out of the way, Tom.'

'No way.'

'Tom, move,' Robbie demanded.

Tom straightened up slowly. 'No, Robbie. She's my sister. I'm not going to let you hurt my sister.'

Robbie and Tom studied each other for a long, tortuous moment.

'Ricky, I know you're here somewhere,' Robbie called out, his eyes never leaving Tom's. 'You've got five seconds to show yourself otherwise I shoot Tom and his sister and then I'm coming after you. Five . . . Four . . .'

Theo could hardly breathe. What should he do? He crawled along the floor towards Ricky who was still crouched behind a display case. So much for his so-called plan. Everything was falling apart, crumbling around him.

'Three . . .'

From the sound of it, Robbie had gone off the deep end. There was no way Robbie would let any of them leave the museum alive to grass on him. Theo knew that as surely as he knew his own name.

'Two . . .'

'All right! All right! I'm here.' Ricky stood up quickly before Theo could reach him.

'And the other boy . . .' Robbie called out. 'You can come out too or your friends get it. And this time I'm not even gonna count.'

Think . . . *think* . . . Theo had to think of something, *fast.*

The display cases . . .

'Show yourself. I'm not going to ask you a third time . . .' Robbie warned.

Theo stood up immediately.

'Now all of you. In there.' Robbie indicated the Irving Room with his gun.

Reluctantly Theo followed the others into the Irving Room with Robbie entering the room last. Theo briefly thought about launching himself at Robbie, but he dismissed the notion at once.

Don't be a doof! he thought.

Robbie would shoot him before he'd taken two steps. And no way could he outrun a bullet. Robbie's gun was very real. Not a toy, not filled with blanks but with real bullets that could kill and maim. And Robbie wasn't playing games. The man was already several sandwiches short of a picnic. They all had to be really careful now. Anything might set him off.

'Robbie, look. The jewels are here.' Tom pointed with a smile. 'Don't lose sight of what we came here for.'

'Shut up. Just shut up,' Robbie roared. 'Everything's gone wrong and it's all your fault. You and your sister. Look at this. Three kids. Count 'em. Three! Scott's missing and Dylan's unconscious.' He pointed his gun at Theo. 'I ought to do you for that alone . . .'

Theo took a small, terrified step backwards. His mouth dried instantly. Sweat trickled down his back like rain on a windowpane. He didn't, *couldn't* take his eyes off Robbie.

'You can wake up Dylan. And Scott's probably just been delayed,' Tom said calmly.

'If anything's happened to Scott, anything at all . . .' Robbie threatened.

Theo could feel Angela look at him but he was careful not to look back . . . That would give them away for sure.

'Robbie, that gun you're holding is the only thing stopping us from leaving here rich and free. If we tie up Ricky and the other one, by the time they're found we'll be long gone. Think about it.'

Robbie frowned at Tom. 'Dylan's our alarm expert. How do we get at the jewels without triggering the alarm?'

'Wake Dylan up!' Tom said as if it was the most obvious thing in the world.

'Tom . . .' Angela began.

'Shut up and stay out of this, Angela,' Tom said harshly.

Angela's mouth snapped shut.

'OK then. I'll bring Dylan around,' Robbie said at last. 'You kids stand against that wall and don't move, unless you want your next move to be your last.'

Theo, Ricky and Angela stepped back against the wall at once. They had no choice with Robbie pointing his gun at them.

'That's more like it. Let's get to it, Robbie.' Tom grinned his relief.

'Hhmm!' Robbie turned around and walked towards Dylan.

Without warning, Tom sprang at him, knocking him to the ground. The gun flew out of Robbie's hand and went off as it hit the ground, shooting into the main hall. Then everything happened at once. Robbie twisted like a snake shedding its skin and punched Tom viciously on the side of his face. Angela raced forward, trying to dodge past the two men on the floor. Theo picked up the security guard's chair next to him and, leaping forward, he smashed it down on the nearest display case. The glass shattered and flew in all directions. Theo dropped the chair immediately to shield his face and eyes from the glass. Instantly an ear-splitting shriek sounded throughout the museum. Ricky jumped over the two men still trading blows on the floor and raced off like the wind. Robbie kicked Tom off him and launched himself towards the gun.

But Angela got there first.

'Give me the gun, Angela,' Robbie ordered, jumping to his feet.

'Stay where you are.' Angela had to shout over the noise of the klaxon.

Tom sprang to his feet, wiping the blood trickling from his nose on the back of his hand. He moved forward, past Robbie towards his sister.

'Well done, Angela. Now give me the gun,' he smiled.

'Angela.' Theo ran over to stand beside her. 'Don't give it to either of them.'

'D'you want it?' Angela asked.

'No fear,' Theo replied immediately. No way did he even want to touch the thing. It was giving him chills just being this close to it. 'Just don't give it to those two either.'

'Angela, don't listen to him. I'm your brother. Give it to me,' Tom said, incredulously.

'There's no way I'm going to let you hand over my property to your brother,' Robbie threatened.

Angela took a step back, looking from her brother to Robbie and back again. She cupped her left hand under her right to steady it, pointing the gun in both Robbie's and Tom's direction. The gun visibly shook in her hand.

Theo felt he should do something, anything but he didn't know what. He could see the fearful indecision all over Angela's face. But it was up to her now. She had the gun and it was her choice.

## Chapter Nineteen

# Family Loyalty

Angela glanced down at the gun. She flicked a tiny switch at the side of it and the chamber fell to one side. Tipping up the gun she let the bullets fall into her hand.

'Theo, lose those,' she said, handing them over.

'Angela, you fool,' Tom shouted.

Robbie leaped forward towards her, rage like nothing Theo had ever seen all over his face. Tom rugby-tackled him to the ground and they were at it again. Theo backed off fast, pulling Angela back with him, in case Robbie should win this bout.

'Let's get out of here,' Theo suggested.

'No, I can't. Tom might need me.' Angela pulled away from him.

'Then let's get the police. We can't handle Robbie. He's a nutter! He probably drinks blood and sleeps hanging upside down from a tree.'

'I'm not leaving my brother,' Angela insisted.

Theo scowled at her. If she didn't leave her brother, then he couldn't leave her. He looked around for Ricky but there was no sign of him. He looked back at Robbie and Tom. They weren't having a boxing match like on the telly. They were punching and gouging and using their whole bodies to hurt each other. It was vicious and nasty and made Theo feel sick.

'Do something,' Angela implored him.

'Like what?' Theo asked.

'I don't know. *Do* something. Robbie's going to kill him.'

Bewildered, Theo looked around for something he could

use. Then he saw a fire hose tucked away in the corner to his right. Maybe he could just douse the two of them. The water in fire hoses came out at quite some pressure. That should be enough to separate the two men.

Then they'll both be cheesed off with you rather than each other! Theo thought.

But he didn't have much choice. Angela was looking at him, expecting him to do something. Theo ran over to the glass-fronted cabinet which housed the fire hose. It was locked. Beside it was a small cabinet which held a key. The instructions above it said 'BREAK GLASS FOR KEY'.

'I need something to break the glass,' Theo said quickly.

'Move.' Angela ran over and hit the glass with the butt of the gun in her hand. The glass shattered instantly. Theo took out the key and opened the cabinet. Taking the nozzle in his left hand, he heaved off the rest of the hose with his right. It was heavy and he couldn't hold it, so he dropped it to the floor. Holding the nozzle, Theo and Angela ran to where Tom and Robbie were still fighting. Both of their faces were covered with blood and one of Tom's eyes had swollen shut. Theo looked down at the nozzle. How did it work?

'It turns on from over there. I'll do it,' Angela said.

She ran over to the fire cabinet and began to turn the large tap beneath the hose.

Theo gripped the hose tightly as he watched Angela turn the tap. Holding it away from him, he pointed it straight at the two struggling men on the ground. The hose coughed. It gurgled. It spluttered. A tiny trickle of water ran out over the end of the hose and dripped pathetically to the floor.

'Angela, nothing's happening,' Theo called out.

'I'm turning it,' Angela called back.

Tom lay groaning on the floor, his face a mass of bruises. Robbie started to stand up . . .

'Today, Angela! Today!' Theo urged.

'I'm doing my best,' Angela snapped.

She was still facing the tap, turning it this way and that, trying to figure out what was wrong. Robbie was on his feet now, and was slowly advancing on Theo like a man-eating tiger ready to pounce.

'It's not working,' Angela said unnecessarily.

Theo couldn't wait any longer. He yelled, 'Angela, shift!' Theo threw the nozzle end of the hose at Robbie in sheer desperation.

Robbie sprang to one side. The hose missed him completely and hit the floor. But before he could take another step, the hose suddenly lurched up, turned back on itself with the force of the water funnelling down it and doused Robbie from the back of his head to his heels.

Robbie spun, his arms raised ready to sort out his new opponent. When he saw it was just a hose, he turned back to Theo, his expression thunderous. This was it. Theo thought Robbie was going to get him for sure. But just at that moment, two policemen emerged from the side doors, followed by Ricky. Robbie looked around desperately for somewhere to hide. Tom stuck out his foot and tripped up Robbie, sending him flying. One of the policemen ran to the main entrance and opened it up. Within moments, cars were screeching to a halt outside the museum, their sirens wailing, their lights flashing. Soon the main hall was swarming with police, most of them busy trying to subdue Robbie, who was fighting back like a cornered rat.

'Are you kids all right? Are you hurt? Do you need to go to hospital?' a policeman asked Angela and Theo, after turning off the fire hose, which was drenching the floor.

Theo shook his head, then handed over the bullets in his hand. Angela handed over the gun without saying a word.

'How did you get here so fast?' Theo asked.

'We've been on special alert ever since the Astral Collection arrived at the museum,' the policeman explained. 'Though I must admit, we thought the alarm going off was just a false alarm until your friend over there found us by the entrance and told us what was going on. If you're all sure you're all right, we'll need you down at the station for your statements.'

'Let me go! LET ME GO!' Tom was struggling to get free from the policeman and policewoman who held him by his arms. 'Angela, help me.'

Theo turned. Tom pulled even harder to be free.

'You're making a mistake. Angela, t-tell them I don't have anything to do with these men. Tell them I came here with you. Tell them I was trying to stop the robbery.'

'Is that true?' the policewoman who held Tom asked.

Angela stared up at her brother, without saying a word.

'Angela . . . ?' Tom said desperately.

'Is that true, Angela?' the policewoman prompted.

The silence in the main hall was deafening as all eyes were turned on Angela.

'I . . . No,' Angela whispered. 'He was with Robbie and Dylan trying to steal the Astral Collection.'

'Angela . . .' At Tom's shocked voice, Angela burst into tears.

Theo put his arm around Angela's shoulder. 'Don't cry,' he said, softly. 'It's OK. It's over now.'

'Angela . . .' Tom's voice held sad resignation.

'I'm sorry, Tom. I'm sorry. But I don't want to live like this any more – scared all the time,' Angela sobbed.

They watched each other, before Tom was pulled away by his police escort.

'You'll find another member of the gang called Scott in the warehouse at 117 Buzan Road. He's in the basement,' Theo told the policeman at his side.

'What's your name, son?' the policeman asked.

'Theo Mosley. And this is Angela. And this is my best friend, Ricky,' Theo said as Ricky came running up.

'I'm Sergeant Goldstein,' said the policeman. 'Taking your statements should be interesting. I mean, how did you even get in here?'

'The same way they did. Angela's brother is a security guard here at the museum,' Theo explained. 'He's the one who let them in via the delivery entrance.'

'The other guard on duty was tied up by Robbie. He's in one of the rooms over there,' Ricky panted.

'Hang on. Haven't I seen you somewhere before?' The sergeant scrutinized Ricky.

'Ricky's been missing since Friday and . . .' Theo began to tell Sergeant Goldstein.

'I'm the one who's been missing. Let me tell it,' Ricky demanded.

'Ricky Burridge . . .' Sergeant Goldstein whistled. 'I thought I recognized you. We've been searching for you for days.'

'You have?' Ricky asked.

'Let's get all of you down to the station,' said Sergeant Goldstein. 'And the first thing I'm going to do, Ricky, is call your mum.'

## Chapter Twenty

# Forgive Me

### 23:48 hrs Tuesday, 20th May

I don't have much time. There's a policewoman outside my door waiting to take me out of here. I begged them to let me stay here by myself. This is my home. But all the grown-ups at the police station said I was too young to be by myself. The policewoman outside says my social worker will process me tomorrow. She makes it sound like I'm a roll of film or a tin of peas or something, rather than a person.

I'm writing this now 'cos I don't know when I'll next get an opportunity to sit down and write.

Tom's in a police cell.

So are the others. I don't care about them. Only Tom. He's in a police cell and I put him there. He wanted me to tell the police that he had nothing to do with Robbie and the others. How I wish I had now. How I wish . . . If I had to do it all over again, I'd say whatever Tom wanted me to say.

But it's too late.

Tom's in a police cell and I'm on my way to a home. Maybe one day I'll look back and think I did the right thing. I hope so. Then maybe this aching pain in my chest will go away.

I've got to go now. The policewoman's knocking on my door.

I'm sorry, Tom. I hope you'll forgive me. You're my brother and I love you but I'm so very tired. I just wanted it all to end. I just wanted it all behind us so we could go home and not jump every time there's a knock at the door or we pass a police officer. That's all. Please understand.

And . . . and forgive me.

## Chapter Twenty-one

# Three Weeks Later

Theo sat with his head in his hands, staring at his essay. Only Mrs Daltry could take what was probably going to be the most exciting adventure of his life and turn it into boring, dull homework. The class had been told to write about the most exciting or frightening thing that had ever happened to them. Mrs Daltry was particularly keen for Theo to write about what she called 'his adventures'. She said he should write down every detail, every moment, but how could he? It hadn't been a fun adventure for Ricky and there were things that had happened between Angela and her brother Tom which weren't really his to tell. He'd tried writing down those bits but it just didn't feel right so he'd screwed up the first two drafts and now here he was with his third attempt and he didn't like this one any better. It made it seem as if he'd done everything himself. And he hadn't.

Downstairs the doorbell rang.

'Don't let that be another reporter,' Theo murmured.

At first, reporters knocking on the door at all hours had seemed exciting. Truth to tell, it made Theo feel kind of important, but the novelty had worn off by the end of the first couple of days. Now the reporters were just a pain in every bodily part!

Well, if it was a reporter, Mum and Dad would soon sort him or her out! They'd had enough of reporters too, especially those who wouldn't take no for an answer – which was ninety-nine per cent of them.

Theo leaned across his small table to push up his window.

Maybe some fresh air would help him think straight because his essay was driving him nuts! And it had to be given in the following morning so time was running out. Theo had to make a decision about what to write and stick to it.

'Hi. Can I come in?' Ricky popped his head round the door.

'Course. You don't have to ask.' Theo beckoned him in.

'What're you up to?' Ricky smiled, strolling over.

'I'm doing the essay Mrs Daltry told us to write,' said Theo. 'She didn't even let me decide for myself what I'd write about. She just told me to write about what happened at the Irving Museum.'

Ricky's smile faded.

'You OK?' Theo asked.

Ricky shrugged. 'Sure. Mrs Daltry said I could write about whatever I wanted. I don't have to write . . . to write about the same as you.'

'So what did you write about?' asked Theo.

'I haven't done it yet.' Ricky shrugged again.

'Are you going to?'

'I don't know.' Ricky began to walk around the room aimlessly. He touched this, he shifted that until he came to stand by Theo's table again.

'Ricky, are you OK?' Theo asked, concerned.

'I guess. Yeah. Sure. I'm great. Why wouldn't I be? Mum lets me have anything I want now. I only have to ask – except she doesn't let me out of her sight and she wants to take me everywhere. She walked me over here and she told me to phone her when I'm ready to leave and she'll come and pick me up.'

'She's just worried, that's all.'

'Yeah, but she doesn't realize that every time she insists on taking me where I want to go, all she does is bring it all back. She won't let me forget what happened.'

'Why don't you tell her that then?'

'I've tried. She won't listen.'

'Then make her listen. Tell her until she hears you. Even my mum wanted to take me everywhere that first week after it happened, and I wasn't the one who was . . . who was kidnapped.'

'No, you weren't,' Ricky said faintly. 'Did I tell you? One of those tabloids that Mum always calls "tacky" offered her a lot of money for my story.'

'Are you going to do it?'

'I think . . . no.' Ricky's voice grew more and more quiet. 'I still have nightmares, you know. I dream that I've lost my hands and my feet and my mouth and I can't speak or shout or anything. Two nights ago I had a dream that there was nothing left of me but my brain and my two eyes staring out, and try as I could, I couldn't make anyone understand what I was thinking.'

'I . . . I'm sorry.' Theo mentally cursed himself for being so ineffectual, but he really didn't know what else to say.

This was the first time Ricky had said a word to Theo about what had happened to him. Theo knew he needed to talk. Hell! He'd spent the last three weeks thinking about very little else himself, but recently he'd begun to wonder if maybe he'd dreamed bits of it. The bad bits. And then he'd see Ricky's face and the shadows in his eyes and know he hadn't.

'I'm sorry, Ricky,' Theo repeated.

'Yeah, well so am I.' Ricky started wandering around the room again.

'Maybe the dreams will stop,' Theo suggested.

'And maybe they won't,' Ricky said with sudden bitterness. 'Those few days when I was a prisoner were the worst days I'll ever have in my life. I'm not going to put them in a stupid story for Mrs Daltry or relive them so some lousy tabloid can sell a few more papers. I just want to forget it. I just want . . . I just want . . .' Ricky's face contorted as he tried to blink back the tears threatening to embarrass him. But it didn't work.

'Sorry,' Ricky sniffed, wiping his hand over his eyes. But the tears didn't stop.

Theo stood up, watching his friend unhappily.

'T-They kept me tied up all the time. They only released my hands and feet to let me go to the loo. They only released my hands and took the tape off my mouth so I could eat. I even had to sleep tied up.' Ricky started to shake as he remembered. 'Robbie . . . Robbie threatened to shoot me if I tried to run away. He dared me to try – he said he needed the target practice.'

Theo gritted his teeth, fury blazing like an inferno through his body.

'I'm sorry I'm crying. I'll stop in a minute,' Ricky sniffed, sitting down.

Theo wished he could think of something to say, but instead he just stood by his table feeling totally useless. He made his way over to his friend and sat down next to him.

'You cry if you want to, Ricky,' Theo said. 'There'd be something very wrong with you if you didn't cry after everything you've been through.'

Ricky buried his face in his hands and wept. After a moment's indecision, Theo put his arm around Ricky's shoulder and hugged him.

## Chapter Twenty-two

# Friends

It was incredible but true. Mrs Daltry was even more boring than usual! Somehow she managed to make the subject of how the Earth was formed as interesting as watching finger-nails grow! Ricky nudged Theo in the ribs. Theo nudged him back. They both glanced at each other and wrinkled up their noses. The classroom door opened.

Theo gasped when he saw who came in. A gasp echoed by Ricky – and everyone else in the class.

It was Angela.

'Hello, Angela. Take your seat,' said Mrs Daltry.

Her head bowed, Angela made her way over to her old table and sat down. Theo and Ricky looked at each other, stunned. What was Angela doing back here? She hadn't been seen since the Irving Museum business. Theo looked across the classroom at her. She looked gaunt and miserable. Theo had seen that look before – on Ricky's face.

After that, everything Mrs Daltry said about how the Earth was formed didn't even get as far as going in one ear and out the other. It just bounced straight off Theo's and Ricky's heads. Neither of them could concentrate. Angela had all their attention.

Years passed – at least that's what it felt like! – before the buzzer finally sounded. Mrs Daltry was first out of the class, a liquorice allsort already on its way to her mouth. Others in the class began to amble out. Angela was busy packing her bag. Theo noticed how she never looked up, never caught anyone's eye, even when someone spoke to her. She'd answer in monosyllables, still packing her bag.

'Come on.' Theo nudged Ricky and they both went over to Angela.

'Hello, Angela,' Theo said quietly.

Angela glanced up quickly. Her glance down again was even faster.

'Hello, Theo.' There was a pause. 'Ricky.'

Theo looked at Ricky. His face was expressionless.

'So how're you doing?' Theo asked.

'Fine,' Angela replied, her nose buried in her bag.

'Are you going to be in our class permanently?' said Theo.

'Yes,' said Angela.

Theo sighed inwardly. She wasn't making this very easy.

'What happened to your brother?' Ricky asked.

Angela looked up, her eyes glistening, her expression hostile. 'He's been remanded in custody. They all have. His solicitor says they're probably all going to prison. So go ahead and gloat.'

'I'm not gloating,' Ricky said quietly. 'Do you live by yourself now then?'

'No. I'm living with my new foster parents.'

'What're they like?' Theo asked.

'What d'you care?' Angela said belligerently.

'Just asking,' Theo replied.

'Listen. I know you two hate me and well, I don't care. I hate you too. And I know you've told the whole class about me and my brother and they all hate me as well. Well, it wasn't my fault. I tried to stop Tom – I *did*. And I'm not going to apologize any more. I'm not.'

Theo opened his mouth to speak but Ricky got in first.

'Now, you listen. We don't hate you. And we haven't told anyone in the class a thing, have we, Theo? All they know is what they read in the papers and saw on telly,' Ricky said. 'And no one's asking you to apologize for anything. It wasn't your fault. In fact, if it wasn't for you, Theo couldn't have rescued me.'

'But I was the one who wrote out the dare which got

you captured in the first place.' Angela stood up, letting her bag drop to the floor. 'You hate me for that at least.'

'At first I did,' Ricky admitted. 'But you wouldn't have written it if you'd known how things were going to turn out. I know that now.'

'Why're you being so nice to me?' Angela asked suspiciously.

'Because I know what it's like to be alone and scared,' Ricky said simply. 'And I can see from your face that that's how you feel.'

'I don't want you to feel sorry for me,' Angela fumed.

'I don't. I think you're feeling sorry enough for yourself. You don't need any help from me,' said Ricky.

'Well, I don't need you or anyone else for that matter. I'm doing just fine on my own.'

Ricky sighed. 'Suit yourself. I just thought we could be friends, that's all. Come on, Theo. Let's go for lunch.'

Ricky walked off without another word. Theo looked from Ricky to Angela helplessly. With a shrug, he turned and ran to catch up with Ricky.

'Ricky . . . ?' Angela stopped them just as they reached the door. 'Can I . . . can I go to lunch with you two?'

Ricky smiled. 'Sure. If you like.'

Angela picked up her bag and ran to catch up with them.

'This doesn't mean I like you two or anything,' Angela said.

'Course not. It doesn't mean we like you either,' Ricky agreed.

'But we've all got to eat,' Theo added.

Theo was the first to smile, with Ricky, then Angela joining in reluctantly.

'Come on. I'm starving,' said Ricky.

And they left the classroom together, discussing just how boring Mrs Daltry had been that morning.

## Chapter Twenty-three

# Nowhere To Go But Up

### 19:00 hrs Monday, 16th June

Today wasn't as bad as I thought it was going to be. I had a long chat with Ricky and Theo at lunchtime and we all walked home together. Colin and some others came over to me when I was eating my lunch and tried to ask me all sorts of questions but Theo and Ricky weren't having any. I didn't have to say a word. Theo called Colin a nosy doof and two-thirds and told him to bog off or else – and from the look on Theo's face, everyone could see he wasn't joking.

It's funny but when I first joined Mrs Daltry's class, I thought Ricky was big and brash and didn't have much going for him and I must admit, I thought Theo was a bit of a wimp. It just goes to show, doesn't it. I got them both completely wrong.

I still miss Tom desperately. Marian, my new foster-mum, says she'll take me to see him if I want. Tom wrote to me, asking me to visit him but I don't know. I'm not sure. To be honest, I'm scared. I don't know how he thinks of me. In his letter he said I'm still his favourite sister and he hopes he's still my favourite brother. I miss him so much. I want everything to go back to the way it was and yet I'm glad it's not like that any more. That makes it sound like I don't even know my own mind and to be honest, I'm not sure I do. Everything is still a jumble in my head.

D'you know, I look back and I still can't believe that all this started with a dare. Ricky was right about that. If I'd known what would come of it I would never, ever have written it. I would've broken my fingers first.

Tom's in prison and I'm all alone and I feel like I've no one to talk to and nowhere to go. At least I felt like that till today. Marian and George – he's my foster-dad – practically frog-marched me to school. What with not feeling well and having to get myself sorted out, I haven't been to school in four weeks. I didn't want to go back today – certainly not to the same school where everyone knows about me, but like I said, it wasn't as bad as I thought it would be.

For the first time in a long, long time I think I may have made two real friends. I guess I should look forward now, not back. What's done is done. What I said before, about having nowhere to go, it's not true. I've just realized. The only place I can go from here is up.

# COMPUTER GHOST

Chapter One

# The Message

To: JDriscoll@JDriscoll.private.uk
From: PDriscoll@PDriscoll.private.uk

Darling Jade,

I miss you so much. You don't know what it's like. I'm so alone here. I can't go forwards, I can't go back. I'm stuck. And I'll be here for ever if you don't do something. Please, please help me. I'm desperate. This is the only way I've found of getting through to you. I can't communicate any other way or with anyone else. God knows I've tried. I guess the reason I can talk to you is that you're the only one still listening to me. You're the only one who still believes in me. As far as everyone else is concerned – including your mother – I'm gone for good. Jade, I need your help. Don't let me down.

All my love,
Dad.

## Chapter Two

# A Brilliant Idea

The noise level in the class was getting louder and louder. Theo stared out of the classroom window beside him, half wondering what had happened to Mrs Daltry. It wasn't like her to be late. Not that he particularly minded that she wasn't here. Mrs Daltry didn't mess about when it came to her class messing about! She was the kind of teacher who took no prisoners! She was very strict, but Theo had to admit that she was also fair. Unlike some of the other teachers, she didn't have favourites and she didn't pick on people without a good reason. Yes, she was definitely one of the better teachers. Not that he'd invite her or any of his teachers to one of his birthday parties!

Theo started in surprise. He was just thinking about her and there she was. He rubbed the grimy glass of the window to get a better look. Mrs Daltry was out in the school grounds talking to the new caretaker, Mr Appleyard. Mr Appleyard had started working at St Christopher's at the beginning of the year and already it was as if he'd been there for ever. Theo wasn't keen on Mr Appleyard. And he wasn't the only one. Mr Appleyard fancied himself as taking over where Hitler had left off. Theo wondered what they were talking about. Hopefully, Mrs Daltry was having a go and giving the caretaker what for! Curious, Theo stood up and opened the window.

'Are you mad?' Ricky rounded on him.

'Theo, shut the window.'

'It's freezing!'

'Theo!'

'All right! All right!' Theo shut the window quickly before anyone else could rant in his ear. Oh well! He'd just have to wonder. Still, the longer Mrs Daltry stayed out there, the longer he could stare out at the clear blue October sky and think. Well, he called it thinking! Mrs Daltry called it wool-gathering. Angela called it daydreaming. Ricky called it space gazing. It was none of those things. It was a time to collect his thoughts, to dream and scheme and use his imagination. It was a time to think about 'what ifs . . .' and 'suppose that . . .' And just at that moment the most magnificent 'what if' he'd ever had in his life occurred to him.

Theo turned to Ricky, his eyes wide and shining like car headlights. 'Ricky, I've just had a brilliant idea!'

'Even if you do say so yourself!'

'Even if I do say so myself!' Theo agreed with a grin.

'Go on then. What is it?' Ricky urged.

Theo's eyes widened even more in delight at the mere thought of it. The only thing he couldn't figure out was why no one had thought of it sooner.

'Ricky, why don't we start up a detective agency?'

'A what?' Whatever Ricky had been expecting, it hadn't been that!

'A detective agency,' Theo repeated. 'Right here in the school.'

'But . . . but where would we get our cases from? And besides, the teachers would never allow it.'

'Then we won't tell them. This will be a detective agency run by us for the other kids in the school. What d'you think?'

'I don't know. I mean, it *sounds* like a good idea but really we don't know anything about being detectives.'

'I do!' Theo contradicted. 'I've been reading *How To Be a Detective in 10 Easy Lessons* and *The Detective's Handbook* and *The Spy's Guidebook* and *Young Detective* and *Everything You Ever Wanted to Know About Being a Detective*.'

'Wow! Why the sudden interest in sleuthing?' asked Ricky.

'Mum and Dad bought me a detective kit for my birthday,' Theo said.

'Oh yeah! You told me,' Ricky remembered. 'But I thought you weren't terribly impressed by it?'

'I changed my mind,' Theo mumbled.

When he caught sight of Ricky's knowing grin, he added testily, 'I can change my mind, can't I?'

''Course you can,' Ricky soothed.

Theo decided not to rise to Ricky's teasing. Especially since Theo knew it was his own fault. He remembered how he'd whined and complained about the present his parents had bought him. But once he'd sat down and started reading all the accompanying blurb and taken a good look at what was actually in the kit, it'd turned out to be not so bad after all. It fact it had turned out to be very interesting – not that Theo would ever admit that to his mum and dad. Not after the way he'd moaned at them for buying him something so feeble!

'So what d'you think of my idea?' Theo persisted.

'Hadn't I better read all that detective stuff too before we start offering our services as detectives?' said Ricky.

'Yeah, yeah!' Theo waved Ricky's observation aside with an impatient hand. 'But what about the cases we're going to solve? We'll only pick really interesting, exciting cases. Only cases that are going to be a real challenge. We'll be like Sherlock Holmes and Watson, Poirot and Hastings, Batman and Robin. We'll be . . .'

'OK class, settle down. The cat's back now!' Mrs Daltry swept into the room, followed by a man Theo had never seen before. The man was tall, with mid-brown hair swept back off his head and a slightly lighter, shortcut, neat beard. His piercing ice-blue eyes looked as if they wouldn't miss much.

'I said settle down. Or we can all practise being quiet during the lunch break later,' Mrs Daltry said, annoyed.

Instant silence.

'That's better. Now this is Mr Dove. He's going to be

taking over this class as your form teacher from next week for the rest of the term.'

Murmurs immediately erupted throughout the classroom. Angela put up her hand.

'Yes, Angela.' Mrs Daltry sighed as if she knew what was coming.

'Where are you going to be, Mrs Daltry?' Angela asked.

Theo smiled. That was Angela. As blunt as ever. Always asking the questions that no one else dared.

'I am going away and I won't be back until the New Year,' Mrs Daltry said.

'Where are you going?'

'If you must know, I'm going to Canada for six weeks.'

'How come?'

'I won a prize and this is the only time the prize organizers will let me go. I have to go next week or I can't go at all.'

'How did you win . . . ?'

'That's quite enough, Angela. If you went to university and did a degree in nosiness, you'd get a first!' Mrs Daltry interrupted firmly. 'Now then everyone, Mr Dove will be sitting in with us for the rest of the week, just to see how we do things.'

'I'm looking forward to it.' Mr Dove directed his smile around the class.

'He doesn't need a week for that. It'll only take about five minutes,' Ricky whispered to Theo.

'Thank you, Ricky, but when I want your opinion I'll ask for it,' said Mrs Daltry.

Ricky and Theo stared at her. How on earth had she heard that? They were sitting towards the back of the class.

'She's got ears like a bat!' Theo whispered, his voice so low that even he could barely hear it.

'And don't you forget it, Theo!' Mrs Daltry smiled.

Theo decided to give up. Much as he was dying to discuss his new idea with Ricky, he certainly didn't want to risk having to sit outside the staff room at lunch time. He'd just have to put his idea on hold until after the lesson.

But it *is* a brilliant idea, he thought to himself. And he felt sure that everyone in the class – no, everyone in the entire *school* would immediately agree with him.

'A detective agency. Are you nuts?' Colin roared with laughter.

Theo tried not to let his annoyance show but he failed. All day, he'd been getting exactly the same reaction. Was he really the only one in the school with any *vision?*!

'Oh, come on, Theo.' Colin wiped the tears from his eyes. 'You must admit that it's a bit of a bizarre idea.'

'No, I don't admit any such thing,' Theo replied testily. 'What's wrong with it?'

'Well, for a start, what d'you know about being a detective?' asked Jack. 'And secondly, this isn't New York. This is St Christopher's! What crimes do you expect to solve in our school?'

'The only crimes here are the school dinners,' Colin added.

'You'd be surprised. There are lots of mysteries that go on in this school,' said Theo.

'Like what?' asked Ricky.

Theo scowled at his friend. Whose side was he on? Ricky got the unsubtle hint and looked suitably contrite.

'Just give us a chance – OK?' Ricky said quickly. 'You'll be amazed.'

'I'm amazed already,' Jack said. 'Theo, you've come up with some weird ideas in your time but this is the best yet.'

Colin started laughing again. And off went Jack and Colin to their first lesson of the afternoon. Ricky and Theo trailed behind them. Theo couldn't believe it, he really couldn't. He had thought they'd be inundated with cases. He really believed they'd have to pick and choose. After he'd had the idea in Mrs Daltry's class that morning, he spent the rest of the lesson going over in his mind the detective techniques he'd learned and working out the best way to keep track of the many cases they were bound to get. He'd even mentally practised turning down those clients unlucky enough to have boring cases.

'I'm so sorry, but we're just too busy . . . Our caseload is phenomenal, astronomical, extraordinary, sensational . . . BIG!!'

'We don't seem to be getting very far,' said Ricky.

'Don't worry. I'm not giving up,' Theo said with determination.

But even as he spoke, he realized that starting his detective agency was going to be more of an uphill struggle than he'd ever imagined.

'We'll just have to convince everyone that they really need us,' said Theo, thoughtfully.

The question was, how?

## Chapter Three

# Reality Like Rot

'I can't believe this place, I really can't,' Theo bristled.

'You'll just have to give everyone a chance to get used to the idea,' said Ricky.

'I think it's a good idea,' Angela added.

Theo, Ricky and Angela were all walking home together. The day had turned out to be a raging disappointment for Theo. He'd stood outside the school gates, trying to convince everyone who came out that his detective agency was going to be the best thing since salt and vinegar crisps. He still couldn't believe the apathy his brilliant idea had been met with. Those who hadn't laughed in his face didn't seem to care much about the idea one way or the other. Reality, like rot, was beginning to set in.

'I can't understand it. I thought people would be queuing up to use us.' Theo couldn't keep the frustration out of his voice. 'Maybe we should advertise?'

'How?'

'I could print off some ads using Mum and Dad's computer tonight,' said Theo. 'Something along the lines of – "Got a problem? Come and see the only ones who can really help you out. Theo and Ricky." Something like that.'

'You'll have to do better than that if you want people to take you seriously. You'll need a better name for your detective agency than "Theo and Ricky's"! That sounds like a restaurant!' said Angela. 'And your ad will have to be eye-catching but discreet. Obvious yet tasteful. Bold yet sincere.'

Ricky and Theo exchanged a look.

'I'm serious,' said Angela. 'Anyway, I doubt if you'll get many girls asking for your help.'

That stopped Theo dead in his tracks.

'Why not?'

''Cause you're two boys. You can't be expected to deal with *girl* problems.'

'Why not?' Theo's frown deepened.

''Cos you're a boy. You won't understand the way we girls do things. The way we think and feel. Girl problems need to be handled in a very special way.'

'What a load of rubbish!' Ricky scoffed. 'We both helped you with your problem not too long ago.'

'Too right,' Theo agreed.

'Yes, but that was a one-off. I'm telling you, you won't get any girl clients – not unless you have a girl helping you out with your cases,' said Angela.

'Ah!' Theo said, as the penny dropped. 'We do have a girl helping us. You!'

'I thought you'd never ask,' Angela grinned.

'Why didn't you just come right out and say that you wanted to be part of our detective agency?' asked Ricky.

'I just did!' Angela smiled.

'I hate it when people don't come out and say what they mean,' Ricky complained, more to himself than to anyone else. He added, 'So what should we do now?'

'You two need to read all the blurb I have on how to be a detective,' Theo said decisively. He dug into his duffel bag and dug out some of his detective manuals which he always carried with him now. '*Don't* lose these,' he ordered, as he handed them over. 'Meanwhile, I'll make up some flyers advertising our services and print them off on Mum and Dad's computer.'

'They don't mind you becoming a detective?' asked Ricky.

'I haven't actually passed the idea by them yet,' Theo admitted. 'But I'm sure they'll say yes.'

'And if they don't?' Angela raised an eyebrow.

Theo had a think about it. 'They won't say no,' he decided.

'How can you be so sure?' Angela persisted.

'I just know. That's all.'

Angela and Ricky exchanged a smile.

'You're not going to tell them, are you?' Angela grinned.

'Nope!' Theo replied. 'And no one likes a know-it-all!'

Theo leaned forward and viewed the computer screen critically. It didn't look *too* bad. His advertisement was all the things Angela had recommended – eye-catching yet discreet, obvious yet tasteful, bold yet sincere.

'Theo, you're a genius!' he murmured.

But just to make sure, he'd print off one to see how it looked on paper. Theo used his mouse to click on the <Print> option and waited impatiently for the printer to finish.

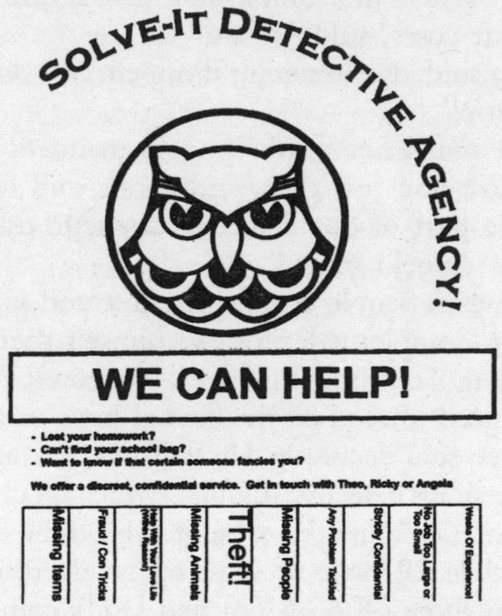

SOLVE-IT DETECTIVE AGENCY!
WE CAN HELP!
- Lost your homework?
- Can't find your school bag?
- Want to know if that certain someone fancies you?
We offer a discreet, confidential service. Get in touch with Theo, Ricky or Angela
Missing Items
Fraud / Con Tricks
Help With Your Love Life (Within Reason!)
Missing Animals
Theft!
Missing People
Any Problem Tackled
Strictly Confidential
No Job Too Large or Too Small
Weeks Of Experience!


Theo nodded as he studied the flyer carefully. He sat back, satisfied.

'Theo, you're a definite genius,' he told himself again.

If this didn't get them some clients with cases to solve, then nothing would!

Chapter Four

# Ignoring You

To: PDriscoll@PDriscoll.private.uk
From: JDriscoll@JDriscoll.private.uk

Dear Dad,

I want to help you, I really do. But I don't know how. You'll have to tell me what you want me to do. Please don't think that I've been ignoring you – I haven't. It's just that it's very difficult to use the PC at the moment. I have to wait until Mum's asleep, or out. She's terrified the same thing will happen to me that happened to you. I've tried to tell her that it won't, but she won't listen.

You don't know how it feels to run to the computer each morning hoping you'll have sent me a message. It's the only thing I have to look forward to. (I have to wait until Mum's having her shower, but if you've sent me a message, it's always worth the wait). Write soon, Dad. All my love, Jade.

## Chapter Five

# The Surprise

'Everyone's talking about your flyers,' Ricky whispered to Theo.

Theo beamed back at him. 'I knew they'd get a response.'

'Let's just hope that none of the teachers get hold of one,' Ricky said, worried.

'Don't worry. I told everyone they weren't to let any of the teachers see them.'

'That doesn't mean they won't,' Ricky pointed out.

They had no time to discuss it further as Mrs Daltry walked into the classroom with Mr Dove. Mr Dove smiled all around again before sitting on a chair against the wall. Theo frowned as he watched their new teacher. The man was a definite wafer! No taste nor flavour! He looked like he wouldn't say boo to a worm, never mind a goose!

I bet he's even more boring than Mrs Daltry, Theo thought sourly.

'Mr Dove will be taking you for your double lesson this afternoon as he's raring to go.' Mrs Daltry looked at Mr Dove like he had only one marble left in his head. 'So I don't want any nonsense now or this afternoon.'

And with that, Mrs Daltry didn't waste any time but got straight down to it.

'Does anyone know what "paranormal" means?'

A few hands flew upwards. A couple more struggled up. The rest stayed down.

'Ricky?' Mrs Daltry prompted.

'It means things that are not quite normal. Things that are above and beyond and outside normal,' Ricky replied.

'Such as?'

'Like being able to move things with your mind . . . er . . . telekinesis, and leaving your body while you're still alive – that's astral projection – and mind-reading and vampires and people who can shape-shift and turn into werewolves and—'

'Thank you, Ricky. I think we all get the idea,' Mrs Daltry said quickly. She added with a smile, 'You seem to know a lot about it.'

'I love fantasy books and films, miss! I don't like anything else.' Ricky grinned.

The rest of the class tittered.

'Hhmm!' Mrs Daltry sniffed. 'Maybe you should crack the occasional school book. Just a suggestion.'

Ricky bent his head, ruefully acknowledging that his school books very rarely got opened.

'The dictionary definition of paranormal phenomena is that which is outside the scope of the known laws of nature or normal objective investigation,' Mrs Daltry continued. 'That's just a long winded way of saying anything which can't be explained using our known laws of science and nature.'

Theo listened to the teacher, surprised. For once, what she was saying was actually *interesting*! What had come over her? An interesting lesson with Mrs Daltry was a paranormal event in itself!

'Does anyone here believe in ghosts?' asked Mrs Daltry.

Immediately, Ricky's arm shot up. Theo stared at him, stunned. Ricky looked at Theo, had a quick look around, then his arm came down faster than a felled tree. Two surprises in less than two minutes. It must have something to do with the subject they were discussing!

'You really believe in ghosts?' Theo still couldn't believe it.

'Yeah! So?' Ricky scowled.

Theo had another look around. Very few people had their hands up and those that did were rapidly reconsidering it.

'Why d'you believe in ghosts then?' Theo asked.

'Theo, who's giving this lesson? Me or you?' Mrs Daltry asked.

'Sorry,' Theo mumbled.

'So Ricky, why d'you believe in ghosts?' Mrs Daltry gave Theo a wry smile before turning to Ricky.

'I just do, that's all,' Ricky replied.

Theo recognized that tone. Ricky was sorry he'd ever admitted to it.

'Have you ever seen a ghost?' Mrs Daltry asked.

Ricky licked his lips carefully. 'Er . . . no,' he answered in a tiny voice.

Mrs Daltry moved on to one of the others who had put their hand up.

Theo elbowed Ricky in the ribs.

'Ricky, *have* you seen a ghost?' he whispered.

'Shush! I'll tell you after the lesson,' Ricky replied softly.

'I'd appreciate that.' Mrs Daltry appeared from nowhere to whisper in Ricky's ear.

She carried on with the lesson, talking about imagination and science and how science fiction often turned into science fact. Mrs Daltry then went on to discuss the power of the imagination in the sciences as well as in the arts. Theo listened with half an ear. As interesting as it was, it still couldn't compare to the fact that his friend Ricky believed in *ghosts*. If Theo hadn't heard it with his own ears, he'd never have believed it. He studied Ricky avidly.

'Stop that!' Ricky hissed.

'Stop what?'

'Stop glaring at me as if I've just sprouted another head or something.'

'This *is* a lesson about the paranormal,' Theo teased.

'I mean it!' Ricky said, annoyed.

'I'm not staring.'

'Yes, you are.'

'I . . . er, well, maybe just a little. You surprised me, that's all,' Theo admitted. 'I would've thought you'd be the last person in the world to believe in all that stuff.'

'Theo, let me know when you've finished so that I can begin again,' Mrs Daltry said testily.

'Sorry. I've finished now,' Theo said quickly.

'I'm glad to hear it.' Mrs Daltry's tone was saccharine. 'And maybe you'd like to sit outside the staff room for the whole of this afternoon's break. That way you'll have plenty of time to come up with a reason why you felt it necessary to chat whilst I was trying to teach.'

'But Mrs Daltry . . .'

Mrs Daltry raised a hand to halt Theo's objections. 'OK then. But the next time I catch you talking that's exactly what will happen.'

Theo pursed his lips, determined not to say another word. Mrs Daltry might be one of the better teachers in the school but sometimes she could be a real bovine creature! A real bovine creature and three quarters!

## Chapter Six

# The Question

'Ricky, when did you see a ghost then?'

The question was out of Theo's mouth the moment they set foot out of the classroom.

The lunchtime buzzer had sounded but Theo's class were all on second lunch so they had half an hour to wait before they could eat.

'What makes you think I've seen one?' Ricky asked.

'Oh, come on!' Theo was insulted. '*How* long have we been friends? I know there's something you're not telling me.'

'Well . . .' Ricky began reluctantly.

'Wait for me then.' Angela came running up. 'Have you two done your French homework?'

'Yep!'

'Yeah. Why?'

'Can I borrow it?' Angela asked hopefully. 'I didn't manage to finish mine.'

'Never mind that now,' Theo dismissed. 'Ricky was just about to tell us about a ghost he saw.'

'You really saw a ghost?' Angela stared.

'It was ages ago when Mum took me up to Scotland after her divorce,' Ricky began. 'We were staying in this bed and breakfast place that used to be a mansion. One morning I was in the dining room and . . .'

'Ricky, did you mean it?'

Ricky turned at the tap on his shoulder. Jade stood immediately behind him, her expression deadly serious. Theo frowned at her. She'd interrupted them just as Ricky was getting to what promised to be the good bit! Mr Dove walked past and gave them all a friendly smile. Everyone shut up until the teacher had turned the corner.

'Did I mean what?' Ricky asked.

'Do you really believe in ghosts?' Jade asked.

'Yes,' Ricky said. 'And if you're going to laugh, you can go away and do it somewhere else.'

'I'm not going to laugh,' Jade replied quietly.

Theo studied Jade's face – there was no sign that she was on a wind-up.

'Theo, do you believe in ghosts too?' Jade asked.

Theo frowned. 'I don't know. I haven't made up my mind about it one way or the other.'

Jade turned to Angela. 'What about you?'

'No.' Angela's answer was immediate. 'No, I don't.'

'You don't think . . . something else, some other part of us lives on when our bodies die?' Jade asked.

'I don't think so. I think when you're dead, you're dead and that's it – end of story.' Angela shrugged.

'And you, Theo?'

'I'd have to think about it.'

'Think about it now,' Jade urged.

Angela, Theo and Ricky exchanged a questioning look. What was all this about? Why was Jade suddenly so interested in talking to them about Mrs Daltry's lesson?

'Come on, Theo. What d'you think?' Jade prompted.

Theo blinked with surprise. 'Er . . . I don't know. I think . . . maybe some part of us might live on after our bodies die, but I certainly don't believe in ghosts in white sheets that go, "Ooo-ooooh!"'

A trace of a smile flickered across Jade's face.

'I don't believe in ghosts in white sheets either,' she said.

'But you do believe in other kinds of ghosts?' Theo prompted.

'D'you think ghosts can use things in this world to communicate with us?' Jade answered Theo's question with one of her own.

'What sort of things?'

'I don't know.' Jade shrugged nonchalantly. 'Telephones, televisions, computers, that sort of thing.'

'I've no idea. But I wouldn't have thought so,' Theo replied. 'What's this all about?'

'I was just wondering.' Jade shrugged, but Theo wasn't fooled by her fake nonchalance for a second.

He watched the uncertainty race across Jade's face. Jade was a quiet girl who kept herself to herself as far as Theo could tell. She was certainly one of the prettiest in the class. She had huge, brown eyes, a ready smile and plaited black hair which was always an immaculate work of art. But over the last two weeks she'd walked around as if she was Atlas, with the weight of the world on her shoulders. Whatever it was that was troubling her, Theo certainly hadn't expected her to talk about ghosts.

'Well? We're listening,' Angela prompted, after a glance at the others.

'It's just that . . . no, never mind!' Jade broke off quickly.

'Go on.'

There was a long silence before Jade spoke.

'My dad . . . talks to me . . .' Jade's voice grew quieter and quieter before tailing off altogether.

Theo gasped. After a quick glance at his friends' puzzled faces, Theo realized that they didn't realize what Jade had just said.

'So? Why *wouldn't* your dad talk to you?' Angela said, confused.

'It doesn't matter.' Jade shook her head and started off down the corridor. 'Forget I said anything.'

'But Jade . . .'

They all watched Jade's rapidly retreating back.

'Did I miss something? Why on earth wouldn't her dad talk to her?' Angela asked.

'Angela,' Theo said, 'Jade's dad died three months ago.'

## Chapter Seven

# Bullet

Angela stared at Theo, thinking she'd misheard. From the look on his face, she knew she hadn't. 'But that doesn't make any sense. He can't have died.'

'He did. He was found slumped over his PC in their house. They reckon he had a heart attack – if I remember rightly,' Theo explained.

'How come you know so much about it and I don't?' Angela asked.

'My mum works for the same company that Jade's dad used to work for,' Theo explained.

'How come you never told me about Jade's dad?' Angela asked, annoyed.

'Can you keep a secret?'

'Yes,' Angela replied, leaning forwards eagerly.

'So can I,' said Theo. 'It was up to Jade to tell you, not me.'

Angela frowned, but Theo knew she'd got the message.

Ricky was still looking down the corridor after Jade. Theo hadn't often seen that serious look on his friend's face, but when he did he knew that Ricky had made up his mind to do something and there was nothing that would stop him.

'D'you think Jade's dad is trying to communicate with her in some way?' Ricky asked.

'Is that what Jade was talking about?' said Angela.

'I don't know, but I think we need to talk to her,' Ricky decided. 'We need to find out exactly what's going on.'

'This afternoon I'd like to talk about how all our lives have been changed due to computers. We're lucky enough to be in the middle of a technological revolution and just as machines changed everyone's lives during the Industrial Revolution, so things for us will never be the same again.' Mr Dove walked up and down, up and down between the class tables. 'Can anyone tell me where you might find computer and microchip technology in your home?'

Hands shot up, including Ricky's. Theo glanced down at his watch. There was ages to go yet before the end of the lesson. Mr Dove was a typical teacher. He was taking a riveting subject like computing and making it as dry as a cream cracker! Eventually Mr Dove waved everyone quiet amid the cries of 'Microwaves?' and 'DVD players, sir?'

'Hands up all those whose parents' jobs are in some way related to computers?' asked the teacher.

More and more hands began to rise into the air. Theo looked around with interest. His mum worked in the marketing department of a computer company. Did that count? Theo decided that it did and put his hand up. Looking around, he saw that Jade had also put up her hand. Did her mum work with computers as well then?

'Jade, how is your mum or dad involved in computing?' asked Mr Dove.

'My dad's a software engineer. He designs games,' Jade replied.

Ricky and Theo exchanged a glance.

'Oh? Any games I might have heard of?' Mr Dove smiled.

*'Planet of the Anvil.'*

Mr Dove frowned. 'I don't think I've heard of that one.'

'That was Dad's new one.' Jade lowered her gaze.

'When will that be available?' asked the teacher.

'D-Dad never finished it,' Jade replied miserably.

Theo held his breath as he waited for Mr Dove to ask why. But to his surprise the teacher didn't ask. All he said was, 'That's a shame.' Then he went on to ask the same question of Amber.

'This is too weird,' Ricky whispered to Theo. 'Jade talks about her dad as if he's still . . . alive.'

'I was just thinking that,' Theo whispered back. 'She mixes up the past and the present tense – did you notice?'

Ricky nodded. 'I'm just surprised that Mr Dove didn't.'

'Would you like to share your comments with the rest of the class? It's Ricky, isn't it?'

'I was just saying that some washing machines and tumble dryers have microchips in them. My mum just bought a washing machine and you can delay the time it starts at by up to nine hours. I was just wondering if that built-in clock mechanism is an example of a special microchip or is it just part of the overall programming?' Ricky said without hesitation.

Mr Dove smiled. 'That's a very good question, Ricky. And it leads us on to a very interesting point . . .'

Theo elbowed Ricky under the table. Very nicely done! Ricky nudged back acknowledging the 'Well done!' contained within Theo's bony elbow. Theo turned to look at Jade again. It seemed to him that she was stuck in the middle of a kind of no man's land. Her dad had died, and yet, according to Jade, he was still talking to her. Was it true? Was there such a thing as ghosts? And if so, was Jade's dad really trying to communicate? What was he saying? What did he *want*? Or was this someone's sick idea of a joke? No wonder Jade was so unhappy. No wonder she mixed up the past and the present. For her they had to be almost the same thing. Theo turned back to the front of the class and shook his head. He had to find a way to help Jade. He just had to.

'Angela! Why are we going in there?' Ricky asked impatiently.

'I need to print out my homework,' Angela snapped back. 'It'll take two minutes. Anyway, why're you in such a hurry?'

'I want to catch up with Jade before she goes home,' Ricky replied. He glanced down at his watch. 'She's talking to Mrs Daltry at the moment.'

'I won't be long,' Angela insisted.

'I'll wait for you out here,' said Ricky. 'I don't want to miss her.'

'Suit yourself.' Angela shrugged.

Theo and Angela walked into the computer room. Theo frowned at Angela. School was over for another day and truth to tell, Theo wanted to go home. It was chicken and rice for dinner tonight, one of his favourites. He looked around. Three times a week, after school, Mrs Sumonu ran the computer club. And even though it was an after-school activity, the room was still three-quarters full. Theo wasn't surprised by the people he saw either. He could've guessed who'd be part of the computer club and he would have got ninety-nine per cent of them right. And the first person he would've guessed at was Toby, better known as Bullet. Theo eyed Bullet warily. Bullet's nickname was well-deserved. You only had to be around him for a minute or so before wanting to leave with the haste of a speeding bullet – and Theo should know. Toby sat directly behind him in class.

The trouble was – Toby was boring and three-quarters!

He ate, slept, lived and breathed computers. Theo loved computers himself, but even he knew where to draw the line. It wasn't even as if Bullet was into computer games. No, he was into the serious stuff like writing his own programs to do nothing that would be of any interest to anyone except Bullet as far as Theo could see. Bullet was also into the hardware side of computers. He was riveted by how computers and modems and screens looked and worked from the inside out. Theo couldn't understand it. As long as the computer worked on the outside, who cared what it looked like on the inside!

'Angela, come on, then,' Theo urged. 'I thought you wanted to print off something.'

Angela looked around, her head moving this way and that.

'There you are, Angela.' Theo pointed to the nearest unoccupied seat in front of a PC.

'No . . .' Angela continued to look around. 'There's a seat over there.'

'But that chair is next to Bullet,' Theo whispered conspiratorially. 'You don't want to sit next to him, d'you?'

A deep, burning blush crept across Angela's face. 'I don't care about that. I just want to use a PC.'

'So what's wrong with that one?' Theo pointed to the PC he'd just indicated.

'Because I like that one over there,' Angela replied, agitated.

Confused, Theo looked from Angela to Bullet and back again. A slow, knowing smile crept across his face.

'You . . .'

'No, I don't – before you say it,' Angela denied vehemently.

'You *do*!' Theo was astounded. 'You fancy Bullet! You need to get your eyes tested asap, and whilst you're at it, you'd better let them look for your brain as well. I think it's fallen out of your nostrils.'

'I don't fancy Bullet,' Angela hissed. 'And don't you dare tell anyone that I do.'

'Your secret is safe with me,' Theo beamed.

'Oh, shut up,' Angela snapped. And with that she marched off.

Theo couldn't resist it. He sauntered across to sit on the other side of Bullet. What on earth did Angela see in him? Bullet was long and gangly and had more pimples than a raw chicken leg. He didn't think much of Angela's taste.

'Hi, Bullet. How're you?' Angela asked, still looking at her own computer screen.

'Huh? Er . . . yes . . . er, I'm OK,' Bullet spluttered.

Angela swivelled in her chair to face him. For the first time she saw Theo was sitting on the other side of Bullet and the instant scowl on her face could've curdled milk. Bullet obviously thought the look was directed at him. He sat back in his chair, terrified.

'Bullet, don't you just hate it when certain people butt in and won't mind their own business?' Angela hissed.

'Er . . . pardon? No . . . yes . . . I guess.'

Giving Theo the filthiest look she could muster, Angela focused all her attention on Bullet.

'So what're you working on, Bullet, I mean, Toby?'

Bullet looked surprised, not to mention flattered.

'I . . . er, well actually, I'm working on a master program to solve things.' Bullet's voice grew quieter but more steady as he started to talk about his favourite subject.

A program to solve things! Theo snorted with disgust. He might've guessed Bullet was writing a program to do his homework.

'What sort of things are you trying to solve?' Angela prompted. 'D'you mean things like science and maths questions, like equations and angles and areas and stuff like that?'

Theo could've sworn that Angela actually batted her eyelashes at Bullet. Pass the sick bag!

Bullet's eyes gleamed. 'Not exactly.' He lowered his voice so that Theo had to strain to hear him. 'I'm writing a program to solve crimes.'

Angela stared at him. And she wasn't the only one.

'You're joking,' she said, uncertainly.

Bullet shook his head emphatically. 'No, I'm not – I promise. I reckon that if you input enough data and that data is analysed and interpreted in the right way, then there's no reason why a computer shouldn't solve crime problems just as easily as it solves maths problems.'

Theo couldn't help it. He was actually interested in what Bullet was saying! First Mrs Daltry, and now Bullet. This was turning out to be a paranormal kind of day and no mistake. Surreptitiously, he tried to draw his chair closer to Bullet's.

'So how does this program work? How do you input all the necessary information and how do you know when you've put in enough and . . .'

'Hang on! Hang on!' Bullet raised a protesting hand. 'I'm just finishing off the program now. Then I'll need a real, live crime to input to test it properly.'

'Can I see how it would work?' Angela pulled her chair closer to Bullet. So did Theo. Bullet turned, startled, as Theo's head suddenly appeared over his shoulder.

'Don't mind me,' Theo smiled. 'I'd just like to see how this works too.'

'I . . . er . . . well, I don't . . . er . . .'

'Angela! Theo! We have to get going.' Ricky popped his head around the door.

'Just a minute.' Theo waved Ricky off impatiently.

'No. We have to go now or we'll miss her,' Ricky insisted.

Reluctantly Theo stood up, followed by Angela.

'I'll have to catch up with you later.' Angela smiled at Bullet.

Pass two sick bags! Theo thought with disgust. As they made their way out of the computer room, Theo turned to Angela.

'Why didn't you just fall down at his feet and kiss them?' he sniffed.

'Theo, I've told you before and I'll tell you again,' Angela rounded on him. 'Mind your own business.'

Chapter Eight

# The Offer

'Why're you lot hanging around out here?'

Angela, Theo and Ricky looked at each other. Each of them had the same expression on their faces. Mini-Hitler had arrived and from the belligerent look on his face they could tell he was in the mood to throw his weight around.

'We're waiting for someone, Mr Appleyard,' Ricky explained.

'Who?'

'A friend.'

'Hhmm!' Mr Appleyard looked at them out of the corner of narrowed eyes. 'Well, why can't you wait for them somewhere else?'

Theo glared at him. What *was* his problem? They were outside the school gates and they weren't causing any trouble, for goodness' sake.

'We won't be much longer. Our friend is just coming,' Ricky soothed the caretaker.

'Hhmm! All right then,' said Mr Appleyard. And he turned to walk back to the school building, just as a few others left the premises.

'That man needs to get a life!' Theo sniffed.

'Too right!' Angela agreed emphatically.

'Hi Jade. Are you OK?'

Startled, Jade turned around. She looked even more startled when she saw who had asked the question – Ricky, with Angela and Theo just behind him.

'Where did you lot suddenly appear from?' Jade asked.

'We've been waiting for you,' said Ricky.

Ricky, Theo and Angela had been standing outside the school gates for at least ten minutes. It was drizzling and from the look of it, the weather was going to get a lot worse. Grey clouds filled the sky. The kind of clouds that were dark, almost charcoal grey, but which seemed to be lit by candle-light from within. Theo hoped it would pour with rain. He liked the rain.

'I didn't see you,' said Jade.

'I'm not surprised. You were in a world of your own,' Ricky smiled.

'What's the matter?' Jade asked with narrowed eyes. 'What d'you want?'

'I . . . er, I wanted to say I was sorry to hear about your dad,' Ricky said.

Jade turned to Theo, then back to Ricky. Theo shifted from foot to foot with unease. 'My dad died over three months ago. What suddenly brought this on?' she asked.

'I just wanted to say that . . . if you ever need any help with anything, then – I'm here. We all are.'

'Are you serious?' Jade raised her eyebrows.

'Totally,' Ricky replied.

'This is just so you can get a client for one of your detective cases, isn't it?'

'It has nothing to do with that,' Ricky denied.

'If I needed any help – which I don't – what makes you think I'd ask you of all people?' said Jade.

Theo was furious for his friend and even Angela, who was better at hiding her true feelings than Theo, gasped at Jade's nerve. But to Theo's surprise Ricky merely smiled.

'Maybe because I'm so unlikely,' said Ricky. 'Then, no matter what you tell me, you know I won't reply in the same way as everyone else.'

Jade frowned but didn't reply.

'Jade, I recognize that look on your face. It reminds me of how I must've looked – and felt – when . . . when I was in trouble a while ago. So I just wanted to say, if you need someone to talk to, I'm here. We all are.' Ricky turned round to Theo and Angela. 'Come on, gang. Let's leave Jade to think it over.'

They all trooped past Jade in silence, leaving her to watch them. Ricky turned round after a few steps.

'Oh, and another thing. I do believe in ghosts,' he said easily.

And with that he carried on walking. Theo couldn't help it. He turned and gave Jade a reproachful look before falling into step with Ricky. She didn't have to be quite so nasty.

'Jade's really rude and sarky. She reminds me a bit of you,' Theo told Angela.

'Thanks a lot!' Angela was definitely *not* impressed.

'No, I mean how you used to be,' Theo amended hastily.

'Thanks a lot!'

'No, I mean . . .'

'Theo, give up while you're behind!' Ricky laughed.

Theo side-stepped a couple of paces away from Angela, giving her a wary look. That hadn't come out right at all. 'Ricky, you still haven't told us about the ghost you saw when you were on holiday,' Theo reminded him, anxiously changing the subject.

'Oh yes. Where was I? I remember. Well, it was late morning and . . .'

'Ricky, wait.'

Theo sighed as Jade came running up to them. It didn't look like he'd ever hear the end of Ricky's story.

'I . . . er . . . I would like to talk to you.' Jade looked down at the front of her left shoe which moved nervously back and forth over the glistening pavement as if she was trying to work a hole in the concrete. 'I don't know how to say this . . .'

'Is it about your dad?' Ricky prompted.

Jade nodded quickly, her expression grateful. Someone else had brought up the subject of her dad first.

'He . . . he talks to me.'

Theo's eyes narrowed. He couldn't help it. If this wasn't a wind-up, then he had no idea what Jade was up to. Was she serious? She couldn't be . . . There were no such things as ghosts. Not that kind of ghost. Not really. Maybe soldiers who died in wars and all those people in the French Revolution who had been guillotined, maybe their ghosts still floated about somewhere, but not everyday people. That was just silly. The more Theo thought about it, the more unlikely he thought the whole thing.

'Theo, I know what that look on your face means.' Jade shook her head. 'I don't blame you. I didn't believe it myself at first.'

'What does your dad say to you?' Angela asked.

'He doesn't actually *say* anything.'

'But you just said he talks to you.'

'Yes, but I meant he . . .' Jade sighed. 'Look, this would be easier if I could show you what I mean. I only live a few minutes away. If you three aren't in a rush to get home, I could show you what I'm talking about. It'll only take five minutes.'

Theo sighed inwardly. He could almost smell his dad's rice and chicken, but he was no closer to getting to it. His stomach rumbled in protest, but Theo ignored it. He looked at Ricky and Angela and shrugged.

'Yeah. OK.' Ricky spoke for all of them.

A relieved smile spread slowly over Jade's face. Theo was startled to realize that he hadn't seen Jade smile in a very, very long time. They walked to Jade's house in silence. A strange, embarrassed hush descended over all of them. It was as if each of them had only just realized exactly *why* they were going to Jade's home. Jade's dad – a *ghost* – actually spoke to her and Jade was going to show them. Theo turned to Jade with a sudden frown, suspicion in his eyes. If Jade was winding them up, then he'd never speak to her again. Never, ever. How would he ever live it down if the word got out that he went to Jade's house to meet her dead father?

Jade turned her head to look at him and Theo quickly looked away.

'I'm not lying, Theo,' Jade said quietly.

'I never said you were,' Theo answered defensively.

'No?'

Theo looked away, feeling guilty and annoyed because of it. Not for the first time, he wished that what he was thinking wasn't always so obviously apparent on his face. It had got him into trouble more than once before. He just couldn't help feeling like they were all inside a joke, just waiting for the punch line. He didn't want the punch line to be at his expense, that was all.

Walking along, Theo began to feel distinctly uncomfortable. He couldn't put his finger on it and yet the hairs on his nape were slowly standing to attention. Frowning deeply, Theo turned around. The road behind them was clear. There were just a couple of cars on the road and yet Theo couldn't shake the wary feeling creeping over him. It was as if . . . as if . . . Theo turned his head again quickly.

'Theo, what's the matter?' asked Ricky.

'Nothing. Nothing,' Theo denied quickly.

He was imagining things, letting his imagination gallop away with him. And no wonder with all this talk about ghosts and ghouls and things that went bump in the night. And yet . . .

*Were they being followed?*

'Theo . . . ?' Ricky prompted.

'It's OK. I'm all right. Nothing's the matter,' Theo replied.

So why couldn't he shake the feeling that they were being watched?

When they reached Jade's house, she dug into her jacket pocket for her front door key. As she turned the key in the lock, she suddenly turned around, nervous.

'You won't say anything to my mum about this, will you? She . . . she doesn't know that Dad talks to me.'

'Don't worry, we won't say a word,' Theo replied immediately.

At Jade's contemplative look, Theo realized that he shouldn't have jumped in quite so quickly. He'd done it again.

'Come on, then,' Jade said. And she opened her front door.

Theo had a last quick look around. He could see nothing and no one out of the ordinary. But then what did he expect? Someone walking along, holding a placard saying, 'Yes, you're right! I *am* following you!' A dark car cruised past them, but apart from that, Jade's street was empty.

The first thing that hit Theo as he stepped into Jade's house, was the smell of air freshener and furniture polish and carpet cleaner and disinfectant. The smells were all mixed up together but distinct nevertheless and they made him want to sneeze. They all stood in the hall as Jade pulled off her jacket and hung it up on one of the coat hooks on the wall.

'Mum, I'm home,' Jade called out.

A woman of about forty appeared immediately.

'It's raining. Don't leave your coat there, Jade. Put it in the bathroom until it dries. Otherwise it'll drip all over the carpet.'

'It's only drizzling, Mum. My jacket barely got wet,' Jade sighed.

'Jade, don't mess up the carpet,' Jade's mum insisted.

With a deeper sigh, Jade removed her coat from the coat hook.

'OK, Mum,' she said quietly. 'I've brought some friends home. Is that all right?'

Mrs Driscoll looked Theo, Ricky and Angela up and down and from side to side. Theo could feel his face begin to burn. He tried to look straight back at Mrs Driscoll but it was hard. He felt like a germ being examined under a microscope.

'That's fine,' Mrs Driscoll said at last. 'As long as they take off their shoes.'

'Mum, please!' Jade protested.

Theo, Ricky and Angela glanced at each other. Was this woman serious? Did she really want them to take off their shoes before they took another step into her house? One look at her face and Theo had his answer. Mrs Driscoll was totally, completely and utterly serious.

'I won't have them tracking mud through the house, Jade,' Mrs Driscoll said firmly.

'We've been walking on the pavement,' Jade said. 'We were nowhere near any mud.'

Mrs Driscoll glared at Jade.

'OK, Mum. OK,' Jade said quickly. She turned to Theo, Angela and Ricky, a pleading look on her face.

'Would you mind? Please.' Her smile was an embarrassed entreaty.

'Shame!' Angela muttered under her breath.

Mrs Driscoll didn't hear it, but Jade did. She chewed on her bottom lip. She was deeply embarrassed and doing her best to hide it from both her mum and her classmates. Theo sure was glad it wasn't his mum who carried on like that. He would never live it down. If his mum did carry on like that, he'd never invite anyone to his house. Never, never, never. Jade must've been desperate to invite them round knowing what her mother was like. Theo had to admit that he was even more intrigued now to find out what was going on.

He bent down to untie his shoe laces. Angela bent down to do the same with her trainers. Ricky kicked off his shoes, which were slip-ons.

'Would you all like something to eat and drink?' asked Mrs Driscoll. 'I could get you some orange juice or some cola and some sandwiches.'

Theo didn't know about the others but he didn't want to take anything from Mrs Driscoll. She'd probably have her plates industrially cleaned afterwards.

'No, thank you,' Theo replied.

Ricky and Angela mumbled the same.

'Mum, can we use the computer?' Jade asked.

'The computer?' Mrs Driscoll's voice was as sharp as a razor. 'No. No, you can't.'

And just like that, it looked like they were going to be scuppered before they'd even started.

## Chapter Nine

# Evidence

'Please, Mum. I'll be very careful – I promise,' Jade replied quickly.

'Jade, you know I don't like you . . .'

'I'll be really, *really* careful,' Jade continued. 'And Ricky, Theo and Angela will be with me all the time so nothing will go wrong.'

Mrs Driscoll took another look at her daughter's companions. 'Jade . . .'

'Please? *Please*?'

'OK, then.' Mrs Driscoll's voice was tiny. 'But ten minutes only.'

'Thanks, Mum.' Jade smiled.

Mrs Driscoll still didn't look happy about it. Her eyes clouded over and her lips turned down. She looked like she was about to change her mind.

'I'll be extra careful, I promise.' Jade smiled.

'I'll rinse off these shoes and put them out in the conservatory.' Mrs Driscoll sniffed. She walked away with their shoes, holding them at arm's length, her head tilted backwards. Jade waited until her mum had left the hall, before turning to the others.

'Mum just . . . Mum . . .' Jade's expression took on a stubborn turn. She pressed her lips together and looked defiantly at all of them.

'All mothers are embarrassing,' Ricky said easily. 'Whenever anyone comes over to our house to visit, my mum breaks out the old photo albums and shows off my photos from the time I was born. I'm surprised she didn't keep one of my old, smelly nappies to show as well.'

Jade laughed.

'You were going to show us something?' Angela prompted.

'This way.' Jade opened the door to the room immediately to their left. It was shrouded in darkness, even though it was still light outside. Theo and his friends stood uncertainly at the door.

'Just a sec.' Jade moved across the room and opened the heavy, dark blue velvet curtains.

It looked better with the curtains drawn, Theo thought. His first, second and third impressions of the room were that it was very cold and uninviting. The walls were a pale blue, the curtains and carpet were navy. Now that Jade had opened the curtains, dust motes swirled in the air like pirouetting dancers. There was a fine layer of dust over most of the furniture. Theo couldn't understand it. With Mrs Driscoll around, Theo would've thought that dust didn't stand a chance. Against the opposite wall, below the window, was a PC. A printer and a scanner sat on a large, wooden table and beneath the table, Theo could see the processor, standing up on its base.

'I'll just switch it on.' Jade pressed the POWER button on the processor. Immediately the monitor on the table crackled into life. Jade switched on the scanner and the printer.

'What has the computer got to do with your dad talking to you?' Angela asked.

Jade slid the PC mouse over its mat, clicking with deft movements as she selected the options she wanted.

'Take a look at this,' she said at last.

Theo, Ricky and Angela gathered around the PC for a closer look.

<Page 1 of 2>
To: JDriscoll@JDriscoll.private.uk
From: PDriscoll@PDriscoll.private.uk

Darling Jade,
How are you? I know these messages frighten

you – and that's the last thing I want. Please don't be scared. I'd never do anything to hurt you – or make you unhappy. I've tried to talk to you before but you couldn't see me. I want you to know that I'm watching over you. I wouldn't let anything or anyone harm you.

This is so bizarre: When I was alive, I was the last one to believe in life after life and here I am clinging on to God knows what and God knows why. No, that's not strictly true. I think I know why I haven't moved up or on or over or whatever the phrase is. It's because I left some unfinished business behind me. Yes, that's a good way to put it – unfinished business. But that's my problem. Or maybe not . . . Jade, maybe you could help

Theo leaned forward to scroll down the page but Jade hit the <ESCAPE> key to clear the screen before the second part of the e-mail could appear.

'This is just one of the e-mails I've received,' Jade said quickly. 'I've had quite a few.'

'Is this really from your dad?' Theo asked what they were all thinking.

Jade nodded. 'At first I didn't believe it either, but it is him. He's said things in some of the other e-mails I've received that only he would know.'

'What sort of things?' Angela asked.

Jade shrugged, careful to avoid catching anyone's eye. 'Different things. For example, two years ago when we were on holiday, Dad and I went out water-skiing. Mum wouldn't give it a try, so it was just me and Dad and the man driving the boat. Well, one of Dad's messages to me told me what the two of us were talking about. There's no way anyone else would have known that. And there've been lots of examples like that.'

'What's this unfinished business your dad talks about?' Ricky asked softly.

Jade licked her lips. For the first time she looked at them directly. 'I . . . nothing. It's not important.'

'Are you sure about that?' Ricky prompted.

'Positive.'

'If you were that positive, I don't think we'd be here,' Ricky pointed out. 'You can't expect us to help you if you only give us half of the story.'

'There isn't much more to tell.' Jade's voice held angry defiance. 'I just needed to tell someone what was going on, that's all. I just needed to know that I'm not imagining things or going crazy.'

'Well, we all saw a message . . .' Theo began.

'But that doesn't mean it's from Jade's dad,' Angela cut in. 'That message could've been sent by anyone.'

'But I just told you that Dad mentioned things . . .'

'But he could've told someone else about your holiday without you knowing it,' said Angela. 'He might've told someone he worked with all about your holiday and they could be the one sending you all these messages.'

'Why would anyone want to do that?' Theo asked.

'How should I know?' Angela said, exasperated. 'All I'm saying is that there are a number of other options to consider before we start believing that Jade's dad is talking to her from beyond the grave and via the Internet!'

'Why is it so hard for you to believe in ghosts?' Ricky frowned. 'Don't you believe in something above and beyond us? Don't you believe in life after life?'

'No, I don't,' Angela said, her voice crackling with bitterness. 'We're alone in this world and when you die, you die. That's it. End of story.'

Theo didn't need to ask. He knew she was thinking about her brother, Tom. Angela's voice always grew cold and hard when she thought about Tom. Theo knew it was just a defence mechanism. Angela's way of trying to stop herself from hurting too much but from her voice, it didn't seem to do much good. Impatient, Ricky turned from Angela to Jade.

'Jade, has your dad asked you to do anything for him?' Ricky asked.

'I . . . not really, no.'

'What does that mean? Not really?'

Licking her lips, Jade's expression finally cleared. She had obviously made a decision about something.

'I want all of you to promise that you'll never talk to anyone about what I'm about to show you.'

'We've already promised,' Theo reminded her.

'I want you to promise again,' Jade insisted.

'We promise.' Ricky answered for all of them. 'You can trust us, Jade. I promise you that too.'

Finally satisfied, Jade turned back to the screen and recalled her last message. Scrolling down, she stepped aside to let Ricky, Angela and Theo read the rest of the message.

<page 2 of 2>

But that's my problem. Or maybe not . . . Jade, maybe you could help me. It would be so wonderful to rest. Simply to rest. I wouldn't even mind if that was all there was to it. I'm so tired. And existing like this . . . it's worse than you can possibly imagine. It's like being stuck in a box with no way out. It's like being stuck in a coffin. This world has become my coffin, Jade. But you could help me to change all that. I did something very wrong and I need your help to put it right. Don't worry, it's not illegal or dangerous. I just need you to deliver something for me. Once this package is delivered I will be at peace. Just saying the word makes me long for it. Let me know when you've found it and I'll give you more instructions. I'm getting weak. Time to go. I know you'll help me. I know I can rely on you.

Dad.

'What package?' Angela asked immediately. Theo raised his eyebrows. Ricky sighed. Theo found himself wishing that for once, Angela wouldn't be quite so direct, quite so blunt. He and Ricky could put up with it because they knew that Angela wasn't as brusque as she sometimes came across but it did tend to put other people's backs up – like now!

'I don't know.' Jade's voice was clipped. 'I wish I did. Dad hasn't said.'

'Your dad wouldn't have asked you to deliver this package unless he thought you knew what he was talking about.' Angela frowned.

Jade bristled like a porcupine. 'Angela . . .'

'Angela, if Jade says she doesn't know then she doesn't,' Theo interrupted quickly.

'I only . . .' Angela trailed off. 'Sorry, Jade. Sometimes I get a bit . . . sorry!'

Jade visibly relaxed. 'Sometimes I get a bit . . . myself!' A trace of a smile flickered across her face.

'Have you spoken to your mum about this?' Ricky asked.

'Not yet. To be honest, I don't think I will.'

'And you haven't spoken to anyone but us about it?' Ricky questioned.

Jade shook her head.

'What exactly did your dad do?' said Ricky.

'He worked for Diadem-21 Software Systems. He's the one who thought up and designed *The Land of Dreams* – amongst others.'

'I thought he worked with Theo's mum in the marketing department,' said Angela.

'I didn't know *The Land of Dreams* was your dad's idea.' Ricky was astounded. 'Theo never told me that.'

'I didn't know,' Theo replied, more than a little impressed himself. 'Jade, I knew your dad was a software engineer but I didn't realize he was responsible for *The Land of Dreams*.'

'What's *The Land of Dreams* when it's at home?' Angela frowned.

Ricky stared at her. 'Where have you been? It's the latest PC game. You have to solve puzzles and defeat the cyborgs and live through your worst nightmares. It's great! It starts when you go to bed and then you find yourself in the middle of a strange, gruesome dream but you can't wake up and then . . .'

'I get the idea, Ricky,' Angela interrupted.

'That was all Dad's idea,' Jade said proudly.

'The only game that comes anywhere near *The Land of Dreams* is *Dyna-Cybo Warriors*!' Theo told Angela.

'Sounds like a classic!' Angela said wryly.

'It is!' Theo enthused.

'Dad's friend, Alex came up with that one – *Dyna-Cybo Warriors*,' said Jade. 'I don't think Dad was too happy about it to be honest. He always refused to mention it and I think he and Alex had a big quarrel about it.'

'Over what?'

Jade shrugged. 'I don't know all the details. All I know is Alex stopped coming over to our house after the game came out.'

'Was your dad jealous?' Angela asked what Theo was wondering.

'Of course not,' Jade denied vehemently.

'Did your dad and this Alex person stop being friends just because Alex came up with a game as good as *The Land of Dreams?*' said Angela.

'My dad's not like that. I don't know if that was the reason – and neither do you,' Jade replied, chips of ice glinting in her eyes.

Angela shrugged. 'I was only saying.'

'Some things you should keep to yourself.' Jade's feathers were definitely ruffled.

'Jade, you should've said about your dad,' Theo said. 'That's amazing. What other games . . . ?'

'Theo!' Ricky interrupted.

'Sorry!'

'Your dad and Alex . . . strange thing to fall out over. A game,' Ricky said thoughtfully. 'Huh! Grown-ups!'

'That's just what Mum said, except she said "Men!" instead of "Grown-ups!"' said Jade.

'So when you two are grown-up men, you'll have no chance!' Angela grinned.

Ricky looked at Theo. 'I think we're being got at!'

'You're not grown-up men yet!' Angela scoffed. 'You've got more brains than most grown-up men!'

'That was a good backhanded compliment.' Jade looked at Angela, impressed.

Much as he was tempted, Theo didn't reply. Angela was obviously remembering her brother and the rest of his so-called friends. They were the ones responsible for Ricky being kidnapped and now they were all in prison.

'Jade, why . . . ?' But Ricky got no further.

'That's enough. Jade, switch off the computer. That's enough.' Mrs Driscoll stood in the doorway, swaying slightly. It was as if she wanted to come further into the room but just couldn't bring herself to do it.

'Mum, can't we just . . . ?'

'No. Switch it off – NOW,' Mrs Driscoll ordered.

Jade and her mum stood watching each other. Long moments passed. Finally Jade did as directed and switched off the PC.

'I think you others should go home now. I'm sure your parents must be wondering where you've got to,' Mrs Driscoll said.

Why doesn't she just lift us up and hurl us out the door? She's not even subtle, Theo thought sourly.

They all stood up and left the room, skirting around Mrs Driscoll who stood at the door like a sentinel. Theo remembered reading a Greek myth once about a scary three-headed, dragon-tailed dog called Cerberus who guarded the gates to Hades, but that dog had nothing on Jade's mum!

'See you tomorrow, Jade.' Ricky smiled.

'Bye.'

'Yeah! Bye!'

Mrs Driscoll followed them out into the hall. Ricky had opened the front door before he remembered.

'Mrs Driscoll, can we have our shoes back please?'

Startled, Mrs Driscoll glanced down at their feet.

'Just a moment.' Mrs Driscoll disappeared towards the back of the house. Moments later she returned carrying a tray lined with newspaper. And on the newspaper sat Theo's, Angela's and Ricky's now cleaned shoes.

'Thank you,' Theo mumbled as he retrieved his shoes. He didn't wait to lace them up either. Mrs Driscoll made him feel too uncomfortable. The moment his shoes were on his feet, he was out of there. And Angela and Ricky weren't far behind him either. Jade stood at the front door, her eyes dancing with what she couldn't say now that her mum was right behind her.

'I'll see you at school tomorrow,' Jade said at last.

'Take care, Jade.' Ricky smiled. 'And thanks for showing us your computer.'

'No problem,' Jade replied.

But Theo watched her face as she shut the door. 'No problem' was an out and out lie. Jade had problems up to her eyebrows – only one of which was her dead father.

## Chapter Ten

# Uncle Pascoe

'So what d'you make of that then?' Angela asked as they walked along.

Theo shrugged. 'I'm not sure what to think.'

'Jade doesn't behave like someone whose dad has just died,' Angela said, more to herself than to anyone else.

'How's she meant to behave?' Ricky rounded on her. 'Where's it written that you have to behave in a particular way? And besides which her dad died three months ago.'

'Three months isn't very long. Three months is nothing . . .' Theo began.

'Ricky, I was just saying,' Angela said defensively. 'There's no need to jump down my throat. It's just that when she talks about her dad, there's no *grief* there.'

'I think she's feels that when she *thinks* about him,' Theo said slowly. 'When she talks about him though it's like . . . it's like . . .'

'It's like he hasn't really gone,' Ricky finished. 'And he hasn't, not if he's sending her messages.'

'D'you really believe those messages were from Jade's dad?' Angela asked, incredulously.

'I don't know. Maybe.'

'You can't be serious.'

'What makes you so sure they *aren't*?' Ricky asked.

'Well, it's a horrible idea for a start.' Angela wrinkled up her nose. 'I mean, the thought of anyone getting messages from their dead dad. But over the *Internet*? Why didn't he just visit her in her house and haunt her like normal ghosts do?'

'Using the Internet was the only way he could communicate with her. He said so,' Theo reminded the others.

'I don't understand you two.' Angela stopped walking and eyed Theo and Ricky speculatively. 'Ricky, it's like you're falling over backwards to believe every word that Jade says to you. And you Theo, you're ready to believe Jade on the evidence of a couple of mail messages which could've been sent by anyone.'

'I never said I believed Jade,' Ricky replied evenly. 'But I'm prepared to believe her.'

'What does that mean?'

'It means that whether or not the messages are from Jades's dad – *she* believes they are and that's what's important,' said Ricky.

They all carried on walking as Angela and Theo thought about what Ricky had said.

'I've had an idea.' Angela grinned suddenly. 'Why don't we use Bullet's new program to see whether or not the messages are genuine?'

'What program?' asked Ricky.

'Angela, what on earth are you on about? Bullet's program is designed to solve crimes, not check out the source of information on the Internet,' Theo pointed out.

'What program?'

'But if someone is trying to trick Jade or pull a fast one then maybe Bullet's program will help us find out what's really happening . . .'

'WHAT PROGRAM?'

'All right, Ricky! All right! Don't get your boxers in a bunch!' said Theo. 'Bullet's written a program to solve crimes – so he reckons.'

'If he says his program solves crimes, then it does,' said Angela, stung.

Theo gave her a knowing, smug look. 'You have got it bad, haven't you?'

Angela's face turned an immediate and deep shade of scarlet.

Amazed, Ricky stared at Theo. 'You're joking. Not Bullet! Come on!'

'I know. I thought she had more taste, but it seems her taste is all in her mouth!' Theo laughed.

Ricky joined in, with his deep, throaty laugh that could probably be heard three streets away.

'Both of you – get stuffed!' Angela flounced off in high dudgeon.

'Oh come on, Angela,' said Theo, still laughing. 'We're only teasing.'

'I don't fancy him. It's a lie.'

'Yeah right!' Ricky grinned. 'Careful you don't trip over your nose, Pinocchio!'

'If you two don't stop, I'll never speak to you again.' Angela fumed.

'Not another word.' Theo tried to suppress his laugh.

Ricky mimed zipping up his lip. Theo joined in and mimed turning a key against his mouth.

'Don't overdo it!' Angela sniffed.

Which set Ricky and Theo off again. And only seconds passed before Angela creased up laughing too.

'Excuse me? Do you three go to St Christopher's School?'

Startled, Theo turned to look at the man who'd spoken to them. He was a man in his mid to late twenties, with wavy, dark brown hair and sparkling, merry brown eyes. He smiled at them and unlike most grown-up smiles, this one seemed genuine. Even so, Theo eyed him warily.

'Do you three go to St Christopher's School?' the man asked again.

Theo nodded.

'Do you know a girl called Jade Driscoll?'

No one spoke.

'I'm trying to get in touch with a girl called Jade Driscoll?'

'I'm not being funny, mister, but we've been told not to talk to strangers,' Ricky said suspiciously.

'I quite understand,' the man nodded.

'These days you can't be too careful. My name is Pascoe DeMille. Jade's my god-daughter. I know her father, Paul, but I've been abroad for the last five and a half years and we've kind of lost touch. In his last letter, Paul said they were hoping to move to a new house and that he was hoping to send Jade to St Christopher's after her primary school. I was hoping to find someone who knew Jade so that I could find out where Paul and his wife, Laura and Jade live now.'

Theo, Ricky and Jade looked at each other – each one waiting for someone else to speak.

'I'm sorry Mr DeMille, but Jade's dad died three months ago,' Theo said at last.

Pascoe stared at Theo, profoundly shocked. 'No . . . Don't say that. He didn't.'

'I'm sorry,' Theo replied, uncomfortably. He turned to Angela and Ricky for help. They weren't going to leave all this to him, were they? But the look on their faces said otherwise. Their eyes danced away from his as they looked at the sky, the houses – anywhere but at Theo and Pascoe DeMille.

'Jade and her mother, Laura – are they all right? Do they need anything? Someone should've let me know . . .' Pascoe was distraught. He turned away from Theo, as if to hide his face.

'Someone should've let me know,' Theo heard him whisper.

Theo felt sorry for the man. He looked devastated. Theo wondered how he'd feel if he suddenly heard that Ricky had died. How long would it take him to get over it – if he ever did?

'Stop it!' Theo muttered sternly to himself. He didn't like the direction his thoughts were travelling in. Ricky wasn't going to die.

Pascoe turned to face them, his expression so sad that Theo caught his breath.

'Do you know where Jade lives? I'd like to see her and her mother.'

'I . . . I'm sorry but I don't think we should give out Jade's address just like that. I'm not being funny but we don't know you . . .' Ricky said uncomfortably.

'I understand. And you're right of course,' said Pascoe. 'In that case could you tell Jade that her Uncle Pascoe is in town and was asking for her. Her mum and dad have had some letters from me over the years so she'll know who I am. If you could ask her to phone me at the Bishop's Arms Bed and Breakfast Hotel. That's where I'm staying.'

Ricky nodded. 'We'll tell her at school first thing tomorrow morning.'

'Thank you. I'd appreciate it,' Pascoe replied. 'I'd be very grateful if you could ask Jade to contact me and not tell her mum I'm here until I've had a chance to speak to her.'

No one replied.

'I know it's rather a strange request but . . . well, Laura and I didn't exactly part on very good terms. I'd love to see her again of course, but I think I'd better speak to Jade first and make sure of my welcome.'

'Oh, I see. OK.' Theo nodded.

'Thank you for your help,' Pascoe said sadly. And he walked slowly away from them.

'You were right not to give out Jade's address,' said Angela, once Pascoe was out of earshot. 'You don't know him from Adam. He could be anybody.'

'Not from the look on his face when I told him about Jade's dad. He was genuinely upset,' said Theo.

'He could've put that on . . .' Angela began.

'Pardon?' Theo couldn't believe his ears.

'He could've been acting.'

'For goodness' sake, he's Jade's godfather,' Theo reminded Angela.

'So he says – but you only have his word for that.'

'True,' Ricky agreed.

Theo shook his head. 'Don't you two trust anyone?'

'I trust you,' Ricky said without hesitation.

'So do I,' Angela agreed. 'But not many other people. And certainly not that man. I mean, Pascoe DeMille? That doesn't sound like a real name for a start. He might be the guy who's sending Jade all those email messages.'

'Why?' asked Theo.

'I don't know,' Angela said impatiently. 'All I'm saying is you're too quick to believe every word anyone says to you.'

'And you're too fast to mistrust and disbelieve everything you're told,' Theo countered.

'So between the two of you, you get it about right,' Ricky soothed, as if he could smell there was a full scale argument coming.

'So what do we do now?' Theo asked, calming down.

'I think first thing tomorrow morning we should grab Bullet and get him to help us,' Angela suggested.

'You can grab him if you want to. Me? I'll keep my hands to myself,' Theo sniffed.

Ricky laughed, adding, 'We must get Jade to trust us. I reckon we still don't have the full story.'

'We can't force Jade to confide in us if she doesn't want to,' said Angela.

'We won't have to force her. I'll charm her,' Ricky grinned.

Angela and Theo looked at each other.

'Poor thing,' Angela muttered under her breath.

Theo looked from Angela to Ricky and back. 'I don't know who I feel most sorry for,' he said. 'Bullet or Jade.'

Chapter Eleven

# Tricks and Lies

'Where've you been?'

Theo skidded to a halt next to Ricky, who stood outside the school gates. He'd run practically all the way from his house and his blood was now roaring in his ears, his knees were aching and he was beginning to get a stitch. He pulled his rucksack back up on to his shoulder where it had been slipping down his arm.

'Sorry, Ricky. I overslept.' Theo bent at the waist and panted to try and get his breath back.

'And where's Angela?' Ricky frowned.

'How should I know?' Theo replied testily.

'She was meant to be here at least thirty minutes before the school buzzer,' said Ricky.

'Take it up with her, not me.' Theo straightened up.

'Am I going to have to do all this by myself?'

'I'm here, aren't I? Stop nagging. You sound like my mother.'

Ricky and Theo glared at each other. The expressions on their faces eased and they each gave a rueful smile.

'Good morning, Theo. How are you this morning?'

'I'm fine, Ricky. What about you?'

'I'm fine. Lovely weather we're having!'

'They did say we might get some rain later!'

Ricky grinned. 'I don't suppose you've seen Angela?' he asked in his politest voice.

'I'm afraid not,' Theo answered.

'What a shame!'

'Can't be helped,' Theo laughed. 'So what's the plan?'

'Let's go and see Bullet and later when Jade arrives we'll tell her that her godfather is looking for her,' said Ricky.

'Is Bullet here already?' Theo raised his eyebrows.

'Are you kidding? Bullet's the first to arrive and the last to leave. You know how he loves computers.'

'I thought he had one at home,' said Theo.

'He does, but his mum and dad have limited him to only one hour on the computer a day.'

'How d'you know?'

Ricky tapped the side of his nose. 'I have ways of finding out these things.'

Theo considered. 'You asked him when he arrived this morning – right?'

'Right!' Ricky admitted. 'A nice bit of deduction on your part!'

'Take notes! I'll make a detective of you yet!' Theo said.

'Come on. Let's go and see exactly what Bullet's new program does.'

Theo and Ricky walked into the school.

Once they were in the computer room, Ricky plonked himself down on the chair next to Bullet, before pulling it right up to Bullet's computer screen.

Theo looked around the room. Apart from Bullet and now themselves, it was empty. But even though it was empty there was still the whirr of the fans in each processor case to break the silence. Theo sat down on the other side of Bullet, enjoying the emptiness and peace in the room but he knew it wouldn't last long. It wouldn't be long now before the room started to fill up.

'Hi Bullet! How's it going?' Ricky grinned.

'Er . . . I . . . I'm fine. How're you?' Bullet smiled. He looked nervous but not particularly puzzled.

He's not surprised to see us, Theo realized.

'Angela warned you we were going to – what was the word she used? – grab you?' said Ricky.

'She did say something about it,' Bullet admitted.

'When did you see her?' Theo asked.

'Last night. She came round to ask if I could help her with her computer homework.'

Ricky and Theo leaned back in their chairs and made faces behind Bullet's back. So much for the element of surprise. Angela really did have it bad!

'So, is it true? Have you really written a program to solve crimes?' asked Ricky.

Bullet nodded, looking suitably modest yet proud of himself.

'Does it work?' Theo asked bluntly.

Bullet's smile of pleasure faded slightly. 'Well, I've only tested it out on one real, proper crime so far.'

'What crime was that?' asked Theo.

'The one where Ricky was kidnapped,' Bullet explained.

All at once, Ricky and Theo became very still.

'And of course that was a slightly different case, because one of you had all the facts and knew what was going on, but . . .'

'Did Angela tell you about that?' Ricky asked quietly.

Bullet nodded.

'I see,' Ricky replied quietly.

'So as I was saying, one of you had all the facts – but of course you two didn't . . . know t-that at . . . the . . . time . . .' Bullet's voice trailed off altogether.

Bullet looked at Ricky, then Theo and back again. He might've been a bit slow when it came to people, but even he could detect the tense undercurrent now flowing through the room.

'I'm sorry. I know I'm not meant to mention it but I thought it would be OK with you two . . . as you know all about it . . . I'm sorry . . .'

'You used what happened to me to test your program?' Ricky asked.

Theo wasn't fooled by Ricky's soft, even tone for a second.

Ricky was a hair's breadth away from going nuclear. And Theo couldn't blame him. He glared at Bullet, willing him to shut up. Couldn't he see what he was doing? Every time he opened his mouth it was only to change feet. Theo hadn't seen Ricky so *furious* in a long, long time.

'Oh yes! I inputted all the data about your kidnapping,' Bullet began eagerly. 'And my program didn't do too badly. As I said, it's not quite the kind of case that I'd designed my program to solve but . . .'

'I'm sorry my getting kidnapped wasn't quite the kind of case you had in mind.' Ricky's voice dripped ice.

'I . . . I . . . didn't mean it like that. I mean . . . I know it must've been horrible for you,' Bullet said, flustered.

'Horrible. Yes, it was . . . horrible,' Ricky repeated, his body tensed up like an overtightened spring.

'I . . . I . . .' Bullet looked horror-stricken as he spluttered his way through another apology. It didn't help that Ricky's expression was now thunderous.

Ricky stood up, the better to glower down at Bullet. Bullet was in real trouble. Ricky was just about to lose it.

'Ricky . . .' Theo warned off his friend. 'Come on, Ricky. Calm down.'

Ricky took a deep breath and his body relaxed visibly. He took another deep breath and slowly sat back down in his chair.

'Sorry Bullet, but what happened to me was more than just some test data for your program,' he said at last.

'I understand that.' Bullet nodded at once. 'And I hope you don't mind that Angela told me about it.'

'If I did mind, it's a bit tough and two-thirds now, isn't it?' Ricky pointed out.

'I promise, it'll go no further,' Bullet said.

'So you were saying about your program?' Theo reminded him, feeling it was time to change the subject.

'Oh yes!' Bullet exhaled gratefully. 'When I tested it on the information Angela gave me, the program said that I should get more information from the person who set up the dare game that led to Ricky being kidnapped in the first place – so it was spot on there. It knew that Angela had more information than she was initially letting on.'

'And what does your program tell you about Jade?' Ricky asked.

'Well, I don't have enough information yet.' Bullet shook his head.

'What information do you need?' said Ricky.

'What've you got?' Bullet replied.

'How much has Angela told you?' asked Theo.

'Just that someone claiming to be Jade's dad sends her email messages and he wants her to deliver a package,' said Bullet.

'Do *you* believe in ghosts?' asked Ricky.

'Oh please,' Theo said hastily. 'Let's not start all that again.'

The last thing he wanted to do was get into another discussion about ghosts. After sleeping on it, he was beginning to wonder if maybe Angela's point of view on this was closer to the truth than Ricky's.

'We haven't got much more information than what you've been told already,' Ricky said.

'I'm brilliant but even I'm not a miracle worker!' sniffed Bullet. 'I'll need more data than that. Besides, I don't see that a crime has been committed and my program is meant to solve crimes, not mysteries.'

'What crimes *does* your program solve?' asked Theo.

Bullet leaned forward towards the keyboard. Theo realized that he'd been just waiting to be asked!

BULLET'S CRIMEBUSTER PROGRAM

Select crime to be solved:

1. Murder
2. Kidnapping

3. Theft (Stealing)
4. Fraud and Cons
5. Bullying – verbal
6. Bullying – physical
7. School-related Crimes

Enter number:__________

'That looks dead impressive and seven-eighths,' Theo couldn't help but admit. 'Does it work? Does it really do all that?'

'Of course it does,' Bullet said with indignation. 'Or at least, I've written all the programs. Now I've just got to get some real cases with proper data to test the programs and make sure they work.'

Theo studied the screen again. 'Couldn't we input the data we already have?'

'Under what heading?' Ricky frowned.

'I was just about to ask that,' said Bullet.

'How about fraud and cons – number 4?' suggested Theo. 'That's all about lying, isn't it?'

'Who's lying?'

'And about what?'

'Jade's dad. Or at least the person who's sending Jade all those email messages and claiming to be Jade's dad,' Theo said.

'You don't know that.' Ricky's frown deepened.

'You don't honestly think that Jade's dad is really sending her messages?'

'I thought Angela was the one with the closed mind, not you,' Ricky countered.

'I don't call it having a closed mind. I call it having a brain,' said Theo.

'Hang on a minute . . .'

'Why don't I try number four and see what the program comes up with?' Bullet interrupted. 'It can't hurt.'

Theo sat back in his chair. Ricky leaned forward. Theo

frowned. He couldn't understand it. Usually he and Ricky never argued – about anything. And yet they had blown up at each other twice in as many days. What was going on? They'd had disagreements before, but never like this. Never so . . . personal. It was as if the very subject of ghosts was stirring up all kinds of nasty things. Not just ghosts and ghouls, but it was forcing Theo to think about death and dying and things he didn't want to think about. Dying was for old people, but his mum and dad were old. And deep down, Theo knew it wasn't just old people who died. Young people died too. Death wasn't choosy. Suddenly, Theo didn't want to do this any more. They were getting into very murky waters here. He didn't want to be forced to think about Jade and her dad. That road led to too many other places that he had no desire or intention of exploring.

BULLET'S CRIMEBUSTER PROGRAM

FRAUD:

Select type of fraud:

1. Fraud involving money
2. Fraud involving jewellery or other possessions
3. Computer fraud
4. Cons and tricks
5. Other

Enter number:__________

'That menu is about as much use as a chocolate teapot,' Theo said impatiently.

'Why d'you say that?' Bullet asked.

'Your menu selections are all too vague. I mean, in Jade's case numbers two, three or four or all of them could apply,' Theo replied.

'You have to pick the one that's most likely to apply,' Bullet said. He was obviously miffed that Theo had found fault with his program.

'OK. How about number four?' Theo suggested.

'Cons and tricks? You really think so?' Ricky asked.

Theo nodded.

'Cons and tricks it is then.' Bullet inputted the number four.

Immediately a series of random numbers and letters scrolled down the screen. Theo sat back, immensely disappointed.

'I thought I'd fixed that bug,' Bullet muttered to himself.

'So much for computer power,' Theo said with disgust. 'We'll just have to use our brains and do it ourselves.'

'I'll have it fixed by this afternoon,' Bullet protested.

'We're not going to hang about waiting for you to fix your program,' said Theo.

'Let me know anything new you come up with and I'll input that data into my program. I'm sure it'll help you,' said Bullet.

Ricky stood up. 'Come on, Theo.' He smiled sympathetically at Bullet. 'Thanks anyway.'

'I will get it working. I will. You wait and see,' Bullet insisted.

Ricky and Theo left the room. Mrs Daltry ambled down the corridor deep in conversation with Mr Dove. Mrs Daltry had a liquorice allsort in her hand, on its way to her mouth. She stopped abruptly when she spotted Ricky and Theo and made a great show of rubbing her eyes.

'A paranormal event in itself. You two are here *early*! Whatever next?'

Ricky grinned. 'We're here to help Bullet with one of his programs.'

'Does he need help?' Mrs Daltry asked, surprised.

'Yep! And in more ways than one,' Theo said, sourly.

'I heard that!' Bullet called out from the computer room.

Theo couldn't help but smile in Bullet's direction. Bullet wasn't too bad. Maybe he was a bit of a computer nut but he was willing to help them. All things considered, Bullet was OK!

'If the two of you are looking for something to do, you can help me and Mr Dove set out the equipment for the first lesson,' Mrs Daltry suggested.

'That would be great,' said Mr Dove. 'It would give me a chance to get to know you better. Mrs Daltry has told me a lot about you.'

'Actually, we were just on our way to the library, weren't we, Theo?' Ricky said with haste.

'Er . . . yes, that's right. We have some research to do.'

'Hhmm!' Mrs Daltry didn't sound too convinced but she let it pass. 'All right then, but just make sure you do go to the library and don't dawdle in the corridors.'

Theo and Ricky scampered off, eager to get away from the teachers before Mrs Daltry insisted on their help.

'So where are we going?' Theo asked, once they were out of Mrs Daltry's earshot.

'To the library, like I said.'

'Why?' Theo asked, surprised.

'I've had an idea. I think I know how we can make sure that it's really Jade's dad trying to communicate with her.'

'Oh yes? I'm all ears.'

'The first thing we need to do is track down the host machine that he's using to send Jade those messages,' said Ricky.

'That information usually comes with the text of the message itself, but I can't remember seeing that in any of the emails that Jade showed us.'

'Yes, I know. We'll have to ask Jade if we can see the messages again.' Ricky pushed open the library door and headed straight for the non-fiction/computing section. This section was over by one of the large library windows and the cold October morning sunlight streamed in, illuminating the books.

'I thought we could . . .' Ricky stopped abruptly when he saw who had beaten them to it. It was Jade.

Ricky made a bee-line over towards Jade, a grin splitting his face from ear to ear. Jade stood watching his approach, her face a mask. Theo felt a strange uh-oh warning chill creep down his spine. Something in Jade's deliberate lack of expression warned him to watch out.

'Hi Jade,' Ricky enthused. 'I think we've come up with a way to help you find out for certain whether or not your dad is really sending those messages . . .'

'He isn't,' Jade said. Her voice was soft, but the tone was firm enough to stop Ricky in his tracks.

'Pardon?'

'I said dad didn't send me those messages. I made them up.'

A long silence followed.

Ricky frowned. 'I don't understand.'

'OK, then. Here it is in words of one syllable. It was just a wind-up. I sent those messages to myself.' Jade turned to Theo. 'You were right after all, Theo. I was just pulling your leg.'

'Why?' Theo asked, his eyes narrowed.

'Why not? I didn't have anything better to do and you two and Angela were obviously looking for something to get you going. So I gave you something. It was your ad about your detective agency that gave me the idea.'

'I don't believe you.' Ricky's voice was ice-cold.

Jade shrugged. 'Suit yourself. But my dad's d-dead. How can he send me Internet messages?'

'But we saw the messages . . .' Ricky began.

'I typed those in myself. I thought it would be a good joke, but I want to stop it now before it goes any further.'

'Why?' asked Theo.

Jade looked confused. 'Why what?'

Theo regarded her steadily. 'Why stop it now? You could've had a lot more fun watching us chase around trying to find out what was going on. So why stop now?'

'I . . . I . . .' Jade got no further. As unexpected as it was shocking, Jade's face crumpled up and she burst into tears.

'Just leave me alone,' she sobbed. And she tried to run past them out of the library.

'Jade, what's going on?' Theo stepped in front of Jade to block her escape. 'You didn't make it all up. I don't believe that for a second.'

'Why?' Jade asked bitterly. 'You were convinced I was lying before. Why the sudden rush to believe me now?'

Theo couldn't answer. He didn't know how to answer.

'You didn't make up those messages, did you?' Ricky asked. There was more than just a question in his voice. A hope against disappointment was mingled in there as well.

'Yes, I did,' Jade said quickly. 'You won't get me to say anything else.'

'Jade, you can trust us. I promise you,' Ricky said earnestly. 'We won't let you down.'

Jade looked around fearfully. Theo did the same, wondering what Jade was looking for. They were quite alone in the library, so why was she so afraid?

'Don't you understand?' Jade's voice was no more than a desperate whisper. 'Dad told me not to talk to you or anyone. He told me that if I do, he won't be able to talk to me ever again. He'll just wander around this earth, unable to rest. Well, I'm not going to do that to him. And I can't lose him again. I won't. *I won't.*'

Jade ran around a now stunned Theo and in seconds she was out of the room. Theo and Ricky regarded each other. Theo didn't like the way things were going – not one little bit. He didn't like the way an icy chill was slowly invading his body, atom by atom.

'If it really is Jade's dad sending her messages,' Ricky began, 'why did he tell her not to talk to anyone about him? I mean, why would he *care*?'

'That's just what I was thinking. Surely he wouldn't mind

that Jade had told us. It can't make any difference to him,' said Theo. 'D'you know what else I think?'

'What?'

'I think there's something very kippery going on here. I think Jade's in danger.'

## Chapter Twelve

# Watching

'So what now, Robin?' Ricky frowned.

'Excuse me but I'm Batman. You're Robin,' Theo argued.

'Yeah, OK. But what now?'

'We're going to have to catch up with Jade and convince her to trust us,' Theo decided. 'If we can't do that, then there's not a lot more we can do for her.'

'We haven't done anything,' Ricky said with sudden anger. 'She needs our help and we haven't done a thing. And I'll tell you something else, if anything happens to her, I'll never forgive myself. Never.'

'Ricky, aren't you taking all this a bit too personally?' asked Theo. At Ricky's scowl, he added hastily. 'I mean, our detective agency was only meant . . .'

'Our detective agency? This has nothing to do with our detective agency,' Ricky said, incensed. 'Jade's in trouble. *Real* trouble – whichever way you look at it.'

'You're remembering when you were in trouble, aren't you?' said Theo.

Silence. Then Ricky nodded.

Theo sighed inwardly. He wasn't sure when this had stopped being just a joke, a bit of fun. Maybe it never was. But one thing was for sure. It was deadly serious now. Ricky would make sure it was treated no other way.

'Let's go and find Jade,' said Ricky.

'What about the information you wanted to look up?'

'That can wait. Finding Jade is more important.' Ricky was out of the library before the sentence was over.

Theo ran after him. Ricky was so determined to help

Jade, even when she told them she didn't want their help. Theo sensed that part of it was because of Ricky's own experiences when he'd been kidnapped but there was more to it than that. Theo ran down the corridor, only a couple of steps behind his friend.

'Where're we going?' Theo puffed.

'Right here. All the girls come in here when they want to be alone or have a cry – I bet.'

It was the girls' toilets. Theo eyed them with distaste. He didn't want to stop here. The boys always passed this part of the corridor in a hurry. And what if someone should see them parked outside the girls' loos? They'd have a mountain of explaining to do. And an even larger mountain of teasing to put up with. Theo shifted uncomfortably from foot to foot.

'You don't know she's in there.'

'No, but it's a good place to start.' Ricky knocked on the door. 'Jade? Jade, are you in there? It's Ricky.'

He put his ear to the door. Silence.

'Jade, I know you're in there.' Ricky turned to Theo and shrugged. He didn't know if Jade was in there or not but he wasn't going to give up now. 'I'm not going away until you come out.'

Still nothing.

'If you don't come out, then I'm coming in,' Ricky warned through the door.

The silence around them deepened. Ricky gathered himself up to his full height. He turned to Theo again. 'Come on, Theo.'

Theo's eyes widened. He shook his head slowly. 'No way! No way am I going in there!'

'Oh come on. There's nothing to be afraid of,' Ricky cajoled.

'Ricky, you're my best mate and I'd do anything for you, but I'm not going in there,' Theo said, adamant. 'The only way you'll get me over that threshold is to knock me out first and drag me in.'

'All right then. I'll go in by myself. You keep watch.' And

without another moment's hesitation Ricky walked into the girls' toilets.

Theo couldn't believe it. His admiration for Ricky shot through the roof. There was no place his friend wouldn't go. No place his friend was afraid of. But mostly Theo felt that Ricky had lost his mind! The girls' toilets! Nervously, Theo looked up and down the corridor, praying that he wouldn't see anyone he knew. And if there was anyone else besides Jade in the girls' loos then it would be all around the school in two seconds flat that Ricky went in there.

Suddenly there came an indignant shriek and Ricky came flying out of the toilets, followed by Jade.

'Ricky Burridge, just what d'you think you're doing?' Jade stormed.

'I did say I'd come in if you didn't come out.'

'Yes, but I didn't think you meant it,' Jade ranted. 'Are you nuts?'

'Probably.' Ricky grinned. 'But we couldn't let you leave just like that. We want to help you.'

'Whether I want you to or not – right?' Jade wiped her damp cheeks with the back of her hand.

Ricky grinned. 'Something like that.'

Jade studied Ricky as if she'd never seen him before. And Ricky didn't flinch, didn't back away. He stood his ground and looked straight back at Jade.

'You're persistent, aren't you?' Jade smiled reluctantly.

'I think the word you're looking for is stubborn,' Theo chipped in.

Ricky grinned. Jade's smile faded to nothing.

'Look, please don't think I don't appreciate what you're trying to do for me. I do. It's just that, I lost Dad once and now he's come back. I couldn't bear to lose him again. Talking to him now, even though it's only by computer, well, it's . . . it's like he never died.'

Theo licked his lips nervously. All kinds of responses flashed through his head but he bit back every one of them.

'Why did your dad tell you not to talk to us?' Ricky asked.

Jade shook her head. 'I'm not supposed to tell you. I've said too much already. If Dad's watching me now, he might decide to stop sending me messages for not doing as he asked.'

'But in that earlier message you showed us, your dad said he could only communicate via email messages on the PC,' Ricky pointed out.

'He meant that's the only way he could talk to me. That doesn't mean that he's not standing right next to you now,' said Jade.

Both Ricky's and Theo's heads whipped round. The corridor was empty. Or was it . . . ? Theo felt an icy knot tighten in the pit of his stomach. The whole idea gave him goose-bumps. What if Jade's dad was right here, watching them? Theo nervously looked around. Now that the thought had entered his head he couldn't get it out again.

'Mr Driscoll, if you are here, I want you to know that Theo and I only want to help,' Ricky said loudly, his voice totally serious. 'We wouldn't do anything to upset Jade. Honest we wouldn't.'

The silence of the corridor echoed back at them. Even Jade looked nervous.

'Didn't your dad like you talking to your friends when he was alive?' Theo asked.

'Are you kidding? Dad loved to meet my friends. He always encouraged me to bring my friends home. He always said the more the merrier.'

'So why would he change his mind now?' Ricky said gently. 'I don't think people change so much when they're dead.'

'He might've done. Maybe dying does things to you.'

Theo had to fight down the strongest urge to laugh – more with unease than with humour – or to waggle his fingers in his ears or crawl away and hide under a table somewhere. He'd never taken part in such a bizarre conversation.

Ricky and Jade were seriously discussing whether or not dying would change a person, apart from in the most obvious way. They were really wondering if it could change your character.

'So what exactly did your dad say in his last message?' Ricky prompted.

Jade looked uncertain, then her expression cleared. 'I'll show you.'

They all walked together to the computer room. Without a word, Jade sat in front of one of the computers, whilst Theo and Ricky pulled up a chair on either side of her.

'What're you all doing?' Bullet asked from the other side of the room.

'Nothing,' Ricky said tersely.

'Can I watch?' Bullet asked.

'No.' All three of them spoke in unison.

'OK!' Bullet replied cheerfully and he carried on with what he was doing.

With deft fingers, Jade signed on to her Internet account and went through the directory of her email messages.

'Have you told anyone else about your dad trying to contact you?' Ricky whispered.

Jade shook her head.

'What about your uncle?' Theo remembered.

'What uncle?'

'Your Uncle Pascoe. We saw him yesterday. He told us to tell you he's staying at the . . . the Bishop's Arms bed and breakfast hotel.'

'My Uncle Pascoe? What're you talking about? I don't have an Uncle Pascoe,' Jade said, confused.

'He said he's your godfather but he's been away. He . . . he didn't know about your dad. When we told him he was really upset. He wanted your address . . .'

'You didn't tell him . . .'

'Of course not,' Theo denied.

'I'll have to ask my mum about him, but I certainly don't

remember him.' Jade frowned. 'Uncle Pascoe . . . ? That doesn't ring a bell at all.'

She turned slowly back to the screen and selected the last message listed.

To: JDriscoll@JDriscoll.private.uk
From: PDriscoll@PDriscoll.private.uk

Darling Jade,

I saw you and three of your friends go into our house yesterday. I hope you didn't tell them about me. I hope you didn't show them the messages I've been sending you. No one must know about me but you. I won't be able to talk to you any more if you tell others about me. Don't even tell your mum. She wouldn't understand. No one understands except you. Have you found my package yet? I need it desperately. Don't stop searching until you find it. Time is running out. And remember, not a word to anyone – or you'll never hear from me again. Remember, I'm watching.

Dad.

Ricky and Theo studied the message carefully.

'Now d'you see why you mustn't become involved. You'll scare Dad away if you do. I've got to sort this out for myself,' Jade whispered.

*I saw you and three of your friends go into our house yesterday . . .*

Theo's blood turned to ice-water. Yesterday, as they entered Jade's house, Theo had had the uneasy feeling that someone, somewhere was watching them. And now his worst suspicions were being confirmed. They *were* being watched.

Theo swallowed hard and clenched his fists, and forced himself to calm down.

'Hang on! Your dad mentioned a package in one of the other emails we saw.' Ricky frowned. 'Didn't he say something about delivering it once you'd found it?'

'That's right,' Jade replied reluctantly.

'What package was he talking about?' Theo asked.

'I don't know. I still haven't found it yet.'

'Do you know where or who you're meant to deliver the package to?' said Theo.

Jade didn't answer.

'Did your dad go into more details about the package in one of his other emails? Maybe in one of the messages that you didn't show us?'

Jade looked away from Theo, chewing on her bottom lip.

'Jade . . .'

'No, Theo,' Ricky interrupted. 'Jade has to make up her mind once and for all about us. We can't push her.'

Anxiously, Theo watched Jade. Ricky was right. They couldn't stop now. It wouldn't be right. Theo wanted to find out what was going on just as much as Ricky did. But it was up to Jade now.

What would she decide?

## Chapter Thirteen

# A Dirty, Rotten Trick

'OK. But you must do what I say with no arguments,' Jade said at last.

'No problem.'

'Agreed.'

'And you can't change your mind or withhold information or anything like that,' Ricky added. 'We're going to see this through till the end.'

The end. What would that be, Theo wondered. And how would they recognize it? Was it simply a case of finding this mysterious package and delivering it? Would Jade's dad really go away and rest in peace once the package had reached its final destination? Somehow, Theo didn't think it would be that simple.

'I guess the first thing I should tell you is . . . I think I found the package this morning,' said Jade.

'What was it?' Theo asked eagerly.

Just at that moment, Angela came through the door. 'Sorry, I'm late. What's going on?' Angela headed straight for them.

'Can we tell her?' Ricky asked carefully.

Jade considered, then nodded. Ricky beckoned Angela closer. For once, Bullet's computer screen did not have one hundred per cent of his attention.

'Jade thinks she's found the package that her dad wanted her to find,' Ricky whispered.

'Oh? What was it then?' Angela asked.

They all turned to Jade, waiting for the answer.

Jade dug deep into her coat pocket. 'I think Dad is after

this.' She took out a small, brown, padded envelope with 'Private' written across it in sloping writing.

'Is that your dad's handwriting? Can you be sure?'

'What's in it?'

'Have you opened it yet?'

The questions came thick and fast. Jade looked slightly overwhelmed.

'Yes, it is my dad's writing. Yes, I am sure. And I don't know what's in it 'cos I haven't opened it yet,' Jade shot back before gulping for breath.

'Well? What're you waiting for?' Angela asked impatiently.

Ricky shook his head. Theo sighed. Angela was at it again! But to everyone's surprise, Jade burst out laughing.

'Angela, I never used to like you – but I do now!' Jade smiled.

'Oh, thanks!' Angela raised her eyebrows.

'I didn't mean that the way it came out,' Jade said quickly. She paused. 'Actually, I think I did!'

'Oh, thanks!' Angela said again.

Angela and Jade smiled at each other.

'I was wondering whether or not I should open the envelope,' said Jade. 'But I think I'll follow Angela's advice.'

'Are you sure?' Ricky asked.

'No.' Jade shook her head after a long pause, 'But I'm going to do it anyway.'

She tore open the envelope immediately, as if she wanted to do it before she could possibly change her mind, and peered in. Her eyes widened in surprise. Theo thought the suspense would kill him. He longed to just snatch the envelope from Jade and take a look for himself but he had to wait. Jade turned the envelope over and shook the contents out into her hand. There were two unlabelled CDs in clear plastic cases.

'Is that it?' Angela asked.

Jade took another look in the envelope, then nodded.

'I wonder why your dad was so desperate for you to find those and deliver them,' Angela mused out loud.

‘Let’s have a look and see what’s on them,’ Ricky suggested.

‘D’you think we should? I mean, I don’t want Dad to . . . to get upset with me.’

‘I don’t see why he’d get upset with you just because we’re trying to help,’ said Ricky carefully.

‘It seems to me that you need all the help you can get,’ Theo added.

‘Your dad should be glad that you’re not alone in this, that your friends are prepared to do what they can to help sort this out,’ said Angela.

‘I suppose so.’ Jade didn’t sound totally convinced.

She looked around and gave a half-hearted smile. Angela was right about that at least. She didn’t want to go through all this alone. She looked at Theo, Ricky and Angela in turn, her gaze speculative. She was surprised at all of them, but especially Ricky. He seemed almost desperate to help her. She remembered that he’d been in serious trouble himself a while ago. She didn’t know too much about it – Ricky had refused to speak about it and Theo had warned everyone off who was even a little bit curious. Was that it? Did Ricky think she was in a similar situation to him and that’s why he was so keen to help? If that was it then he had got hold of totally the wrong end of the stick.

Jade still remembered the howl of anguish that had erupted from her when her mum had told her about her dad. She had refused to believe it, as if not believing it would somehow change the fact that her dad had died. And then the weeks and weeks of anger. Anger at her mum, anger at her dad, anger at the world. Anger that she had buried deep within as she turned in on herself, terrified to let out what she was really feeling. She wouldn’t go back to that again. At least this way, she had something, some small part of her dad to talk to.

And if she was right about Ricky’s motives for helping her, what about the others? What was in it for them?

'Why are you all doing this?' Jade couldn't help asking.

'Doing what? Helping you?' asked Theo.

'This isn't just so you can have a case for your new detective agency?' Jade asked suspiciously.

'This has nothing to do with Theo's idea about starting a detective agency and you know it,' Ricky said calmly. 'Stop trying to push us away. It won't work.'

Silence. Then Jade smiled. 'So which disk should I try first?'

'Either one,' said Ricky.

Jade placed a CD in the disk drive and pulled her chair closer to the keyboard. 'I'll see what's on the disk first before I do anything else.'

They all watched as Jade moved the mouse and clicked on icons to display the disk contents.

```
> DIR A:

> LOST IN CYB01.PGM
  LOST IN CYB02.PGM
  LOST IN CYBO TEST3.PGM
  ATLANTIS.PGM
  ATLANTIS1.PGM
  ATLANTIS2.PGM
  DIARY.EXE
  INSTALL.EXE
  SETUP.EXE
```

'What are those files then?' Bullet's voice came out of nowhere, making everyone jump.

'Bullet, this *is* private,' Theo pointed out.

'That's OK. I'm not about to tell anyone, am I?' Bullet said cheerfully. 'And besides, I reckon Jade needs my help. I'm the computer expert in this room.'

'And modest with it,' Theo muttered.

'I don't believe in false modesty,' Bullet replied with a beaming smile. 'So what're all those files then?'

'Look, more and more people seem to be getting involved in this,' Jade said firmly. 'I want everyone in this room to promise that it won't go any further. I'll tell you four and that's it. No more.'

'We promise,' everyone said immediately.

'All right then,' Jade said. 'To answer your question, Bullet, I don't know what these files are.'

'Step aside then.' Bullet elbowed his way to the computer and stood over Jade like a vulture, waiting for her to stand up. Eyebrows raised, Jade got to her feet.

'Let me try and install it. That seems like a good place to start,' said Bullet.

Everyone watched avidly as Bullet ran the INSTALL program. The message <PLEASE WAIT> flashed up on the screen.

'Whilst we're waiting for that, I'll let Dad know that I think I've found what he's been asking for,' said Jade.

Jade moved to the next screen and started up her Internet account using her name and password.

'Don't tell him that you're trying to find out what's on the disk though,' Theo warned.

'Don't worry. I wasn't going to,' Jade replied.

To: PDriscoll@PDriscoll.private.uk
From: JDriscoll@JDriscoll.private.uk

Dear Dad,

How are you? I think I've finally found what you're looking for. I'm sorry it took so long but I was looking for a big parcel rather than a small, padded envelope. The envelope has two CD-RW computer disks in it. Is this what you were after? If so, what should I do next? Will I be able to see you? Please let me know. I'd love to see you. I wouldn't be frightened – honest. I'm at school, but I'll wait around in the computer room for a while in case you're able to reply to this message immediately.

Love,
Jade.

Jade clicked on the <SEND> button before standing up. She joined the others to see how far Bullet had got.

'It's asking me to insert the other CD now.' Bullet explained the self-evident message on the screen.

'Go on then,' Angela prompted eagerly.

Bullet inserted the second CD into its drive and pressed the <ENTER> key as directed. All at once, it was as if the hard disk drive went crazy. It spun and clicked and whirred in a frenzy.

'These disks don't have a virus on them, do they?' Bullet asked worried.

'How should I know?' Jade replied.

'I think I should have run the virus checking software first.' Bullet's eyebrows knitted together with anxiety.

'Mrs Sumonu is going to hit the roof if you've introduced a virus onto one of her precious computers,' Ricky pointed out unhelpfully.

'I should definitely have run the virus checking software,' Bullet muttered. 'Mrs Sumonu is always saying that if we bring disks in from outside, we must make sure they're clean first.'

'I'm sure it'll be OK,' Theo said doubtfully.

'At least this is a stand-alone computer,' Bullet said. 'We should be grateful for that.'

'Bullet, you're so clever! What does that mean – stand-alone computer?' Angela asked.

Theo shook his head as he watched Angela. The tone of her voice and the expression on her face conjured up a single word in his mind – simpering!

'It means that if Jade's disks do contain a virus, at least it won't be passed down the school network to all the other computers in the room,' Bullet explained. 'The three machines on this side of the room haven't been connected up to the school network yet.'

'I really don't like the sound of that.' Theo pointed to the processor casing.

The disk drive sounded like it was revving up to take off. Then all at once, the noise stopped. Bullet watched the screen, waiting for some clue as to what just happened.

'It wants a password now to continue.' Bullet frowned.

They all turned to Jade, expectantly.

'Don't look at me. You all know as much as I do now.' Jade shook her head.

'What was your dad's name?' asked Bullet.

'Not was. *Is*,' Jade corrected, firmly. 'His name *is* Paul.'

No one spoke. Theo shifted uncomfortably in his seat. Jade really didn't believe that her dad was dead. And thinking about it, if her dad could still talk to her, if he could still communicate, then surely he wasn't really dead – not in the real sense of the word. Theo wasn't sure what to think any more. Death and dying and being dead were subjects he didn't like to think about. They were taboo subjects and as soon as they entered his head, he always pushed them out again. It was as if just to think about them was to invite them in to do their damage. Theo didn't want that. And try as he might, he just couldn't get comfortable around Jade when she talked about her father. Truth to tell, he was afraid that the death of her dad might somehow be . . . contagious.

'I'll type your dad's name in as the password,' Bullet suggested. 'Although I'd be really surprised if your dad had chosen anything as obvious as that.'

He hadn't. A warning message flashed on the screen.

INVALID PASSWORD. 1 OF 3. PLEASE TRY AGAIN.

'Bullet, what does that mean? 1 of 3?' Angela asked.

'I'm not sure,' Bullet said slowly. 'I'll try another password.'

'Which one this time?' asked Ricky.

'I'll try Jade's name,' said Bullet.

And although he could type using all ten fingers, Bullet typed in J-A-D-E using only his index finger to ensure that every keystroke was correct.

INVALID PASSWORD. 2 OF 3. PLEASE TRY AGAIN.

'I thought so.' Bullet withdrew his fingers from the keyboard as if it had suddenly turned white hot.

'You thought what?' Ricky questioned.

'I've got one more chance to get the password right,' Bullet replied.

'And if you don't get it right?'

'The best that will happen is the installation program will just stop,' said Bullet.

'And the worst?' Theo didn't want to, but he had to ask.

'It depends on how malicious the installation program is,' Bullet replied. 'It can be anything from wiping out the directory it was being installed into, to erasing the whole hard disk.'

'It can't do that . . . can it?' Ricky asked aghast.

'Easily,' Bullet said grimly.

'But that hard disk has got lots of people's classwork and homework on it,' said Ricky.

'I know. We won't be too popular if the disk gets wiped.'

'No kidding,' Theo scoffed. 'Now tell us something we don't know.'

'Maybe we should quit while we're ahead?' Angela suggested.

'But we can't give up now. You all said you'd help me. You're not going to give up at the first hurdle, are you? Jade protested.

'We can still do this. I'll backup the hard disk first, just as a safety precaution. Then we can try re-installing the software on your dad's disks again,' said Bullet.

'Go on then, ' Jade agreed reluctantly.

Bullet put a blank CD into the second CD drive and tried to get a file listing. But the installation program wouldn't let him.

Bullet hit the <ESCAPE> key. Nothing happened. He pressed it again. Then pressed it simultaneously with the <CTRL> key. Still nothing happened. Bullet's expression was stony as he tried <ALT> with the <F4> key, <CTRL> and <C> together and <CTRL> and <Y> together. But he was still in the installation program.

'Just take the disk out of the drive,' Theo suggested.

Bullet pressed the eject button but nothing happened. He tried again. Same result.

'There's one last thing we can try but if this doesn't work, we've got problems.' He shook his head.

'Should we start panicking yet?' Ricky asked, eyebrows raised.

'Not yet,' Bullet replied.

He tried holding down the <CTRL> <ALT> and <DEL> keys all at the same time.

WARNING: IF THE COMPUTER IS RESET AT THIS TIME, ALL DATA ON THE HARD DISK WILL BE ERASED. PLEASE ENTER THE INSTALLATION PASSWORD.

'I think we can start panicking now.' Bullet slumped in his chair.

'So are you going to try another password then?' Jade asked.

The screen from which Jade had sent the email to her dad beeped loudly.

'Dad's replied to my message.' Jade jumped out of her chair and moved over to the other screen.

Immediately everyone gathered around, watching avidly as Jade displayed the message on the screen.

To: JDriscoll@JDriscoll.private.uk
From: PDriscoll@PDriscoll.private.uk

Darling Jade,

Thank God! Thank God you've found my package at last. I was beginning to lose hope of you ever finding it. Yes, it's exactly what I've been waiting for. Here's what I want you to do. DON'T TRY TO READ THE DISKS! That's most important. After school, I want you to take them to the shopping centre. At exactly four-thirty, I want you to drop the package into the bin outside The Body Shop. Then you're to go home. I'll send you a message at exactly five o'clock – and I'll have a surprise for you, but only if you've followed my instructions to the letter. Remember, don't tell anyone about me and don't show my messages to anyone. I'll be watching you. All my love.

Dad.

'I don't know who's sending you those messages, but it's a dirty, rotten trick if you ask me.' Bullet scowled.

Startled, Jade asked, 'What d'you mean?'

Bullet was surprised. 'Well, that obviously can't be your dad because he's been asking you for ages to find this mysterious package – but if it really was your dad, he'd have known where the package was from the beginning.'

'He might've forgotten,' Jade said quietly.

'Yeah right!' Bullet scoffed. 'And even if he had forgotten *where* it was, he wouldn't have forgotten *what* it was. So why does he keep referring to it as 'the package' all the time? And since when does a ghost need a package to be dropped off in a bin outside The Body Shop? If your dad wanted to get rid of the package, he could've told you to throw it in the nearest bin in school or anywhere. And if he did want the package, surely he would've told you to put it on his grave or something? And what would a ghost want with a couple of disks? Angela told me what your dad used to do for a living. I reckon your dad must've been working on something really important and someone out there is trying to get their hands on it.'

The room was as still as an early Sunday morning. You could've heard a feather drop.

Bullet looked around the room, confused. 'I mean, that's what you all reckoned – right?'

Still no one spoke.

'I just thought it was a nasty trick.' Bullet defended himself, even though he wasn't sure why. 'Someone has obviously got hold of your dad's email account and password and they've been trying to get you to do their dirty work for them.'

Theo looked down at the floor. If, at that moment his life depended on it, he still couldn't have looked at Jade. He, Angela and Ricky had each tried to tell Jade the same thing but she'd never listened. And in his heart, Theo could understand why. But now Bullet had come right out and hit the nail smack dab on the head. Bullet had come straight to the point where Theo and the others had danced gingerly around it. And truth to tell, Theo had begun to wonder if maybe, just maybe, the email messages might actually be from Jade's dad?

'It is a nasty trick, isn't it?' Jade's voice was barely more than a whisper.

Only now did Theo dare to glance up. Silent tears streamed down Jade's cheeks.

'I'm sorry. What did I say?' Bullet asked distraught. '*What did I say?*'

'Excuse me.' Jade ran out of the room.

'Will someone please tell me what I said?' Bullet pleaded.

Ricky turned to him. 'It's not your fault, Bullet. You only told her the truth, that's all.'

'I don't understand.'

'Jade believed those mail messages really were from her dad,' said Theo.

Bullet's eyes widened like dinner plates. 'You're joking.'

Theo, Ricky and Angela all shook their heads.

'I wonder though,' Angela said thoughtfully. 'I wonder if Jade really did believe that those messages were from her dad? Or did she just want to believe it?'

'Does it make a difference?' Ricky asked.

'No, I guess it doesn't,' Angela sighed.

'What about these disks?' Bullet asked. 'What should I do with them?'

'Are you going to try and put in the password? You've got one more go left,' said Ricky.

'Maybe we shouldn't fiddle about with the disks whilst Jade isn't here,' Angela suggested.

'The best way for us to help her is to know what we're dealing with,' Ricky argued.

'Any suggestion for the last password?' Bullet asked.

No one answered. Bullet shrugged.

'Does anyone know Jade's mum's name?'

'Laura.' Theo remembered Pascoe DeMille mentioning it.

'OK then. Here goes nothing.' Bullet took a deep breath and typed in L-A-U-R-A.

Immediately the disk drive sounded like it was winding up about to explode.

'What's happening?' Theo asked urgently.

'I think the program is wiping the hard disk,' said Bullet. 'I was afraid that would happen.'

'Wiping the whole disk?' said Ricky.

Bullet nodded. 'Mrs Sumonu is going to dance on our heads.'

'Can't you just stop it?' Angela chipped in.

'That would probably make it worse not better. The best thing we can do is wait for the disk to be wiped clean and then try to load up as much as we can onto it again,' said Bullet.

'Can you do that without Mrs Sumonu finding out?' Theo asked.

'I can reload the operating system and all the software applications, but I can't reload everyone's work.'

'Let's hope everyone who used this computer kept backups of their data.' Ricky crossed his fingers.

'The trouble is,' Bullet glanced down at his watch, 'loading up the operating system and all the software will take at least two hours. Class starts in five minutes.'

'We'll tell Mrs Sumonu we'll reload all the deleted software tonight after school,' Theo suggested.

'No way,' Ricky interjected. 'We're going to put the disks in the bin outside The Body Shop just as the mail message said. Tonight we're going to find out just who's doing this to Jade and why.'

Chapter Fourteen

# The Messenger

'Thank goodness for that. I thought this day would never end. We should head straight for the shopping centre,' said Theo. 'We need to plant these disks well before five o'clock. The person sending the messages needs to believe that Jade left them there.'

'But suppose our "messenger" is already there?' Angela said.

'We're going to have to take that chance,' Ricky said.

Ricky looked no happier about it than Angela but they didn't have much choice. They'd just have to play it according to the email message and watch each other's backs. School was over at long last and now they had some business to take care of. Theo just wished his stomach would quieten down.

'Jade should be here,' Ricky sighed.

'She's far too upset. This isn't a game for her,' said Angela.

'It's not a game for me either,' Ricky replied. 'Someone is trying to mess with Jade's head. I just want to find out who and why.'

'You're . . . you're the ones I spoke to yesterday, aren't you?'

Theo jumped. And he wasn't the only one. They'd all turned the corner and there stood Pascoe DeMille.

'Er . . . yes, we gave Jade your message,' Theo said hastily.

'What did she say?'

'She didn't recognize your name,' Ricky said slowly. Theo could see the deepening suspicion in his friend's eyes.

'It's been a while since I saw her. I would've been more

surprised if she had remembered me,' Pascoe sighed. 'Did you tell her where I'm staying?'

'Yes, we told her that as well,' said Ricky.

'How is she doing?'

'Not too well,' Angela chipped in before Ricky could answer.

Pascoe bent his head momentarily. When he looked up again, his eyes were shimmering with unshed tears. 'I wish . . . I wish there was something I could do for her. Something I could do to make all this easier for her.'

'Were you good friends with her dad then?' Ricky asked.

'I guess you could say that.' The merest trace of a smile flickered across Pascoe's face. 'We went our separate ways a while ago though. He disagreed with my choice of profession.'

'Why? What do you do?' Angela asked straight out.

'I am . . . or rather I was an actor. Not a very good one. Not a very successful one. Paul told me I was wasting my time but . . .' Pascoe shrugged.

'Did you quarrel about it?'

'Angela!' Theo said, exasperated.

'I'm only asking.' Angela defended herself.

'Yes, we did quarrel about it,' Pascoe admitted.

'Jade's dad seemed to have quarrelled with a lot of people,' Angela said. 'He quarrelled with one of his friends at work about some game or another.'

'Oh yes . . . *Dyna-Cybo Warriors* . . .' said Pascoe thoughtfully.

'How come you know about that?' Theo asked.

'Letters. We kept in touch.'

'I thought you said you'd lost touch with each other,' Ricky reminded Pascoe.

'Yes, we did.'

Well, which one was it? It couldn't be both. Something didn't add up. And in the space of five seconds, he'd changed his story twice.

'D'you know Paul's friend, Alex?' Pascoe asked lightly.

Angela shook her head. Ricky and Theo didn't move.

'Well, Alex is a nasty piece of work. Take some advice, steer well clear. The only one Alex cares about is Alex,' said Pascoe.

'How d'you know that?' asked Ricky.

'You'd be surprised.' Pascoe stared at them without even blinking. His voice held an intensity that had Theo shifting back away from him. There was definitely something about Pascoe DeMille that was not quite right.

'You three take care of yourselves. And remember to stick together,' Pascoe said.

And with that he marched off past them and round the corner.

'What on earth was that all about? What did he mean by his last remark?' asked Angela.

'I have no idea. And did you have to volunteer quite so much information?' Theo rounded on Angela.

'What're you talking about? I barely spoke to the man,' Angela said amazed. 'What's the matter with you?'

'I don't trust that man. I think we should be careful of him. For all we know, he could be the one sending Jade those messages,' said Theo.

'You'll be blaming it on the man in the moon next,' said Angela.

'Don't you think he knew a lot of stuff for someone who lost touch with Jade's family years ago?' Theo suggested sardonically.

'I don't know. Maybe he's been catching up since we saw him yesterday,' Angela said.

'Yeah, right!' Theo shook his head. Angela swung from not trusting a word anyone said to taking people at face value. She was such a 'what you see is what you get' kind of person that she found it hard to believe that everyone else wasn't the same. It gave Theo a headache.

The shopping centre was busy and noisy, with people bustling here, there and everywhere. The smell of burgers and pizzas wafting down to them from the food hall made Theo feel slightly sick. The last time he had felt like this was when Ricky had been kidnapped and he and Angela were about to confront the kidnappers. A queasy, uneasy feeling plucked at his stomach like a vulture over meat.

Shouldn't we call the police or something?' Angela whispered.

'And tell them what?' asked Ricky. 'That someone claiming to be the ghost of Jade's dad asked her to dump some disks outside a shop in the centre and we're waiting for him to pick them up?'

'Ricky, I think Angela's right. The last time we were in a situation like this, we almost left it too late before calling the police,' Theo remembered. He looked around nervously as he spoke.

'I wish Jade was here,' Angela couldn't help saying. 'We're doing this for her. It feels strange her not being here.'

'All the more reason to make sure we don't fail,' said Ricky. 'Did you see her when her mum came to pick her up this afternoon? She couldn't stop crying.'

'I don't think Bullet's ever going to forgive himself,' Angela admonished. 'You should've warned him before letting him say all those things about the messages Jade was getting.'

'He didn't give us a chance.' Theo defended himself and Ricky. 'He just launched straight in.'

'It wasn't his fault, it needed to be said. It's just a shame that Jade had to hear it that way,' Ricky sighed.

'D'you think Jade is OK?' Angela said, concerned. 'Maybe after this we should go to her house and make sure?'

'Her mum won't thank us,' Theo pointed out.

'Is that going to stop us then?' asked Angela.

Theo shook his head. 'Nope!'

'I wonder if someone will come for the disks,' said Ricky, glancing down at his watch. 'We've been here for over an hour now and nothing's happened.'

'I've got to go home soon. I told Mum I'd be home by six,' said Theo.

'That's what I told Marian,' said Angela, talking about her foster-mum.

'I hope someone turns up soon. I'd like to take a good look at the person who's doing this to Jade.'

'Who d'you think is responsible for all this?' Theo asked.

'I have no idea.' Angela shrugged. 'I did wonder if maybe this had something to do with Jade's dad's friend, Alex.'

'Why him?'

''Cos apart from Jade's mum and your mum, I don't know anyone else connected with Jade's dad,' Angela admitted.

'We don't have a big list of suspects, do we?' Theo admitted.

'We don't need a big list of suspects. This isn't an Agatha Christie mystery,' Ricky dismissed. 'All we need to do is wait to see if someone picks up the package and then take it from there.'

'Shouldn't we separate?' Angela suggested.

They all considered.

'Maybe we'd better not?' Theo said uncertainly. 'Just in case?'

Strange that Pascoe DeMille's words about staying together should crop up in his head at that moment.

'OK.'

'Agreed.'

'Time to keep our eyes open and our mouths shut,' said Ricky. 'We wouldn't want to miss Jade's package getting picked up.'

'If it does get picked up,' Angela pointed out.

'If we can see the person who picks it up,' Theo added.

Ricky and Angela looked at him. 'Well, you never know,' Theo mumbled. 'We might all be wrong. Maybe it is Jade's dad after all.'

'I thought I was the one who believed in ghosts, not you,' Ricky said, surprised.

'I'm trying to keep an open mind,' said Theo, loftily.

'But not wide open,' Angela said with sarcasm.

'Shush!' Ricky admonished.

And they all shut up. The centre was full of late afternoon shoppers, laughing, smiling, scowling. Was one of them waiting to see if some disks were dropped into the bin outside The Body Shop? Or was someone else waiting . . . ? For the life of him, Theo couldn't tell which worried him more – the watchful gaze of the living or the dead. So here he was with Ricky and Angela waiting for something to happen.

And then it did. But it wasn't what any of them had been expecting.

A tall woman with auburn hair and dressed in an expensive, brown business suit strode up to the bin and looked down into it. With a frown of distaste she rummaged through it, obviously searching for something specific. Then a Cheshire cat smirk spread slowly over her face. She picked up the envelope Jade had found with *Private* written on it and pushed it into the larger than average handbag over her shoulder. She took a quick look around, and marched back the way she came.

'Come on,' Ricky hissed. 'Let's follow her.'

They ducked around the escalators where they were hiding and started weaving in and out of the people milling around them.

'We've got to keep up with her. We can't lose her now,' Ricky urged.

The woman marched with a purpose, keeping a straight line down the middle of the shopping centre. Theo thought his heart would stop when all at once she turned and looked behind her. Theo, Angela and Ricky immediately stopped in their tracks and looked anywhere but at her. Angela smiled at Theo and said, 'D'you fancy a McDonalds instead?'

'Nah! I'm not that hungry.' Theo shook his head.

'It's OK. She's moving again,' Ricky said after a moment.

'Phew! Fast thinking there, Angela,' Theo smiled.

'We're not out of the woods yet,' Angela pointed out.

They continued after the mystery woman, until all at once Ricky broke into a run.

'Oh no! She's taking the lift. Hurry up!'

They all belted towards the lift the woman had just stepped into. Ricky reached it first, just as the doors were closing. He slipped in sideways, whilst Theo and Angela watched in horror as the doors shut in front of them.

'What do we do? What do we do?' Theo tried to quash the panic which was beginning to rage in his stomach.

'Press the button for the other lift. I'll watch to see where this one stops.' Angela pointed to the floor indicators between the two lifts.

Theo pressed the button, willing the second lift to move down faster. 'Come on! Come on!' He clenched his fists, fear and frustration fighting within him.

'First floor. Car park level one. Car park level two. The lift has stopped on car park level two.' Angela pointed up at the lift indicator. 'Now it's stopping at car park level three.'

'So which floor do we go to?'

'Both of them. We'll start with car park level two first,' said Angela.

'If they're on level three, we'll never find them that way. They'll be out of the car park and half way to Scotland before we've even finished searching level two.'

'If you've got any better suggestions, now is the time to open your mouth,' Angela fumed.

Theo knew she wasn't angry with him. She was worried about Ricky, just as he was. Suppose the woman in the lift with him realized that Ricky was on to her. Where was Ricky now? Was he safe? Theo remembered the last time Ricky was in trouble. He wasn't going to go through all that again. But a terrible sense of déjà-vu swept over him.

At last the lift arrived. To both Angela and Theo's annoyance and intense frustration a woman pushing a pram got into the lift with them.

‘Hurry up, Sam. I haven’t got all day,’ the woman called out to the girl of four or five standing outside the lift.

And neither have we, Theo thought, glaring at the girl, and willing her to get in the lift.

‘Samantha!’ The woman yelled, exasperated. She turned to Angela and Theo, smiling apologetically.

‘I want a doughnut! I *need* it!’ Samantha burst into tears and turned around to trot down the centre after her doughnut.

‘SAMANTHA!’ The woman pushed the pram out of the lift and headed after her daughter.

‘Thank goodness for that.’ Angela pressed the button for the second floor of the car park. Nothing happened. She pressed it again and kept her finger on it. The doors shut so slowly, it was as if they were doing it on purpose. At long last the lift started to move, but it moved upwards as if it was on great-granny pedal power.

‘I could run up the stairs backwards faster than this,’ Theo complained.

Angela pressed the destination lift button over and over again. It didn’t make any difference. The lift continued crawling upwards. Theo could’ve wept with frustration. Finally they reached the second floor of the car park. The moment the doors were a body width apart, Angela and Theo were out of there. The lift opened straight out into the car park which at this time of day was full of cars. A hollow kind of silence echoed at them from all directions. Theo turned his head this way and that, desperate for some sound, some noise, some clue as to what was happening.

Nothing. No tall woman in a brown suit. And no Ricky.

‘Should I call out for him?’ Angela whispered.

‘We’d better not. We might make things worse rather than better,’ Theo decided.

‘Then we’d better split up. Back here in ten minutes.’ And Angela was off.

‘Angela, no. We should stay . . .’ But Theo was talking to himself.

What should he do now? Catch up with Angela so that they could stay together or try and find Ricky by himself? They would cover more ground apart but Theo wasn't happy about it at all. After a glance down at his watch, he turned and headed in the opposite direction to Angela. He scanned left and right, right and left for Ricky, wondering if he should dismiss his own advice and call out for his friend. The car park was vast, with bays going off in all directions. When his mum and dad came here with him for the weekly shopping, they always complained about the way the car park was designed. Unless you were lucky enough to park near a lift or you had years of experience of hunting round the car park, you stood no chance of finding your car until you were old and grey. Theo didn't know what to do for the best. He broke into a jog, moving up and down between the aisles of cars.

Still nothing.

Theo glanced down at his watch again. The ten minutes were up. He'd go back to the lift and if Angela hadn't found Ricky either then Theo was going straight to the police. The sudden, sharp click of heels made Theo freeze. He ducked down behind the nearest vehicle and stealthily made his way from car to car towards the noise. He tried to peep his head up, but ducked it down again when he saw two people only metres away from him. One was the woman in brown from down in the shopping centre but the man had his back to Theo. Praying that they hadn't seen him, Theo wondered what he should do next. Eyeing the ground with distaste, he gritted his teeth and lay down flat to look under the adjacent cars. Two pairs of feet – a woman in brown shoes with high heels and a man in grey lace-up shoes and dark socks with bright dayglo green stripes stood two cars away. Could he get a bit closer? Keeping low, Theo crept around the first car. He was beginning to differentiate between the soft voices.

'You stupid woman! Why didn't you check first?'

'I didn't want to draw attention to myself. It was bad enough having to go through the bin in the first place,' the woman replied with low anger. 'And don't call me stupid!'

'If the shoe fits!' said the man. 'Couldn't you tell these weren't the right CDs?'

'How was I meant to tell that without a computer? Or was I meant to read the disk with my fingernail?'

'The great big labels marked *My First and Second Sing-Along CDs* should have given you just a slight clue!'

'Don't talk to me like that. You wouldn't have got this far if it wasn't for me.'

'And exactly how far is this far?' the man fumed. 'As far as I can see we're right back where we started.'

'Maybe Paul just mislabelled the CD to throw us off?'

'See for yourself,' the man said, exasperated.

Theo had to risk it. Slowly, oh so slowly he crept around behind the voices until he was behind the car they were standing next to. It was an olive green sports car with a licence plate showing it was this year's model. Theo straightened up just the merest fraction to peer through the back window. He could see the profile of the woman but, frustratingly, the man still had his back to him. But now Theo could see they were using a laptop computer which was perched on top of the sports car. If he could just get a tiny bit closer . . .

Theo's knee hit against the bumper of the car and the noise was like a cannon going off. Theo ducked back down but it was too late. The voices stopped immediately. Theo could hear footsteps heading in his direction. His heart pounded, his blood roared in his ears, he was going to be sick.

Move! *Move!* he told himself, but his feet refused to listen. Swallowing down his terror, Theo jumped up and ran like a rabbit, too frightened even to look back. He could hear two sets of footsteps racing after him.

'Come back here,' the man yelled belligerently.

'He heard us. He was listening,' the woman raged.

Theo willed his legs to run faster. He ignored his lungs screaming for air and his heart ready to burst and the stitch in his side like a plunging knife. He ran and ran.

'No! In the car! Quick!' The man's voice yelled out behind him.

And still Theo didn't look back. It was only when he heard the footsteps retreating that he dared to slow down and even then he was half afraid it was a trick. He turned but there was no one behind him. Sure he was going to have a heart attack at any second, Theo stopped to catch his breath.

Why had they stopped chasing him? He was what seemed like kilometres away from the lift and there was no one around. Theo still couldn't believe that he'd been so clumsy, so stupid as to alert them to his presence. He was so busy watching them to make sure that they couldn't see him that he'd forgotten to pay attention to the back of the car. They had heard him and given chase but at least he was safe now. Only . . . why had they given up so easily? Why had they stopped chasing him?

And then, horrifyingly, Theo realized why they had stopped running after him. They had gone back to their car and now it was heading straight for him.

They were going to try and knock him over . . .

# Chapter Fifteen

# The Accident

Once again, Theo took off. One word played over and over again in his head. *RUN!* If he could just reach the lift. If he could just run fast enough . . . But he could hear the car behind him getting nearer and nearer. Its engine roared like a ravenous lion about to pounce and Theo knew it was only a few metres behind him now. They were really going to run him down . . .

'Theo, over here.'

The voice came out of nowhere. Theo didn't stop to work out who had called him or to work out the exact location of the voice. He had to get away, that was all he knew. He turned on the run and veered towards the voice.

'This way! Get down! Quick!'

Theo barely registered the fact that it was Pascoe DeMille. All he had on his mind were the occupants of the car who were trying to catch up with him.

'Down!' Pascoe pushed Theo down beside a black Land Rover and then squatted down himself. Both crouching, they frog-hopped their way behind the Land Rover and behind several cars, before stopping. Pascoe placed a finger over his lips as the two of them listened for the approach of the green car.

'Where did he go?' The woman's voice rang out over the low, steady purr of the car engine.

'He can't have got far.'

'We'd better go. We can't risk staying here any longer. Someone might see us.'

'Never mind. I'll deal with Theo Mosley and Jade . . .'

Theo didn't hear any more as the car drove off. But he didn't want to hear any more. He'd heard enough. The man and the woman in the car knew his *name* . . . How did they know who he was? Theo could taste the fear in his mouth. It was as dry as feathers and burned like acid.

Pascoe straightened up and dusted himself off. 'I warned you to stick with your friends.' He shook his head.

'How did you know we should stay together?' Theo stood up and eyed Pascoe warily.

'I'm psychic!' Pascoe smiled. 'You'd better get back to the lift. Angela and Ricky are worrying about you.'

'Hang on! Where did you come from? How come you're up here helping me?'

'Actually, I was up here loading my groceries into my car,' Pascoe replied. 'I saw what was going on and thought you needed some help, that's all. It really looked like they were trying to . . . Well, I'm sure they weren't . . .'

'I think they were,' Theo argued. 'Shouldn't we go to the police?'

'I'd rather not get involved in the police – if it's all the same to you.'

'Why not?'

'I have my reasons,' Pascoe said, evenly.

'How did you know we'd be up here? Have you been following us? How did you know all this was going to happen?' Theo still couldn't get over the feeling that Pascoe's arrival had been a little too timely, his intervention a bit too convenient. Was Pascoe in on this with the woman in brown and the man with the stripy socks? And now that Theo was thinking a little more calmly, there was something about the man in the stripy socks that was familiar. If he could just put his finger on it . . .

'I'd better get back to my car,' Pascoe said. 'Just be careful, Theo – OK?'

'How d'you know my name?' Theo stepped back from Pascoe.

The more the man opened his mouth, the more Theo suspected that Pascoe DeMille was not everything he claimed to be.

'The man in the car that was chasing you mentioned a Theo Mosley. I just assumed it was you.'

But Pascoe had called his name before that. Theo was sure of it.

'Aren't you going to do something to help?' Theo tried. 'That man said he was going to deal with Jade as well – not just me.'

'Don't worry. He won't get the chance.' Pascoe's face was as hard as granite as he stared down the car park. Then he looked at Theo and his face relaxed into a smile. 'Not with you and your friends on the job.'

And with that, Pascoe headed off down the car park. Theo watched him for a few moments, a deep frown creasing the skin on either side of his mouth. Theo turned and made his way back to the lifts.

No! I can't just leave it there, he shook his head vehemently.

Pascoe had to do *something* – even if it was just telling the police what had happened. He couldn't be that ineffectual, even if he was a grown-up. Theo turned back, ready to argue with Pascoe.

But there was no sign of him.

Theo looked up and down the rows of cars, but Pascoe was nowhere to be seen. His frown deeper now, Theo ran back to the lifts. Angela and Ricky were just entering one of them as he ran up.

'Wait! Wait for me!'

'Theo! We were just about to go to the police.'

'Where on earth have you been? We were worried sick.'

'Where were *you* then?' Theo asked Ricky, annoyed.

'The woman rumbled me. When I didn't get out on this floor, she pressed the button for the next one up. And when I didn't get out there either, she pressed the button for the ground floor and accused me of playing about with the lifts.

I had to get out on the ground floor and then she went up again,' Ricky explained.

'So with all that wandering up and down the car park lifts, we must've just missed each other,' added Angela.

'But never mind that,' Ricky dismissed. 'Theo, what happened to you?'

'Simple. The woman in brown met her accomplice – it was a man but I didn't see his face. Then they both heard me eavesdropping and tried to run me over with their car.'

Ricky and Angela stared, but Theo's expression was too grim for this to be a joke.

'Are you all right?'

Theo nodded.

'Are you sure?'

'Yes.'

'Let's go to the police. This is getting serious.' Now Ricky's face was as grim as Theo's.

'That's not all,' Theo added.

'I would've thought that was enough,' Angela said, eyebrows raised.

'Guess who helped me get away from the two in the car?'

'Who?' Angela and Ricky asked in unison.

'Pascoe DeMille.'

'Pascoe!' Angela was stunned. 'What's he doing here?'

'Shopping – or so he said,' Theo replied.

'Lucky he was here then,' Ricky said slowly.

'Isn't it just?' Theo agreed.

Silent moments passed before anyone spoke.

'Hhmm . . . d'you think Pascoe is working with the other two or is he after the disks for himself?' asked Angela.

'I think he's working alone or for someone else we haven't come across yet,' Theo said at last. 'Otherwise why would he help me out?'

'Unless he's trying to lull you into a false sense of security?' Ricky suggested.

Theo shook his head. 'I don't think so. I think he was

genuinely helping me but maybe he knew that we'd substituted other CDs for the real ones.'

'How would he know that?' Angela frowned.

'I don't know. I'm only guessing,' Theo said impatiently. 'All I do know is that it's too much of a coincidence that he should just appear like that.'

'Mrs Daltry says that sometimes coincidences do happen,' said Angela.

'Yes, but Mrs Daltry . . .' And then it hit Theo. He stared at his friends. His mouth dropped open and stayed open. He couldn't believe it. And yet . . . and yet he was sure he was right.

'What's the matter?' asked Ricky, concerned.

Theo shook his head. He must've made a mistake. He *must* have . . . It was ridiculous – preposterous. And yet, the more he thought about it . . .

'Come on Theo, sick it up!' said Angela.

Should he or shouldn't he? Theo wondered if he should tell his friends of his discovery. What if he was wrong? The trouble was once he had said it, there was no turning back. So he had to be sure . . .

'Nothing. Never mind.' Theo couldn't tell his friends about his revelation. They'd never believe him for a start. And suppose he *had* got it wrong? There'd be hell to pay. But he was so *sure* he was right . . .

'Don't tell us it's nothing when we can see from your face that that's a blatant lie,' frowned Ricky. 'What's up?'

Theo made a conscious effort to think of something else so that Ricky couldn't read his expression. He was surprised the name of the person he had in mind wasn't blazoned across his forehead.

Theo was convinced he knew who had tried to knock him over.

But knowing it and proving it were two different things. He'd just have to find a way to prove it first – and that meant setting a trap. It wouldn't be fair to get his friends involved until he was absolutely certain. Especially after everything Ricky and Angela had already been through.

Theo's heart began to thump a slow, fearful tattoo in his chest, as if it knew and was protesting his decision.

'It's OK.' Theo attempted to smile. 'I thought I recognized the woman in the brown suit, but I didn't.'

'Oh, OK. Let's pop in and see Jade on our way home,' Ricky suggested.

'Fair enough,' Angela agreed.

Theo didn't speak. His mind was overwhelmed by the course of action he was contemplating. If he was wrong he would be in the worst trouble of his life. But if he was right . . . Not only would he be in trouble, he'd be in *danger*. Theo wondered if he should tell his friends of his suspicions. It'd be so much easier to have company on this. Theo sighed inwardly. He was being selfish. He'd make one hundred per cent certain first and then he'd tell them.

An unwelcome question formed in his mind and refused to budge. If and when he needed his friends' help, would he be in a position to get it?

## Chapter Sixteen

# The Secret

'Hello, Mrs Driscoll. May we speak to Jade please?'

Mrs Driscoll's look could've felled an elephant at ten paces. She was not pleased. Glancing down at her watch, she asked, 'Do you have any idea what time it is?'

'A quarter to six,' Ricky said. 'We won't stay long. We all have to be home by six o'clock.'

'Jade's been very upset. She's in her bedroom asleep and I don't want to disturb her.'

'It's very important that we see her. We have some important news to tell her,' Theo said earnestly.

Ricky and Angela glanced at Theo.

'I think it's rather late to be . . .'

'Mum, it's OK. Please can I talk to them?' Jade walked down the stairs and towards the door.

'Jade, I . . .'

'*Please*, Mum.'

'Just five minutes then. Is that understood?'

Jade nodded. Mrs Driscoll glanced down at everyone's shoes.

'You can all stay in the hall but you're not to go into the front room or any of the other rooms,' she sniffed.

And with that she went into her front room and shut the door.

It was obvious that Jade had been crying – and not just a little either. Her eyes were puffy and swollen and her mouth drooped like a wilting flower.

'Jade, I need to talk to you – in private.'

It was hard to say who was more surprised – Jade or Angela and Ricky.

'Theo, what's going on?' Ricky frowned.

'It's OK. I just want to ask Jade something,' said Theo.

'So why can't you ask it in front of us?' asked Angela.

'Because I can't. Please, just give me a minute,' Theo pleaded.

Reluctantly, Angela and Ricky stepped back as Theo stepped forward.

'Ricky, what's Theo up to?' Angela asked, suspiciously.

'I have no idea,' Ricky replied.

Ricky tried to keep the hurt out of his voice at Theo's lack of confidence in him. He wasn't sure that he was totally successful. Since when did Theo keep secrets from him? Didn't Theo trust him any more? Ricky just couldn't work it out. He leaned his head forward to try and hear what Theo and Jade were whispering but they were speaking too softly for him to make out more than the occasional word. Now Jade was shaking her head vehemently. Theo spoke more urgently than before. He was obviously trying to convince Jade of something, but she didn't look happy. Jade looked over in Ricky and Angela's direction and said something to Theo. Now it was his turn to shake his head. Curiosity burned through Ricky like acid. Why was Theo shutting him out? What had he done? Maybe Theo blamed him for the fact that they'd all been separated in the car park and Theo had been in danger. But Ricky would never have jumped in the lift with the woman in brown if he'd known what was going to happen. When Ricky had been kidnapped, Theo had saved his life, not to mention his sanity. For a long time afterwards, Theo was the only one he could talk to about the experience.

Ricky shook his head slowly, unhappy with the direction his thoughts were leading him. He just wished the sour feeling in the pit of his stomach would go away. If Theo didn't trust him any more, why didn't he just come out and say so? Jade and Theo walked back towards them.

'Why did you want to see me?' Jade asked Ricky and Angela.

'I don't know if Theo just told you this, but a woman tried to pick up the disks you found,' said Ricky. He looked directly at Jade. He couldn't look at Theo. 'We followed her up to the car park above the shopping centre, where she met another man but we lost them.'

'What Ricky's trying to say is that we're not much further forward,' said Angela.

Jade looked at Theo. 'Theo seems to think we are.'

'Any thoughts you'd care to share?' Angela asked with fake nonchalance.

'No,' Theo said simply.

For once Angela had no reply.

'Oh Angela, before I forget, d'you have Bullet's home phone number?'

'Yes.'

Theo waited for Angela to carry on but she didn't.

'Can I have it please?'

'Why?'

''Cos I need to talk to him about something.'

'What?'

'Angela . . .' Theo said, exasperated.

'OK, OK!' Reluctantly Angela gave Theo the number. Theo wrote it down on the back of his hand.

'Anyway, we'd better get going,' said Theo to Jade. 'We don't want to get you into trouble.'

'It's all right,' Jade shrugged.

Ricky and Angela were the first ones out of the front door. Theo turned back to Jade just before he stepped over the threshold.

'We're . . . we're sorry about what happened earlier today – about the things Bullet said. None of us meant to upset you.'

At first Theo thought Jade wasn't going to answer. He winced as he realized he was just dragging painful memories to the foreground again. He was about to shut the door when Jade stopped him.

'Theo, don't worry about it. I guess . . . I guess I had to hear it. I think deep down I knew that Dad . . . that Dad was gone. It's just that this was my chance, you see. It was my chance to say all the things to Dad that I never got to say when he was here. It was a way of holding on to him.'

'I understand that,' Theo nodded.

He leaned forward and whispered something in Jade's ear. She smiled, but it didn't last long. She regarded Theo and said, 'Just be careful, OK?'

'Careful is my middle name,' Theo grinned.

And with that he shut the door.

They all walked along in silence.

'You've become very secretive all of a sudden,' said Angela.

Theo shrugged. It wasn't exactly as if he could deny it.

'Don't we get to hear what's going on then?' Ricky asked.

Theo looked at Ricky. Ricky was looking straight ahead. Theo sighed. He'd known at Jade's house that Ricky was upset with him. Theo wasn't the only one who had difficulty hiding his true feelings.

'Soon. I just have to check something first. OK?'

Ricky shrugged. Theo sighed again. Ricky was even more upset with him now, not that he'd ever say as much.

'Well, this is my street. I'd better get going before Mum breaks out the bloodhounds,' said Theo lightly. 'I'll see you both tomorrow.'

'Yeah.'

'Sure.'

Angela and Ricky walked away without a backwards glance. Theo watched them go with a heavy heart. He longed to call them back and tell them exactly what was going on but he couldn't. He just couldn't. As he'd explained to Jade, this was something he was going to have to do all alone. And the thought of it terrified him.

Chapter Seventeen

# To Catch a Thief

Ricky's face was thunderous as he watched Theo deep in conversation with Bullet and Jade. Last night was bad enough, but now Theo seemed to be rubbing Ricky's face in it. When Ricky had arrived at school that morning, Theo was standing by the school gates. Ricky had made the mistake of thinking Theo was waiting for him. Theo soon put him right.

'I'm not waiting for you. I'm waiting for someone else,' Theo told him in no uncertain terms.

Theo hadn't exactly said, 'Now get lost!' but it was there, in his tone of voice.

If Theo didn't want to be friends any more, why didn't he have the courage to just come right out and say so? Why make it clear to everyone in the class that he and Ricky had fallen out, without telling Ricky how or why first? Ricky couldn't understand why Theo was doing it. In fact, Ricky would've said that Theo was the last person to behave like that.

'Good morning, everyone.'

'Good morning, Mr Dove.'

Everyone scooted back to their places. Mr Dove hitched up his trouser legs and sat on the edge of the table, facing his class.

'I'll be taking you for your double lesson this morning,' Mr Dove smiled.

Theo looked out of the window. He sat up in surprise when he saw Pascoe DeMille standing in the school grounds, looking up at Theo's classroom window. Jade obviously hadn't been in touch with him yet. Pascoe spotted Theo and waved frantically. Theo turned to look at Jade who sat at the back of the class. She looked terrible. Theo wondered if she'd managed to get any sleep at all. As if she knew she was being watched, Jade turned to him. Her expression was sombre as she nodded to him before facing the front of the class again. Theo watched Mr Dove as he walked up and down the class handing out worksheets. Pascoe would just have to wait. Theo had more important things on his mind at the moment. He picked up his duffel bag and emptied its contents on to the table. Now where on earth had he put it?

'Hello, Theo,' Mr Dove smiled as he searched for a free space to put Theo's worksheet on the table before him.

'Hello, sir,' Theo replied.

'It looks like you've brought everything including the kitchen sink to school,' Mr Dove said drily.

'Sorry, sir.'

'What're you looking for?' asked the teacher.

'My pen,' explained Theo.

'It's right there in front of you,' pointed the teacher.

'No, that one doesn't work,' Theo said.

'Then why carry it around?' Mr Dove smiled.

Theo shrugged, embarrassed. He used his forearm to sweep everything back into his bag.

Mr Dove moved on.

'You can use one of my pens if you like,' Ricky offered.

'No, it's OK,' Theo declined.

Theo turned to talk to Bullet. 'Bullet, can I borrow a pen and your ruler?'

'Oh? Oh! Er . . . yes, of course.' Bullet handed it over.

'What's wrong with my pen?' Ricky said quietly.

'I prefer Bullet's.'

'Suit yourself.'

'I will,' said Theo.

'Theo, I just said no talking,' Mr Dove frowned.

'Sorry, sir. I didn't hear you,' Theo apologized.

'That's because you were too busy talking. I think you'd better stay behind at break and write me a page on why sometimes it's better to open your ears rather than your mouth.'

Theo lowered his head. 'Yes, sir.' It certainly hadn't taken Mr Dove long to show his true colours.

Ricky frowned at the teacher. 'But that's not fair, sir. Theo was only asking for a pen and a ruler.'

'Never mind, Ricky.' Theo glared at his friend. 'Leave it. You'll just make things worse.'

'I'd listen to Theo if I were you – unless of course you'd like to join him at breaktime.'

'No, he wouldn't,' Theo answered for Ricky.

Ricky shut up – more because of the way Theo was glaring at him than because of anything the teacher said. There was no doubt about it. Somehow, in some way, Ricky had lost his best friend.

Theo looked out of the window again. Pascoe was still there staring up at the school. From across the school grounds, Theo could see Mr Appleyard striding purposefully towards him – and it didn't take super vision to see that Mr Appleyard was not pleased to find a stranger in the school. Theo scowled at Pascoe. The last thing he needed was for Mr Appleyard to get antagonized. If Pascoe wasn't careful, he'd blow all of Theo's carefully laid plans.

The rest of the double lesson passed without incident. It also passed without Theo and Ricky saying one word to each other – which was a first. At last the buzzer sounded. Ricky leaped up and crammed his work into his bag.

'Theo, I don't think we should sit together any more,' Ricky said tonelessly.

There was no disguising the shock on Theo's face. Ricky frowned. Had he made a mistake? Maybe Theo did still want to be friends after all.

'Ricky, I . . .'

'Theo, up here please, where I can keep an eye on you,' Mr Dove ordered.

Theo got his things together and after a brief, abject glance at Ricky, he moved to the front of the class. Theo watched, dejected, as the rest of the class trooped out to enjoy the morning break.

'Theo, sit down and get on with it, or are you waiting for an engraved invitation?'

Theo waited for Jade, the last one out of the classroom, to close the door behind her. He turned back to Mr Dove and eyed him speculatively.

'Theo, are you going to sit down or not?' Mr Dove was beginning to get cross now.

'I think not,' Theo said at last.

'I beg your pardon?'

'I don't see why I should sit down for someone who tried to knock me over,' Theo said simply.

Mr Dove stared at him. His mouth opened and closed like a drowning fish.

'And please don't insult my intelligence by denying it. I know it was you.'

Mr Dove burst out laughing. 'Theo, I take my hat off to you. In my time, I've heard some amazing excuses and accusations from children trying to get out of the work I set them, but this one is in a class of its own.'

'I know it was you. I recognized your voice.'

'Let me get this straight. You claim that someone almost accidentally knocked you over and you're blaming me?'

'First of all, it was no accident, you meant to do it. And second of all I recognized your voice.'

'So you never saw the face of this person who came at you?'

'No, I didn't. But then you already knew that. You must've known there was no way I could see your face from the back of the car where I was hiding. And when you drove at me, the last thing I was going to do was stop and turn to get a good look at you.'

'I haven't a clue what you're talking about, but maybe we should both go to the headmistress and get this sorted out.' Mr Dove's voice was now winter ice. 'You can tell her your accusation.'

'I think that's a good idea,' Theo agreed. 'I'll tell her how I know it's you because you're wearing the same yuky socks with the bright green stripes that you were wearing yesterday in the car park. I might not have seen your face, but I did see those.'

Mr Dove glanced down at his feet and back up again. 'You can't see my socks.'

'I could when you perched on the edge of the table when you came in this morning. And I'll tell her that I was behind your car and I made a scratch on it. That was the noise that alerted you to the fact that someone was listening,' Theo lied on the spur of the moment. 'There's no way I could've seen or been near your car since but I bet I can describe the shape of the scratch on your car's paintwork perfectly. And I know it's your car because I waited by the entrance to the school car park this morning and saw you drive in. It was the same dark green sports car that tried to knock me over.'

'I see,' Mr Dove said slowly. 'I don't think we'll go to see the headmistress after all.'

'Er . . . I think I'd rather, if it's all the same to you.' Theo edged back nervously.

'I've had just about enough of your interfering.' Mr Dove took a step forward. 'If it wasn't for you and your friends I could've been long gone by now.'

'So you admit that you did try to knock me down?'

'I'm only sorry I missed.'

Theo took another step backward. Mr Dove took another step forward. It was as if they were both involved in some fearful, macabre dance.

'I know you've got the disks I want. Hand them over and no one will get hurt.'

'You mean, *I* won't get hurt.'

Mr Dove smiled – an evil, oily smile that made Theo want to race for the door, but he had to stand his ground.

'Something like that,' Mr Dove agreed.

'You've made a mistake, I haven't got the disks.'

'I saw them when you emptied your bag on the table earlier.' Mr Dove lurched forwards without warning and grabbed Theo by the arm. 'Hand over those disks or I will wring your scrawny little neck.'

'I don't know what you're talking about . . .' Theo gasped.

'*Planet of the Anvil* – does that ring any bells?' asked Mr Dove.

'Let go of my arm. You're hurting me.'

'Give me your bag. GIVE ME YOUR BAG NOW!' Mr Dove started to shake Theo.

'Here.' Theo slipped his duffel bag off his shoulder, but he couldn't stop it from falling on the floor because Mr Dove was still holding his other arm.

Mr Dove released Theo and picked up the bag at once. He started rummaging through it.

'So all this was just to get hold of Jade's dad's disks?' said Theo.

Mr Dove didn't reply.

'I bet you're not really a teacher at all, are you?'

'As a matter of fact, I am a qualified teacher. It's just not what I do any more. I've found something a lot more lucrative.'

'Yeah, like stealing other people's disks.'

'It's not the disks. It's what's on them.' Mr Dove smirked as he took out the two CDs from Theo's bag.

'What's so special about an unfinished game?'

'It isn't unfinished. *Planet of the Anvil* is very much complete. And it's going to make us a fortune.' Mr Dove waved the disks at Theo. 'But there's something else on here that's a lot more important.'

'Like what?'

'Like none of your business.' Mr Dove tapped his nose.

'I'm out of here. And if you know what's good for you, you won't follow me.'

Mr Dove headed for the door.

Theo thought for a moment. 'Something that's a lot more important? Oh, I know what you're talking about. You mean the file containing the proof that *Dyna-Cybo Warriors* was Jade's dad's idea and not Alex Reeves'. Yes, I guess that would be more important.'

Mr Dove froze in his tracks. He turned, his expression pure rage. 'What did you say?'

'Nothing,' Theo said quickly. 'Didn't you say you had to be going?'

'How d'you know about that file?'

'A friend of mine analysed the disk and managed to break the code and read the files. He's the one who told me that Jade's dad had managed to hack into Alex's computer and had retrieved the file with his initial voice notes, as well as the copies of some memos that went back and forth between him and Alex discussing the idea. That's why Jade's dad and Alex had their big quarrel, isn't it? Alex nicked every file referring to the new game from Jade's dad's computer and then passed the game off as his own. It's all in Paul Driscoll's diary file on the first CD. The other CD contains his new game which he was determined that Alex wouldn't get.'

'I think you'd better come with me,' Mr Dove said stonily.

'I'd rather not.'

Mr Dove made a dive for Theo, but Theo was ready for him and jumped out of the way. He raced towards the door, but Mr Dove was quicker. Just as Theo managed to wrench open the door, Mr Dove's longer arms slammed the door shut. He grabbed Theo's upper arm and squeezed until Theo couldn't feel his fingers.

'You're going to come with me to my car and if you do anything to draw attention to yourself – anything at all – I'll make sure that you are very, very sorry. I hope for your sake that I make myself crystal clear.'

Theo gulped and nodded. He tried to prise Mr Dove's fingers off his upper arm but the man wasn't letting go.

'You're hurting me.'

'You should've thought about that before you decided to stick your nose in where it wasn't wanted.'

'But I'm not the only one who's figured out what's going on.' Theo said desperately. 'What's the point of taking me with you?'

'You'll buy us some time.' Mr Dove's gaze darted around the classroom like a cornered rat. When he was satisfied that they were really alone, he said, 'You're not to say a word to anyone. D'you understand?'

'Yes.'

Mr Dove's grip on Theo's arm tightened.

'D'you understand?'

Theo winced and nodded.

'How did you get into our school anyway? I mean, how did you know Mrs Daltry would win a holiday and be away so you could take her place?' Theo gritted his teeth against the pain in his arm. He had to keep talking. He had to wait for a chance to catch Mr Dove off guard.

'Who d'you think arranged for her to win the holiday in the first place?' Mr Dove said scornfully. 'Alex and I put up the money. It cost us, but we'll get it back. Jade's dad's new game is going to make us rich.'

Theo stared at him. 'But . . . but you couldn't guarantee you'd take her place . . .'

'Yes, I could. It was just a question of being in the right place at the right time. I was at the local supply teacher agency when this school rang up for Mrs Daltry's replacement – and here I am. Now no more talking.'

Mr Dove opened the door and marched out into the hall, dragging Theo after him. He froze when he saw the crowd in the corridor waiting for him. There stood Jade, Bullet, Ricky, Angela and – looking very perplexed – Mr Appleyard.

'Did you get it?' asked Bullet.

Theo dug into his trouser pocket and before Mr Dove could stop him, he threw a mini tape recorder to Bullet who caught it one handed.

Bullet pressed the OFF button and smiled. Mr Dove looked from Theo to the crowd before him and back again.

'You . . .'

'Every word,' Theo grinned. 'Now let go of my arm.'

In a daze Mr Dove did as Theo ordered. 'What's going on?' Mr Appleyard was annoyed. 'I thought you said there was a rat up in the classroom.'

'There is. You're looking at him,' Bullet replied. 'Could you make sure he doesn't go anywhere while I get one of the teachers to call the police?'

Without waiting for a reply, Bullet raced down the corridor to the staff room.

'You're the new supply teacher. Mr Dove, isn't it?' asked the caretaker.

'He's not a teacher at all. He tried to knock me over,' said Theo.

'You're not going to believe the word of these kids over me, are you?' Mr Dove laughed lightly.

Mr Appleyard's eyes narrowed. 'I know these kids. And while they get on my nerves, I don't think they'd lie about something like this. Not something that could get them into so much trouble if it was a lie. But on the other hand, I don't know you from a hole in the ground! So I think you'd better stay exactly where you are.'

If Mr Appleyard had looked around at that moment and seen the looks on the faces of Theo and the others, his head would've doubled in size. Theo was amazed. Mr Appleyard was actually going to help them. Theo had always planned with Bullet that he'd do something to get kept behind by Mr Dove. The plan was for Bullet to get Mr Appleyard the moment the class was over. Theo reckoned the caretaker was a better bet than one of the teachers who would never believe anything against another teacher. But Mr Appleyard's reaction was always the biggest worry. He could've turned round and called them all liars. As it was, Mr Appleyard's suspicious, wary eyes were still on Mr Dove.

Mr Dove looked up and down the corridor. Quick as a snap, he made a break for it, racing for the stairs at the end of the corridor.

'Oh no you don't!' Mr Appleyard was the first to move. He chased after Mr Dove, but it was Angela who rugby tackled Mr Dove to the floor. Theo, Ricky and Mr Appleyard piled on top of him to make sure he couldn't get up and try to escape again.

'Get off me! GET . . . OFF . . . ME!' Mr Dove yelled.

'Yeah, right!' Ricky scoffed.

Jade walked up and around them to look down at the squirming ex-teacher.

'You're the one who sent me all those mail messages, aren't you?'

Mr Dove didn't reply.

'You must've found out Dad's password and you've been sending me emails pretending to be him. How could you? How could you be so mean?'

'You had something we wanted,' Mr Dove sneered, not in the least bit repentant.

Jade drew herself up to her full height and looked at Mr Dove as if he was something nasty she had just stepped in. 'I've just figured it out. You work for Alex, don't you?' Jade asked.

'Who's Alex?' Mr Dove said curtly.

'Don't worry,' Theo told Jade. 'The tape proves he does know Alex Reeves.'

'Even if I do, you can't prove she had anything to do with this,' said Mr Dove.

'She?' Theo was astounded. And he wasn't the only one.

'Jade, you never said that Alex Reeves was a woman,' said Angela.

'Didn't I? I thought I did,' Jade replied.

'Is she a tall, pretty woman with dark brown hair down to her shoulders?' Theo asked.

Jade nodded. 'Why? D'you know her?'

'She was with him when they tried to knock me over,' said Theo.

'My sister's much too smart for any of you,' Mr Dove scoffed. 'By the time she's told her side of the story, the police will think you're crazy.'

'Your sister?' Jade whispered.

'I should've guessed. Well, I might not have seen your face yesterday evening, but I did see hers – more than once,' Theo reminded Mr Dove. 'And with that tape and everything you just said, I think I'll manage to convince the police.'

'And Theo, don't forget, Angela and I saw her too,' said Ricky. 'We saw her take the package out of the bin in the precinct.'

Mr Dove's face fell. Bullet came running down the corridor with at least three other teachers behind him.

'Mr Appleyard, just what d'you think you're doing? Get off Mr Dove at once – and that goes for the rest of you,' Mr Cookson ordered.

'Not a chance,' Mr Appleyard replied. 'Not until the police get here.'

Mr Cookson looked around and frowned deeply. 'Would someone mind telling me exactly what's going on?'

## Chapter Eighteen

# Friends

Ricky, Theo, Angela, Jade and Bullet all sat around the same lunch table. They were very aware of the looks they were getting from the rest of the dining hall.

'This has got my detective agency off to a flying start,' Theo said with relish.

'Whose detective agency?' Angela raised an eyebrow.

'*Our* detective agency,' Theo amended.

'Are you still going through with that? Haven't you had enough excitement to last you a lifetime?' Jade frowned.

'Nah! I'm just getting into it,' Theo grinned. 'Besides, with the five of us in this detective agency, there won't be a case we won't be able to crack.'

'The five of us? You mean . . . you mean, I'm included?' Bullet asked amazed.

'Of course you are. You're our computer expert,' Theo said with impatience. 'I thought that was obvious.'

'I'm included.' Bullet grinned around the table.

'I'm the brains of the outfit,' Theo continued. 'Bullet can be the computer expert, Angela can be the heavy and do all the strong arm stuff . . .'

'Thanks!' Angela said, indignantly.

'Ricky will be the second lot of brains and Jade can look after the girlie problems.' Theo's grin was even broader. 'I've got it all worked out.'

'Girlie problems? That is outrageous! What a cheek!' Angela's indignation knew no bounds now.

'OK, brains! If you're so clever, tell me how Mr Dove

knew that I'd told you about the emails I was getting,' Jade challenged.

'That's easy,' Theo grinned. 'Remember when you first came up to us in the corridor and asked if we believed in ghosts? And d'you remember how Mr Dove passed us in the corridor and we all shut up until he turned the corner? Well, I reckon he turned the corner but he didn't carry on walking to the staff room. I think he just stood there and listened to our conversation. He probably guessed what you had on your mind. And then when you took us to your house, I was sure we were being followed . . .'

'You never said!' Ricky frowned.

'I thought maybe I was imagining things, but now I don't think so. I think Mr Dove was behind us. That's how he knew you'd confided in us, Jade,' said Theo. 'I mean, what else would we be doing at your house?'

Jade looked at Theo, impressed. 'Theo, you just might make a detective yet!'

Theo nodded happily. Nothing could dampen his mood. Mr Dove had been taken away by the police and although they'd had to spend the rest of the morning explaining what had happened, it seemed like Mr Dove and his sister were definitely going to get what they deserved. The police wanted each of them to go round to the local police station within the next twenty-four hours with their parents to make official statements. Theo was more than willing. He was just a bit worried about how he was going to explain the whole thing to his mum and dad first.

'You'll all be glad to know that I think I've finally got my Crimebuster program working, so it's at your disposal, Theo,' Bullet announced. 'It's just a shame it had a couple of bugs in it before this, or it might have led you to the truth sooner.'

'And then again . . .' Theo teased.

'Just a minute, Theo,' said Ricky. 'I've got a huge Tyrannosaurus Rex bone to pick with you.'

Theo sighed. Was he the only one who was *happy* about the outcome?

'Go on, then,' Theo said, his head resting on one of his hands.

'Just what did you think you were doing by not telling me what was going on?'

'You and Angela have already been through enough, don't you think? It wouldn't have been fair to drag you into this – especially if I was wrong about Mr Dove. I didn't want to get the two of you into any more trouble after everything you went through during the kidnapping incident.'

'Theo, that wasn't your decision to make,' Angela said angrily. 'You should've told me and Ricky what was going on right from the start and let us make up our own minds.'

'Too right!' Ricky agreed.

'But you wouldn't have said no, even if you wanted to,' Theo shrugged.

'Theo, don't you ever do that again,' Ricky said, his voice so quiet that Theo almost didn't hear what he said.

Everyone else around the table grew quiet too. They could all tell that Ricky was furiously angry.

'We're friends. You don't shut friends out like that,' Ricky fumed.

'But I was only doing it *because* we are friends.' Theo tried to defend himself.

'I told him that he should tell both of you what was going on,' said Jade. 'But he wouldn't listen.'

'He does tend to think he knows everything, doesn't he?' Bullet added.

'What is this? Get at Theo hour?' Theo said indignantly. 'Anyone else?'

'I mean it, Theo.' Ricky still wasn't mollified. 'Don't you ever do that again. Do you understand?'

Theo nodded. 'Friends again?'

It took a few moments, but at last Ricky nodded.

'Then why do you still have a face like a handful of mince?' Theo teased.

Reluctantly, Ricky smiled. Theo realized that it was going to take a while for Ricky to fully forgive him – but he would. Bullet turned to Jade.

'I'm sorry about what I said about the email messages you were getting,' Bullet said seriously. 'I never meant to make things worse.'

'I know that.' Jade managed a smile. 'It wasn't your fault. It was just a bit . . . I'll be all right. It'll take a while, but I'll be all right.'

Silence.

Theo tried to think of something to change the subject. 'Oh, are you going to get in touch with Pascoe DeMille then? He was hanging around the school earlier, probably looking for you.'

'That's not funny, Theo. In fact I think it was very cruel of all of you to play a trick on me like that,' said Jade.

Bewildered, Theo looked at his friends but from the expressions on their faces they were at as much of a loss as he was.

'You know what I'm talking about,' said Jade.

'I haven't a clue,' Theo denied.

'Pascoe DeMille,' Jade said impatiently. 'You know very well that years and years ago my dad tried acting for a while before he went into computing. That was before I was even born and a long time before we moved to our current house. His stage name was Pascoe DeMille. He used the same initials as in his real name.'

Paul Driscoll . . . Pascoe DeMille . . .

Theo stared at Jade in stunned silence. He wasn't the only one.

'Are you saying . . .' Angela's voice came out in a high-pitched squeak. She coughed and tried again. 'Are you saying that Pascoe DeMille is . . . was your *dad*?'

'Of course not,' Jade replied. She looked around the table. 'If you lot aren't having me on, then someone's playing a joke on *you*.'

'D'you have a photograph of your dad?' Ricky asked quietly.

Jade nodded. 'I've got lots of photos.'

'Can we see them?'

Jade dug into her bag and took out a tatty envelope. She emptied its contents over the table. Family photographs fanned out everywhere. There were photos of Jade's dad by himself, photos of Jade and her mum and dad on holiday, in the house, in the garden. Theo could understand Jade carrying around all those photos. In her shoes he would do the same. After a moment's hesitation, everyone reached out to pick up the photos for a closer look.

'I didn't get to see this Pascoe DeMille person.' Bullet looked at the photos with interest. 'Did he make himself up to look like Jade's dad then?'

Ricky, Angela and Theo looked at each other. Theo felt a chill trickle down his back then snake its icy way through the rest of his body.

'Jade, the man who spoke to us, the man who helped us – it was this guy.' Ricky pointed to the man in the photograph he was holding. 'There's no doubt about it. The man we met was a lot younger, but it was definitely this man.'

'It can't have been. That's my dad.' Jade frowned deeply.

'I know,' said Theo. 'It all makes sense. That's why he was helping us. We must've been talking to your dad's gh . . .'

'Theo,' Angela interrupted. 'Do me a favour and don't finish that sentence.'

'Wow!' Ricky breathed. 'It's just like when I was in Scotland with Mum and one morning, I was downstairs in the dining room and I saw . . .'

'Ricky,' Theo raised a hand. 'No more ghost stories. I think I've heard enough about ghosts to last me a lifetime.'

And for once, no one argued.

# LIE DETECTIVES

# Prologue

'Are we really going to go through with this?'

The night rain battered at the window as if trying to get through it. The woman sipped her mineral water, unable to disguise the way her hand was shaking. The ice in her drink clinked and clinked again against the sides of her glass. She could almost imagine it was beating out a coded message.

*Don't do it! Don't do it!*

She put the glass down with a bump, some of its contents sloshing out onto the coffee table. She stood up to close the curtains. They should've been closed ages ago. Even though this flat was on the second floor of the tallest building for streets around, she still felt nervous about the possibility of being watched. More often than not she closed the curtains before she even switched on the lights in the flat. She wasn't usually so careless. They had agreed that they couldn't take any chances. It wasn't like her. She turned around.

'Is there really no other way?' she whispered.

The man shook his head. 'You know there isn't. We don't have any choice. This latest invention of his is milking the company dry. If we don't stop him – and soon – the company will be worth about ten pence, if we're lucky. DemTech is just as much ours as it is his.'

'Couldn't we . . . fight him in court or something?'

'Darling, we've been through all this before. On paper DemTech belongs to him. In court we wouldn't have a leg to stand on. And d'you think I'd be suggesting we do this if there was any other way?' the man replied softly. 'He's taken over financial control of this project himself so I can't find out what it's really costing the company, but I know it's a lot more than he's stated publicly. We've both worked too long and too hard to let DemTech go down the drain now.'

The woman sighed her agreement but her expression was far from happy. She sat down next to the man on the settee. 'I'm scared. I think . . . I think he may know about us . . .'

The man raised a sceptical eyebrow.

'Don't look at me like that,' the woman argued. 'I'm telling you, he's on to us.'

'What makes you think that?'

'Over the last couple of days he's been making some very peculiar comments. Strange comments – about you and how hard you work and about me and how he wouldn't have got this far without me fighting at his side and in his corner. Stuff like that.'

'Maybe he means it.'

'Yeah, right!'

The man poured himself some mineral water from the bottle on the table. 'OK. What else?'

'Someone logged on to my computer earlier today and went through most of my files. That's why I wanted to see you tonight.'

The man sat bolt upright. 'Did they get . . . ?'

'Don't worry. I'm not that stupid. I removed all our stuff from my computer a couple of days ago.'

'And you reckon Darius was the one who logged on to your computer?'

'Who else would have access to it?'

The man wiped a hand over his forehead. 'We'll need to act fast then – just in case. He's going on some ridiculous school visit tomorrow which should prove the ideal time and place to . . . to get him out of the way.'

'Tomorrow?' the woman said, aghast. 'So soon?'

'Darling, look at us. Look at the way we live. Sneaking around corners and hiding like criminals when we've done nothing wrong. And it's all thanks to Darius Marriott. I can't even tell my family about you because of him. I'm sick and tired of living this way.'

'So am I, but this is so . . . so . . . *final*.' The woman took a deep breath to try and control herself. 'Once we've done this, there's no turning back.'

'I know. That's why I have to know that you're beside me on this. I have to know I can count on you.'

The woman bowed her head. Silent moments passed. When she looked up, her expression was no happier but it now held resolve. 'If there's no other way . . .'

The man smiled his relief. 'There isn't. We can't afford to hang about for much longer – not if he really does suspect something. I just need to know that the Lazarus suit will do what we want it to do.' The man continued to whisper even though they were quite alone.

'That part of it is fine. It's all been set up. We just need to make sure that one of us is close enough to set it off,' the woman replied.

They watched each other for several tense seconds.

'Are you sure there's no other way?' the woman asked again.

'I'm positive. We've got to get rid of him once and for all.'

'OK. I trust you, you know that.' The woman sighed.

'Darling, think of it. We can be together openly. We won't have to creep off to another city once a week just to be together.'

'I know. But I don't want anything to go wrong . . .'

'It won't. No one knows about us – no one. And by this time next week, Darius will be gone for good and you and I will own DemTech. And most important of all, we can be together openly, without all this sneaking around.'

'I wish I had your confidence.' The woman shook her head.

'Don't worry, I have enough confidence for both of us. This time tomorrow, Darius Marriott will be out of the picture – permanently.'

Chapter One

# Detecting Lies!

'Is that it then?' Theo whispered.

Bullet nodded.

'Does it work?'

'I don't know,' Bullet admitted. 'I only finished it late last night.'

Theo leaned in closer. Bullet held a rectangular gizmo about the size of a large calculator. It gave off a faint hissing sound like an untuned radio. It consisted of ten buttons numbered zero to nine, two small dials and an LCD screen which took up at least a third of the gadget. A small antenna stuck out of the top of the gizmo.

'What's that?' Angela, who sat on the other side of Bullet, pointed to the contraption in Bullet's hands.

'A lie detector,' Theo supplied before Bullet could open his mouth.

'What's it for?' asked Angela.

Bullet and Theo exchanged a look. 'Detecting lies?' Theo suggested.

Angela's face flamed as Theo and Bullet exchanged another wry look. 'Theo, there's no need to be quite so sarky.'

'Then don't ask stupid questions!' Theo grinned.

'It wasn't a stupid question . . .' Angela was beginning to raise her voice now.

'Shush, you two. Before you have all the teachers over here,' Bullet whispered.

Theo and Angela both sat back abruptly in their chairs. Theo had a quick glance around. Bullet was right. They were already getting a disapproving frown from Mr Cross – cross by name and cross by nature! Theo looked away, only to catch sight of Mrs Daltry scowling at them. Oops! Quickly, Theo looked up at the stage, wondering for how much longer this assembly was going to go on. They'd only been in the hall about ten minutes, which was nine minutes too long as far as Theo was concerned. Mrs Nash, the deputy head, was half-way through reading out the school announcements.

'What happens when your machine detects a lie?' Theo whispered out of the side of his mouth.

'It bleeps, unless I turn the sound off first. And it's got a built-in microtape recorder to record conversations and there's a recording chip in it which records the exact moment or moments in the conversation when lies were told,' Bullet explained. 'This lie detector can monitor a person up to ten metres away, it can record conversations of up to thirty minutes and it can indicate the sentences that are untrue.'

'Does it sweep the floor as well?' Theo raised a sceptical eyebrow.

'Does it work?' Angela couldn't help asking.

'As I said, it's not fully tested yet but there's no reason why it shouldn't.'

'And just how does it know when someone's lying or not?' Theo asked, after looking around to make sure none of the teachers could see them talking.

'When people lie, they change the way they speak without realizing they're doing it. Their words might become faster or slower, or higher or lower. Of course, the closer I am to the person being tested, the better it works and the more accurate the results. It's similar in principle to a voice stress analyser except my invention is much more sophisticated.'

Theo sniffed but said nothing. That was Bullet! As modest as ever!

'But once someone knows you're checking to see whether or not they're lying, they can change the way they tell their lies so that they fool your machine,' said Ricky, leaning across Theo.

'That's why it's better if the person I'm testing doesn't know they're being tested,' Bullet explained. 'It also uses Doppler radar techniques to detect and monitor body changes. Then this lie detector interprets all the data . . .'

'This is turning into a Heathrow job,' Theo sighed.

'Huh?'

'This is going over my head!' explained Theo. 'But it'll be interesting to see if it works.'

'Of course it works. *I* made it,' sniffed Bullet.

'So who are you hoping to catch out in a lie?' Angela asked.

'No one in particular. I'm just testing it. I thought I'd try it out on our new headmaster,' Bullet whispered back.

'Mr Unbar?' Angela said, surprised. 'What d'you reckon he's lying about?'

'He's a grown-up and a teacher. So he's bound to lie at least once every five minutes,' Bullet shrugged. He continued to fiddle with his gizmo.

'That's a bit cynical, isn't it?' Angela raised her eyebrows.

'After everything you've been through with your brother, I'd have thought you'd be the first to agree with me,' said Bullet.

Angela didn't answer. She turned away to stare straight ahead. Theo gave Bullet an angry look.

'What did you have for breakfast this morning? Tactless on toast?' said Theo.

Bullet looked at him, surprised. Then he turned to Angela. 'Sorry. I didn't mean that the way it came out.'

'Never mind. It doesn't matter,' Angela shrugged.

'Angela, are you OK?' Theo asked, concerned.

'Yes, I'm fine.'

Bullet looked down at his gizmo which was pointing in Angela's direction. A downward arrow flashed intermittently on it.

'What does that mean?' Theo pointed.

'Angela's lying,' Bullet whispered in Theo's ear. He turned

back to Angela. 'I really am sorry. Sometimes my mouth goes to work before my brain has had a chance to kick in.'

'OK,' Angela nodded. The faint trace of a smile on her face disappeared as swiftly as it had appeared.

Theo gave Angela one last look before turning back to the stage. Angela still didn't speak about her brother Tom much, even after all this time. Her brother was still in prison and Angela was the one who'd put him there. No wonder she couldn't bear to talk about him. Bullet should've known better.

'And now I have a wonderful surprise for all of you,' said Mr Unbar as he took over from Mrs Nash up on the stage.

'Yeah, right!' Theo muttered. What their new headmaster thought was a wonderful surprise and what Theo might think was a wonderful surprise were bound to be two different things. Theo didn't need Bullet's lie detector to spot that little fib.

'As part of our school's policy to have visits from prominent people in industry, we are very lucky to have Mr Darius Marriott here with us today,' the headmaster continued.

Bullet sat bolt upright and stared up at the stage as if he'd been stung. Well, maybe not stung – Bullet was allergic to wasp stings – but slapped at any rate. Theo frowned as he looked at Bullet. He'd never seen such a look of intense concentration and excitement on Bullet's face before – not even when Bullet had finally managed to get his program to solve crimes working.

'Darius Marriott, as I'm sure most of you already know, is the head of DemTech Industries. Over the last decade, his company has invented at least half of the new labour-saving devices we have in our homes today. DemTech are also leaders when it comes to medical, technological and military innovations.'

At the few murmurs of distinct disapproval floating around the hall, Mr Unbar continued hastily. 'And another division of his company invented the now classic game *Operation Blaster*.'

The murmurs of disapproval were now mixed with whispers of appreciation and anticipation. Theo gave a sniff of derision. Mr Unbar never used one word where fifteen would do. If he meant that DemTech invented loads of gadgets used in hospitals and by the army then why didn't he just come right out and say so.

'So let's give him a big welcome,' Mr Unbar smiled.

The hall erupted into spontaneous applause as a tall man wearing a white shirt and navy blue cords came on to the stage. Beneath his shirt but clearly visible, he wore a strange-looking black-grey waistcoat or vest with sleeves down to his elbows.

'Hello everyone,' Darius Marriott said with a smile. 'I'm here today because I'm hoping to convince all of you of how wonderful science is! I'm hoping that some of you will become scientists and maybe some of you will come and work for my company.'

Theo switched off. He didn't want to be a scientist. He wanted to be a famous detective, more famous than Sherlock Holmes and Hercule Poirot and Batman and Miss Marple put together. He'd be a private detective with swish offices somewhere in Central London and all the major cities around the world. He'd have a number of other private detectives working for him, but he'd be the best. He'd be so famous, he'd be on chat shows and in the papers and people would come to him to solve their most perplexing cases.

*Ladies and gentlemen, it gives me great pleasure to introduce as my next guest Sir Theo Mosley – the greatest detective of the 21st century. The greatest detective the world has ever seen!*

Theo drifted away, imagining the big house he'd buy and the plush offices he'd work from and all the money he'd have in his Swiss bank account until a sharp elbow in his ribs brought him back to reality. He glared at Ricky who grinned back at him.

'Now can anyone guess what I'm wearing under my shirt?' asked Darius Marriott, looking around the hall.

Darius proceeded to unbutton his shirt and take it off so that everyone could have a better look at the waistcoat underneath. Nervous giggles sprung up around the hall. The teachers gave each other dubious looks.

'Don't be shy!' Darius smiled. 'What am I wearing?'

Silence. Then a couple of hands were raised tentatively in the air. A few more hands went up. Darius pointed to Angela, who was one of the brave ones.

'Is it a bullet-proof vest?'

Theo wasn't the only one to burst out laughing. What a ridiculous answer! Trust Angela!

'You've been watching too many James Bond films!' Ricky leaned across Theo and Bullet to whisper to Angela.

'It might be,' Angela defended herself.

'Actually that's a very good guess,' said Darius, looking around. 'And this suit uses similar technology for some of its components.'

The laughter died down. Angela looked around with a vindicated, smug smile on her face.

'But it's not right,' Darius Marriott continued. 'How about you? What d'you think it is?'

'Is it for concealing things?'

'No.'

'Is it some kind of jet pack for flying above the traffic?'

'No. But I wish it was,' Darius Marriott smiled. 'What a good idea!'

'Is it an invisibility suit?'

Theo gave a snort of derision. He turned his head, craning his neck to see who had come up with that daft idea. The guesses were growing more and more bizarre! Bullet put up his hand.

Darius Marriott pointed at him. 'Yes?'

'Is it some kind of medical device?'

'What makes you say that?'

'It's the sleeves really,' said Bullet. 'They only go down to your elbows which makes me wonder if somehow they're for taking your blood pressure, 'cos they always take your blood pressure at about heart level.'

'Well done! When you leave university you must apply for a job at my company,' Darius Marriott smiled.

Theo gave Bullet a congratulatory dig in the ribs. Unfortunately, Angela chose that precise moment to do exactly the same thing. Bullet doubled over as if he'd been punched in the stomach.

'Are you OK?' Darius Marriott asked, concerned.

Bullet sat up, wincing as he breathed. 'Yeah, I'm fine.'

Theo caught sight of Mrs Daltry glowering at him and Angela. He sighed. He didn't have to be Einstein to know that the moment they were out of the hall, Mrs Daltry was going to have a rant.

'What I'm wearing is the result of a new project my company is working on called the Lazarus project. Lazarus was a man who, according to the Bible, was brought back to life by Jesus. We call this a Lazarus suit – even though really it's only a Lazarus waistcoat or jacket at best. But Lazarus suit sounds so much better, doesn't it?'

More than a few nods and smiles agreed with Darius.

'In fact some of you may have seen me talking about this Lazarus suit last week on the telly. Or perhaps some of you have seen articles about the Lazarus suit in the national papers? It was formally announced two weeks ago. And you'll have to forgive the poetic licence,' Darius continued. 'This device is well named because that's what the suit ultimately sets out to do. Another good name for it would be the suit of life. Our suit is designed to be worn by those who might need medical attention literally at a moment's notice. This Lazarus suit can take your blood pressure and monitor your heart rate. It can even administer medicines and some medical treatments. And what's more . . . what's . . .' Darius Marriott's voice slowed and trailed off altogether. His eyes became glassy and he began to sway backwards and forwards.

Mr Unbar, the headmaster, stood up slowly, a frown on his face. 'Mr Marriott, is everything all right?'

Darius Marriott tried for a smile and missed by several kilometres. 'I . . . I . . .' Then he suddenly lurched like a puppet being yanked off the ground before falling over on to his side. All the teachers sprang up at once and they weren't the only ones. Bullet leaped to his feet, his gizmo still hissing and crackling in his hand. Mr Unbar rushed over to Darius Marriott, who now lay still on the stage floor. Theo didn't know what to do, what to say. Was this a joke?

'Is this part of Mr Marriott's demonstration?' Angela whispered.

'I don't know,' Theo replied slowly. 'But I don't think so. I think this is real.'

Murmurs and anxious whispers broke out all over the hall. Mr Unbar put his fingers to Darius Marriott's neck, only to cry out and instantly draw his hand away. Clenching and unclenching his fingers, he looked up and down Darius's body. From where he was sitting, Theo could see Darius Marriott's body jerk suddenly then stop, then jerk again as if he was having a fit. Shaking his hand, Mr Unbar tentatively tried again. Unclipping Darius Marriott's Lazarus suit and pulling it off, the headmaster placed his ear to the prone man's chest. He sat up and tried to take Darius's pulse again, feeling both his neck and his wrist.

'Someone phone for an ambulance,' said Mr Unbar, his face grim. 'Quickly. This man is dying.'

## Chapter Two

# Shock

'D'you think he's OK?' Bullet's voice was barely a whisper.

Theo shrugged. They all watched out of the classroom windows as Darius Marriott was carried away on a stretcher by two paramedics. The school gates were quite a distance from the classrooms and even further away from the assembly hall. A good width of a football pitch away at least. Theo didn't envy them, having to carry Darius Marriott all that way. As for Theo and everyone else in the hall, they'd all been bundled out of the assembly hall so quickly, Theo's head was still swimming. So much for his first thought that maybe this was some kind of joke.

'Not a very good advertisement for his own suit, is he?' said Angela.

'What's that supposed to mean?' Bullet rounded on her at once, his eyes blazing.

Theo exchanged a sigh with Ricky, then shook his head. Angela had all the subtlety of a charging rhino! Bullet and Angela made a good pair.

'I just meant . . .'

'Yes . . . ?'

'I just meant that if he's had a heart attack then maybe his suit should have . . . I don't know . . . saved him somehow,' Angela tried to explain.

'How d'you know that his Lazarus suit didn't save him?' Bullet fumed. 'How d'you know that he wouldn't be dead now if it wasn't for his Lazarus suit?'

'I was only saying, Bullet. Don't bite my head off,' Angela replied.

'Don't open your mouth and talk rubbish then,' Bullet said in no uncertain terms.

Theo watched as Angela's face went as stiff as a board.

'Calm down, Bullet,' Ricky soothed. 'Angela didn't mean anything by it.'

'I'm going to see if I can visit my . . . visit Darius Marriott in hospital,' Bullet announced.

'What on earth for?' asked Theo.

'To make sure he's all right,' Bullet replied, with angry defiance. 'Darius Marriott has been my hero for I don't know how long. I want to make sure he's OK.'

'Why don't you just send him a card or something?'

'No, I want to see him. I can't wait any more. I have to tell him . . .'

Angela, Ricky and Theo waited expectantly for Bullet to finish his sentence.

'Tell him what?' Ricky prompted.

'It doesn't matter.'

'Bleep! That's a lie for a start,' Theo said drily.

'Come on, Bullet,' Ricky urged. 'If you can't tell us, who can you tell?'

Bullet took a deep breath. He looked around uncertainly, blinking rapidly the way he always did when he was trying to make up his mind. 'It's just that . . . Never mind. You wouldn't believe me if I told you.'

'Try us,' said Ricky.

'It's just that . . . that's my dad they're taking to hospital,' whispered Bullet.

Theo's jaw hit the floor. It was a toss up as to whose eyes were the widest open. Angela, Ricky and Theo looked at each other, then quickly back at Bullet as if they couldn't bear or didn't dare to let him out of their sight.

'Come again?' said Theo.

'Darius Marriott is my father,' Bullet said, his voice firmer this time.

'Since when?' asked Theo.

'What d'you mean "since when"? That's a funny question. He's been my dad all my life,' Bullet said, a hint of impatience in his voice.

'Glad to see I'm not the only one who can ask stupid questions,' Angela sniffed.

'No, I meant . . .' Theo shut up. He wasn't quite sure what he meant. He was in shock – complete, total and absolute!

'So will you help me see him?' Bullet asked.

'Hang on!' Ricky frowned. 'When you answered his question in the assembly hall, Darius Marriott didn't seem to treat you any different to anyone else. He didn't *act* like you were his son.'

'That's 'cos he doesn't *know* that I'm his son,' said Bullet.

'Whoa! Whoa! You're doing another Heathrow job on me.' Theo shook his head. 'He's your dad and he doesn't *know* it?'

'That's right. He and my mum broke up before I was born,' Bullet explained. 'They used to work for a software house and Darius was my mum's boss.'

'Your mum was married to Darius Marriott?' asked Theo.

'No. They used to go out together. Mum was his secretary years and years ago. Then Mum became pregnant with me and she left the company,' said Bullet.

'Why?' asked Angela.

'She didn't want him to feel that he had to marry her just 'cos she was having me,' Bullet replied.

'Did she tell him he was going to be a father?' asked Angela.

'No. I just said that.'

'And your mum told you all this?' Ricky's frown was deepening.

'Not in so many words, but yes.'

'What does that mean – not in so many words?' asked Ricky.

'Mum told me about it. She didn't actually come right out and say that Darius Marriott is my father but I put two and two together.'

'Are you sure you didn't put two and two together and come up with seventeen and three-quarters?' asked Ricky.

'I'm telling you, Darius Marriott is my dad. We even look alike,' Bullet insisted.

Theo had always reckoned that Bullet was the spitting image of his mum but now that he'd seen Darius Marriott up close, he and Bullet did look a little bit alike. A teensy-tiny little bit.

'Are you saying that in all these years he's never been to see you? Not once?' asked Ricky.

'No, he hasn't. But how could he? He didn't know about me. Mum never told him.' Bullet shrugged. 'But that doesn't matter. Because I'm going to visit him in the hospital and I'll tell him who I am and then we'll be like a real family.'

Theo shifted position uncomfortably. Did Bullet really think it would be that simple? Did he really believe that all he had to do was go up to Darius Marriott, say, 'Hi Dad, I'm your son!' and Darius would hold out his arms, cry out, 'My son! The child I never knew I had!' and that would be that? Chewing on his bottom lip, Theo wondered if maybe he was being too cynical. Maybe he'd been around Angela for too long. Maybe Darius Marriott would welcome Bullet with wide open arms.

'I think you should take this one step at a time,' Ricky said carefully. 'Are you sure you've got the whole, full story from your mum?'

'Of course,' Bullet frowned. 'As I said, she told me some things and I worked out the rest.'

'But are you sure you're right?' asked Ricky.

'What're you trying to say?' Bullet suddenly went very still.

Ricky backed off immediately. 'Nothing. I just think you should be very careful of your facts, that's all.'

'I am. I wouldn't have told you that Darius Marriott was my father unless I was absolutely sure.' Bullet's voice was frosty.

'You've seen it on your birth certificate?' asked Angela.

'Mum says she's lost it.'

'Why don't you send off for a copy, then?' Angela suggested.

Bullet stared at her. 'I never thought of that.'

'When are you hoping to visit your dad then?' asked Ricky.

'If not tonight, then definitely tomorrow. It's Saturday tomorrow so Mum shouldn't mind.'

'Are you going to tell her what you're up to?' asked Angela.

'No. I'll visit my dad first and make sure everything is all right and then I'll tell her,' Bullet replied.

'Wait till tomorrow afternoon and then we'll all come with you,' Ricky stated.

Bullet wasn't the only one who was surprised. Theo stared, then glared at Ricky. Weren't they supposed to be going to the cinema tomorrow afternoon?

'You want to come with me?' Bullet couldn't believe it.

'If that's OK? We won't get in the way – honest.'

Bullet shrugged. 'If you want to come along, that's fine.'

'Am I coming too?' Angela asked, puzzled.

'Of course,' Ricky replied before Bullet had a chance.

Theo forced the frown from his face. Ricky was up to something. That much was obvious. But what? Why was it suddenly so all-fired important that they go with Bullet when he visited his dad?

'OK. I'll try and find out from one of the teachers which hospital my dad's been taken to,' said Bullet.

'And if you can't?' Theo couldn't help asking.

'Then I'll phone around tonight when I get home. I'll phone every hospital in the country if I have to,' Bullet replied. 'Once I find out, I'll give you a call and you three can meet me outside the appropriate hospital tomorrow afternoon at two.'

'That's fine.'

Their attention was called back to the window as the ambulance sped away from the school. A number of teachers stood by the school gate, talking to Mr Unbar. Soon, they turned and headed back into the school. Theo walked back to his desk with everyone else. He didn't want to be caught gawking by Mrs Daltry. Theo searched in his bag for his workbook. Then he remembered that he'd left it on Mrs Daltry's table the night before. With a sigh of impatience, he got up and went to the front of the class. Yes, he was right. There it was. Theo picked it up and turned to head back to his desk. He saw that Bullet was the only one still standing at the window. And the look on Bullet's face stopped Theo cold in his tracks. No one else could see Bullet's face, only Theo – and Theo wished at once that he hadn't.

Never before had Theo seen such a look of complete and utter longing. In fact, the look on Bullet's face went far beyond longing. It was yearning and loneliness. And intense, white-hot hope. And it was directed not at anyone in the class but out of the room and out of the school. It was for the man being rushed to hospital in the ambulance. Theo felt as if he had just spied on something very personal. He just hoped that Bullet wouldn't be too disappointed if things didn't go the way he was obviously imagining they would.

## Chapter Three

# Visiting Hours

Theo stood outside the main entrance to the local hospital, wondering for the umpteenth and three-quarters time what on earth he was doing there. It was a warm, clear, early spring afternoon. The wind wasn't nearly as biting as it had been at the beginning of the month. In fact there was a pleasant breeze blowing. And where was Theo spending the rest of his day? Stuck in a hospital, that's where! This was a wild goose chase and no mistake. And what's more, it was embarrassing. Of course Darius Marriott wasn't Bullet's dad. The whole idea was just . . . silly! It was a crazy idea, mixed with more than a little wishful thinking. So what if Bullet's mum had worked for Darius Marriott years and years ago? They might even have been an item for a while. But that didn't make Darius Marriott Bullet's father. At the tap on his shoulder, Theo spun around. Angela and Ricky stood behind him.

'Where's Bullet?' asked Angela.

'At home, if he's got any sense,' Theo sniffed, adding for good measure, 'Which is where we should be.'

'Why d'you say that?' asked Ricky.

Theo looked at him, surprised. 'Isn't it obvious? This is just a waste of time.'

'Darius Marriott might be Bullet's dad. Stranger things have happened,' Ricky said lightly.

'D'you really believe that?' Theo stared.

'What? That stranger things have happened?'

'No. That Bullet's story is true,' Theo said with impatience.

'I don't know. But . . .'

'But Bullet believes it's true and for now you're prepared to go along with that.' Theo sighed. 'This is just like you, Ricky. When Jade said her dead dad was sending her e-mail messages you believed her, too.'

'No, I believed that she believed it. And I didn't think it was impossible,' Ricky contradicted. 'If I remember rightly, it was you two who said that it was a trick or Jade was lying or misguided. But what about Pascoe DeMille?'

'Never mind about who or what Pascoe was,' Theo interrupted. No way was he going to speculate about Pascoe DeMille again. It gave him the creeps just to think about the guy. 'We're talking about Bullet and his dad. What're we going to do?'

'We're Bullet's friends so we're going to be here to help him if and when he needs us,' said Ricky.

'We're nuts to get involved in the first place,' Theo said.

'For once, I agree with Theo.' Angela stuck in her five pence worth. 'This has nothing to do with us. This is between Bullet and his so-called dad.'

'Hi, everyone.' Bullet's voice behind them had everyone turning around guiltily. Chewing his bottom lip, Theo wondered just how much of their conversation Bullet had heard. Bullet looked cool and collected, far calmer than the rest of them. But Theo wondered just how calm Bullet really felt inside. After all if Darius Marriott *was* Bullet's father, then this would be the first time Bullet spoke to him. Bullet would introduce himself as Darius Marriott's son and after that anything could happen.

'Let's go in,' Bullet said.

'Is Darius Marriott definitely in this hospital?' asked Angela.

Bullet nodded. 'He's in the Wellington Ward on the third floor.' At Ricky's questioning look he added, 'I phoned last night and again this morning just to make sure. My . . . my dad's only going to be at this hospital until eight o'clock tonight. After that they're moving him to a private hospital across town and then I won't get a chance to see him. So it's now or never.'

'How d'you know all this?' Angela queried.

'I told you. I phoned and asked.'

'But why would they tell you?' Angela persisted. 'I thought that sort of information was confidential.'

'Not to family members and I'm his son,' Bullet replied.

Was it Theo's imagination or was there something in Bullet's tone of voice which challenged them to contradict him?

'So what's wrong with him, then?' asked Angela.

Theo had wanted to know that too, but he wasn't sure how to frame the question. He might've guessed that Angela would come right out and ask.

'They think he might have had a heart attack but he's out of intensive care already and they reckon he'll make a full recovery,' said Bullet.

'Does your mum know you're here?' Angela narrowed her eyes.

Theo shook his head. Angela got worse, she really did. Bullet glared at her. He just stared, not answering her question.

'Only asking,' Angela defended herself.

Theo wondered about Angela and Bullet. At one point Angela had been mad keen on Bullet. But if she was still keen on Bullet and he was keen on her, then they had a very strange way of showing it.

'Well, we can't stay out here all day. Let's go in,' Ricky said at last.

They trooped into the hospital in silence with Bullet leading the way, followed by Ricky and Angela. Theo hung behind the others. He was worried. Worried sick. He and Bullet hadn't been friends very long but they were friends now and Theo didn't want to see Bullet . . . disappointed. And this whole business had DISAPPOINTMENT written over it in great big flashing capitals!

'How do we get to Wellington Ward, please?' Bullet asked the receptionist.

'Along there, turn left, take the lift up to the third floor and then along to the end of the corridor,' the man behind the reception desk answered. He pointed the way, indicating the directions with his hand without once looking at them.

'Thanks,' Bullet mumbled.

Without another word they all followed the receptionist's instructions. Apart from their trainers squeaking on the polished floor, no other sound from the group could be heard. As they entered the lift, Theo thought, 'If someone doesn't say something soon I'm going to . . . I'm going to . . . laugh or shout or bark at the top of my voice. Anything to break this silence!'

They stepped out of the lift and the strange quiet that surrounded them stepped out with them. In the distance the hospital sounds carried on as normal, but Bullet and the others walked in their own bubble of quiet concern. The corridor stretched out before them, with signs hanging down from the ceiling at regular intervals and doors and stairs leading off on both sides. They were all the way down the corridor before anyone spoke.

'Bullet, when you go in to see your dad, we'll wait outside,' Ricky suggested.

'Can't we go in with him?' Angela asked, surprised.

'No, we can't,' Ricky replied, getting annoyed for once. 'What Bullet and his dad have to say to each other is their own private business and nothing to do with us.'

Angela flushed red at Ricky's rebuke but before she could answer, they'd reached the double doors which led to Wellington Ward. Bullet took a deep breath and pushed at the doors. A huge ward spread out before them but only the patients in the first bay were visible. Immediately to their right was the ward office. Bullet marched straight up to the office and tapped smartly at the door even though it was open.

'Yes? Can I help you?' The sister in the room looked up from the report she was reading.

'I'm looking for Darius Marriott.'

The sister turned to glance up at the clock on the wall behind her. She frowned. 'Visiting hours don't start for another ten minutes.'

'We don't mind waiting,' Bullet said.

Theo couldn't understand how Bullet could be so calm. He was a nervous wreck and it wasn't even his dad.

'And you are?' The sister looked at Bullet pointedly.

'My name is Toby. Darius Marriott's my dad.'

The sister glanced up at the clock again. 'Oh. Well, I suppose I can make an exception just this once. But I mean just this once – d'you understand?'

'Yes, sister.' Bullet grinned gratefully. 'So which bed is he in?'

'Bed number fifteen. He's in a side room straight up the corridor and to your right.' The sister bent her head to continue reading her report.

'Thanks.' Bullet was already on his way when he spoke. Theo walked faster to catch up with Angela and Ricky. He risked a glance in their direction. It was hard to tell what they were thinking. Maybe it was just him. Maybe he was being unnecessarily anxious about what was about to happen.

All too soon they reached a door with the number fifteen on it. Bullet turned to look at them all, took a deep, deep breath and then pushed open the door. Darius Marriott was reading a newspaper. The doctor, a tall man as skinny as clock hands at six o'clock with a very tidy moustache and dark brown hair swept back off his face, stood over Darius. He held a hypodermic syringe in one hand and in his other he held the intravenous drip line which ran into a vein in Darius Marriott's left arm. Both Darius and the doctor turned their heads at Bullet's entrance. Bullet hovered uncertainly at the door. Darius Marriott had a query on his face – nothing more. The doctor frowned, let go of the drip and slowly replaced the plastic protective cap back on the hypodermic needle. Bullet stepped into the room, still holding the door open.

'Yes? Can I help you?' asked the doctor, placing the syringe on the cabinet next to the bed.

Bullet couldn't tear his gaze away from the man in the bed. Theo's heart felt like food processor whisks on the fast setting. He couldn't have been more nervous, more apprehensive, if he was the one about to talk to his father for the first time.

'Can I help you?' The doctor repeated impatiently. He took hold of Darius's hand and slid his fingers up to his wrist to take his patient's pulse as he spoke.

'I . . . I've come to see my dad.' Bullet could hardly get the words out.

'You've got the wrong room,' Darius Marriott said tersely. 'There's no one else here. I don't share this room with anyone.'

'No . . . you d-don't understand . . .' Bullet stammered.

'I'll just take your blood pressure, Mr Marriott, and then I'll go,' said the doctor. He picked up the sphygmomanometer or blood pressure machine on the table beside the patient and placed it on the bed.

'What don't I understand?' Darius Marriott asked Bullet, as the doctor unrolled the blood pressure cuff and wrapped it around his forearm.

'Mr Marriott, I'm . . . I'm Toby Barker. You're my dad.'

'You're . . . you're not a doctor. Who are you?' Ricky's voice held fear and belligerence. '*Who are you*? What are you doing to Bullet's dad?'

Stunned, Theo turned from Ricky to the doctor. If he hadn't seen it for himself, he never would've believed it. The expression on the so-called doctor's face changed in the blink of an eye. He let go of Darius's arm and snatched up the syringe again. Bullet leaped forward as the doctor pulled the plastic cap off the needle and lunged for Darius Marriott. But Bullet was on him in an instant, knocking the syringe out of his hand. It flew across the room and hit the wall.

The bogus doctor lashed out, knocking Bullet off his feet.

He snarled out a curse and leaped for the door. Theo ran over to Bullet, who lay collapsed on the floor. Ricky and Angela barred the doctor's exit. They dodged and darted around him, two terriers yapping at a giant's heels.

'Get out of my way,' the man raged.

Angela and Ricky didn't answer. Nor did they take their eyes off the man. The man roared his frustration. His eyes sparked so much they could've lit matches. His hands lashed out and thrashed about as he tried to grab hold of Angela and Ricky to yank them out of his way. But they always managed just to evade his hands. With a leap, the man grabbed hold of Angela's arm but she twisted like a striking cobra and was immediately out of his grasp. Suddenly, the man charged headfirst for the door, like some kind of demented bull. Angela and Ricky jumped out of his way – only just in time. The door banged open and the man raced down the corridor in an instant.

'Stop him. Someone stop him,' Angela yelled.

But she was too late. As the sister stepped out of her office to find out what all the commotion was about, the exit doors were already swinging shut.

'Stop him! Call the police.' Angela was jumping up and down and screaming at the same time.

'Bullet? Bullet, are you OK?' Theo asked urgently.

Bullet rubbed his head as he sat up slowly. 'Yeah, I'm fine. He just took me by surprise, that's all.'

'Are you sure you're all right? You're not hurt?'

Bullet got to his feet. 'I'm fine, I promise. But what about my dad?'

## Chapter Four

# A Mistake

Doctor Nolan, a nurse, a woman wearing a business suit and two police officers – one in plain clothes, the other in uniform – were all crowded into Darius Marriott's room. Theo, Bullet and the others were wedged against the wall watching what was going on. Darius Marriott looked like death on a bad day. One moment he stared straight ahead profoundly shocked, the next moment he blinked like a stunned owl, the next moment his lips pursed and his eyes narrowed with fury. He didn't know what to think – or feel.

'How are you feeling now, Mr Marriott, sir?' asked the woman. She'd introduced herself as Mrs Tracer, an executive manager at the hospital. Theo wondered why she didn't wet her lips and kiss Darius Marriott's feet while she was at it. How grovelly could one woman get?

'I'm feeling fine – thanks to that boy over there.' Darius Marriott looked directly at Bullet but there was no trace of a smile on his face. Bullet's head dropped, he could no longer meet his father's gaze.

Was that all the man had to say? 'Thanks to that boy over there'? Theo shook his head. If he was in Darius Marriott's place, how would he feel? To be confronted with a son he'd never seen, a son he never even knew existed, and a threat to his life in the same five minutes – that would be enough to knock anyone for six. But Theo thought he would have had more to say to Bullet than his dad seemed to.

'Mr Marriott, we're going to get the substance in this hypodermic syringe analysed at once,' said Detective Sergeant Reid, the CID policewoman in plain clothes. 'And we'll get to work on circulating your initial statements and your descriptions of the phoney doctor.'

'Just what was it that made you suspect the so-called doctor in the first place?' the uniformed officer asked.

They all turned to look at Ricky. Theo had been wondering the same thing himself but in all the confusion and commotion he hadn't had the chance to ask.

'Well, first of all he was trying to take Mr Marriott's pulse on the little finger side of his wrist when everyone knows you take a pulse from the thumb side of your wrist. And then, when he tried to take Mr Marriott's blood pressure, he put the cuff around Mr Marriott's forearm instead of his upper arm,' explained Ricky.

'It was very observant of you to notice. Well done!' said DS Reid.

'This is bizarre. Why would anyone want to harm me?' Darius Marriott shook his head.

'People in your position rarely get where they are without making enemies,' said DS Reid. 'It could be some crackpot out to make a name for himself by harming you but I'm betting the motive is a tad more personal or mercenary.'

'What d'you mean?'

'Well sir, to put it bluntly, who stands to gain by your death?'

Theo wondered at the bewildered look on Darius Marriott's face. It was as if he had never even considered the question. Moments passed and still Darius stared, too aghast to utter a word. They weren't DS Reid and Darius Marriott any more – they were Medusa and her victim!

'That's enough, officer,' said Dr Nolan. 'I won't have Mr Marriott any more upset than he already is.'

Darius raised a hand. 'It's all right, doctor. I want that fake doctor found just as much as the police do, more so in fact. If someone's trying to kill me I want them found.'

'So who has a motive to get rid of you?' asked DS Reid.

'No one as far as I know. When I die, some of my money

will go to various charities and some members of my staff, but the bulk of my fortune goes to the co-directors of DemTech and to my wife, Samantha.'

'And where is your wife now, sir?'

'She's in New York visiting Daryl Matthewson, an old friend of hers,' Darius answered.

DS Reid made a note of the New York address and phone number in her notebook. 'Has your wife been informed that you're in hospital?'

'I'm not sure.' Darius frowned. 'My Personal Assistant Jo Fleming was here last night and again this morning. She said she's been trying to get in touch with Samantha but she's had no success.'

'How long has your wife been in New York, sir?' asked the sergeant.

That's just the question I would've asked, Theo thought to himself – pleased that he was thinking along the same lines as the CID woman.

'Almost a week now.'

'Does she often go abroad by herself?'

'Sometimes. It isn't always possible for us to go on holiday together. I have a very busy schedule.' Darius Marriott shrugged.

He didn't look terribly bothered by that fact either. Theo couldn't imagine his mum and dad ever taking separate holidays. The thought would never occur to them. Theo regarded Darius Marriott. He took a long, hard look. And in that moment, Theo decided that he didn't like Darius Marriott very much. Correction! He didn't like him at all. There was something about him . . .

'Look! I really must insist that everyone leaves at once.' Dr Nolan put her foot down. 'Whilst Mr Marriott is in this hospital he's my responsibility. He may already have had a mild heart attack and I'm not prepared to let my patient take any more chances.'

'OK, doctor. OK.' DS Reid turned to the patient. 'I've got

your address and your preliminary statement but later on I'll need to ask you a few more questions,' she said.

'You have my card. Just make an appointment with my PA and I'll make myself available,' said Darius.

Reluctantly the police, the nurse and the hospital official all left the room. Theo and the others stayed where they were. As far as Theo was concerned, he wasn't leaving until someone came right out and told him to leave. He wanted to know what was going on, more for Bullet's sake than his own, but even so! The doctor frowned in Theo's direction. Theo glanced at Bullet, Angela and Ricky. From the determined looks on their faces, they weren't about to volunteer to leave either. But just as the doctor opened her mouth to evict them, Darius said a surprising thing.

'It's OK, Doctor, I'd like them to stay.'

The doctor looked like she wanted to argue, but in the end she decided against it.

'Doctor, I thought you'd ruled out the possibility of a heart attack,' Darius Marriott continued, before the doctor could change her mind.

'We're still trying to work out exactly what happened. At first we thought you'd had a heart attack but your ECG readings were normal and your blood test results all came back normal as well. You have no previous history of heart attacks and no heart attack symptoms so we're at a bit of a loss to explain what happened.'

'Er . . . maybe there's something you should know. I wasn't going to say anything but maybe it will help you to pin down the reason why I collapsed. And I didn't like to say in front of the police and the others,' Darius said. 'Just before I . . . I keeled over, something happened with my suit.'

'What suit?'

'My Lazarus suit,' Darius Marriott provided. 'It's a Lazarus waistcoat or jacket actually but that doesn't sound as good! It's been designed as a first stop medical defence system. It's meant to be worn by anyone who may need medical assistance in a hurry. It can monitor your blood pressure and pulse rate and, based on your past medical history, it can administer any necessary drugs using a hypodermic needle system. It's going to make my company a fortune.'

'Never mind the advertisement! What suit are you talking about? Hold on. Is it that dark grey waistcoat thing you were wearing when you collapsed?'

Darius nodded.

'What has this suit got to do with your heart attack?' Dr Nolan frowned.

'I felt the suit give me an electric shock just before I hit the ground,' Darius replied.

'An electric shock? Where?'

'Over my chest.'

'But it was the shock that probably stopped your heart,' the doctor stared. 'Don't you realise that defibrillating a healthy heart can stop it?'

'De-what?' Theo couldn't help asking.

'Defibrillating,' Ricky provided. 'If your heart has stopped or it's not beating properly, they sometimes give you an electric shock over your chest to get your heart to contract then start beating properly again.'

'Mr Marriott, why would your suit defibrillate your heart in the first place?' Dr Nolan asked.

'I don't know. And that's what worries me. The Lazarus suit has so many fail-safes built into it that it should never do that unless there is no other choice. The suit would never, *ever* enter defibrillation mode unless it registered that the wearer's heart had stopped beating.'

'Why didn't you tell one of us this information before now?'

'Because I can't afford any adverse publicity for my project. The Lazarus suit is too important to me.'

'I'd say your Lazarus suit contains a few bugs that need to be sorted out before anyone else wears it.' Dr Nolan couldn't keep the anger out of her voice. 'Do you realize you could've been killed? Whose stupid idea was this device of yours?'

'Mine actually.' A trace of a smile flickered across Darius's face.

Dr Nolan didn't look the slightest bit embarrassed. 'Well, you've done better, Mr Marriott. You've done much better.'

'I've been thinking about this and the only thing I can think of is that the suit somehow malfunctioned or was tripped remotely. I was wondering if maybe, with all the gadgetry in the school hall, my invention was somehow given a false signal or a signal that confused it. If that was the case, it might've thought my heartbeat had become dangerously irregular, or had stopped altogether,' Darius said, more to himself than to anyone else.

'What kind of false signal?' asked Dr Nolan. 'I thought this suit of yours had all its components in the one place?'

'Yes, but it can be set up so that someone with the proper equipment can monitor your vital signs from a remote computer. The range is limited but it still works. That computer then communicates with the Lazarus suit using radio waves. If my suit somehow picked up radio waves from another source, that might've triggered the malfunction.'

Every bone in Theo's body turned to mush. It felt like there were a thousand spotlights all trained on him, burning into his skin, making his blood boil in furious panic. Horrified, he turned to Bullet. He couldn't help it. Ricky and Angela were doing the same thing and Theo knew that their expressions mirrored his own. Bullet's lie detector . . . Was Bullet's lie detector responsible for almost killing his dad?

Theo took one look at the horror-stricken expression on Bullet's face and immediately looked away again.

'What's the matter?' Darius Marriott wasn't slow to pick up on the atmosphere very apparent in the room.

'I . . .' Bullet looked around, then turned back to Darius. 'I invented a lie detector and I was trying it out in the assembly hall yesterday morning.'

'A lie detector? So?'

'So it uses radio waves . . .' Bullet's voice was little more than a murmur, but in the stunned silence of the room it was loud enough.

'You mean *you're* responsible for my suit almost killing me?' Darius straightened up, his expression thunderous.

'It was a mistake. I didn't mean it. I didn't know,' Bullet pleaded.

'You tried to *kill* me.' Darius Marriott was incredulous. 'You stupid idiot! I ought to call the police back here to arrest you on the spot.' Darius looked like he was about to leap out of the bed and throttle Bullet.

'I'm sorry . . .'

'Sorry? Sorry doesn't cut it. You shouldn't mess about with things you know absolutely nothing about. And then you have the nerve to tell me that cock-and-bull story about being my son. I should have you arrested for that, as well.'

'Now wait just one minute,' Ricky exploded.

'No, Ricky.' Bullet shook his head.

'I'm not going to stand here and let him talk to one of my friends like that.' Ricky refused to be quiet. 'You've got a short memory, mister. All of us, including Bullet, just saved your life – or have you forgotten that? Someone was in here with a syringe and they were obviously out to get you. It was probably that same person who somehow tried to fiddle about with your Lazarus suit by remote control. You've got no right to blame Bullet when you have no proof that he had anything to do with it. What kind of father are you?'

'I'm not any kind of father,' Darius snorted derisively. 'That's why I wanted all of you to stay behind. I won't have that boy or any of you going around spreading lies about me. I don't know what kind of game you four think you're playing but I want to nip this in the bud before it goes any further.'

'What're you talking about?' Angela scowled.

'You four have obviously cooked up this little scheme between you to get money from me or something. Let me tell you right now it's not going to work.'

If Theo's mouth dropped open any further, cars would soon be driving through it! He couldn't believe his ears. Did Darius Marriott really think that they were out to extort money from him? One look at the grown-up's face and Theo had his answer.

'You must be seriously nuts!' Ricky fumed. 'We wouldn't take a thing from you if we were starving hungry and you were giving away free doughnuts. We're here 'cos Bullet, I mean, Toby, told us you were his dad and we're his friends so we wanted to lend him moral support.'

'If Toby or whatever his name is told you that, then he's lying.'

'No, I'm not. My mum is Teresa Barker. She used to be your secretary and you two used to go out together. Mum told me so.'

'Teresa Barker . . .' Now it was Darius's turn to look dumbfounded. 'Tessa is your *mother*?'

Bullet nodded. 'Only her close friends call her Tessa. Everyone else calls her Teresa.'

'And she told you that I was your father?'

Bullet nodded again.

Darius shook his head slowly, never taking his eyes off Bullet. 'You're not my son,' he said at last. 'Either your mother or you is mistaken – or lying.'

'Why would Mum lie about it?'

'I don't know. Maybe she's the one after my money, and she sent you to do her dirty work for her.'

Bullet took a step forward, his fists clenched. 'You take that back.'

'I didn't mean that the way it sounded,' Darius said impatiently.

Theo snorted under his breath. Darius had meant it *exactly* the way it had come out. A tense silence reigned.

'Bullet, maybe we should wait for you outside?' Ricky suggested uneasily.

Bullet immediately shook his head. 'No, you're my friends. I'd like you to stay.' He turned back to Darius. 'Besides, I knew he'd deny it. That's why my mum left him when she found out she was pregnant with me. She knew he'd do his best to find a way to wriggle out of it. That's just the type of man he is.'

'Now wait just a minute. Did your mother tell you that?'

'No. You just did,' Bullet replied bitterly.

A strangely stricken look swept over Darius's face. Theo just wanted to get out of there. He'd never felt so in the way, so horribly intrusive, in his entire life.

'Look, you don't understand,' Darius began.

'Oh, yes I do. I understand perfectly,' said Bullet. 'I'll be going now. I think I've wasted enough of your time.'

Bullet turned and walked out of the door, leaving Theo and the others with no choice but to follow him.

## Chapter Five

# If We Hadn't Turned Up

'What a slime bag!' Angela voiced her opinion the moment the door to the side room had shut behind them. 'Bullet, you're better off without him.'

'Angela, not now,' Ricky said impatiently.

'But he is.'

'Angela. Shut up,' Ricky hissed.

'Excuse me.' Bullet walked down the ward without another word.

'Angela, for goodness' sake! How would you feel if you were Bullet? Just remember what it was like when it was you and your brother in trouble,' Ricky rounded on her.

'I didn't mean . . .'

'You never *mean* to say these things, but you do!' said Ricky.

Angela looked down the ward to where Bullet was walking away from them without a backward glance. 'Toby, hang on. Wait!' Angela pelted down the ward after him.

'You were a bit hard on her,' Theo said to Ricky. 'She means well.'

'Angela has to learn to think before she opens her mouth,' Ricky said, not a hint of an apology in his voice. 'It was bad enough for Bullet to have to listen to that man who's supposed to be his father without Angela making things worse.'

They started walking down the ward.

'Ricky, what's the matter with you?' Theo asked curiously. 'It's not like you to be so . . . so impatient and judgmental. What's wrong?'

Ricky sighed. He looked towards the closed side room door. 'I guess Darius Marriott just got to me, that's all.'

'Why?' Theo asked.

'If you must know, I think . . . I think I . . . envy Bullet. At least his dad is here for him to find and be with. My dad's in another country and isn't the slightest bit interested in me. I guess that's why Darius Marriott got to me. He shouldn't . . .' Ricky got no further.

At that moment the side room door opened and Doctor Nolan stepped out. She called down the ward to Ricky and Theo. 'Could you come back please? Mr Marriott would like to see you. Where're the other two?'

Theo looked down the ward corridor but Angela and Bullet were nowhere to be seen. 'They've gone.'

'Then you two had better step in. But you're not to upset Mr Marriott, d'you understand?' said the doctor.

'That works the other way round as well,' Ricky muttered.

Theo didn't want to see Darius Marriott again. He'd had enough of that man to last him a lifetime and beyond. He looked at Ricky. If Ricky refused to go in, then so would he – but nothing doing. Ricky walked into the room. Theo had no choice but to follow.

'You wanted to see us.' Ricky's tone was clipped.

'Where's . . . Toby?' Darius asked.

'Your son has gone,' Ricky said deliberately. 'I guess he didn't want to stay where he wasn't wanted.'

Darius regarded Ricky. Ricky returned his gaze without flinching.

'Do you know Toby's address?' asked Darius.

'Yeah,' said Ricky.

Silence.

'Could you possibly give it to me?'

'Why?' Ricky said bluntly.

'Ricky!' Theo's voice held a warning.

'It's a perfectly reasonable question.' Ricky turned back to Darius. 'Why?'

'I think I may have been a bit . . . hasty. I want to sit down with Tessa and Toby and talk about this . . . situation,' Darius replied.

Ricky scrutinized Darius as long moments passed.

'Have you got a piece of paper and a pen?' Ricky asked at last.

Darius removed a notepad and a fancy fountain pen from his bedside cabinet. He held them out to Ricky. After a moment's hesitation, Ricky moved forward to take them. Writing quickly, Ricky soon handed the pen and pad back to Darius who immediately looked down at the pad to see what Ricky had written.

'I know where that is,' Darius nodded.

'Mr Marriott, if you don't mind me asking, who d'you think that bogus doctor was?' Theo couldn't help asking.

'I have no idea.' Darius's shrug of the shoulders was a little too nonchalant. 'I've been wondering that myself.'

'So you didn't recognize him?' Theo persisted.

'Of course not.'

'What did he tell you he was doing?' asked Theo.

Darius shrugged again. 'He said he had some medicine for me which had to be administered via my drip.'

'Did he say what it was?'

'No and I didn't ask.' Darius began to frown. Theo knew he had to get the next question in quick!

'Your Lazarus suit, have you worn it before?'

'Yes, but not outside our research lab. We still have more tests to run before we can get them formally safety-tested.'

'D'you really think they'll sell loads?' Theo asked.

'Of course. If I wasn't already a millionaire then the Lazarus suit would certainly make me one.'

'And what happens if they don't sell loads?'

'What d'you mean?' Darius's frown was back with a vengeance.

'If they don't sell, will you lose a lot of money?' asked Theo.

'I don't see what . . .'

'I wouldn't ask if it wasn't important,' Theo interjected.

'If you must know, quite a lot of my company's money, not to mention my own, is tied up in this project,' said Darius. 'And that's all I'm prepared to say on the subject.'

'Thanks,' Theo said thoughtfully.

'I can't believe I'm answering the questions of a little kid!' Incredulous, Darius shook his head, speaking more to himself than anyone else.

Little kid indeed! What a cheek! Theo glared at Darius, who didn't seem to notice.

'Are you going to be a reporter or a chatshow host when you grow up?' Darius asked Theo.

Theo shook his head, still feeling peeved at being called a little kid.

'You should seriously consider it,' said Darius drily. 'You have a way of getting people to talk to you before they even realize what they're doing.'

'Theo's going to be a world-famous private detective,' Ricky smiled.

Theo scowled at his friend. What did Ricky think he was playing at? Theo's ambition was a secret, shared with only a few close friends.

'Is that right?' Darius raised his eyebrows. 'That's very interesting.'

'I'm only thinking about it. There are a lot of things I'd like to do,' Theo said defensively.

'Well, fascinating as all this might be, I think it's time you two boys left now. Mr Marriott needs to rest,' Doctor Nolan said.

'We were just going anyway,' said Ricky. 'Mr Marriott, good luck with Bullet, I mean Toby, and his mum.'

The only indication they got that Darius had heard was the curt nod of his head. Ricky and Theo left the room.

'Don't tell anyone else about my wanting to be a private detective.' Theo rounded on Ricky at once.

'Is it such a big secret?' Ricky asked, surprised.

'Yes. I don't want the whole world to know yet – and certainly not Darius Marriott,' said Theo.

'Why not?'

'I don't like him – and I don't trust him. And a detective has to trust his instincts.'

'Why did you ask him all those questions?' Ricky asked.

'There's something very funny going on here,' Theo replied.

'Like what?'

'I don't know what – *yet*. But I intend to find out.'

'Oh dear!' Ricky sighed. 'Theo, I don't think we should stick our noses into Bullet and his dad's private business, however much we might like to.'

'I have no intention of doing anything of the kind. But Darius Marriott almost died at our school. And if we hadn't turned up at this hospital when we did, he might've been dead now. That needs investigating. And we're just the ones to do it.'

Ricky held up his hands. 'Theo, don't say it! Please don't say it!'

But, grinning, Theo said, 'This is a job for the Solve-It Detective Agency!'

## Chapter Six

# Motive

'Where's Bullet?'

Ricky and Theo were outside the hospital building now. Angela was there waiting for them. Bullet wasn't.

'He went home,' Angela sighed.

'What did you say to him?' Ricky asked, eyes narrowed.

'Nothing. I didn't say anything tactless,' Angela defended herself. 'I apologized, that's all.'

'How did he seem?' Ricky asked. 'Was he all right?'

Moments passed before Angela answered. 'To be honest, I don't think he was. I think, if I wasn't with him . . .' Angela didn't finish her sentence. She didn't have to.

'What should we do now?' Ricky asked Theo.

Theo considered. 'I think the first thing we should do is find out as much about Darius Marriott, his family and his company, DemTech Industries, as we can.'

'In one afternoon?' Angela said dubiously.

'We'll carry on next week if we have to,' Theo decided.

'*If?* There's no if about it. It'll take us ages to find out any useful information,' frowned Angela. 'And finding out about DemTech and Darius Marriott wasn't exactly how I had planned to spend my half-term. I wanted to . . .'

'Bullet needs us,' Ricky interrupted.

Angela huffed impatiently. 'OK! OK! So how exactly are we supposed to find this info?'

'The Internet, of course. Where else?' Theo smiled.

'I'll go to the library and see what I can find out from the newspaper archives and the company records,' Ricky suggested.

'Good idea,' Theo agreed.

'I'll go with Ricky,' said Angela.

'Meanwhile I'll go home and use Mum and Dad's computer. Hopefully, it won't take me long to find out a thing or two about our friend Mr Marriott,' said Theo.

'So when are we going to meet up?' asked Ricky.

'Tomorrow at three in my house – unless I phone to say otherwise. OK?' Theo replied. 'See you.'

The three friends split up and headed in their different directions. Theo hadn't the first clue what he was looking for. What did he hope to find? What did he know so far? Some man had tried to inject goodness only knew what into Darius's intravenous drip. The police had bagged the syringe and would analyse the substance in it, but how would Theo ever get the results of their analysis? That was the first problem. And then there was this so-called Lazarus suit. Had it malfunctioned on its own or did Bullet's lie detector have something to do with it? Or was there another explanation? With each step he took, Theo's lips became more compressed. There was a mystery here all right, but how would Theo get access to all the information he needed to solve it? And then there was Bullet. If Darius did turn out to be Bullet's dad, then in a way that would make what Theo had to do a lot simpler. On the other hand, it would make Bullet's life a lot more complicated. Theo had decided he didn't like Darius Marriott and nothing had happened to make him change his mind.

Theo stopped walking abruptly, making the woman who was walking behind him swerve to avoid him. Oblivious to her impatient look, Theo stood still as he thought. In the Solve-It Detective Agency's last case, Theo had made the mistake of not taking Jade's predicament seriously until it was almost too late. He didn't want that to happen again. Bullet was a mate. Theo wanted it to remain that way. And secretly, Theo couldn't help agreeing with Angela. Not having Darius Marriott for a father would be no loss as far as he was concerned. The man was a cold fish. But Theo knew he'd have to set his own feelings aside. He had to do what he could to help Bullet and the first step was to sign on to the Internet using Mum and Dad's computer.

Two hours later, Theo sat back and tilted his head in every direction to massage his tired neck muscles. He was exhausted and his eyes felt like they were perched precariously on two matchsticks. He felt like he'd read through at least a whole novel's worth of data. But at least he'd made progress. Theo looked down at the A4 sheets of paper beside his chair. He'd found at least fifteen pages of information about Darius Marriott and DemTech that was worth printing out. And nothing he'd read had changed his mind about Darius Evan Marriott. The man had been married three times, his third wife being Samantha McRae – now Samantha Marriott – who was currently in the States. Darius was forty-five and had started up DemTech Industries when he was twenty-six. DemTech stood for Darius Evan Marriott Technologies and Darius seemed to take the credit for every invention to come out of his company even though most of them were designed and researched and built by his employees. Darius was a multi-millionaire but as far as Theo could see that was the only thing he had going for him. Once again, Theo studied the organizational chart he'd drawn up for DemTech.

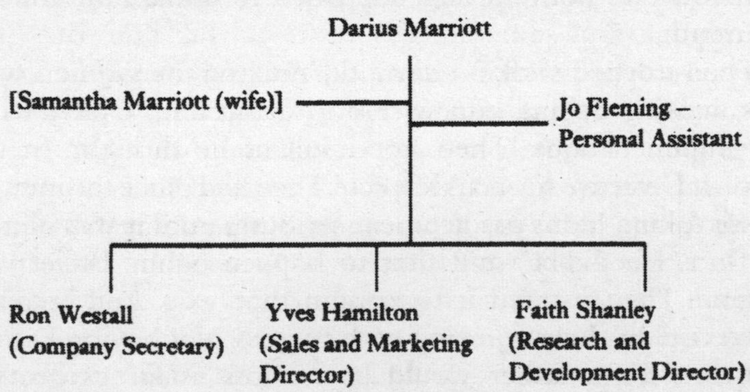

He had photos of Darius and all his company directors. He had their full backgrounds and CVs. Ron Westall, Yves Hamilton and Faith Shanley. In their photos, they all looked shifty as far as Theo was concerned. He had more information than he knew what to do with and yet, in a way, it felt as if he had nothing. Any of them, all of them or none of them could've been responsible for the attempt on Darius's life. With Darius out of the way, maybe one of them or all of them would take over DemTech. Maybe one of them had a mind warped enough to believe that that was a strong enough motive for *murder*. What were the usual motives for murder? Greed? Jealousy? Fear? Did any of those apply here? It was hard to know without knowing the people involved.

And murder was a serious business. Not something Theo wanted to get anywhere near. And not something he wanted his friends mixed up in either. If one of the directors was responsible for the attempt on Darius Marriott's life, it was a job for the police. Theo was in danger of getting in way over his head. 'Cos if one of the directors *was* involved, what was to stop them from trying again? Which one of them could it be?

Theo didn't know the directors so it was a bit pointless to speculate about their motives. He did know Darius, though. He'd met the would-be victim so he'd have to concentrate on him first. And it was strange, but Darius seemed to recover remarkably quickly from the initial shock of learning that someone was trying to kill him. But then what else was he supposed to do? It wasn't as if he could lock himself in his hospital room and refuse to come out ever again. Maybe Darius had more than an inkling as to who was trying to get rid of him? It had to be someone close to him. Someone who maybe knew about him being at their school, but who certainly knew that he was in hospital. The first thing to establish was exactly what had happened to Darius Marriott on their school stage. Was it Bullet's lie detector that had caused his dad's accident? It seemed very unlikely but Theo couldn't rule it out. Only one person would know whether or not the lie detector was involved and that was Bullet himself. Gathering up the DemTech data off the floor, Theo ran out of the room and downstairs.

'Mum, can I go round to Bullet's house?'

'What? Now?' Mum glanced down at her watch. 'It's almost six o'clock.'

'It's really important,' Theo pleaded. 'And I'll be back in an hour, I promise.'

'I don't know, Theo. It's a bit late to go visiting. Can't you leave it until tomorrow?' asked Mum.

'No, I can't. I really can't. It's very important, Mum.'

Theo's mum regarded him with a frown. A huge grin spread over Theo's face. 'Thanks, Mum.'

'I didn't say yes,' Theo's mum protested.

'Thanks, Mum.' Theo was already in the hall and heading for the door.

'An hour.' Theo's mum stressed as she followed him. 'I want you back in an hour and you're to go straight to Bullet's house and then straight home again. D'you understand?'

The front door was open. 'No problem. See you later.'

'Theo . . .'

Theo didn't wait to hear any more. He needed to see Bullet. Bullet was the key to this whole mystery.

## Chapter Seven

# The Unexpected Guest

'Hi, Miss Barker. Is Bullet in?'

'Hello, Theo.'

Theo took a good look at Bullet's mum. It was as if he was seeing her for the first time. Usually she received the briefest of glances to make sure she hadn't sprouted two heads or something and then Theo swept past her on his way to find Bullet. But now that he knew a bit more about her, he was more interested. She was a lot younger than his mum. Theo reckoned she was in her early thirties at the very most. Theo's mum was Jurassic, in her mid-forties and climbing. Or was the word deteriorating! Bullet's mum had short hair parted on one side and swept back off her face and dark brown, twinkling eyes. And she always wore leggings or jeans. Theo had never seen her in a skirt or a dress.

Bullet's mum turned with a frown to look at the clock hanging on the hall wall. 'Is something wrong?'

'Oh no. I just wanted a quick word, that's all,' Theo assured her.

'Hhmm. Well, you'll have company. Ricky and Angela just arrived saying the same thing.' Bullet's mum missed Theo's start of surprise as she turned to take another quick look at the clock. 'Come on in, then.'

Theo stepped into the house and Bullet's mum shut the door behind him. 'They're all in the living room. I wish I knew why you all look so serious.'

Bullet's mum's voice was mildly curious, inviting Theo to confide in her, but Theo didn't answer. He walked into the living room. Bullet was sitting at his computer – naturally!

– whilst Angela and Ricky sat on the sofa. And it didn't take a clairvoyant to realize that there was a very frosty atmosphere in the room. Nodding his hello, Theo sat down next to Ricky. Bullet's mum looked around the room.

'Would any of you like something to eat or drink?' she asked.

'No, thank you.'

'No, thanks.'

Theo shook his head.

'I . . . er . . . I have some things to get on with in the . . . er . . . upstairs, so I'll leave you all to it,' Bullet's mum said.

Even when Bullet's mum had shut the living-room door behind her, still no one spoke. And then, without warning, Bullet sprang out of his chair.

'So why are you here, Theo? To tell me how you've been sticking your nose into my private business as well?' Bullet raged.

'Pardon?'

'You heard me. These two,' Bullet waved a dismissive hand at Angela and Ricky, 'these two have been telling me how you all decided to stick your noses in where they're not wanted.'

'We're only trying to help you,' Theo protested. 'We thought as we all have a week off, we could . . .'

'Who asked for your help?' Bullet blazed. 'I certainly didn't. And as for helping me, are you sure having another stupid case for your rotten detective agency didn't come into it somewhere?'

'Theo never even mentioned our detective agency,' Angela stormed back at Bullet.

Theo bent his head, guiltily. He *had* been thinking about the Solve-It Detective Agency, it was just that Angela hadn't been present at the time – but that wasn't all there was to it.

'Bullet, you're not being fair. We're just trying to help,' said Ricky quietly.

'Help with what? I don't need your help. I told my dad that I'm his son and he wasn't interested. That's it. End of story.'

'But what about that bogus doctor in his hospital room? Don't you want to find out what that was all about?' Theo couldn't help asking.

'And what about when he keeled over on our school stage yesterday morning?' said Ricky. 'I don't know about you, but I want to know what's going on.'

'Why?' asked Bullet.

His question momentarily threw all three of them.

'That's a strange question,' Angela frowned. 'Someone's out to get your dad. Aren't you interested in finding out who and why?'

'No,' Bullet answered immediately.

Angela opened her mouth to respond but Ricky placed a restraining hand on her arm and shook his head. Theo was barely aware of the front doorbell ringing outside the room. He was so wrapped up in what was going on in Bullet's living room, he was barely aware of anything else.

'Are you really not interested?' Ricky asked.

'That's right.'

'Don't you even want to know if it was your lie detector yesterday that made Darius's Lazarus suit malfunction?' Theo couldn't believe Bullet could be that blasé about what had happened.

'Now that I've had a chance to think about it and test it out again, I know it *wasn't* my lie detector,' Bullet replied.

'How d'you know?' Theo asked.

'Because it's not possible. I . . .' Bullet got no further.

At that moment the door opened and to Theo's stunned amazement, in walked Bullet's mum followed by Darius Marriott. A collective gasp echoed in the room as they all regarded the unexpected guest. And Theo wasn't the only one who looked as if he'd just been slapped around both cheeks with a dead trout. Bullet's mum looked like she'd just seen a ghost. Looking at her, Theo tried to determine whether Darius's arrival was a nice or nasty surprise but her face was now shuttered off, an expressionless mask.

'I see I'm interrupting,' Darius said easily.

'No, not at all. Bullet's friends were just leaving,' Bullet's mum said meaningfully.

Theo, Ricky and Angela immediately stood up.

'Yes, that's right, Mr Marriott. We were just leaving,' said Ricky. He turned to Bullet. 'Don't worry, Bullet. We won't be troubling you with this matter any more if you don't want us to.'

'Where're you going?' Bullet asked.

'We've got to go home,' Ricky said. 'Besides . . .' Ricky turned to look at Darius Marriott. He didn't need to say anything else.

'Could you stay, please?' Bullet asked.

Theo looked from Ricky and Angela to Darius and then back to Bullet. He wondered who Bullet was talking to.

'Toby, I don't think . . .' his mum began.

'It's OK, Mum. My friends know that he's my father.' Bullet's voice was lemon-bitter as he turned to face his dad. 'And they know just what he thinks of the idea, too.'

'They know *what*?' Bullet's mum asked sharply. 'How could you tell them or anyone else such a thing?'

'Why not? It's true, isn't it?'

'This isn't something I care to discuss in front of all and sundry,' snapped Bullet's mum. 'And Toby, I'll thank you not to broadcast this family's private business.'

'If I can't tell my best friends then who can I tell?' Bullet replied.

It was funny the way things worked. A few minutes ago, Bullet was on the verge of throwing them out and never speaking to any of them again. And now here he was, declaring that Theo and the others were his best friends. Theo could feel his face begin to burn as he looked around the room. He was embarrassed – he couldn't help it. He felt totally out of place, like a fifth wheel or a third leg.

'Tessa, I would like to talk to you and Toby in private, if you don't mind,' said Darius.

'Bullet, we do have to be going now,' Ricky interjected when Bullet would have protested further. 'We'll see you tomorrow or Monday. Just call if you need anything – OK?'

Reluctantly, Bullet nodded. As they left the room, Theo looked up at Darius. Why was he here? What was he thinking? What was he *after*? Oh, to be a fly on the wall! Theo trooped out after the others but not before he'd given Darius a long, hard look and made sure that Darius knew he was being scrutinized. If Darius did anything, anything at all to upset Bullet, then Theo would find some way to pay him back.

'You just see if I don't,' he thought, hoping that his thoughts were clearly readable on his face. He couldn't help it, but he still didn't like Darius Marriott and what's more he didn't trust him, either. Not one little bit.

## Chapter Eight

# Where There's A Will

'So he didn't phone you either?' Ricky asked.

'Nope,' Theo replied, disappointed. 'I was hoping he would but . . . no.'

'Not one call all last week?'

'Not a peep. Not a beep.' Theo shook his head. 'Is he here yet?'

'No. He wasn't outside. And he's not in the computer room either,' Ricky said, amazed.

Monday morning – and every school morning come to that – always found Bullet in the school's computer room, fiddling with one of his programs. But not today.

Angela sighed. 'I called round to see him last Sunday, Tuesday and again yesterday.'

Ricky and Theo stared at her.

'You're joking!'

'You never!'

Angela raised her eyebrows. 'Of course I did. What was I meant to do? Sit at home and wonder all week?'

'That's what we did,' Ricky pointed out.

'Yeah, well, I couldn't wait that long. I wanted to make sure that Bullet was all right.'

'You are so nosy!' Theo told her with a mixture of admiration and irritation.

'The nosiest,' Ricky agreed. 'So how was he? Was he OK?'

'I'm not going to tell you,' Angela sniffed.

Ricky and Theo looked at each other, puzzled. 'What d'you mean you're not going to tell us?'

'You two are just hypocrites!' said Angela. 'You stand there condemning me for being nosy and then, with the next breath, you ask me to share the results of my nosiness! You two need to get together and make up your minds what you really want.'

Theo had to admit that Angela had a point. 'OK, sorry. Now tell us what happened.'

'Not until you admit that you like me to be nosy 'cos it means I do your dirty work for you.'

'We admit it. We admit it!' Ricky said, exasperated. 'Now, what happened?'

'Bullet and his mum weren't in – at least, not any of the times I called round,' Angela shrugged. 'And I phoned them every evening at seven and there was no answer.'

'I wonder where they were all week.' Ricky voiced the thought in all their minds at that moment.

The classroom door opened and as if on cue, in walked Bullet. Bullet was usually one of the last ones to come into the classroom. He worked up until the last possible moment on the computers in the IT Lab. But when he did come into class, usually he made a beeline for Theo and the others. But not today. With just a faint smile in their direction, Bullet walked straight over to his chair and sat down at his table. Angela, Theo and Ricky exchanged a glance, wondering what was going on. Theo led the way as they walked across the classroom.

'Hi, Bullet. How goes it?'

Bullet shrugged. 'Fine.'

'Everything all right?' asked Ricky.

'Yeah, fine.'

'Did you have a good week?'

'Yeah, great.'

Was that all he had to say to them? Theo tried and failed not to get annoyed.

'So what did Darius want when he came round to your house that Saturday, then?' asked Angela.

Bless her! Theo had to bite his lip to stop himself from laughing outright.

'If you must know, Angela, he came to apologize,' said Bullet. 'He said that not only am I his son but that he's glad I am. We sat and talked for a long while and then he took us out to dinner.'

'Why the sudden change of heart?' Theo couldn't help asking.

'I think my announcement that I was his son was just as much a shock to him as it was to me when I found out. It never occurred to me that he would be fazed by the news,' Bullet replied.

Theo remained silent. It all sounded very reasonable. Very plausible. And yet . . . And yet. Darius had been more than adamant that he was not Bullet's dad. And now he'd done a whole one hundred and eighty, welcoming Bullet with open arms. What was he up to? Theo sighed inwardly. Maybe the man wasn't up to anything. Maybe he really had changed his mind. Theo sighed again. He'd have to watch this cynical, pessimistic attitude that he seemed to be developing!

'I'm glad for you,' Theo said sincerely.

Bullet grinned. 'Thanks.'

'And where were you yesterday and all last week?' said Angela.

'Pardon?' blinked Bullet.

'Where were you? I knocked for you a couple of times and I phoned you every night last week,' said Angela.

'If you must know, Mum went to stay with my aunt whilst I spent the week with my dad – and I'm getting more than a little tired of you, Angela.'

'Huh?'

'Since when did I have to report to you?'

'I wasn't expecting you to report to me. I was just concerned.'

'Don't you mean "prying"?' Bullet asked scornfully. 'My dad said I should be careful about my so-called friends now. He said a lot of people will only want to be my friend so that they can get to him through me.'

Theo's mouth dropped open so fast, he nearly dislocated his jaw – and he wasn't the only one. This seemed to be a continuation of the conversation they'd had in Bullet's living room over a week ago, only it had taken a bizarre and much more hurtful twist.

'Thanks a lot. We're not your friends because of your dad,' Angela said with indignation.

'And why would we want to get to your dad? I don't even like the man,' Theo fumed.

'Bullet, you've got a nerve. We were your friends long before your dad arrived on the scene,' Ricky reminded him furiously.

'No, you weren't. I was just a nerd who happened to know his way around a computer. That's the only reason you talked to me in the first place,' Bullet said.

'That's not true. I mean, that's not the whole story,' Theo amended at Bullet's sceptical glance. 'OK, that might've been why we first started talking to you but we all considered you our friend after that.'

'You obviously didn't feel the same way,' Ricky said quietly.

Theo recognized that tone at once. Bullet had gone too far. Even Bullet seemed to recognize that maybe he'd said too much.

'I'm sorry. I didn't mean that the way it came out. But my dad said that now he's changed his will, I have to choose my friends very carefully,' Bullet tried to explain.

'Now he's done *what*?' asked Theo, the rest of Bullet's sentence lost on him.

Bullet looked around, then beckoned them closer. 'I'm only telling you three this because . . . because I know that you're my friends really,' Bullet whispered. 'But my dad changed his will last Thursday. His lawyer visited him whilst I was at his penthouse flat. He's left some of his money to his staff and some close friends, but he's left his company, DemTech Industries, to *me*.'

No one said a word at that. Not even Angela. They all stared goggle-eyed at Bullet. It didn't even cross Theo's mind that this was a wind-up. Bullet was too earnest, too serious.

'But I want you all to promise that you won't tell another living soul. I promised Dad I wouldn't tell anyone, so you've got to promise, too. OK?'

'We promise.' Theo raised his right hand. Angela and Ricky did the same.

'Why is he leaving you his company?' Theo asked when his voice had fully returned.

''Cos I'm his son, of course!' Bullet replied, eyebrows raised.

'Yes, I know. But you've only known the man for five minutes. He can't have changed his will already,' said Theo.

'Well, he has.'

'Why?'

'What d'you mean?'

Theo grew more and more puzzled by the second. 'I mean, what's his rush? If he really has changed his will, why did he change it so quickly?'

'I'm his son.'

'Yes, but . . . Ricky, what d'you think?' Theo appealed to his friend to back him up. Surely he wasn't the only one who thought this whole thing was bizarre. Ricky shrugged and said nothing. Theo frowned at him, trying to decipher his expression but Ricky's face was a mask. Theo turned to Angela. He felt sure that her expression mirrored his own.

'But why isn't he leaving the company to his wife, Samantha? What does she get?' Theo continued.

Bullet frowned. 'Dad never mentioned her. I guess she'll get his money and I'll get the company. Or maybe they have one of those special agreements that rich people make when they don't want to lose all their money. One of those pre-nuptial agreements?'

'Twit!' Ricky laughed. 'Rich people make pre-nuptial agreements before they get married. It's so they can protect their money if they ever get divorced. I've never heard of an agreement to cut out the other person if one of you dies.'

'Just because Dad never mentioned it, doesn't mean he didn't leave her anything,' Bullet defended rigorously. 'Besides, maybe Dad's set it up so that she already has all the money she needs.'

'From what I've seen, rich people never have all the money they need. They never have enough.' Theo shook his head. 'But congratulations, Bullet. That's brilliant news. Good for you.'

Bullet smiled. 'To be honest, I don't even care about the money. I'd always planned to be a famous inventor and make my own money. What I can't get over is saying the word "Dad"! My dad! I still can't quite get used to it. It's wonderful. All these years without a dad and suddenly I've got one – and it's Darius Marriott.'

Ricky lowered his head.

'What did your mum say about all this?' asked Theo.

'She was furious with me at first. She never told me the name of her boss all those years ago, so I had to do some digging. All she said was that she and a man she'd worked with had been very much in love and she became pregnant and decided to leave without telling him.'

'So how did you pin it down to Darius Marriott being your dad?' asked Theo.

'Mum stopped working when she was pregnant with me and she only started working again when I was seven. I found some old pay-slips she'd hidden away and then used the Internet to track down DemTech. There were only a handful at DemTech at the same time as my mum. It wasn't hard to find out who Mum was working for.'

Ricky used his elbow to nudge Theo in the ribs before nodding in Angela's direction. Angela was staring at Bullet, a strange expression on her face.

'Angela, you're very quiet,' said Ricky.

Angela never took her eyes off Bullet. The hurt in her

eyes was being overtaken by a hard, sombre look that Theo hadn't seen in a long, long time. 'I don't want to be accused of sticking my nose in where it's not wanted.'

'Angela, I . . .'

'Excuse me.' Angela didn't wait for Bullet to finish. She turned abruptly and walked off.

'I didn't mean to upset her,' Bullet mumbled.

'Yes, you did,' Ricky contradicted. 'Angela liked you and stuck up for you long before anyone else gave you a chance and you were really mean to her.'

'Yes, Saint Ricky. Sorry, Saint Ricky.' Bullet bowed with sarcasm. 'Who d'you think you are?'

'I know who I am. And that's not someone who thinks he can switch his friends on and off like a tap whenever it suits him,' Ricky snapped.

'I don't do that.'

'That's exactly what you're doing. A moment ago you said you were telling us about your dad's will 'cos we're your friends, but now you're acting like a cow pat again,' Ricky told him straight.

'Listen, I don't need you or anyone else in this rotten school. My dad says he's going to pay for me to go to a private school so I don't have to mix with people like you any more.'

*People like you!* Theo opened his mouth to tell Bullet exactly where he could stuff his private school but Ricky got in first.

'Bullet, you needn't worry about "people like us" polluting your breathing air any longer. See you around.' Ricky walked off without a backward glance.

Theo scowled, wanting to tell Bullet exactly what he thought of him but he was so angry he knew if he opened his mouth, his words would fall out in an inarticulate, furious jumble. He took a deep breath, and another and another.

'You've had a dad for exactly ten days and money for less than a week and look at how it's changed you,' Theo said slowly and quietly. 'If you ask me, you were better off without either of them.'

'But no one did ask you. So you can push off along with Ricky.'

'I don't mind if I do,' Theo told him. 'Oh, and as for my birthday party two weeks on Saturday, don't bother coming. I'm sure you don't want us riffraff inflicting our lower-class germs and bacteria on you.'

Theo turned to walk away. Bullet called out after him, 'I wasn't going to come anyway. My dad's taking me out.'

Theo refused to turn back to dignify Bullet's boast with a response. As far as Theo was concerned, the Solve-It Detective Agency was now back down to three people. Jade, who was meant to be part of the agency, had moved with her mum up to Manchester to be closer to the rest of their family. Theo and the others had been really sorry to see her go, but as for Bullet . . . His was definitely a case of good riddance to bad rubbish. Theo couldn't believe the change that had come over Bullet. Bullet didn't seem to know what he wanted. He talked about Theo and Ricky and Angela being his friends and yet in the next breath he insulted them with a nastiness that took Theo's breath away.

Was that really what money did for you? If it was, then Theo wasn't sure that he wanted to be rich. No, he took that back! He did want to be rich, but he'd handle it a lot better than Bullet. He wouldn't be moronic enough to think that he was better than all his friends just because he had more money than them. He wouldn't dream of insulting his friends in the way that Bullet had just done. It was as if Bullet reckoned they didn't have any feelings.

Theo couldn't help sighing as he sat down next to Ricky. There was no doubt about it. Sudden money seemed to do strange things to a lot of people's minds. And so many rich people seemed to be so miserable. Mind you, Theo would rather be miserable with money than without! It was better to be miserable in comfort. Theo turned his head. Bullet was watching him and Ricky, with a strange, almost forlorn, expression on his face. An expression which disappeared almost as soon as Theo looked at him, to be replaced by something that Theo had no trouble interpreting. Theo gritted his teeth. If Bullet didn't stop looking at him like Theo was something nasty he'd just trodden in, Theo was going to march across the room and tell Bullet one or two things about himself. Just who did he think he was? It'd be a long time before Theo forgot what Bullet had just said. He wasn't going to forgive him that easily either. Giving him the filthiest look he could, Theo turned his head away, utter contempt in his every gesture. He risked a quick glance at Bullet to see if he had made his feelings for his former friend clear. Bullet purposely avoided Theo's eyes. Theo gave a slight smile of bitter satisfaction. So much for his ex-good-friend Bullet Barker. If Theo never spoke to him again, it would be too soon.

## Chapter Nine

# Reckoning

'Why did you drag me down here to the car park?' The man looked around anxiously. 'We shouldn't be seen together like this.'

'You're the one who told me not to talk to you in the office. You said Darius probably had the place bugged,' the woman reminded him.

'I wouldn't put it past him.' The man looked around the empty car park again. 'So what's so important that it couldn't wait until tonight?'

The woman sighed and shook her head. 'I think we should call a halt. We should quit while we're behind.'

'No way. No one suspects us. We're OK.'

'But he's changed his will,' the woman replied, anguished. She began to pace up and down, rubbing her hands together in an agitated mime of washing them clean.

'Yes, I know.'

'Don't you understand? He's changed his will. That changes everything.'

'No, it doesn't. It just means we have to get rid of the boy before we deal with Darius.'

The woman froze in her tracks. 'You can't be serious. Getting Darius out of the way is one thing. But getting rid of his son is something else again.'

'Darling, we have to. We haven't got any choice.' The man took the woman by the arms and hugged her tight. 'We can't stop now. We just can't.'

The woman pulled out of his grasp. Bitterly, she said. 'Your plan to use the Lazarus suit to get rid of Darius failed. He survived and we were moronic enough not to let things be. We should've quit then but no, you had to hire someone to try again – and they got caught.'

'It wasn't Jake's fault. He said those kids came in just as he . . .'

'I don't want to hear it.' The woman turned her head away.

'Darling, listen to me. We can't stop now. We're both up to our necks in this – and we both have too much to lose.'

'So what do we do now?'

'I don't know. Jake's panicking and he's bleating to get paid. He wasn't supposed to get any more until . . . until Darius was no longer a problem. But now that the police have his description, he wants to disappear as soon as possible – and of course that takes money.'

'We haven't got it. You tell him that.'

'I already have,' the man said with impatience. 'But he doesn't want to hear it. I'm afraid he might try something . . . foolish.'

'Where did you find this guy?'

'That hardly matters now. The point is, we're stuck with him.'

'Look! I just want to forget about the whole thing,' the woman said firmly. 'We should just keep our heads down.'

'What about Jake? He wants money.'

'Well, he can't have it.'

'He could make a great deal of trouble for us.'

The woman shook her head. 'Not without making a great deal for himself too. He's hardly likely to complain to the police, is he?'

'He might do. And he knows who I am,' said the man.

'He doesn't know me.' The woman managed her first slight smile since the meeting had begun. 'And I can provide you with an alibi for the time when he tried to pull that little stunt at the hospital.'

'I don't think that would work. I was in a bar around the

corner from the hospital waiting for him. I'm sure someone there could recognize me,' the man argued.

'How could you be so stupid?'

'I didn't expect him to tell me he'd failed,' the man snapped.

It was a long time before either of them spoke. The woman said at last, 'It's only a matter of time before Darius finds out about you and me and then he'll put two and two together and he'll come up with the right answer.'

'That's why we need to act quickly.'

Long moments passed as the allies regarded each other. 'OK then. I'll carry on with this – because I love you,' the woman said sadly. She drew herself up to her full height. 'If we're going to get rid of the boy, it should be soon.'

'Good!' The man drew a sigh of relief. 'I knew you wouldn't let me down. Don't worry. I'll tell Jake that he still has some work to do.'

Chapter Ten

# Look Out!

'D'you two think this is all my fault?'

'Huh?' Ricky looked at Angela, surprised. 'What on earth are you talking about?'

Angela shrugged. 'The way Bullet turned on the three of us. I know you two think I'm really tactless and nosy as well, but I didn't mean to . . .'

'Angela, stop talking rubbish,' Ricky dismissed. 'Bullet's behaviour had nothing to do with you being tactless. Besides, he should be used to that by now!'

School was over for another day and the three friends were walking home. It was a wet and windy Thursday afternoon and as far as Theo was concerned, the weather suited his mood. For four whole days, none of them had exchanged a single word with Bullet. Deep down, Theo had to admit that he actually missed his former friend. He hated the icy silence that had descended between them. And what was worse, neither Angela nor Ricky had mentioned Bullet since the big bust-up. But since Monday, whenever the three of them were together, they'd all lapse into strange silences where it was obvious that they were all thinking about the same thing.

With a sigh, Theo looked up at the sky. It was peculiar weather for the end of May. Until that morning the last week had been unseasonably hot and breezeless. Theo remembered reading somewhere that hot, breezeless weather made people a lot more irritable and short-tempered. If that was the case, then it would explain a lot as far as Bullet was concerned. Maybe now that it was raining and the air was cooler, things would get back to normal.

'It's just that, I can't help thinking that I somehow made things worse between all of us, not better.' It was plain to see that Angela was brooding about the events of the last few days.

'Forget it, Angela. Bullet just thinks he's too good to walk on the same planet as us, that's all,' Theo sniffed.

Ricky shook his head. 'I don't know. I don't think so. I think it's more than that.'

'What d'you mean?' asked Angela.

'It's just that I've now had a couple of days to cool off and think about it. And d'you know something? When Bullet was saying all those things to us, it was as if it wasn't him saying them at all. It was as if someone else – maybe that Darius Marriott bloke – was talking through him,' said Ricky thoughtfully.

Theo raised his eyebrows. 'That's a bit fanciful, isn't it? I reckon it was just Bullet the wazzock talking!'

Ricky shrugged, but said nothing.

'I don't know what's going on,' Angela said, bemused. 'Bullet and I used to be such good friends. At one time I actually fanc . . . I mean, I liked him a lot!' Angela amended, her cheeks flaming red. 'But now, it's like every time I open my mouth I annoy him.'

'Maybe we're not giving him a chance,' suggested Ricky. 'Bullet's got a lot to deal with right now. Maybe we should all just . . .'

'Ricky! Theo! Just a minute, Angela!'

They all turned to see Bullet come puffing up behind them. He had to cross a broad road to get to them and he gave the briefest of glances to his left and right before charging across. Without warning, a dark car seemed to rev from a standstill to an instant eighty kilometres an hour and it came racing towards Bullet, who had now reached the middle of the road. Theo was the first to see it.

'NO!' Theo yelled a warning.

'Bullet, look out!'

Bullet turned his head and saw the car racing towards him. Shock froze him to the tarmac. Ricky leaped forward – but Angela beat him to it. She dashed into the middle of the road, just as the car was almost upon Bullet and shoved him out of the way. Angela tried to dive after him, but she wasn't so lucky. The side of the car hit her and Angela was knocked into the air. And in that moment, Theo's heart stopped beating. As Angela hit the ground, Theo could hear the THWACK-CRACK from where he was standing. And when Angela hit the ground, she stayed perfectly still, her eyes closed. The car roared up to the next corner, its brakes shrieking as it raced around it. And now Theo's heart was racing. In a shocked daze, Theo looked up the road but it was too late. The car had gone. Ricky was already squatting down at Angela's side. Icy cold, Theo walked slowly to the middle of the road. Already a crowd was beginning to gather and the cry was going up for an ambulance and the police.

'Is she . . . ? Is she . . . ?' Bullet whispered.

Angela lay crumpled up on her side, her leg bent at a very peculiar angle beneath her. And the road beneath her head glistened red with a thin trail of blood running from her forehead.

'She's still breathing – but she's in a bad way,' Ricky said grimly.

A short, broad man with a crop of dark hair squatted down next to Ricky. 'Let's try and make her more comfortable . . .'

'NO!' Ricky shouted. 'No. You mustn't move her. We have to wait for the paramedics to arrive. If you move her you could make things worse, not better.'

'He's right. You shouldn't move accident victims,' a woman from the ever-growing crowd joined in.

'Did anyone see the car that did this?' asked the short, broad man.

'It raced off around the corner,' another man from the crowd volunteered.

'Did anyone get the licence plate number?' someone else asked.

Stricken, Theo looked up the road in the direction the car had driven off. He'd been so shocked, so stunned by what had happened he couldn't even remember his own name when it was all going on, much less the licence plate of the car. He tried to think back. What colour was the car? Dark blue. Navy blue. What make was it? He didn't know. He wasn't sure. If only he'd been more together. Then he could've noted all the details for the police. He was useless. Some detective he was. Angela had been knocked over in front of him and he couldn't say whether it was a man or woman driving and all he could remember was that it was a medium-sized, navy blue car. Even Ricky had been quicker off the mark than he had been.

'She . . . she pushed me out of the way . . .' Bullet's tremulous voice was just one of many. If Theo hadn't been looking at him at the time, he would never have caught what Bullet said. 'She pushed me out of the way. She saved my life.'

All around, the crowd were asking each other what had happened, what they should do, where was the driver of the car that had hit the girl. The questions buzzed round and around Theo's head like hungry bluebottles.

In the distance an ambulance siren could be heard, getting closer and closer.

'Theo, take Bullet to your house. And don't leave until I get there.' Ricky's sudden command was harshly said.

'I . . . What about the police and the ambulance people and . . . ?'

'Never mind all that. I'll tell them what happened. Just take Bullet and go,' Ricky ordered.

Theo took another look at Ricky's stony expression and grabbed Bullet by the arm. 'Come on, let's go.' Theo pulled him away from the crowd.

'I want to stay here.' Bullet tried to pull his arm out of Theo's grasp.

'No, you can't. Come on. You're coming home with me.'

'No way. I want to stay with Angela. I want to make sure . . .'

'Bullet, don't be so stupid. You've got to come to my house where it's safe,' Theo hissed at him. Part of the fury in his voice was directed at himself although Bullet had no way of knowing that. 'The driver of that car was after *you*. He was trying to *kill* you and if it hadn't been for Angela he would've succeeded. We've got to get you somewhere safe. Now come on.'

Chapter Eleven

# More Questions Than Answers

'Who would want to kill me?'

Theo kept silent. Bullet was sitting at Theo's work table in his bedroom, his expression still glazed and dazed. Theo glowered at Bullet, but Bullet didn't seem to notice. Theo told himself that he was being unfair. What had happened wasn't Bullet's fault any more than it was Angela's, but after everything that had happened over the last few days, Theo found himself resenting the fact that it was Angela being whisked off to hospital in Bullet's place. It wasn't that he wanted to see Bullet injured or hurt in any way, but it wasn't *fair*.

Theo's scowl deepened as he felt guilty for the direction in which his thoughts were taking him. Theo decided he'd better keep his mouth shut. Rage bubbled in him like lava in a volcano. He knew he was just waiting for any excuse to lash out and the closest person to hand at the moment was Bullet.

'I don't understand. Who would want to kill *me*?' Bullet whispered again.

Theo forced his lips together tight, tight, tight. He turned away from Bullet. If he heard that one more time . . .

'I mean, who would want to . . . ?'

'Oh, for goodness' sake!' Theo exploded. 'Don't be so stupid. You spent Monday morning boasting about your dad leaving you everything in his will. Well, you may be ecstatic about it but it's obvious you and your dad have cheesed someone else off!'

The horrified expression on Bullet's face as he turned to face Theo had him feeling even more rotten.

'I'm sorry,' Theo said grudgingly. 'I shouldn't have blurted it out like that but Bullet, start working those brain cells. You may know a lot about circuits and computers and microchips and that, but you don't know much about people – especially adults.'

'You really think my life is in danger? That it was deliberate?' Theo could barely hear Bullet's voice now.

'I've been thinking about that.' Theo forced his voice to be calm and collected. 'The car came straight at you. It started up when you began to cross the road. So yes, I do think it was deliberate.'

Bullet stared at Theo but didn't answer.

'I didn't get it at first either. When Ricky told me to take you straight to my house it took a couple of seconds for the reason why to click into place,' Theo admitted.

'You're faster on the uptake than me.' Bullet's lips were a thin slash across his face as he spoke. 'Seems I've been getting a lot of things wrong recently.'

'What d'you mean?'

'Never mind.'

Theo didn't push it. He didn't envy Bullet one little bit. What was the point of having millions coming your way when you couldn't even cross the street – literally. Theo's thoughts slid back to Angela. He sat down on his bed and sighed.

'I wish Ricky would hurry up and get here. I wish I knew how Angela is doing.'

'Why did Angela do it?' At Theo's questioning look, Bullet said, 'Why did Angela save my life after all the vicious things I said to her?'

'Maybe she reckoned it was worth saving? Or maybe she just acted on the spur of the moment and didn't realize what she was doing?' Theo provided with a certain malicious relish.

'If she dies . . .'

'Don't say that. Don't even think that,' Theo stormed. 'Angela will get better – and soon. I just know it.'

'You know more than me then.'

'Bullet, I swear if you don't shut up I'm going to chuck you out.'

'Sorry.'

'Anyway, why were you chasing after us?' asked Theo.

'Pardon?'

'Before the accident. You were running after us. What was that all about?'

'Oh yeah!' Bullet turned away from Theo. 'I . . . I wanted to catch all of you together. I wanted to apologize for all the things I'd said.'

'And you reckoned an apology would make up for it,' Theo said scornfully.

'No. But it's all I have,' Bullet said quietly. He suddenly covered his face with his hands. 'I'm so confused. Dad told me that I have to . . . to think and act like his son now, but . . .' Bullet broke off, the look on his face expressing clearly that he felt he'd said too much. He looked at Theo defiantly, daring him to comment. Theo turned away, determined to keep his mouth shut.

They sat in silence, apart from each other, not even facing in the same direction. The seconds turned into long, painful minutes and still no one spoke. Just when Theo thought he was going to explode with the silence, the door burst open, making both Bullet and Theo jump.

'Ricky!' Bullet leaped to his feet.

'Your mum sent me straight up,' Ricky told Theo.

'How's Angela? Is she OK? Is she badly hurt?' Bullet asked anxiously.

'She woke up as the ambulance arrived. She's broken her leg and has a concussion but the paramedics will know more when they get her to hospital,' Ricky told them.

'I thought you were going with Angela to the hospital,' Theo said.

'I wanted to, but the ambulance woman told me that I couldn't because I'm not a relative. She said I could visit Angela once she was comfortable in hospital,' said Ricky.

'Did Angela mention me at all?' asked Bullet.

Ricky nodded. 'She asked if you were OK. I told her you didn't have a scratch on you.'

Ricky and Theo stood facing Bullet. The tension in the room was a tangible thing, charged like summer lightning.

'Go on. Why don't you just come right out and say it? It should've been me, not Angela, in hospital now.'

'Don't be ridiculous. Why would I wish it was you instead of her? The thought never even crossed my mind,' Ricky said angrily.

Theo hung his head. He knew he couldn't say the same thing.

'Don't lie. I know you reckon this is all my fault.'

'Look Bullet, when you're ready to talk sense and stop feeling sorry for yourself, let us know.' And with that, Ricky deliberately turned his back on Bullet.

'Are you sure Angela's going to be OK?' Theo asked. 'I've been sitting here worried sick.'

'I can only tell you what I was told.' Ricky shook his head.

'I want to visit her as soon as possible,' said Theo.

Ricky nodded his head in agreement. 'OK, we've got to find out who was driving the car that tried to knock down Bullet. It's a shame we can't see a copy of Darius Marriott's wills – both new and old. That would give us a list of suspects to start from.'

'Why do we need to see the old will?' Theo frowned.

'Because of what happened the Friday before half term,' said Ricky. At Theo's blank look, he continued. 'I think Mr Marriott's heart attack – if that's what it was – was not as spontaneous as it looked.'

'Why?' asked Bullet.

Ricky completely ignored him.

'Why? Because of the bogus doctor?' asked Theo.

'Mainly that. But also this Lazarus suit. If it can be activated by remote control but only at a limited range, how do we know that there wasn't someone nearby who set it off, hoping it would kill him? Then Mr Marriott's own invention would've been blamed for his death. If I wanted to get rid of him, then that's how I would do it.'

'D'you think that's what happened?' asked Bullet.

'Hhmm! Did you hear something?' Ricky asked Theo lightly.

Theo shrugged. It was hard work pretending Bullet wasn't in the room, but this was where they found out once and for all where Bullet stood. If he left the room and left the house, then that would be that and Theo and Ricky would be on their own.

'Did Mr Marriott come to our school with anyone else?' Ricky asked. 'That might be worth finding out. And we need to know exactly how close another person has to be to send remote messages to the Lazarus suit.'

'But what about Bullet's lie detector?' said Theo.

'What about it?' asked Ricky.

'I thought that had something to do with Mr Marriott's Lazarus suit being activated,' said Theo.

'Certainly, we can't rule it out. But in light of what happened at the hospital, it'd be one ginormous coincidence if Bullet's lie detector made Mr Marriott's suit malfunction and then someone used that opportunity to try and bump him off.'

'But coincidences do happen,' Theo pointed out.

Ricky nodded in reluctant acknowledgement. 'It'd be nice to know exactly how this lie detector works and how the Lazarus suit works, to see if one could have really set off the other.'

'I can tell you that,' said Bullet eagerly. 'I can show you the lie detector and Dad's Lazarus suit.'

'But our first aim should be to find out exactly what's in this new will,' Ricky mused.

'Stop ignoring me. I'm sorry – OK. I'm sorry.' Bullet pulled Ricky around to face him. 'And I can probably get you a copy of the will.'

'So you're with us now, are you?' Ricky asked coolly.

'Yes, I am.' Bullet replied at once.

'How can you get the will?' Theo asked.

'The lawyer brought it round for Dad to sign yesterday,' said Bullet. 'Dad keeps all his important papers and documents in the safe in his study, so I might be able to get hold of it for you to see. Or maybe I could just copy it on to Dad's computer using his scanner and then print it out.'

'How d'you know where your dad's likely to keep the new will?' asked Ricky.

'Well, he kept the old will in his safe so I don't see why he wouldn't keep the new one there too,' Bullet replied.

'You learned all this in a couple of weeks?' Theo asked, impressed.

'Dad showed me his safe when he showed Mum and me around his flat two weeks ago,' said Bullet.

'He lives in a flat?' Theo was surprised.

'A penthouse flat. He has flats in New York, Paris, Rome and Sydney too.'

Theo wasn't surprised!

'What about the safe combination?' asked Ricky.

'The safe's digitally coded and on an electronic timer,' said Bullet.

'So?'

'So I have a device at home that can handle that,' Bullet smiled.

'Don't tell me. Let me guess. A device you made yourself?' said Theo.

'Natch!' Bullet agreed with no attempt at modesty.

'Pardon?'

'Naturally. Natch,' Bullet explained.

Theo and Bullet regarded each other, slowly smiling. And the harsh words of the last couple of days were, if not forgotten, then on their way to being forgiven.

'What's our plan of action?' asked Ricky.

'Mum and I are going round to Dad's for dinner tonight. I'll see if I can get hold of a copy of Dad's will then,' said Bullet.

'How is your mum with all this?' Theo couldn't help asking.

'She . . . she wasn't too happy, but she says she's getting more used to the situation now,' Bullet admitted. 'When she first found out what I'd done, she hit the stratosphere. When she'd finally cooled off, we sat down and talked for four hours straight. She told me I should've told her what I was doing. But how could I? I didn't want to hurt her feelings. I didn't want her to think I was looking for something better.'

'Is that what she thought?' Ricky stared.

'Until I put her straight,' Bullet sighed. 'She didn't think she'd given me enough information to work it out and she reckons I should never have gone to Dad and told him who I was without speaking to her first.'

'Well, it's done now,' said Theo.

'Any chance that she and your dad . . . ?'

'No. None at all. Mum made that very clear,' said Bullet. 'Besides Dad's married now, anyway.'

They sat in a moment's silence, contemplating just how complicated Bullet's life had suddenly become. With all the weird things happening to him, it was no wonder he was acting very peculiarly!

'OK then. You're going to try and get hold of a copy of your dad's will for us to see. Just don't get into trouble over it,' said Theo.

'Don't get caught, then you won't get into trouble,' Ricky said bluntly.

Theo sighed deeply. 'The trouble is, we have far more questions than answers at the moment.'

'But not for long,' Ricky replied without hesitation.

'If someone is trying to get me out of the way, I hope we get the answer to all our questions before they succeed,' said Bullet.

Only the hiccupy catch in Bullet's voice belied the evenness of his words. He wasn't as collected about this as he was trying to make out. Theo didn't expect him to be either.

'Bullet, Ricky and I will come with you if you want to

go to the police. In fact maybe that's what we should do, before you get hurt.'

'I've got no proof.' Bullet shook his head.

'We're your proof,' Theo insisted. 'We'll tell the police how that car came straight for you. And Angela's your proof. She's in hospital, isn't she?'

'Yes, but the driver might have been drunk or just not looking where he or she was going,' Bullet argued.

'Then why didn't the driver stop?' asked Theo.

'I don't know, all right? Some drivers just don't stop when they've been in an accident. It happens,' said Bullet.

'Bullet, you need to think very seriously about this,' Theo stated. 'I'm not waiting for someone to put me, you or any of us in the hospital – or worse – to satisfy your need for concrete and absolute proof. You're waiting to get proof over our dead bodies!'

'Don't you dare say that,' Bullet shouted. 'All I have to do is think about Angela and what happened to go icy-cold inside. It should've been me and it could've been a lot worse. Don't you think I don't know that? I'm not *stupid*.'

'Calm down, Bullet. Theo never said you were,' Ricky soothed.

No, but there was no doubt about it. Hanging around Bullet was getting to be a dangerous occupation. The driver of the car hadn't been after Angela. He or she had been after Bullet. And look what had happened. Theo sat up with a start. He'd just thought of something else. Something that was making his heart jump.

'You . . . you don't think the driver will try to get to Angela?' Theo whispered.

From the stunned look on Bullet's and Ricky's faces, it was obvious they hadn't considered the possibility either.

'You don't think the driver will think that Angela looked into the car and can identify him or her?' Theo continued.

'No! No.' Ricky's protest at the idea burst out of him. 'Angela was too busy pushing Bullet out of the way to see anything or anyone else.'

'Yes, but does the driver know that?' Theo persisted.

'Of course. I'm sure Angela never took her eyes off Bullet,' Ricky said firmly.

Theo nodded slowly, clenching his fists. He had to get a grip! If he wasn't careful he'd be jumping at shadows.

'It's just that, if there's even a chance that the driver might try to get to Angela in the same way he or she tried to get to Mr Marriott, then we really should go straight to the police,' said Theo.

'It won't happen,' said Bullet.

'You're sure of that?'

'Yes. The driver wanted . . . wants me. Angela has nothing to do with this. Besides, I won't let anything else happen to Angela – or any of you.'

'Like you can do anything about it,' Theo dismissed.

'I'm the one the driver wants. So can you just shut up about it, please?' Bullet yelled.

'No, we can't,' Ricky joined in. 'If something were to happen to you too, we'd never forgive ourselves. If you go to the police, they'll be able to protect you.'

'I'm not going to the police and that's all there is to it,' Bullet said fiercely.

'Why not?'

'I have my reasons.'

'Care to share them?' Theo asked after a brief pause.

'No.'

'We could go without you?' Ricky suggested, steel in his voice.

'I'd deny everything,' Bullet shot back at once. 'I'd tell them you're making it all up.'

Theo opened his mouth to argue, only to snap it shut again. What was the point? Bullet had obviously made up his mind. What did he hope to achieve with his ostrich act? That wouldn't make his dilemma go away. There were no two ways about it. Someone was after Bullet and if they didn't find out who and stop them, Bullet didn't stand a chance.

## Chapter Twelve

# Shadows And Shadows

'Theo, Ricky's on the phone.'

'Mmmm! Urgmmm!' Theo pulled up the duvet further around his neck and allowed himself to drift off again.

'Theo! Ricky said it was urgent.'

Reluctantly, Theo opened his eyes. He glanced at the clock radio on the floor beside his bed. Then he groaned. 'Mum, it's six-thirty in the morning.'

'Why don't you tell Ricky that? He's your friend, not mine.' Mum stood in the doorway, wearing her dressing-gown. And she didn't look too pleased either.

Theo dragged himself out of bed and rubbed his eyes. So this was what half-past six on a Monday morning looked like! As far as he was concerned, if he never saw it again it would be too soon. Stumbling to his feet, Theo made his sleepy way downstairs.

'You had better be at death's door,' Theo said the moment the phone receiver was to his ear.

'Good morning to you too!'

'It's not the morning. It's the middle of the night,' Theo grumbled. 'What d'you want?'

'Charming! I need you to meet me at the corner opposite the newsagent's at seven-fifteen,' said Ricky.

'You must be joking. I'm going back to bed.'

'No, you can't. Bullet's at his dad's flat. He wants us to meet him there before school.'

'Why?'

'He wouldn't say. He just said it was very important.'

'But it's so early,' Theo protested.

'You're not saying anything that I haven't already said to Bullet. But he said it was urgent so I said we'd be there.'

'Couldn't you go by yourself?' Theo said hopefully. His bed was calling to him and Theo was finding it hard to resist.

'Theo, don't be so lazy,' Ricky said impatiently. 'Get out of bed and I'll see you in forty-five minutes.'

And with that Ricky put down the phone. Theo sighed, forcing his eyes to stay open. A shower would wake him up, but the problem was coming up with a plausible explanation for why he wanted to leave the house so early.

'Mum, Dad!' Theo called as he headed back up the stairs. 'I've got to go round to Ricky's. He's panicking about our test today.'

Theo's mum appeared bleary-eyed from her bedroom. Behind her, Theo could hear his dad snoring.

'You're going round to Ricky's before school?' Theo's mum couldn't believe her ears. She pinched her arm. 'I'm obviously still asleep. It takes a cannon to wake you up and an earthquake to get you out of bed.'

'Well, I'm not happy about it, but Ricky needs my help.' Theo yawned.

'Helping Ricky revise is all very well, but make sure you're not late for school.' Theo's mum wagged her finger.

'Yes, Mum. I'm off for a shower.'

'Would you like some bacon and eggs on toast?' Theo's mum asked.

'Oh, yes please.' Great! He was going to get breakfast before he left the house.

'So would I!' Theo's mum nodded and headed straight back into her bedroom.

'Very funny, Mum,' Theo called after her, but her bedroom door was already closing. Calling himself all kinds of a fool for falling for his mum's strange sense of humour yet again, Theo had his shower and got dressed. Grabbing a cold chicken drumstick and a carton of apple juice from the fridge, Theo set off to meet Ricky.

'This had better be as important as Bullet thinks it is,' Theo fumed.

'Shush! Keep your voice down.' Ricky nodded his head in the direction of the suited man who sat two seats in front of them.

'Why would he be listening to our conversation?' Theo whispered.

'He got on at the same stop as us and the bus is practically empty, yet he chose to come and sit back here with us.'

'So?'

'So I'm just keeping my eye on him, that's all,' Ricky whispered tersely.

Theo looked at the back of the man who sat before them. He had light brown hair and wore glasses but that was all Theo could make out.

'It's just a man on his way to work,' said Theo.

'Probably.' Ricky shrugged. 'But it doesn't hurt to be . . . cautious. Anyway this is our stop.'

'I still can't believe I'm doing this,' Theo grumbled as he and Ricky got off the bus. 'I must need my head examined.'

'Stop moaning,' Ricky groaned. 'You're giving me a headache.'

Ricky and Theo started walking past some of the cleanest, swishest-looking buildings Theo had ever seen in his life. He and Ricky exchanged a look.

'How the other half do live!' Theo said drily.

'How the lucky five per cent do live!' Ricky amended.

'So where's this flat then?' asked Theo.

'It's not a flat. It's an apartment,' Ricky corrected loftily.

'Where is it then?' Theo looked behind, wondering if perhaps it was back the other way. But what was that? Was it his imagination or had someone ducked into an alleyway a little further down the road? He turned to Ricky, wondering if his friend had seen the same thing, but Ricky was busy looking for the number of the building before him. Frowning, Theo looked down the road again. He was certain someone had ducked out of sight when he turned. Theo walked slowly back the way he'd come. Back towards the alleyway.

'Theo, where're you going? It's this way,' Ricky beckoned.

'I just want to check something out,' Theo called back. He ran the rest of the way to the alleyway and looked down it. Neither its smell nor its appearance were particularly inviting. It was strewn with boxes and rubbish and other things that looked entirely less savoury. And it was dark – towering buildings rising like giants on either side of it. There was no one there and, as far as Theo could see, no one would want to go down there, either. And yet, somewhere in there amongst the shadows . . . Theo shivered. The whole alleyway had turned into a malevolent presence.

'Theo, are you coming or what?' Ricky called impatiently.

Taking one last look, Theo turned and walked back to Ricky. They carried on walking together.

Ricky started reading off the numbers of the buildings. 'Fifty-nine to sixty-nine. It must be the next building along.'

Theo turned sharply. A man walking behind stopped to look at one of the buildings.

'Ricky, I think we're being followed,' said Theo.

Ricky turned around. 'What? Are you sure?'

'No,' Theo admitted. 'But I'm sure that man was hiding in the shadows of the alleyway and now he's pretending to be looking at that building.'

'Wait a minute. Isn't that the man who was sitting two seats in front of us?' asked Ricky.

Theo stared. 'Is it?'

They both turned all the way around to look at the man they suspected of following them. The man took a piece of paper out of his pocket and looked down at it before looking back up at the building. He turned around and walked in the opposite direction away from them.

'Maybe we're both a little jittery.' Ricky shrugged.

'And maybe we aren't,' Theo countered.

The front of the next building consisted almost entirely of marble and glass. Behind a huge desk against one wall sat two uniformed security guards. The foyer of the building consisted of huge plants and glass and mirrors. Theo had never seen anything like it. Theo and Ricky looked for a doorbell for Darius Marriott's apartment but there was none. Instead there was a bell to press for Reception. Raising his eyebrows, Ricky pressed it. Theo could see the two security guards watching them. Then he heard a loud click. Ricky pulled at the door and they entered.

'Can I help you?' asked the older of the security guards.

'We're here to see Bullet, I mean Toby Barker. His dad is Darius Marriott. He asked us to meet him here.'

'Just a moment.' The security guard picked up one of the two phones on the desk in front of him and looked Theo straight in the eye. 'Hello, Mr Marriott. I have two children down here who say they're here to see your son . . . Yes, sir.' The guard turned back to Theo and Ricky. 'And your names are?'

'Theo Mosley. And this is Ricky Burridge,' Theo provided.

The security guard repeated the information over the phone. 'Yes, sir . . . No, sir . . . Very good, sir.'

Three bags full, sir! Theo thought, eyebrows raised. What was it about Darius Marriott that had all the grown-ups around him bowing and scraping? The man's farts were probably just as smelly as everyone else's!

'Take the lift over there and press the button marked P,' ordered the security guard.

Without another word, Theo and Ricky did as they were told. Only when the lift doors had shut behind them did they speak.

'Have you ever seen anything like this?' Theo asked. 'This

lift has got a better carpet in it than we've got in our whole house! And this building is something else. Mr Marriott must be rolling in it.'

'He probably has a room in his apartment full of money and he goes in there every day and just jumps up and down and rolls about in it,' Ricky sniffed.

'Ah! But is he happy?' Theo asked seriously.

He and Ricky looked at each other. 'Yes!' they said in unison.

The lift doors opened. Bullet and his dad stood outside an open door beyond which Theo and Ricky saw the biggest living room they'd ever seen. Darius wore a royal blue shirt, a golden yellow tie and a navy blue suit which fitted so well it had to have been made for him.

'Hello, Mr Marriott.'

'Good morning, Mr Marriott.'

'Morning. I can't stop. Help yourself to whatever.' Darius rushed past them into the lift.

'Bye, Dad.'

Darius just had time to wave before the lift doors closed.

'In a hurry, was he?' said Ricky, drily. 'So Bullet, I'm bursting to know what was so all-fired urgent that you had to drag us out of bed at six o'clock in the morning.'

'How come you're here and not at home?' asked Theo.

'I spent the weekend with my dad. It's OK. Mum said I could.'

'You're round here a lot these days, aren't you?' Ricky said thoughtfully.

'Is your mum here too?' Theo asked.

Bullet shook his head. 'She wouldn't come even though Dad invited her. But she said she understands that me and Dad want to get to know each other better. I sometimes wish . . .'

'Wish what?' Theo prompted when Bullet shut up.

'It's just that it would be so perfect if Mum and Dad . . . Well, there's no use talking about it. It's not going to happen.' Bullet shrugged.

Theo and Ricky followed Bullet into the penthouse. Only when they were inside the apartment, could they appreciate the living room's true size and splendour.

'Wow! This isn't a living room. Clear all the furniture out of the way and two professional teams could play a decent game of football.' Theo whistled appreciatively.

One wall of the living room was entirely made of glass and the view was spectacular. They could see most of the town and out into the countryside beyond. The sky was a clear, morning blue and in the distance Theo could see a plane banking. He walked over to the window and looked out over the town, wondering if he'd be able to make out his house from here.

'Where's your dad gone, then?' asked Ricky.

'He had to leave for an emergency meeting,' said Bullet.

'So where's the fire?' Theo turned to ask.

'I wanted to show you around and show you some things before his housekeeper arrives. We're only going to be alone for about another twenty minutes, half an hour at the most,' Bullet explained.

'I thought you were going to scan your dad's will into his computer and get a printout.' Theo frowned.

'I don't want to risk it. I don't want to risk taking anything out of this apartment that I shouldn't. Dad told me that he's got security devices all over the place.'

'What kind of security devices?' Theo and Ricky looked around anxiously.

'I can't see anything,' Ricky said slowly, still checking the corners of the vast room.

'That's the thing. I've looked everywhere and I can't see the first hint of a security device. Dad's security is brilliant.' Bullet grinned.

'So how are we going to see the will?' Theo asked. 'I don't want to do anything that'll have shutters banging down and lights flashing and will get Tweedledee and Tweedledum at the desk downstairs up here.'

'I think we're OK as long as we don't try to take anything out past the front door,' Bullet said.

'You don't sound too sure,' said Ricky.

'I'm not,' Bullet admitted.

'What explanation did you give your dad for inviting us round here?' asked Theo.

'I asked him if you could come round before school to help me revise for our test today,' Bullet explained.

'And your dad was OK with that?'

Bullet smiled. 'He believed me. Why shouldn't he? Besides, I think he thought I just wanted to show off his apartment to you.'

'Can't think why!' Theo said wryly, looking around again.

'Come on. This way. We'd better get cracking before the housekeeper arrives. The safe is in Dad's den.'

Suppressing the urge to make a sarky remark, Theo followed behind Bullet who led the way to one of the rooms on the right, leading off the living room. The den consisted of a large mahogany table upon which sat a PC screen, printer, scanner and speakers. The floor was polished parquet wood with a huge rug in the centre of the room. The rug was a revelation in itself. Its pattern consisted of three white peacocks displaying their snow-white tail feathers, whilst between them and around the edges smaller midnight-blue and turquoise peacocks tried to peck at them. And the peacocks were so beautifully embroidered, Theo expected them to burst out of the rug and take wing at any second. Around the walls there was shelf after shelf of books. Theo walked around, curious about the sort of things a millionaire liked to read. It was all non-fiction. And most of the books were about military whatevers. Military machines. Military strategy. Military tactics. Military doodahs – past, present and future. Theo wrinkled up his nose. How boring. Apart from the large table with all the computer equipment on and under it, there were two huge black leather chairs beneath each window and one wall of the den was covered in paintings, most of which Theo recognized as famous ones done by people like Monet and Van Gogh. Theo's mum and dad liked paintings – especially Impressionist paintings – but they bought the posters and then framed them. Theo was in no doubt at all that every painting in this room was the real thing. He couldn't help wondering, did Darius Marriott own those paintings because he liked them and they gave him pleasure, or did he own them so that he could say he owned them?

'Dad calls that his picture wall.' Bullet smiled.

'It's a great room,' Ricky said.

Theo didn't think so. In spite of the morning light streaming through the window, the room was cold and dark and uninviting.

'Dad's safe is under the rug.' Bullet headed straight for it. 'Help me roll it back.'

They all helped to roll back the rug until more than half of the floor was exposed. Pulling the rug out of the way, Theo and Ricky went back to Bullet to check out the contraption in the floor. And there it was – a rectangular door, a little smaller than the cupboard doors in Theo's kitchen at home. It was made of a silver-coloured metal. In the middle of the door was a keypad. Theo had expected a round tumbler device with numbers all around it like they always showed on the telly. Bullet took a small device out of his pocket, like a thick compass with two antennae sticking out of it. Also attached to it were two earpieces on a longish cable, like the earpieces sometimes supplied with a portable CD player.

'That's your safe cracker, is it?' Theo asked.

Bullet nodded, putting the earpieces in his ears.

'So how does it work then?'

'It sends a phased series of tones and pulses to the opening mechanism microchip and analyses differential micro delays in response times so that . . .'

'Nope, forget it. It's another Heathrow job already.' Theo waved away the explanation which had already lost him.

'When you try a random number for the combination, the computer takes a different amount of time to say "no" based on how wrong the number is. By timing the delay you can home in on the right number pretty quickly.'

'Hang on.' Theo frowned. 'With a keypad you could have any number of numbers and in any order. I don't see how your device is going to help in this instance.'

'I know all the numbers except the last one and I know the last one consists of three digits,' said Bullet. 'So all I have to do is find that last three-digit number before Mrs Frayn the housekeeper arrives.'

'Go on then. Do your stuff,' said Ricky, glancing down at his watch. 'But hurry up.

We still have to get to school after all this. I'll wait by the door and warn you if anyone comes in.'

Ten minutes later the safe still wasn't open.

'Bullet, we're running out of time,' Theo said anxiously.

'I know. I know. I'm doing my best,' Bullet replied.

Another seven minutes passed before the safe door finally clicked open.

'At last!' Ricky breathed a sigh of relief. He went back to the centre of the room to get a better look. Hanging down on suspended rods were hanging files, each containing papers and more papers.

'I think Dad's will is in here somewhere.' Bullet started hunting through the hanging files.

'What's the rest of this stuff?' Theo couldn't help asking.

'Research notes on new inventions, notes on the Lazarus suit, that kind of thing. Plus details of most of Dad's bank accounts around the world.'

'He's got more than one account?' asked Ricky.

'Of course,' said Bullet, as if it was the most natural thing in the world. 'Ah, here it is. Dad's will.'

Ricky and Theo gathered in closer, eager to see what it contained. They all read in silence for a couple of minutes.

'All that legal jargon is a bit hard going but as far as I

can see, you get everything apart from a few thousands scattered around to some of his staff and some of his favourite charities,' Theo said at last.

'Yes, but have you seen this bit?' Ricky turned to the third page of the will. 'If Bullet dies before Mr Marriott then the terms of the old will apply.'

'Bullet, what were the terms of the old will, d'you know?'

'Yeah, Dad told me. As far as Dad's DemTech shares are concerned, Ron would've inherited twenty-five per cent, Yves and Faith would've got eleven per cent each and Jo was due to get four per cent.'

Theo's expression grew pained as he did some less than rapid mental totting up. 'Hang on. That doesn't add up to one hundred, that only adds up to fifty-one.'

'Dad's only got fifty-one per cent of the company's stock. At the moment, Ron has fifteen per cent, Faith and Yves have thirteen per cent and Jo has eight per cent of the company.'

'But – have I got this right? – according to the old will, if your dad's shares were split between the four of them, none of them would've had outright control of DemTech. Ron would've inherited the most, giving him – my head hurts! – forty per cent of the company, but that's not enough to run things,' Theo pointed out.

'Maybe Dad didn't want any one of them running the company. Or maybe it was a device to make them all work together? I don't know.' Bullet shrugged.

'Your dad told you an awful lot about himself and his company in a very short space of time,' Ricky said speculatively.

'We've had great talks.' Bullet beamed. 'We had a lot of catching up to do.'

'But why would he tell you so much about his wills and the DemTech set-up and the rest?' Ricky persisted.

''Cos I'm his son, of course,' Bullet said, surprised that Ricky even had to ask.

'It's just that . . .'

'What was that?' Bullet's head turned immediately towards the door. 'Quick! Give me the will.'

Bullet snatched the will out of Ricky's hands and stuffed it back into its hanging file before slamming the door shut.

'The rug! Quick! The rug!' Bullet hissed.

Theo rolled and Ricky leaped in the rug's direction. Bullet sprang out of the way as Ricky and Theo rolled it out like pushing a barrel. They straightened up the rug just as the door opened.

'Hello, Mrs Frayn . . .' Bullet's voice trailed off as they all stared at the woman who entered the den.

If this was Mrs Frayn then she was like no other house-keeper Theo had ever seen. She wore a bright red evening dress and a midnight-black mink coat. And something told Theo that it wasn't fake fur.

'Well now. Who might you three be?' the woman asked. 'No, don't tell me. Let me guess.' She pointed straight at Bullet. 'You're Darius's long-lost son. Correct?'

Bullet gulped and nodded.

The woman scrutinized Bullet as if he was under a micro-scope. It wasn't that Theo and Ricky were forgotten. It was as if they weren't even there. They were of no more interest than passing ants on the pavement.

'Toby Barker . . .' The woman breathed Bullet's name, her tone dripping with the smile on her face although, for the life of him, Theo couldn't see what was so amusing. The woman looked around, before turning back to Bullet.

'Tell me,' she said at last. 'How much would it take to make you and your mother disappear?'

## Chapter Thirteen

# Mrs Marriott

'I don't understand.' Bullet's voice came out in a squeak.

'You're obviously after my husband's money but I'm back now. And I'm going to make sure you don't get one brown penny from Darius's will. So I'll ask you again, how much will it take for you and your mother to make yourselves scarce?'

'I don't want Dad's money,' Bullet replied indignantly. 'That's not what this is about at all.'

'No?' Mrs Marriott crossed the room, overpoweringly sweet perfume wafting behind her. It made Theo want to sneeze. 'Then exactly what is this all about?'

'I just wanted to see Dad. I wanted . . . I want to be with him,' said Bullet.

'There's no room for you in his life, or mine,' said Mrs Marriott.

'That's not what Dad said,' Bullet told her.

'But then he wouldn't. Darius always leaves it to me to do all his dirty work for him.' Mrs Marriott's laugh was a tinkling bell. No one could deny that she was very beautiful. She had shoulder-length auburn hair and deep green eyes framed by the longest eyelashes that Theo had ever seen. Some people might've looked silly wearing an evening dress at this time in the morning, but she didn't.

'Did my dad tell you to get rid of me?' Bullet's voice was barely above a whisper.

'Of course not. But he will do,' said Samantha. 'At the moment, you're a new experience for him. He's never played at being a daddy before. He'll soon get bored.'

Never before had Theo witnessed such a display of vindictive spite. This woman was a real piece of work. She reminded Theo of a swaying, spitting cobra, mesmerizingly dangerous. He longed to open his mouth to defend his friend but he was only too aware that it was none of his business.

'Dad isn't like that.' Bullet tried to defend himself.

'No?' Mrs Marriott shrugged out of her coat and trailed it behind her on her way to the door. 'I've known him for a lot longer than you. Allow me to know my own husband.'

'Dad is kind and generous and he loves me,' Bullet shouted at her.

Mrs Marriott laughed like a drain at that. 'That's what you think? Darius loves no one but himself. You'd do well to remember that – then you won't be too disappointed.'

Bullet clamped his lips together, not trusting himself to say another word.

'What are you three boys doing in here anyway?' Mrs Marriott suddenly turned her gaze on Ricky and Theo. She looked slowly around the room, then down at the rug.

'Ah! Have you been at Darius's safe? I hope you broke in and tore up that ridiculous will. I know the combination number if you're having trouble,' Mrs Marriott smiled.

'We don't even know where Mr Marriott's safe is,' Theo tried.

'Of course not,' Mrs Marriott said in mock empathy.

'What makes you think we were looking at Mr Marriott's safe?' Ricky asked carefully.

'Darius insists that the biggest white peacock, there in the middle, always faces due north – which is that way.' Mrs Marriott pointed towards the picture wall. 'That peacock always has his beak directly facing the Degas in the middle of the wall.'

No one spoke.

'I'd turn the rug around before the housekeeper or my husband comes home if I were you three.' Samantha Marriott turned and headed out the door, calling back over her shoulder, 'I'll be seeing you.'

'Not if I see you first,' Bullet muttered under his breath.

Samantha turned immediately. 'But that's where you're wrong, Toby. You and I will be seeing a great deal of each other. I'm back now. And don't you forget it.' And Samantha swept out of the room, quietly closing the door behind her.

'Whew! I feel like I've just stepped out of a tumble dryer,' said Ricky.

And Theo knew exactly what he meant. 'Come on. Let's change this rug around before anyone else notices that we've shifted it.'

As they all helped to turn it back to its correct position, Ricky put into words what everyone else was thinking, 'Why did she warn us? I mean, what was in it for her?'

'Maybe she's going to tell Dad that I was investigating his safe?' Bullet ventured.

'But now she has no proof – unless of course she was lying about the way the rug lies,' Theo said slowly.

'I hate to say this, 'cos I didn't like her at all, but I don't think she was lying somehow,' Ricky said slowly. 'I think she hates your guts, Bullet, but I don't think she was lying to you.'

Theo considered. 'No, I don't think so either.'

'So what do we do now?' Ricky asked.

'Let's get out of here.' Bullet headed for the door. 'Besides, there's something else I wanted to show both of you.'

'What?'

'Dad's suit of life as he calls it. His Lazarus suit.' Bullet led the way out of the den and into another room off the main living room.

'What's this room?' asked Ricky, pointing to the room Bullet indicated.

'It's my bedroom when I'm here,' Bullet explained. 'It's one of the guest rooms.'

He led the way into his room and closed the door. The Lazarus suit lay on his bed.

'Why did you want to show us this?' asked Theo.

''Cos I want you two to be my witnesses,' said Bullet. 'I've tested it backwards, forwards and sideways and my lie detector doesn't set it off.'

'It's not exactly the same conditions,' Theo ventured. 'No one was wearing it.'

'I was,' Bullet stated.

'What?' Ricky and Theo spoke in horrified unison.

'You nutter! It might've killed you,' Ricky ranted.

'No way. I know Dad's invention works. Besides, I tested it range-wise, height-wise, frequency-wise, amount of light-wise and every other wise I could think of. My lie detector doesn't activate this suit. In fact the only thing my lie detector does is switch the suit off. It doesn't do anything else.'

'This thing has an on/off switch?' Theo said, confused.

'No, not really, but it has a number of electronic components. If any of those components are activated, then using my lie detector nearby stops them from working. In effect it switches all the electronic components off.'

'Including the defib . . . defibrillation bit.' Theo tried to remember the word.

'Including that.' Bullet nodded.

'So how exactly does it work?' Theo reached out a tentative hand towards the suit.

'Just as Dad said. It's designed to be ultra-thin so that it can be worn under a shirt and a proper suit. The high collar would be hidden by a shirt with a proper collar and it has a mechanism in it to take the pulse in your neck. There's a cardiac massage unit, a defibrillation device – but that's only ever used as a last resort – it can take your blood pressure and it can administer injections like insulin in times of emergency.'

Theo broke out his notepad.

'What're you doing?' asked Bullet.

'I'm taking notes. I want to draw this thing just so I don't forget what all its bits and pieces do. It might be important.'

'Just remember that the details of this suit are strictly confidential,' Bullet said anxiously.

Theo nodded and carried on drawing.

'Do you think your dad's Lazarus suit will be successful?' Ricky asked.

'I don't know,' Bullet replied. 'All the really successful inventions involve things that have mass-market appeal so that lots and lots of people will buy them. But apart from presidents and prime ministers and famous film stars and maybe royalty, I don't really see who else would buy it. It's going to be hideously expensive to buy and cost even more money to maintain, monitor and operate.'

'If the price is really high, your dad's company will still make a huge profit even if they only sell a few thousand worldwide, won't it?' asked Ricky.

Bullet shrugged doubtfully. 'That's the theory.'

'I see you have better business sense than my husband.' Samantha Marriott had appeared from nowhere to stand in the doorway. Bullet jumped and he wasn't the only one. Where had she appeared from? How long had she been standing in the doorway? Theo could've sworn he'd shut the door behind him as he entered the room.

Samantha Marriott reminded him of a snake in more ways than one.

'I only came in here to say don't you three have school to go to or something?' asked Mrs Marriott. 'Not that it's any skin off my nose if you go or not. I just don't want to get blamed for not mentioning it.'

'We were just leaving . . . Mrs Marriott.' Bullet stumbled over her name.

A slight smile played over Samantha's lips. 'Toby, as you're obviously uncomfortable saying my name, you can call me . . . Mrs Marriott.'

No doubt she thought she was being hilariously funny.

'Enjoy yourselves, sprogs. I'm off for a hot bath and a cold glass of champagne.' Mrs Marriott swept out of the room, leaving the door wide open.

'What an old trout!' Ricky breathed.

'She was right about the time though,' Theo said, glancing down at his watch. 'We'd better get a move on or we're going to be late.'

'Theo, you go on ahead. I want to talk to Ricky about something,' said Bullet.

'Then I'll wait too,' Theo began.

'No, you go on ahead. We'll meet you at school,' Bullet said firmly.

Theo stared from Bullet to Ricky and back again. He tried – and failed – not to feel hurt by his exclusion. What had he done? Why were they shutting him out? Confused, he didn't move.

'I'll show you to the door,' said Bullet.

'Don't bother. I can find my own way out,' Theo snapped.

Fine! If they didn't want him, if he was getting in the way, then he would leave. Right now. Theo marched out of the room and headed for the front door. He could sense Ricky and Bullet watching him. He fully intended to keep going without a backward glance. He fully intended to take a leaf out of Mrs Marriott's book and leave the front door wide open, but somehow it didn't happen.

'I'll see you both at school then?' Theo turned and asked uncertainly.

Relief broadened Bullet's smile. Standing slightly behind Bullet, Ricky shrugged apologetically. He obviously had no idea why Bullet wanted him to stay behind. With a nod, Theo left the apartment, shutting the door quietly behind him.

# Chapter Fourteen

# No Doubt

Theo watched the classroom door like a circling hawk watching a rabbit. Where were Ricky and Bullet? What if something had happened to them? First Angela, then Ricky and Bullet. Theo felt like he was losing sight of all of them. The previous night, Theo had phoned Angela's foster-mum and dad to find out how Angela was doing but there'd been no answer. In the end, Theo had phoned the hospital but all they would say was that Angela was comfortable.

'Theo? Why has the door suddenly become so fascinating?'

'Sorry, Mrs Daltry.' Theo snapped back to the here and now.

'You've been staring at that door for the last ten minutes. What am I missing?' asked the teacher.

'Nothing, Mrs Daltry. I . . . I was just thinking,' Theo said quickly.

'Could you think by staring at the whiteboard instead of the door, please?'

'Sorry!' Theo mumbled. He turned to the whiteboard, making a great show of reading every letter Mrs Daltry had written. She raised her eyebrows but didn't say anything.

Where *were* they? If anything had happened to them . . . At that moment, the door opened slowly. Ricky and Bullet immediately entered the room and made a beeline for their chairs as if hoping the teacher wouldn't notice them.

'Excuse me! What time in the morning do you two call this?' asked Mrs Daltry.

'Sorry, Mrs Daltry,' Ricky began.

'We . . . we missed our bus,' Bullet added.

'Ricky, since when do you need a bus to get to school? You live two streets away.'

Ricky and Bullet exchanged a quick look. 'I went to meet Bullet,' Ricky tried to explain. 'So I had to get a bus to his house and then a bus back here again.'

'The next time, let Toby come to school on his own. Then you'll both be on time,' Mrs Daltry said, annoyed. 'Now hurry up and sit down.'

Ricky quickly sat down next to Theo. Bullet sat at his table.

'Everything OK?' Theo whispered.

'So-so,' Ricky whispered back. 'Ssh! I'll tell you later.'

'I'd appreciate that,' Mrs Daltry drawled from the front of the classroom.

Theo bent his head over his work. The last thing any of them wanted or needed right now was to antagonize Mrs Daltry and her bat ears!

Theo turned in his seat the moment Mrs Daltry was out the door, her bag of liquorice allsorts in her hands already. Most of the others in the class were close behind. 'OK, give! What's going on?'

'Bullet wanted to talk to me about something. But that's not the important thing right now,' Ricky dismissed with a wave of his hand. 'Theo, the thing is, you were right. We *are* being followed. Someone followed us to school.'

Icy drips careened down Theo's back. 'Are you sure?'

'No doubt about it,' Bullet replied, joining them.

'So what do we do?' Theo asked.

'I don't know,' Bullet admitted.

The three friends looked at each other. No one wanted to say out loud what each of them had in their minds.

'What was this morning all about?' asked Theo at last.

'Pardon?'

'Why did you want Ricky to stay behind at your dad's flat?' asked Theo.

'This was one of the reasons.' Bullet pulled a scrunched up, grubby envelope out of his duffel bag and passed it to Theo. Gingerly, Theo fished the letter from its envelope. Holding it by its corners, Theo regarded Bullet, who looked away. Theo unfolded the sheet of paper and began to read the two typed lines in the middle of the page.

*Toby Barker,*
*Be careful you don't get stung.*

Theo turned to Bullet. 'What is this supposed to mean?'

Bullet shrugged. 'I think it's meant to be a threat.' At Theo's puzzled frown, Bullet continued. 'The person who sent it obviously knows that I'm allergic to wasp stings.'

Theo stared at the piece of paper before him, before turning back to Bullet. 'D'you really think that's what it means?' he asked, aghast.

Bullet shrugged. 'I can't think what else it could be referring to.'

'Who knows you're allergic to wasp stings?'

'Mum and you guys. Family and friends. It's not a secret. I have to walk around with a hypo of adrenaline and wear a medic alert bracelet – you know that.'

'So anyone could've found out,' Theo mused. 'What're you going to do about this letter?'

'See if I get any more.'

'When did you get this one?' Theo asked, reading it one more time before handing it back.

'Yesterday,' Bullet replied.

'But yesterday was a Sunday. The postman doesn't deliver on a Sunday,' said Theo.

'It was hand-delivered some time yesterday morning, apparently. It was waiting for me when I went home to get my school bag,' Bullet explained.

'Let me see the envelope again,' said Theo.

Bullet handed it over. Theo scrutinized the back and the

front of the envelope. It was a plain white, self-seal envelope with the words 'Toby Barker' typed on the front and underlined. There was no address and no stamp.

'Why couldn't you have mentioned this at your dad's flat? Why did I have to leave?'

Theo didn't miss the conspiratorial glance which flashed between Ricky and Bullet. 'What're you two not telling me?' Theo hoped his voice didn't sound as hurt at the exclusion as he felt.

Silence.

'You're not going to tell me, are you?'

'It was nothing to do with you, Theo,' said Bullet. 'Not really. I just wanted Ricky's advice on something.'

Theo had to bite back his retort that his advice was every bit as good as Ricky's. If Bullet wanted to confide in Ricky about something and not him, then he'd just have to leave them to it.

'I suppose I'd be wasting my breath asking you to go to the police?'

Theo had his answer from the expression on Bullet's face.

'Aren't you frightened?' Theo asked, more than a hint of exasperation in his voice. 'First Angela's accident and now this. If it was me I'd be camped on the doorstep of my local police station. You wouldn't be able to get me out of there.'

'It's not that simple.'

'It is from where I'm standing,' Theo dismissed.

'But you don't have your dad to consider from where you're standing,' said Bullet.

'Pass that by me again.' Theo frowned in an effort to unravel Bullet's sentence.

'I mean, if someone's after my dad, then I want to be there to help, not locked up under police protection somewhere. Dad doesn't know about this and I want to keep it that way,' said Bullet. 'And besides, if I'm out and about, then maybe whoever it is will concentrate on me and leave my dad alone.'

Stunned, Theo turned to see what Ricky's reaction was to all this. Ricky was slowly shaking his head.

'You're not thinking or saying anything that I haven't,' Ricky sighed. 'Bullet's determined not to get the police involved – at least not yet.'

'Bullet, I'm sure your dad can look after himself much better than you can.' Theo couldn't let it rest there. He had to try and make Bullet see sense.

'He needs me.'

*Not as much as you need him.* The words almost fell out of Theo's mouth but he managed to bite them back just in time.

'Bullet, I'm sorry but I think this has gone far enough. If you won't go to the police then I will.' Theo made up his mind.

'No!' Bullet exploded. 'I don't want you to.'

'It's for your own good. I'd never forgive myself if something happened to you or any of us.'

'It won't.'

'Oh, you can guarantee that, can you?' Theo said with sarcasm.

'It won't,' Bullet repeated.

'And I'm going to make sure of that. As soon as school is over this afternoon I'm going straight to the police . . .'

'And what're you going to tell them?' Bullet drew himself up. His eyes took on a steely glint.

'I'll tell them about that letter for a start.' Theo was well aware that he was about to lose a friend – and maybe for good – but what choice did he have? If Bullet wouldn't go to the police, then he would.

'What letter?' asked Bullet.

'The letter in your hand.' Theo pointed.

'What letter?' Bullet asked again.

'That one . . .' Theo's voice trailed off as he realized what Bullet was up to.

'I don't know what you're talking about. I never received any letter,' Bullet stated as if to drive the point home.

Theo and Bullet glared at each other without even blinking. Suddenly Theo made a lunge for the letter in Bullet's hand. Bullet pulled his hand away, jumping backwards at the same time. Theo only just missed – but miss he did.

'You try that again and I'll . . .'

'You'll what?' Theo challenged. 'You're acting like a real . . .'

'Look, this isn't getting us anywhere,' Ricky intervened. 'If Bullet doesn't want to go to the police then we need to come up with a different strategy.'

'You can't agree with what he's doing?' Theo asked, aghast.

'That's not the point, is it?' Ricky shook his head. 'The police are out. So what do we do to flush out the person who's behind all this? That's what we have to work together to decide.'

Casting a filthy look in Bullet's direction, Theo swallowed the anger rising in him like bile and sought to control his temper. 'Will someone *please* tell me what's going on?'

'We've told you all you need to know, Theo,' Ricky said quietly. 'Let it go.'

'Oi! You three. You know you're not allowed to be in here durinq breaktime.' Mr Appleyard the caretaker stood at the open classroom door, waving them out.

Theo looked around. They were alone. Everyone else had left the classroom. Theo had been so wrapped up in what was going on with Bullet and Ricky that he hadn't even noticed.

'Come on. I haven't got all day,' Mr Appleyard snapped.

Theo followed Ricky and Bullet out of the classroom, but the caretaker was way down the list of things on his mind. Ricky and Bullet had all his attention. Why was he being excluded? What were they up to?

'I know how we can go forward from here,' Bullet said as they left the classroom and Mr Appleyard behind. 'I think we should go and see my dad after school.'

'Your dad? You mean at his office?' Theo questioned.

Bullet nodded. 'It's not far. And that way we'll have the chance to see the people he works with. I'll phone him this lunch time and arrange it. Agreed?'

'Agreed.' Ricky spoke for both himself and Theo.

And Theo couldn't help resenting it. And the way they told him some bits and kept other bits secret. But going to Mr Marriott's was a good idea and as he couldn't come up with a better one, he kept quiet.

The next step was to suss out Mr Marriott's colleagues, and once that was done then they'd all be in a better position to figure out who wanted Darius Marriott and Bullet permanently out of the way.

## Chapter Fifteen

# Office Life

'Can we see Mr Marriott, please?' Bullet asked.

'Mr Marriott? Mr Darius Marriott?' the receptionist questioned.

Theo glared at her. How many Mr Marriotts did they have in the building, for goodness' sake?

'Yes, that's right. Can we see him, please? He's expecting us,' said Bullet.

'He is?'

'That's right. He's my dad.' Pride laced every beaming word. Theo smiled faintly to himself but said nothing.

'Just a moment.' The receptionist picked up the phone receiver and pressed four numbers in quick succession. She gave the three boys a suspicious look before swivelling her chair away from them and cupping her hand over the mouth piece before she spoke.

Theo raised his eyes heavenward. This woman wouldn't have been out of place working for the American CIA.

'What's your name?' the receptionist asked Bullet.

'Toby. Toby Barker.'

'And your names?'

'I'm Ricky Burridge and this is Theo Mosley,' said Ricky.

The receptionist swivelled her chair away from them again. She whispered into the telephone receiver, nodding, then shaking her head as she spoke. A few moments later she put down the receiver, a look of surprise on her face. 'Take the lift up to the third floor. You'll be met.'

'Thank you.' Bullet smiled, more than a hint of smugness turning up his lips.

Theo and Ricky followed Bullet to the lift. Theo turned to look out of the glass-fronted reception area into the street beyond.

'What's the matter?' Ricky asked.

'D'you think we're still being followed?' Theo asked tentatively.

Ricky turned to look out into the street too. 'I don't know. If we are being followed then they've got better at it.'

Theo nodded his agreement as they all stepped into the lift. Ricky checked the buttons in the lift. 'Seven floors! Does the whole building belong to your dad?'

Bullet nodded.

'Wow!' Ricky whistled, impressed.

They entered the lift and headed up to the third floor.

'Why are we here again?' Theo asked drily.

'Moral support,' Bullet answered at once. 'Plus three heads are better than two or one.'

'You didn't think that earlier this morning,' Theo muttered.

'Pardon?'

'Nothing.' Theo looked away from the speculative glance being directed at him by Ricky. Theo knew he was being silly, but he couldn't help it. Being excluded still rankled. The lift doors opened and they all stepped out.

'Hi. Toby?' A woman with impossibly red hair and a wide smile beamed at all of them.

'Yes, I'm Toby.' Bullet put out his hand.

'And Ricky?'

Ricky nodded.

'And you must be Theo.'

'That's right.' Theo nodded as well.

'Welcome. Darius said you might be popping in this afternoon for a tour. I'm Joanne Fleming. Call me Jo – everyone does. It's great to meet all of you at last. Toby, Darius has told me so much about you.'

'Has he?' Bullet was pleased.

'Are you kidding? He's spoken of nothing else. I must

admit, it was a bit of a surprise for all of us when we heard he had a son. A long-lost son you might say. But now he's found you – or you found him.' Jo grinned.

Ricky and Theo exchanged a glance. Goodness, but this woman could chat! She hardly paused to draw breath. But Theo liked her! She was friendly and bubbly. Theo suspected that most people would like this woman. They walked through the double doors at the end of the short corridor to find themselves in a large, open plan area with offices running down one side of it.

'Let me introduce you to some of the people your dad works with.' Jo walked almost as quickly as she talked. Theo had to practically trot to keep up with her. 'This is Yves Hamilton's office. He's our Sales and Marketing Director.'

They approached an office with a painted wooden door and fluted, frosted windows on either side of it. Jo rapped smartly on the door and, without waiting for a reply, opened it immediately.

A black man with short hair at the sides and no hair at all on top, turned around in his chair to face them, his fingers still poised over his computer keyboard. He wore gold-rimmed glasses which dominated his face. His jacket was slung over his chair and his sleeves were rolled up to his elbows.

'Hi, Yves. This is Toby, Darius's son, and his friends, Ricky and Theo.'

'Is it now? Hi, there.' Yves stretched out his hand to Bullet, who shook it. He waved to Theo and Ricky who stood behind Bullet, out of reach. 'So what brings the three of you to this neck of the woods?'

'Dad said he'd show us around.'

'Ah yes! Your dad warned . . . told us about changing his will. So I suppose it's only right. All this is going to be yours one day.' Yves smiled.

Bullet returned the smile uneasily. 'Not for years and years yet.'

Yves nodded but didn't reply.

'So what exactly do you do, Mr Hamilton?' Theo asked.

Yves looked at Theo with surprise. Theo realized that the man had forgotten he was standing there. Bullet had all of his attention.

'I'm in charge of making sure that we market and sell our products in the most cost-effective, efficient and profitable way possible.' Yves smiled.

'D'you do that all by yourself?'

Yves burst out laughing. 'Thank you for your confidence in my super-human abilities but no, I don't. I have a team of about one hundred and thirty in this country alone. The sales staff are based at our other offices up and down the country, although most of the marketing staff are based in this building.'

'Didn't I see you a couple of weeks ago at our school when Mr Marriott came for a visit?' bluffed Theo.

Yves Hamilton's smile vanished. 'That was the morning Darius had his heart attack, wasn't it?'

Theo nodded.

'You couldn't have seen me. I was in a marketing strategy meeting all morning.'

'My mistake.' Theo shrugged. 'I thought I saw you there but I've obviously got it wrong.'

'Jo, you were there, weren't you?' Yves turned to Darius's personal assistant.

'Yep! At the back of the hall watching. Faith was there too – which is just as well because when it all happened, I'm afraid I lost it. Faith accompanied Darius to the hospital and I came back here. It gave me quite a shock to see Darius keel over like that, I can tell you.' Jo shrugged. 'Thank goodness he's OK now.'

'I still think he should be taking it easy. He's trying to do too much.' Yves shook his head.

'You know Darius,' Jo smiled. 'The doctor at the hospital told him that it probably wasn't a heart attack so he signs himself out and he's back to work a couple of days later. You can't keep a good man down!'

'Well, I'll tell you what I told him. He's being too hasty. He should give himself time to recover. If it wasn't his heart giving him a warning, then it was something going wrong somewhere in his body. You don't just hit the deck for no reason. He needs to slow down.'

'Yes, Yves. I'm sure Toby and his friends didn't come here to hear your views on Darius's health.'

Yves Hamilton looked at Toby sheepishly. 'I guess I'm simply a fusser at heart! It's just that your dad is not only my work colleague but a very good friend. I'd hate to see anything happen to him.'

'Well, sorry to interrupt you, Yves. I'll let you get on with it. Next stop – Faith Shanley's office. She's our R&D director.'

At Ricky's puzzled look, Theo supplied, 'Research and Development director.'

'Oh.' Ricky nodded his thanks.

They moved along to the next office. There was no need to knock, for this door was already open.

'Hi, Faith.'

Faith Shanley slammed shut the drawer she'd been rummaging in before she looked up. She was pretty in a cold, detached sort of way. She had jet-black hair and the lightest blue eyes Theo had ever seen. They were so light as to be almost colourless. It gave her the strangest appearance.

'Are you busy?' Jo smiled.

'Yes I am, actually,' Faith declared icily. She glared at Toby, then Ricky and Theo.

'This is Toby Barker, Darius's son. And these are his friends, Theo and Ricky.'

Faith Shanley continued to scrutinize them all without saying a word. Finally she barked out, 'Shouldn't you three be in school?'

'School's over for today,' Bullet informed her.

'Already? It's only four-thirty.'

'School finishes at three-thirty.'

'That early? No wonder you children leave school not knowing your backside from a hole in the ground!' Faith snorted with disgust.

Charming! Theo glared at the R&D director. With her people skills – or the lack of them – Theo wouldn't let her direct traffic, much less the research and development department.

'Jo mentioned that you were at our school when Darius collapsed on our school stage.' Ricky shook his head. 'It must have given you quite a shock.'

'I was in the car waiting for him. The first I knew about it was when the ambulance pulled up.' Faith frowned. 'I promised myself when I left school that I'd never set foot in another one and I'm a woman of my word.'

'Yes, er . . . I can see you're busy, so we'll leave you to it.' Jo hustled them out of Faith's office and moved them down to the next one. 'Don't mind Faith. She's been a bit . . . preoccupied over the last couple of weeks.'

Theo looked at all the secretaries and other workers busy at their computers in the open plan office. Talk about living in each other's pockets. In the open plan you couldn't even make a phone call with any degree of privacy. He'd hate to work anywhere quite that exposed. Anyway, the situation wouldn't arise. He was going to be a world-famous, first-class detective.

'Now this is Ron Westall's office. He's the company secretary. I don't know if you know this Toby, but Ron started DemTech with your dad.' Jo popped her head around the door and looked around the empty office. 'Now where's he got to?' Jo straightened up to look around the rest of the open plan. 'Oh well! He'll turn up.'

'If Ron Westall started the company with Mr Marriott, why does DemTech stand for Darius Evan Marriott Technologies?' Theo asked.

'I'll answer that,' a voice piped up from behind them.

Theo swung around. An older man than Darius with chestnut-brown, wavy hair, twinkling blue eyes and a friendly face grinned at them. The silvery strands in his hair were many. He kept running his fingers through his hair in an effort to stop it flopping down over his face.

'I'm Ron Westall. And to answer your question, I've always been a "get on with it behind the scenes" kind of guy. Darius has always been better at presenting our ideas than me, so I let him get on with it. But the first couple of successful inventions DemTech engineered were based on ideas I had. I had the ideas, Darius put up all the money. Another reason the company is named after him.'

'But we couldn't do without you.' Jo smiled.

'Jo, you're too good to me.' Ron's smile broadened.

'Are you going to the dance on Saturday?' Jo asked.

'Will you be there?'

Jo nodded.

'Then of course I will,' Ron beamed.

'Ron, you are such a flirt,' Jo said drily.

'What dance?' Theo whispered to Bullet.

'It's the DemTech annual company summer dance. They're all going to some swish hotel,' Bullet whispered back.

'Jo, d'you know if Yves and Faith are going on Saturday night?' asked Ron.

'They both said they were – although Faith said she might have to duck out early.'

'She always says that, and then she's one of the last ones to leave!' Ron chuckled. 'Anyway, I'd better get back to my office. I wouldn't want to be accused of slacking.'

Ron walked off with a wave. Jo carried on walking down the corridor formed by the offices on one side and half-partitions on the other. 'This office at the end here belongs to your dad. I think his wife is in there at the moment but I'm sure she won't be too long.'

They all stopped outside Darius's closed door. Theo could

hear Samantha Marriott's muffled voice through the door and she didn't sound happy.

'I don't think so . . .' Samantha's voice was becoming louder and more shrill.

Theo heard the lower baritone of Darius's voice, although he couldn't make out the words.

'You can't do this to me, Darius.' Samantha's words rang out loud and clear. 'I won't be treated like a pair of old shoes.'

'At least old shoes were once of some use. You're just . . .' The rest of Darius's inaudible answer seemed to make things worse, not better.

'I'll make you pay for this – I swear I will.' Samantha was practically screaming by now.

Without warning, the door burst open and Samantha came careering out to crash straight into Jo.

'Did you have a good time, listening at the keyhole?' Samantha sneered.

'I did no such thing, Mrs Marriott,' Jo replied evenly. 'We were just waiting for you to come out.'

Only then did Samantha realize that Jo wasn't alone. Her eyes narrowed into wafer thin slivers of dislike when she saw Toby.

'Come to inspect your inheritance, have you? Let's hope you live long enough to enjoy it.'

'Mrs Marriott, I think that's enough,' Jo said quietly.

'Who d'you think you're talking to?' Samantha rounded on the PA. 'You're just the hired help around here and don't you forget that.'

'Jo is absolutely right.' Darius's ice-cold voice piped up from behind his wife. 'That will be quite enough.'

The look Samantha Marriott directed at first her husband and then Jo was scalding. Without another word she marched off.

'Don't take any notice of Samantha.' Darius smiled at Toby. 'She's a toothless dog with a very loud voice! Come in. Come in! Welcome. Thanks, Jo.’ Darius shut the door after Ricky had entered the room, leaving Jo outside.

‘Have you just arrived? What’ve you seen so far?’

‘Jo introduced us to the other directors of DemTech,’ said Bullet.

Darius smiled. ‘Good! Now then . . . let’s see . . . How would you like to see our research and development labs? I’ll show you where we’re testing the Lazarus suit.’

‘That’d be great, Dad,’ Bullet enthused.

‘Yeah. Thank you, Mr Marriott,’ said Ricky.

Theo nodded his thanks. This Darius Marriott was a world apart from the one in the hospital. Maybe the last couple of weeks spent with Bullet had started to mellow him out a bit.

‘This way then,’ said Darius, cheerfully.

They all trooped after him as he led the way to the lifts.

‘Er, Darius, you have the Chivers meeting in less than five minutes.’ Jo came running after him.

‘Make them comfortable and tell them I’ll be with them in about fifteen minutes,’ Darius said.

‘But Mr Chivers . . .’

‘Jo [illegible]’ Darius’s smile had disappeared[illegible]

Jo’s sunny expression shut up like a penknife. ‘Yes of course, Darius.’ She nodded quickly. And she scurried back to her table outside Darius’s office.

‘Sorry about that.’ The smile appeared again.

As they stepped into the lift, Theo cast Darius a speculative look. This man was a right Janus – a man with two faces. The public face he used to impress people and make the world think he was wonderful, but his private face was a lot nastier. And Theo knew which one he believed to be Darius Marriott’s true face.

He risked a look at Bullet who was laughing at some joke his dad had just told him. Even Ricky was laughing. They might have been fooled by Darius’s act but Theo most certainly wasn’t. Darius might have acknowledged Bullet openly as his son, he might even have left him an awful lot of money in his will, but there was more to it than that. All this was moving much, much too fast. The introductions, the will-changing, the invites to DemTech and the apartment. It was as if Darius wanted the whole world to know that he was accepting his son with open arms. But Theo just couldn't shake the feeling that Darius was up to something. Something which might cost all of them, but especially Bullet, very dear indeed.

## Chapter Sixteen

# Opinions

'Here we are! Seventh floor! Everyone out.' Darius was the last one out of the lift. 'This way to the labs.'

The more Darius spoke, the less impressed Theo was with him. 'I don't know who he thinks he's fooling with his *Willy Wonka* impersonation,' Theo thought with a scowl.

'This floor contains our testing labs. The sixth and seventh floors of this building are used for research and development in its initial stages. I have other R&D facilities up and down the country, of course.'

'Of course,' Theo muttered.

Darius and Bullet turned to look at him. Darius's smile wavered only slightly.

'Anyway, at the moment the testing labs are all concentrating on the Lazarus suit,' Darius continued

'Which was your idea, Mr Marriott – wasn't it?' Theo asked politely.

'Yes, as a matter of fact it was,' Darius replied, his mask of bonhomie never slipping.

'Aren't you afraid someone will try to steal your idea?' Ricky asked.

'Not with the security I have in this building. People know about the Lazarus suit now, of course. It was officially announced over a month ago now. But they don't know about any of the components or the technology used. I'm sure any number of my competitors would sell their souls for one of our prototype suits but it's not going to happen.'

Ricky looked around, scepticism on his face.

'The doors may look like wood, but they're solid steel

with locking mechanisms we designed ourselves here at Dem-Tech. The windows are all made of toughened glass so that nothing short of rapid machine-gun fire at close range could make so much as a dent in them. Believe me, no one's walking out of this building with anything that doesn't belong to them – and the Lazarus suit is *mine*.'

Darius opened the nearest door to the lift. Three people occupied the room – one man and two women, each wearing white overalls. One sat at a computer, the other two sat at the huge table in the middle of the room. Three or four computers were situated on the only other table against the far wall. Books lined one set of shelves and electronic instruments lined another. High up on the wall there was a ventilation grille, about three times the size of the one in the bathroom in Theo's house. A fire extinguisher and a smoke alarm where the glass had to be broken to raise the alarm were hidden away in one corner of the room. The occupants of the room sat on padded wooden stools which didn't look at all comfortable.

That's probably Darius Marriott making the chairs uncomfy to make sure that no one falls asleep on the job, Theo thought.

'Hi, Sam. How's it going?' Darius asked the man at the middle table.

'Fine thanks, Mr Marriott,' Sam replied. 'The testing is going very smoothly indeed.'

'That's what I like to hear.' Darius rubbed his hands together. 'So we're still on schedule?'

'Yes, sir. No problem.'

'How do you test something like the Lazarus suit?' Theo couldn't help asking. 'I mean, don't you need people to act as guinea pigs?'

The room went strangely quiet at that. Tense moments passed, before Darius laughed lightly.

'We test it as much as we can using computer simulations. And we have anatomically correct robots or dummies which are programmed to display any number of symptoms for our Lazarus suits to deal with.'

'Oh I see,' Theo said doubtfully.

He wondered what he had said to make everyone pause like that.

'And these suits are just for presidents and prime ministers and that?'

'Not at all. Our suits come in all shapes and sizes,' Darius denied.

'They're for anyone who can afford them,' a woman piped up from across the room in front of a computer.

Darius turned and lasered her with his look. The woman immediately turned back to her computer, suddenly very busy.

'Dad, can we see some of your other labs?' Bullet asked quickly.

Darius started, almost as if he'd forgotten about them for a moment. 'Yes, of course. Right this way.'

Darius took them into some more of the labs on the seventh floor. In one lab, a short woman was putting on a Lazarus suit, adjusting the straps across her chest and waist to ensure a snug fit.

'How d'you know which medications to put in the suit?' Bullet asked.

'That's all worked out beforehand, based on each individual's medical history,' Darius answered.

'And how d'you set it up?'

Theo frowned at Bullet. Why did he want to know that? What difference did it make? Bullet turned to face Theo as if he'd heard the unspoken questions.

'Just interested,' he said, defensively.

Darius proceeded to explain exactly how the appropriate syringes with the necessary medication should be attached to the suit.

'And my suit will do the rest,' he finished with a flourish.

'It's a very, very clever idea, Dad,' Bullet enthused. 'I hope

I can come up with something half as good when I'm an inventor.'

By the time Darius had showed them around the R&D labs on the sixth floor as well, Theo had to admit he was very impressed. The testing labs were like nothing he'd ever imagined. One contained a mockup of an intensive care hospital ward, another contained a number of different-sized suits at various stages of development and all the labs contained more electronic gadgetry than Theo had ever seen in his life.

'This lot must've cost a fortune,' Theo whistled. For the first time he was beginning to appreciate just how rich Darius Marriott really was.

'DemTech have spent over thirty million on the Lazarus suit already,' Darius shrugged. 'But it's all going to be worth it.'

Theo nodded. He could well believe it. He wouldn't have minded being shown around again as it was a lot to take in at just one go, but unfortunately it was getting late.

'Thank you so much for showing us around, Mr Marriott,' Ricky said sincerely. 'It was great – really interesting.'

'My pleasure,' Darius smiled, escorting them back to the lift. 'It's the least I could do. After all, you did help to save my life.'

'Oh yes! By the way, Mr Marriott, did the police ever tell you what was in that hypodermic syringe left by the bogus doctor?' asked Theo.

Darius's expression immediately became strangely watchful. 'Ever the detective, eh! As a matter of fact, they did tell me. Apparently it was potassium chloride. It would've made my heart stop almost immediately and everyone would've assumed I'd had another heart attack – fatal this time.'

'So someone was still trying to make it look like an accident,' Theo mused to himself.

'Well, at least all that nonsense is over now.' Darius's smile missed his eyes by kilometres. 'So thank you for your concern but there's no need to worry.'

'Did the police catch the person responsible, then?' Ricky asked.

'No, I did,' Darius replied.

Theo and Ricky stared at him, astounded.

'Bullet didn't tell us the person who tried to harm you had been arrested.' Ricky faced Bullet with accusatory eyes.

'I didn't know,' said Bullet. 'But I'm so glad, Dad.'

'You must be very relieved.' Theo thought about how he'd feel if he had the sword of Damocles suddenly removed from over his head. Relief wouldn't begin to describe it.

'Yes. It is good news,' Darius agreed evenly.

Good news! Is that all he had to say? Good news? Theo looked at Darius suspiciously and all at once he knew beyond a shadow of a doubt that Darius was lying. But why? *Why?*

'I was sorry to hear about your friend's accident. Toby tells me the driver jumped a red light and hit Angela and never stopped.'

'I don't understand. What . . . ?'

A swift elbow in the ribs from Ricky halted the rest of Theo's sentence.

'Yeah! I don't understand how anyone could do something like that either,' Ricky said. 'But at least Angela's doing OK in hospital. We're going to visit her tomorrow.'

'Give her my best, won't you,' said Darius.

Ricky nodded.

'So you're all off home now?' Darius asked as the lift arrived.

'Yes.'

'That's right.'

'What about you, Toby? Will you be having dinner at my apartment or with your mum? I'll give you a lift home afterwards if you have dinner with me.'

Bullet thought for a while. 'With Mum I think.'

'Then I'll see you all soon,' Darius said.

'Oh, hang on. Sorry, Dad. I've left my duffel bag in lab number four. I'll just go and get it.' And before anyone could say a word, Bullet was off. An embarrassed silence descended as they all tried to find something to say.

'How did you catch the person who tried to . . . harm you?' Theo asked at last.

'I don't think I should say. It's now in the hands of the police and I'm not supposed to talk about it until after the court case,' Darius replied.

Or at least until you've had a chance to make up a reasonable story, Theo thought, making sure his expression stayed perfectly neutral.

'Have all those people in the offices on the same floor as you been at this company a long time?' asked Theo.

Darius didn't attempt to hide the suspicious look on his face. 'Ron and I started the company and Faith and Yves came on board within the first year.'

'It's lucky it wasn't any of them, then.' Theo decided to try his luck.

'None of them have any reason to try and get rid of me. They all have plenty of shares in the company and they're each paper millionaires because of it. Even Jo my secretary has shares in DemTech. She's a very rich woman too.'

'What's a paper millionaire?' Theo asked.

Darius looked annoyed. 'It means that they all have shares which are worth a great deal of money if they were to sell them – which they can't, unless they sell them to me.'

'Why can't they sell them to someone else?'

'Because the shares were signed over to them on the strict understanding that each of the shareholders had to hold on to their shares for a minimum of fifteen years, or sell them back to me at the price they originally bought them for. They all signed contracts to that effect. I'm not having DemTech carved up by big conglomerates trying to buy all the shares they can, so that they can take over my company. And if any of the other stock holders so much as live together, never mind get married, one of the parties has to give up all rights to their shares. In effect the shares come back to me.'

'So if Yves and Faith or Ron and Faith get married, one of them loses their shares? Is that right?' Theo wanted to make sure that he hadn't misunderstood.

Darius nodded. 'Correct. The person with the largest amount of shares has to give them back to me.'

'And if something should happen to you?' asked Ricky.

'Then of course my fifty-one per cent stock holding in the company goes to Toby. But nothing is going to happen to me. I intend to be around for a very, very long time.'

'Of course,' Theo said. But before he could say anything else, Bullet appeared.

'Here it is. I've found it.' He held up his bulging duffel bag.

They all trooped into the lift.

'Toby, phone me tomorrow and let me know how you are – OK?'

Bullet nodded. 'See you, Dad.'

And the lift doors shut.

'I'm glad everything's worked out OK between you and your dad,' Theo said carefully.

Bullet and Ricky exchanged a glance. Neither of them spoke. Once again, Theo found himself wondering just what on earth was going on.

## Chapter Seventeen

# Visiting Hours

'Hi, Angela. We can't stay long. How're you feeling?'

'Why can't you stay long? You've only just got here.' Angela struggled to sit up a bit more. 'And you lot took your time visiting me. I was beginning to wonder if I had bad breath or something!'

'You've finally guessed, huh!' Ricky grinned.

Angela's look spoke unspoken volumes!

'I see you're back to normal,' Theo said drily.

'All apart from my leg here.' Angela pointed to the plaster cast which covered most of her right leg.

'How does it feel?' Ricky asked.

'Itchy! What's the matter with you, Bullet? You're very quiet.'

Bullet looked at the curtains surrounding Angela's bed, he looked up and down the hospital ward, he looked everywhere but directly at Angela.

'I . . . er . . . I just wanted . . .'

'You wanted to get down on bended knee and kiss my itchy big toe and thank me for saving your life.' Angela grinned.

Urrgghhh! Theo broke out in a cold sweat at the thought of it.

'Well, I wouldn't go that far,' Bullet laughed, now looking at Angela.

'But something like that – right?'

'Something like that,' Bullet agreed.

'So how have you lot been getting on without me? Have you made any progress?'

'Some,' Ricky said after a brief glance at Bullet.

'But not as much as we should have made by now,' Theo added.

'Let's hear it then,' Angela prompted.

They spent the next ten minutes arguing about what had happened after Angela was taken to hospital, bringing Angela up-to-date with everything that had taken place.

'So who's on our list of suspects?' asked Angela.

Bullet and Ricky turned expectantly to Theo. 'I think it has to be someone who'd benefit from Darius Marriott's death.'

'You had to read fifty million "How To Be A Detective" books to reach that conclusion?' Angela was not impressed.

'If you'll let me finish!' Theo sniffed. 'As I see it, that narrows our list of suspects down to Darius Marriott's wife, Samantha; Ron Westall, the company secretary; Faith Shanley, the R&D director; or Yves Hamilton, the sales and marketing director. Under Darius Marriot's old will they'd each get another block of shares when Darius died but not enough for any one of them to get controlling interest of DemTech. But under the new will Bullet here will get fifty-one per cent of all the shares in the company which means it'll be his. But if something happens to Bullet and his dad, then the co-directors of DemTech are laughing.'

'What about Jo Fleming?' Ricky frowned.

'What about her?' asked Theo.

'Well, she's got some shares in the company too – remember?' Ricky pointed out.

'Oh yes . . . I'd forgotten about her.'

'So who do you think is responsible for all this?' asked Angela.

'I don't know,' Theo replied slowly. 'I still can't get over the feeling that I'm missing something – something obvious and vital. I know it has to be one of the directors of the company or Samantha Marriott but I still can't work out who. At the moment Faith Shanley's my favourite suspect.'

'Why?' Bullet asked, surprised.

'She looks and acts like she could wrestle a shark with one hand tied behind her back,' Theo said.

'That doesn't make her a killer,' Ricky pointed out.

'So who do you think it is, then?' asked Theo.

'Someone else,' Ricky said mysteriously.

'Like who?'

Ricky shook his head, unwilling to say anything further.

'Come on, Ricky. Stop being so mysterious,' Angela cajoled.

'It's just that I've been doing a little detective work of my own,' Ricky admitted. 'And I suspect something about one of DemTech's directors.'

'What?' Theo asked, exasperated.

'I'm not going to say until I have proof.' Ricky shook his head.

'Ricky, this is Theo, Bullet and Angela you're talking to,' Theo said, annoyed. 'You don't need concrete proof to make us believe you.'

'I know. But if what I suspect is true, then I want to be sure of my facts.' When Theo opened his mouth to argue further, Ricky stated, 'Theo, Darius Marriott is Bullet's dad. I want to be absolutely certain I'm not making a mistake before I do anything to upset either of them or jeopardize their relationship.'

'And might it come to that?' Bullet asked quietly.

Ricky didn't answer. The look on his face said that he thought he'd said too much already.

'What I will say is this,' Ricky said at last. 'Bullet, you're not to trust any of the staff at DemTech. If anyone, anyone at all from that company, phones you and says they want to see you – for whatever reason – make sure you take one of us along with you. D'you understand?'

Bullet nodded.

'This is really important, Bullet. D'you understand me? You're not to trust anyone from DemTech.'

'I get it. I get it.' Bullet frowned.

Everyone stared at Ricky. None of them had ever before heard that note of urgency in his voice.

'Ricky, stop it.' Bullet frowned. 'You're . . . you're making me nervous.'

'I hope so,' Ricky said seriously. 'I really hope so. 'Cos if you don't do as I say – it'll probably be the last thing you ever do.'

Theo wasn't going to let him get away with that. 'Ricky, d'you remember when Jade was convinced her dead dad was sending her e-mail messages and I thought I'd discovered who the real culprit was?' Theo reminded his friend. 'I set a trap to catch him and I didn't tell you what I was doing.'

Ricky's lips thinned. He knew what was coming next.

'D'you remember how you went ballistic when you found out what I'd done?' Theo continued relentlessly. 'And now you're doing exactly the same thing. If it wasn't OK for me, how come you can do it?'

'I was wondering that myself,' Angela piped up.

'I agree with Theo.' Bullet put in his five pence worth. 'And this has more to do with me than any of you. I don't think you should shut me out like this.'

Theo glared at Bullet. There was a lot of shutting out going on. Ricky looked at Angela lying on her hospital bed and then at Theo and Bullet. 'It's just that . . . OK. I was planning on going to the Family Records Centre on Saturday.'

'The what?'

'The Family Records Centre in Islington. They keep records of all births, marriages and deaths in England and Wales. Ricky explained.

'Why're you going there?' Theo questioned.

'To test a theory. And if my theory is right, then I'm hoping to set a trap for the ones doing this. I think that's the only way to flush them out.'

'Are they open on Saturdays?' Theo asked.

Ricky nodded. 'I checked.'

'I'm going with you,' Bullet said at once.

Looking straight at Ricky, Theo said, 'So am I. And don't bother arguing because you'll just be wasting your breath.'

'We can't all go. Bullet, you'd better stay behind,' Ricky said.

'But . . .'

'We'll let you know what we found out as soon as we get back. I promise,' Ricky interrupted. 'You're going to have to trust us.'

'What about this trap you're going to set? I can help with that, surely?' said Bullet.

'Actually, I did want you to do something for me . . .' Ricky admitted reluctantly. 'Are you going to see your dad tomorrow?'

'Yeah. I was planning to pop into his office after school. Why?'

'I need you to spread some information about. The thing is, it'll be dangerous.' Ricky's voice faded to a whisper.

'Just tell me what you want me to do,' Bullet said with determination.

'We're going to set a trap,' Ricky added sombrely. 'But I'm worried we'll be the ones caught in it.'

'Is that why you didn't want to include any of us?' Bullet asked. 'Just in case things went wrong?'

'Yes. These people have already proved that they'll stop at nothing to get what they want. I just don't want any of us to get steamrollered whilst we're trying to catch them out.'

'But Dad said the police have already arrested the person behind all this,' Bullet reminded them.

'If someone has been arrested for your dad's attempted murder, then the police have the wrong person. I'm sure of it.' Ricky's voice was grim.

They all digested Ricky's last statement in silence.

'And you think more than one person is involved in this?' Bullet said.

Ricky nodded. 'And I think they're covering each other's tracks, or your dad would've found them out by now.'

'Is it two people who work for Dad?'

Ricky nodded. 'I think so. And if I'm right, a visit to the Family Records Centre will prove it.'

'And if you're wrong?' Angela asked.

'Then Bullet and his dad are in even more danger.'

'How d'you work that out?' asked Theo.

'Because we'll have narrowed down our list of suspects and the person or people doing this will have to act even more quickly. Time will no longer be on our side,' Ricky said. 'You see, that's the problem. With all this, I might actually make things worse.'

## Chapter Eighteen

# Bait

'I still can't believe it.' Theo shook his head.

It was five-thirty in the evening. Ricky and Theo were on their way home from the Family Records Centre, both their expressions grim. The tube train was jampacked with late afternoon shoppers returning home and Ricky and Theo stood next to each other, squashed against the door.

'What made you suspect?' Theo couldn't keep a trace of admiration out of his voice.

'Something she said – and watching the two of them together,' Ricky replied.

'Well, they completely fooled me. Lucky you were more on the ball than I was,' Theo said. Though he couldn't help feeling that in some way, he had failed. He should've been the one to make the connection. He should've picked up on the clues, too.

'Theo, it's not that I cracked it, or you cracked it. We solved this together.' Ricky correctly interpreted the expression on his friend's face.

'It's not that so much. It's just that . . .'

'It's just that we make a good team,' Ricky insisted.

Theo smiled. 'That's exactly what I was going to say!'

'What we have to do now is use this information to drag them out into the open. We have to make them show their hand,' said Ricky.

'How d'you intend to do that?'

'Bullet's already taken care of that bit back home,' Ricky said with satisfaction.

Theo was startled. 'He doesn't know . . .'

'No. How can he when we only found out for certain about an hour ago? But yesterday when he went to his dad's office, I asked him to tell everyone what you'd be up to this afternoon. He was to try and make sure that all the staff on the third floor of DemTech got to hear about your forthcoming visit to the Family Records Centre. I told him to make sure the info was given out in a casual way as if he was just making conversation.'

'Hang on a minute. *My* visit?' Theo asked, astounded.

'Yes, you! That way we can use you as bait and I'll be there to make sure that nothing bad happens to you.'

'Thank you very much!' Theo exploded. 'If you're going to use me as bait, you could've told me first.'

'I'm telling you now.'

'Thanks for nothing. So when we get home, there could be some lunatic just waiting to run me down or anything.'

'It won't come to that – I told you. I'm here to make sure that you're perfectly safe.'

'You can't guarantee that. Ricky, you . . .'

'This is where we get off. Come on.' Ricky pulled Theo past the already closing tube train doors. 'I'll go with you to your house and then I'll disappear for half an hour if you don't mind.'

'Why?'

'I've got one last thing to check at the library.' Ricky glanced down at his watch. 'And I'd better hurry up before it closes.'

'What d'you need to check?'

'Some DemTech annual accounts information and I want to look up something on Darius Marriott.'

'What?'

'I'll tell you once I've got the info.'

'Oh Ricky, don't start all that again. I thought we'd got all this "my surname is Mystery and my middle name is Secret" nonsense sorted out.'

'I'll tell you when I've been to the library – not before,' Ricky insisted stubbornly.

'Before you disappear, why exactly did Bullet want to talk to you alone in his dad's apartment the other day?' Theo couldn't help asking.

'He wanted my advice about something.'

'I know that. What? And why didn't he want my advice too?'

Ricky sighed. ''Cos you live with your happily-married mum and dad. Bullet was like me until a couple of weeks ago. There was no dad on the scene.'

'Oh . . .' Theo couldn't argue with that. 'So what did Bullet ask you?'

'His dad wants Bullet to come and live with him permanently. Bullet just wanted to know what I'd do in his shoes. But I was sworn to secrecy, so don't go blabbing.'

'Of course not.' Theo frowned. 'So what's Bullet going to do?'

'He's not sure. But he thinks he'll stay with his mum.'

'Is that what you'd do?'

'Oh yes!' Ricky replied without a moment's hesitation.

There was something in his voice. Some strange hard edge that Theo hadn't heard before. 'What's the matter?' Theo questioned.

Ricky shook his head.

'Come on. Something's obviously troubling you.'

'Never mind. Just leave it,' Ricky dismissed.

Theo glared at Ricky, oblivious to the impatient glances being directed at him by those trying to leave the station. Fine! If Ricky wanted to play that game then Theo wasn't about to spoil his fun.

'All right then. Be like that,' Theo said at last.

They walked back to Theo's house, chatting about nothing in particular, rather than the subject uppermost in both their minds. Until, running out of things to say, they both fell silent. Theo couldn't understand what was going on with this whole business. For the last few days, he'd felt as if he was constantly fifteen minutes behind everyone else.

Secrets . . . That was it. Everyone seemed to have secrets. And he was so close to what was going on, he felt as if he couldn't see the wood for the trees. He'd never really known what that saying meant before, but now its meaning was all too clear. He was too close to Bullet and Ricky to see things objectively. Maybe that's why Ricky had had an inkling as to who might be responsible for all this mayhem before he had. He felt as if he'd done nothing but worry for longer than he cared to remember. He was worried about Bullet and Angela and Ricky and even Darius Marriott. Still, now that they had found the information they were looking for, maybe they could get somewhere at last. The proof of what they had found wouldn't be posted to them for another four or five days though. Finding the data on the Family Records computer was one thing. Getting a proper printout of that data was apparently something else entirely. They'd handed over their money, but they couldn't get the certificate they'd paid for, for a minimum of four days. Theo just hoped and prayed that they *had* four days. If Bullet had spread rumours about what he'd been doing that day, then even four hours seemed optimistic.

And at that moment, Theo made a decision. He'd go home and wait for Ricky. And then tomorrow without fail, they'd go to the police with what they knew. And if Bullet and Ricky wouldn't go with him, then he'd go by himself. He was no one's sitting duck and at the moment, that's exactly what he felt like. It wasn't a pleasant feeling. Theo quickly turned his head. There were people milling about here, there and everywhere. Was one of them watching him? What if he was being followed? What if . . . ?

Stop it! Theo told himself firmly. He was OK. Even if Bullet had managed to pass on the message about his so-called solo trip to the Family Records Centre, there wouldn't have been time for the guilty parties to have arranged anything. He was safe – but only if he went to the police the very next morning. Now that the decision had been made, Theo felt strangely comforted. All he had to do was hold on for one more night.

Outside Theo's house, Ricky said, 'Right then, now you're safely home, I'll see you in a little while. I've only got fifteen minutes before the library closes.' And Ricky was already turning around and heading back the way they had just come.

'Ricky . . .' Theo called after him.

'Tell me later,' Ricky called back, breaking into a run.

With a sigh, Theo turned and went into his house. He had a foot on the bottom step when his dad came out of the living room.

'Hi, Theo. How was your day?'

'Informative,' Theo told his dad. He headed up the stairs, pulling off his jacket as he went.

'Just a sec. You got a message from Bullet. He wants you to meet him at the DemTech building. He said he and his dad will meet you there and his dad will give you a lift home again,' said Theo's dad. 'I don't know what all of you have been up to recently but I do know that I've hardly seen you.'

'When did Bullet phone?'

'About an hour ago. He said it was urgent.'

Theo glanced at his watch. 'I'm just going to pop out for a while. Dad, Ricky's going to come round later. When he does, could you tell him where I've gone and that I'll be back soon.'

'All I seem to do around this house is take messages for you,' Theo's dad grumbled. 'And I never get one word of thanks either.'

'Thank you for taking my messages, Dad,' Theo said deliberately.

'It's too late.' Theo's dad sniffed with mock indignation. 'Thanks should be spontaneous, not prompted.'

'Later, Dad,' Theo called, as he headed out of the door.

'Not too much later, Theo,' his dad called back at once.

'I want you home within the hour – without fail. We'd see more of you if you were a lodger instead of our son. I don't know why your mum and me . . .'

Theo didn't hear any more. He walked briskly down the garden path, breaking into a run once he hit the road. He didn't know why Bullet wanted to see him but it was obviously important.

'Name?'

Theo stared at the intercom. He peered through the glass to look at the uniformed security guard who had asked the question.

'Name?' The voice came again, edged with impatience.

'Theo. Theo Mosley.'

'Ah yes. You're expected,' said the security guard.

There was a buzz and a click and the door swung open. Theo walked straight up to the security guard who sat behind the reception desk.

'I'm here to see . . .'

'Yes, that's right. Take the lift up to the third floor. You'll be met.'

'Is this place open all the time?' Theo couldn't help asking.

'Yep! Seven days a week. Twenty-four hours a day,' the guard replied.

Theo headed over to the lift. DemTech was nothing if not efficient! He stepped in and pressed the button to go up to the third floor, speculating about what Bullet and his dad wanted to say to him. The lift halted and the doors slid open with a hiss.

'Hello. Theo, isn't it?' Jo Fleming stood right in front of the lift, a notepad in her hand.

'Hello, Miss Fleming,' Theo said, surprised. 'I was meant to meet Bullet, I mean Toby, and his dad here.'

'Oh, yes. Darius mentioned it. They've gone up to one of the labs on the seventh floor,' said Jo. 'I'll take you up.'

Jo led the way to the lift and they headed up to the top

floor in silence. Theo struggled to find something to say, but failed. He glanced at Jo, who had a preoccupied look on her face. Theo used the opportunity to scrutinize her. She was a dark horse and no mistake. Theo knew she'd been at DemTech for quite a few years now. He couldn't help wondering just what she really thought of her boss. Darius Marriott didn't seem like exactly the easiest man in the world to get along with. For a start, this woman always seemed to be working. It was Saturday and she was still in the office. Didn't she have a private life? Even when Theo was a great detective, he'd still make sure he had time for a personal life and to have some fun. Otherwise what was the point?

'Here we are,' said Jo.

Theo stepped out into an eerie silence which was a total contrast to the noise and organized chaos present when Darius Marriott had shown them around.

'Is it always this quiet on a Saturday?' Theo asked.

'No, not usually. Most of the quality assurance and testing staff work on Saturdays and some work on Sundays, too. It's just that most people are at the company knees-up tonight,' Jo replied as they walked down the corridor. 'I'm just on my way there now. Here we are. Bullet's in there.'

Theo opened the door and walked in. 'Hi, Bullet. What was so . . . ?'

The door banged shut behind him. Theo spun around – but he was too late. With a resounding click, the door was locked.

## Chapter Nineteen

# No Way Out

'What on earth . . . ? What's the matter?' Bullet asked urgently.

'Jo's locked the door,' Theo replied. He started rattling the door handle. 'Let us out! LET US OUT NOW!'

'Don't worry, Theo. We're going to deal with Toby – and then it's your turn,' Jo called through the locked door.

'What d'you mean?' Theo's blood ran liquid nitrogen cold. 'OPEN THIS DOOR.'

'Sorry, Theo, but you've left us no choice. If what we've got lined up for Bullet doesn't work for you too, Ron's got a little something waiting for you on – or should I say off – the roof of this building.'

'Jo, the joke's over. Let us out – *please*. Come on! You can't do this . . .' Theo pulled even harder on the door handle, but it was useless.

Beyond the door there was now nothing but an eerie silence. Theo shook the door handle, wondering if there was some way to force it open. Nothing doing! There was no way a big, heavy security door like that was going to give, no matter what Theo did to it.

'What's going on? What's she up to?' asked Bullet.

'I have a horrible feeling I know,' Theo said through gritted teeth. 'But I don't understand . . . Bullet, why did you want to see me?'

Bullet looked puzzled. 'What're you talking about? You left a message with my mum saying that you wanted to see me at the DemTech building. You said it was a matter of life and death.'

'But that's the message *I* got – that you wanted to see me,' said Theo.

And all at once, it became very clear what was going on.

'Bullet,' Theo fumed. 'Ricky and I found out that Jo Fleming and Ron Westall are married. According to the old will, if anything should happen to your dad, combined they'd have enough shares to take over the company.'

'But then Dad changed his will . . .' Bullet breathed. Realization like Antarctic water flowed over him.

'And they know that I've spent the day at the Family Records Centre finding out that the two of them are married. And d'you remember what else the DemTech stock contract said? If by any chance, any of the directors should even so much as live together, one of them would have to give up their shares, no arguments, no questions.'

'But why lock us in here? They can't keep us here for ever. We'll just shout until someone lets us out.'

'Everyone's away at the summer party, so we won't be found until tomorrow. And I think Jo and Ron have got more than an overnight stay locked in this lab lined up for us.'

'Oh, great! I am in BIG trouble. Mum's going to do her nut if I come home late again.'

'Your mum! What about my mum and dad? Dad gave me strict instructions to be home early tonight. And Ricky's going to come round and I'm not going to be there.'

Theo and Bullet looked around the empty lab. He looked up. Directly above them was the roof – but there was no way out to it from here. The vent high up on the wall was too high to reach and much too small to crawl through.

'What now?' Bullet asked.

'I guess we sit tight and wait for someone to let us out,' Theo replied.

'But why on earth would she lock us in here in the first place?'

Theo walked around the lab looking for something,

anything that would help him to prise open the door. Four computer terminals sat on the large table against the far wall and on the middle table were various electronic components, most of which Theo had never seen before and none of which could be used on the door.

'It's getting hot.' Theo tugged at the neck of his sweatshirt. What had Jo done? Turned off the air conditioning? She must've done. The temperature in the room seemed to be leaping up. 'Aren't you going to pull off your jumper?'

Bullet shook his head. 'I'm cold.'

'You're kidding! I'm sweltering.'

'Yes, but . . . Oh-oh! I think the heat is the least of our problems. Look!' Bullet pointed up at the ventilation grille high above their heads. Theo looked up and saw a wasp crawl out of the grille and sit on it for a moment. Then out came another one. Then another. And another. Soon the grille was heaving with wasps, sitting on the grille, buzzing angrily. Theo turned to look at Bullet, who edged backwards away from the wasps until his back was against the opposite wall and he had nowhere else to go. Theo started edging backwards, too. More and more wasps were coming out of the grille now, buzzing in shared fury.

Theo ran for the door. He rattled the handle frantically. 'LET US OUT! SOMEONE, PLEASE! LET US OUT!'

'Theo, no. Don't shout or jump up and down,' Bullet called out to him.

The wasps were on the move now. In twos and threes and fours they left the grille to begin flying around the room. Theo ran back to Bullet.

'Bullet, where's your hypo of adrenaline?'

'It's in my bag,' Bullet said slowly.

'Where's your bag?' Theo desperately looked around the lab. 'Bullet, where's your bag?' he repeated when Bullet didn't answer.

'It's under Jo's desk. She said I should leave it there for safe-keeping,' Bullet whispered.

Theo stared at his friend, horror-stricken. 'I never should've come up here with Jo. I knew it was her and Ron – so why did I do it? How could I have been so stupid?'

'You weren't to know,' Bullet dismissed quickly.

'But I did know. Jo was the only one in the school hall with Darius when he visited our school. We knew that if the Lazarus suit malfunction was triggered by remote control using a computer, the computer would still have to be quite close. Jo Fleming is the only one who could've possibly done it. She must've had a laptop or one of those PDAs. Faith was too far away in a car outside the school grounds. I had all the pieces, I just didn't put them together.'

'Never mind Jo. What about us?' Bullet's voice was stiff with fear.

More and more wasps emerged from the grille and took flight.

Theo pulled off his sweatshirt. 'Quick! Wrap this around your head and stuff your hands in your pockets.'

'No, Theo.' Bullet shook his head. 'If you get stung by this many wasps it could kill you, too.'

'But just one sting could kill you. I'll take my chances.'

'I can't let you do . . .'

'Bullet, we haven't got time for this,' Theo protested impatiently. 'Put this around your head. Come on.'

Reluctantly, Bullet wrapped the sweatshirt around his head, leaving only a very little of his face exposed. Theo glanced down at his shirt and trousers. Suddenly they seemed as flimsy as tissue paper.

'I'll try and break one of the windows.' Theo picked up a stool.

'But Dad said . . .'

'Any better ideas?'

Bullet shut up. Theo ran over to the window by the door and holding the stool with two hands, he heaved it at the glass. The stool bounced off the window, sending a shooting pain straight up Theo's arms. Ignoring the pain dancing around his shoulders, Theo tried again. And a third time. It was futile. The stool was coming off worse than the window. Theo dropped the stool in disgust.

'We'd both better get under that table,' he announced.

'Wasps can fly under tables as well as over them, you know.'

'It's better than nothing,' Theo replied, pulling Bullet after him. 'Come on. Hurry!' Theo was having to shout over the noise of the wasps in the lab now. And still they kept coming. Theo and Bullet kneeled down under the computer table, both watching the grille. The wasps in the lab had to number at least one hundred and probably a lot more. Theo felt numb with fright. He'd never felt anything like it before, even when confronted with Angela's brother Tom and his so-called friends at the Irving Museum. Goodness knows he'd been scared enough then but this was much, much worse. Because Bullet was with him and Bullet was allergic to wasp stings and his adrenaline hypodermic syringe was outside the lab. It was only four floors below them but it might as well have been on the moon. Every time Theo had been in trouble before, it was down to him to find some way out. He could run or hide or call the police and although he'd been in some dangerous situations, there'd always been some way out. But not now. They were stuck in a lab full of wasps and the glass was toughened and the door was locked. There was no way out. What would happen if Bullet got stung? Theo knew the answer to that one and that was the trouble.

A wasp buzzed near his face. Theo swatted out with his hand to push it away.

'Don't do that. You'll just antagonize them more,' Bullet whispered.

Theo dropped his hand at once. 'Cover your face, Bullet. Quick, before – OW!' Theo snatched his hand off the floor and cradled it against his body. Already a lump was forming on his forearm around the wasp's sting.

Bullet pulled the sweatshirt off his face. 'Theo, are you OK?'

'BULLET, SHUT UP AND COVER YOUR FACE,' Theo yelled. 'OWW! OUCH!'

The air was thick with wasps now. Theo couldn't see across the room and for all his big talk he wasn't sure how many more stings he could take.

'Theo, Jo's not going to open this door until I'm out of the way.' Bullet pulled the sweatshirt off his face and spoke behind his hand. 'With me out of the way, you stand a chance of escaping.'

Bullet crawled out from under the table and took Theo's sweatshirt off completely. Theo sprang after him.

'Bullet, are you out of your mind? Get back under . . .'

But Theo was too late. Wasps surrounded them like shrouds. Theo could feel stings like red hot pinches up and down his body. It was swelteringly hot in the room and getting hotter all the time and his skin felt like fires were breaking out all over it. But that wasn't the worst of it. Bullet was in trouble. He was surrounded by wasps.

'Can't . . . breathe . . .' Bullet choked out, pulling at the neck of his jumper and the shirt underneath.

Theo rugby-tackled Bullet to the floor and half pushed, half dragged him back under the table. He swatted out in every direction, trying to keep the wasps away from Bullet, oblivious to the stings they gave him in his desperation to help his friend.

'Bullet? Toby, speak to me. Are you all right?'

What a stupid question. Bullet's face and hands were puffed up like balloons and his lips and eyelids were horribly swollen. Theo grabbed hold of Bullet's wrist, searching for a pulse – and not finding one. His fingers darted back and forth over the inside of Bullet's wrist. Nothing. Theo felt for a pulse in Bullet's neck but he wasn't sure exactly where to press his fingers. He knocked the wasps off Bullet's jumper and put his ear down to Bullet's chest. Nothing. And that's when Theo knew. Bullet's heart had stopped beating.

Theo's whole body was on fire now. He was pain personified. And the buzzing . . . If only the buzzing would stop.

Theo closed his eyes, his head still resting on Bullet's chest. He had to do something to escape from the intense, white-hot pain lancing up and down his body. He'd close his eyes. That's what he'd do. He'd close his eyes and allow himself to sleep, to move outside and beyond his body where the pain couldn't reach him.

A small part of Theo's mind told him not to sleep. To stay awake. To fight. But he couldn't. He was in agony and it was driving him crazy. If he didn't escape and soon, he wouldn't escape at all. Just to close his eyes, to allow his mind to drift away from his body . . . Theo did just that. And his last conscious thought was that Bullet was dead and he was dying.

Chapter Twenty

# Live Saver

It was the smell that hit Theo first. An antiseptic, disinfectant smell which instantly told Theo that he was in hospital. But he couldn't remember why. He struggled to open his eyes and the instant they were open he saw them. Hundreds and hundreds of them. Thousands and thousands of them. Wasps. Theo cried out. And they were instantly gone.

'Theo? It's all right, darling. Mum and Dad are here. You're OK now.'

Theo looked over at the anguished faces of his parents. 'I'm in hospital.' It was a statement, not a question.

'That's right.' Theo's dad tried to smile, his eyes shimmering.

As Theo became more awake, he was aware of his head pounding like a woodpecker's beak. He tried to raise his hand to his head but, startled, he saw that it was swathed in bandages. Only then did he remember everything.

'Bullet. Where's Bullet? We have to help him. He . . .'

'Theo, calm down. Toby's fine. In fact he's in better shape than you are. He was only stung a couple of times on his hands and once on his face. The rest of his body was very well padded and protected.'

'But he's allergic. One sting alone can kill him,' Theo said, anguished.

'Yes, but he was well wrapped up to disguise the fact that he was wearing one of his dad's prototype Lazarus suits. He'd added his adrenaline syringe to the suit and it saved his life. Apparently he's been wearing it for the last couple of days – just in case.'

'The Lazarus suit? Why didn't he say?'

'You'll have to take that up with him,' Theo's mum said, an edge to her voice. 'Ricky and Toby told me what's been happening from their point of view but now I want to hear it from you. I want to know exactly what you've been up to – from the beginning.'

Theo kept his explanation as short as he could, but at the end of it he was still exhausted. But not too exhausted to catch the look exchanged between his parents.

'Theo, this must stop. If you get involved in something like this again, I want you to give me your word that you'll come to me or your mother and you'll tell us what's going on.'

'But I was never in any real danger – not until we were locked in the lab with the wasps, at any rate,' Theo argued.

'Yes, but look what happened then,' said Theo's dad at once. 'You were stung more than ten times and if Mr Marriott's detective hadn't been on the spot, it might've been a lot, lot worse.'

'Mr Marriott's what? His detective?' asked Theo.

'Apparently Mr Marriott appointed detectives to protect you, Ricky and Toby after Angela had her accident. He was worried that something else might happen.'

Theo digested this piece of news. So he'd been right. There *had* been someone following him – but the man had been on his side.

'The man looking after you managed to drag you and Toby out of that lab just in time.'

'What about the detective hired to look after Bullet? He should've been able to let us out of the lab almost immediately.' Theo frowned. 'Where was he?'

'He was hiding out in the gents' toilets,' said Dad. 'He didn't realize Jo and Ron would make their move so quickly.'

'He was a fat lot of use then,' Theo sighed, closing his eyes at the waves of fatigue washing over him. 'So Toby's OK? You're sure?'

'Positive.'

'What about Jo Fleming and Ron Westall?' Theo struggled not to succumb to his exhaustion. He wanted to know what had happened to the ones who'd done this to him.

'They've both been arrested and charged. And it's only a matter of time before the police get the man they hired to get rid of Darius.'

'So they didn't try to do that bit themselves?'

'No. Jo has confessed to everything. Apparently, they needed someone who could pretend to be a doctor and give Darius Marriott his fatal injection. Darius would've recognized both of them at once. Besides . . .'

Theo didn't hear any more. His eyes, already as heavy as lead weights, closed of their own accord and he was out of it.

'Hello. How're you feeling?'

Theo forced himself to focus on Ricky's voice. 'I'm OK. How do I look?'

'D'you really want me to answer that?'

Theo sighed and sat up. 'That bad, huh?'

'That bad and worse,' Ricky stated. 'Can I sit on your bed?'

'Yeah! No problem.'

Ricky perched at the edge of the bed, pushing with his feet against the floor to steady himself.

'Where're my mum and dad?'

'They've gone to get something to eat. They've barely left your side in over twenty-four hours.'

'Twenty-four hours?' Theo asked, aghast. 'Have I really been out that long?'

Ricky nodded.

'So is it true? Have Jo Fleming and Ron Westall been arrested? Are they really the ones responsible for all this?'

'That's right. Of course I knew it was Jo when she said she'd been standing at the back of the assembly hall when

Darius came to visit our school. She was the only one close enough to set off the Lazarus suit by remote control.'

'What made you suspect that Jo wasn't working alone, though?'

'You didn't see her face when she introduced us to Ron at the DemTech offices. She was looking at him the way your mum and dad look at each other and he was looking back in exactly the same way. And then she started rubbing the ring finger of her left hand – even though she didn't have on a wedding ring.'

'You're joking!'

'No, I'm not. She wasn't aware that she was doing it, but I noticed. And it made me wonder. And once I knew they were married then we had a motive right there. Their combined shares would give them control of the company once Darius was out of the way,' said Ricky. 'And Bullet told me that Ron had been dead set against Darius's Lazarus suit idea from the beginning. Ron thought it was a waste of money.'

'It saved Bullet's life,' Theo pointed out.

'Yes, it did,' Ricky said thoughtfully. 'He snaffled one from an empty lab that day he left his duffel bag behind.'

'So he left his bag behind on purpose,' Theo realized.

Ricky nodded.

'Where's Bullet now?'

'In the ward across the corridor. He's going to visit you a little later.'

Theo raised his eyebrows. 'Is he up and about already?'

'Yep! The doctors reckon he can go home tomorrow at the latest.'

Theo leaned back against the pillows. He felt strangely . . . flat. The whole world had moved off and up and on without him. Jo and Ron had been arrested and he hadn't seen it. Bullet was going to be all right and he hadn't witnessed it. He was out of things. It wasn't a very comforting feeling.

'At least you're doing well, Ricky. You're the only one of our group who isn't in hospital,' Theo laughed.

Ricky didn't join in.

'What's the matter?' Theo asked, his smile fading.

'I should've been there,' Ricky exploded. 'I knew what might happen. I should've been there. That's why I told you not to leave the house without me, but you went anyway. You . . . you could've been killed.'

Theo stared at Ricky, who was more distraught than Theo had ever seen him. 'Ricky, look at me. I'm OK. I could've been killed but I wasn't.'

'Yes, but you . . .'

'Ricky, I'm fine. I promise,' Theo insisted. Ricky's mouth snapped shut. He didn't look very happy, nor particularly convinced but he stopped arguing. 'So what will happen to Ron and Jo now?'

Ricky shrugged. 'Bullet told me that his dad wanted the police to drop the charges but nothing doing.'

'Drop the charges?' Theo stared at Ricky. 'Has Mr Marriott lost his mind?'

'No. Mr Marriott has lost something a great deal more precious to him,' said Ricky.

'What d'you mean?'

'I think Mr Marriott has been dipping into his company's reserves to finance his Lazarus suit. I think DemTech isn't worth as much as everyone thinks it is.'

'What makes you think that? And since when were you interested in financial goings-on?'

'Since we became involved in this whole business,' Ricky replied. 'D'you remember when Mr Marriott told us that the Lazarus suit cost over thirty million in development last year alone?'

'Yes. So?'

'Last year DemTech reported profits of just over twelve million. That's what I went to the library to check,' said Ricky.

'And if he hadn't spent the thirty million on the suit it would've been forty-two million instead.' Theo frowned. 'What's your point?'

'In the official accounts and the shareholders' reports, DemTech is down as having spent only seven million on R&D throughout the whole company in the last year,' said Ricky. 'I think Mr Marriott accidentally let slip to us what the real cost was.'

'Well, he can afford it.' Theo still didn't see what the problem was.

'But can he?' Ricky said. 'I think that in their own twisted way, Ron and Jo were right. I think that Darius has been dipping into his own company's funds in order to finance the R&D on his Lazarus suit. I reckon that's why he wanted to drop the charges against Ron and Jo, because otherwise there might be external auditors and all sorts going through the company's books to see just what's been going on.'

'But as company treasurer, wouldn't Ron have known all about it?'

'Not necessarily. I think he more than suspected,' said Ricky. 'That's probably why he wanted to stop Darius – before Darius bankrupted the entire company.'

'But what proof do you have of all this?' Theo asked.

'Yes, I'd be very interested to hear that, too.'

Theo's and Ricky's heads snapped around. Darius Marriott was standing right behind them. Theo looked around him but luckily Darius was alone.

'Go on, Ricky. I'd like to hear how you intend to prove what you've just said,' said Darius.

Ricky didn't answer. Both he and Theo sat perfectly still, watching Darius Marriott with unblinking eyes. Darius looked around the ward before turning back to the two boys.

'Because I'll tell you now,' said Darius. 'It's all perfectly true. I've been borrowing money from the DemTech pension fund and from my company's staff saving scheme to invest in my new invention. But if you go to the police now, DemTech will go down the drain and Toby's future will go right along with it. In a few months' time, once my Lazarus suit is on the market, I'll be able to replace every penny I've taken and no one will be any the wiser. So I'll ask you again, what d'you intend to do about it?'

'You deliberately changed your will knowing that the person or people after you would go after Bullet instead,' Ricky said quietly. 'You put your own son in the firing line, whilst you hid behind him.'

Darius's lips tightened. 'I hired private detectives to protect him – to protect all of you.'

'But you wouldn't have had to do any of that if you hadn't changed your will in the first place,' Ricky pointed out. 'From the moment I heard you'd done that, I knew what kind of father you were. I knew what kind of man you were. I knew you had to be mixed up in something shady because you're incapable of doing anything else. You don't care about your son Toby any more than you care about the stranger in the next bed. Toby was just a convenient decoy. Someone you could use to get the people who'd tried to kill you out into the open.'

Theo sat frozen to the bed. He couldn't believe what he was hearing and yet every word Ricky uttered clicked into place and made perfect sense.

'Spare me the lecture please. I'll ask you again. What d'you intend to do about it?' Darius repeated icily.

Ricky looked at Theo, then back at Darius Marriott. 'Nothing,' he said, softly. 'I'm not going to be the one to tell Toby what his dad really is. I'm not going to be the one to tell him that his dad doesn't care a kidney bean about him.'

A slow smile spread across Darius's face, as if he'd expected no other answer. Theo longed to yell at him, shout out to the whole ward and the whole world just what Darius Marriott had done. But he knew he wouldn't.

'Hello, Dad. Hi, Ricky, Theo,' Bullet called out from a few beds away as he strode up the middle of the ward.

'Hi, son.' Darius gave Ricky and Theo a look of pure triumph before he turned to Bullet. 'How're you feeling?'

'I'm fine. I'm more worried about Theo. He covered my body with his to stop me being stung. He saved my life.'

'I think my Lazarus suit did that, Toby,' Darius laughed.

'That as well!' Bullet agreed. 'I owe my life to Angela, Theo and your Lazarus suit respectively! So Theo, are you OK?'

'I'm fine.' Was that really his voice? So distant?

'You don't sound it!' Bullet said, concerned.

Theo forced himself to smile, and forced the smile into his voice. 'Toby, I'm fine.'

'Now I know you're not. You've never called me Toby in your life!' said Bullet.

Ricky and Theo looked at each other and grinned.

'I'll never be able to thank you for what you did for me,' Bullet added, looking embarrassed. 'You're a good friend. Both of you, and Angela – and I won't forget it.'

'Bullet, if you're going to get all mushy, I'll turn my head, shall I?' asked Ricky. 'Then you can give Theo a kiss without my seeing it.'

'Ricky, why don't you . . . ?'

'Toby!' Darius admonished.

'. . . Go and play in the traffic!' Bullet finished.

'Bullet, just remember Ricky, Angela and I will always be your friends – OK?' Theo couldn't help saying.

'OK.' Bullet grinned happily.

Theo looked up at Darius. Something told him that with a father like Darius Marriott, Bullet was going to need all the friends he could get. But for now, it was over and Bullet was safe. And at that moment, that was all that mattered.

# About the author

**MALORIE BLACKMAN** is acknowledged as one of today's most imaginative and convincing writers for young readers. *Noughts & Crosses* has won several prizes, including the Children's Book Award. Malorie is also the only author to have won the Young Telegraph/ Gimme 5 Award twice with *Hacker* and *Thief!* Her work has appeared on screen, with *Pig-Heart Boy*, which was shortlisted for the Carnegie Medal, being adapted into a BAFTA-award-winning TV serial. Malorie has also written a number of titles for younger readers.

In 2005, Malorie was honoured with the Eleanor Farjeon Award in recognition of her distinguished contribution to the world of children's books.

In 2008, she received an OBE for her services to children's literature.

www.**malorieblackman**.co.uk